ROBERT L. FORWARD

RESCUED FROM PARADISE

JULIE FORWARD FULLER

BAEN

ACKNOWLEDGEMENTS

The authors wish to thank the following people for their help in various technical and literary areas: Bruno Augenstein, Patrick Carrick, Martha Forward, Charles Fuller, Gerald David Nordley, Hans P. Moravec, Charles Sheffield, Vernor Vinge, and Mark Zimmermann.

Most of the art was expertly prepared by the great group of graphic geniuses at Multi-Graphics in Marina Del Rey, California.

Contents

Prometheus 1
Eden 10
Loading 19
Delivery 34
Births 44
Flouwen 58
Jollys 87
More Room 118
Spawning 129
Hearing 146
Teachers 165
Follow On 170
Tools 182
Dam 189
Rescue 196
Wave 203
Tablet 213
Demonfish 227
Interpreters 243
Lava 267
Aloha 285
Solarians 312
Leaving 327

Contents

PROMETHEUS

George looked out one of the large view windows on the slowly rotating interstellar sailcraft. The strange worlds drifting by on the other side of the thick glass were illuminated with the deep red glow of Barnard—six lightyears distant from Earth.

How much they knew—now—of the strange forms life took on those beautiful planets! On one planet, brilliantly colored, almost immortal blobs of intelligent living jelly surfed with joy in oceans of ammonia; on another lived acre-sized creatures—half plant and half animal—that carved majestic underground cities out of ice; on a third were amazing walking trees with freely-flying eyes that were now befriending the humans who had been marooned on their Edenlike tropical globe.

With a sigh, he pushed away from the view window and floated over to the command console on the control deck of the lightsail starship *Prometheus*. The thought of his comrades stranded down on the planet below had reminded Colonel George Gudunov of his neglected duties. He placed the chordic keypad in his lap and stared at the blank screen. Since the accident had happened, all the responsibility, all the decisions, and—especially— all the reports, were left to him.

He had always respected and even loved General Virginia Jones, but it was at times like these that George missed the stocky black Marine the most. While "Jinjur" had been in command here on *Prometheus*, these reports back to Earth had been her responsibility. She had been good at it, dictating to the computer all the relevant facts about their exploration trip in proper "official report" jargon.

George, to his sorrow, had found that dictating always led to his getting lost on tangents. His reports became long rambling essays on the wonder and beauty of all that surrounded them. His joy in his life here on this exploration trip to the stars was not supposed to be included in the official reports, and yet the enthusiastic scientist in him could not keep his feelings from coming out. Only slow and painful typing, where every word had to be pecked out a letter at a time, could force George to become more frugal with his delight. It wasn't that he felt any less strongly, only he begrudged the effort that was necessary. Consequently, each report meant hours spent in front of this damn blue screen . . . when he would much rather be getting on with the discovering, the exploring, the joy, of living this fascinating life here among the stars.

It was also at these times that he almost envied Jinjur. She might have had her space-wings clipped and be trapped on the surface of a planet, but it was an alien world, full of fascinating secrets that were waiting to be ferreted out . . . with no reporting required afterward.

George sighed and began typing. . . .

The primary mission task at the present time is to get the necessary survival supplies to the ten members of the crew who crashlanded on the moon Zuni. The only vehicle suitable for landing supplies is a robotic amphibious exploration crawler, and only four crawlers and their aeroshells are left. Although the ship's computer James and its Christmas Bush motile could construct additional crawlers using the onboard mechanical fabrication facility, the facility does not have the capability to manufacture the large ceramic aeroshells needed for atmospheric reentry. Thus, in consultation by radio with Mission Commander General Jones, a decision has been made to use the four crawlers for supply drops at approximately six year intervals. After that period, additional landers hopefully will be available from the expected follow-on mission, due in approximately twenty-five years.

Because of the long time between drops, it is essential that each of the crawlers carry as much payload as possible. The first amphibious exploration crawler has been stripped of all nonessential equipment, sensors, and shielding, and its hull reconfigured as a cargo hauler. The maximum payload it can now safely carry has been increased to fifty kilograms. A major portion of that payload will be vitamin pills. Although the current diet of native foods seems to be life-sustaining, we cannot take the chance that it is inadequate. In an attempt to lower their level of dependence on these imported vitamins, we are also shipping the seeds of those plants we have with us here on Prometheus. If the crew can grow these grains and vegetables, then further shipments of the vitamins supplied by those plants can be reduced, allowing for the import of equipment and tools to improve the lives and aid the research of the scientists on the surface.

Because of the stranded party's decision to bear children despite being trapped in such primitive, although idyllic, surroundings, we have also included a selection of medical supplies including obstetrical forceps and child-sized medical instruments. Fortunately, the immune systems of the stranded party have been able to cope well with the native micro-organisms, which have evolved no methods to overcome the body's defenses, so no medicines except pain-killers are needed.

Here George paused and looked around the twenty-meter-diameter circular control room that constituted the bottom deck of Prometheus. It was nearly empty. With only nine crew members left on board to operate the apartment-building-sized vehicle around the clock, three crew members were always asleep in their private apartments, and three were taking care of household or personal chores somewhere else, leaving only three to operate the ship and the science instruments.

Captain Tony Roma was at the navigation console controlling the gigantic lightsail, three hundred kilometers across, which provided propulsion for *Prometheus*. Tony was discussing with the ship's semi-intelligent computer, James, the best way to configure the sail to handle the drop in light pressure when the sunlight emitted by the star Barnard was temporarily cut off during the upcoming eclipse. The conversation was nearly inaudible, since Tony's softest words were picked up by an extended "hand" of the tarantula-sized six-armed computer motile "imp" that stood on his shoulder, multicolored laser lights blinking brightly from the tips and joints of its multitude of "fingers." The fine metal fingers on another "hand" of the imp placed near Tony's ear vibrated into invisibility and from the vibrating tips emanated the voice persona of James as it conversed with Tony in the constrained and correct tones of a professional servant.

Linda Regan was at the science console, her personal imp formed into a band over the top of her head. With its glittering laser lights, it looked like a multigemmed tiara. From the imp, one arm reached out to pick up her voice, one arm touched behind her ear to monitor her health, while two arms formed a set of stereo headphones over her ears. She muttered a command and a clanking sound came from the circular science instrument rack in the center of the control deck as a large telescope rose up out of its storage position and moved inward to look down through the two-meter-diameter science dome built into the floor of the deck.

George, looking for any excuse to avoid having to write, pulled the sticky-hook patches on the seat of his uniform loose from the loop pile of his console chair. Propelled by a careful kick, he floated over to a position next to the telescope, where he could look out the science dome at the upcoming eclipse. Looming large and close below him was the fingernail moon of Earthlike Zuni, home of the alien Jollys, and now, perforce, ten of his fellow crew members. Beyond Zuni was its primary, the gaseous giant Gargantua, four times more massive than Jupiter. Slowly setting behind the thinly illuminated limb of Gargantua was the dwarf star Barnard, shining with a color like a charcoal fire. Off to one side of Gargantua, George could see the three other large moons of Gargantua: Ganymedelike Zulu—the ice-covered-ocean home of the alien icerugs and coelasharks; Titanlike Zouave—a smog-covered iceball; and Marslike Zapotec—dry and dead. Beyond Zapotec was the infinity-symbol-shaped double-planet Rocheworld—home of the alien flouwen and the gummies. The two lobes of Rocheworld didn't quite touch, but they were so close to each other that they shared a common atmosphere, and each lobe was distorted by the other's gravity into a distinct egg shape.

As George watched, Barnard set behind Gargantua, and with the glare gone, the stars came out. The black circle that was Gargantua took a twenty-degree chunk out of the sky, but George instantly recognized the constellation of Orion below it. The constellation was different when seen from Barnard, however; in addition to the three stars in Orion's belt as seen from Earth, there was now a fourth star, a yellow one at the right end. It was Sol, the home to which he would never return, six lightyears away in distance and an eternity away in time—for *Prometheus* was on a one-way exploration journey designed to last the entire lifetime of the crew.

The imp on George's shoulder noticed a rare tear of homesickness welling up in the corner of George's eye, and detached a subportion from itself that was identical in form, but thirty-six times smaller. George, used to the constant ministrations of the imp, didn't even notice as the miniature imp crawled across the side of this face to pick up the tear and carry it away to a ventilation duct, its hind "feet" whirring like miniature propellers as it flew through the air. With a sigh, George pushed himself back from the instrument rack, floated to his place at the command console, and picked up the chordic keyboard. He paused, fingers flexing, as he thought back over their journey.

Prometheus had started out on its six-lightyear voyage to the stars with a crew of twenty—ten men and ten women—most in their late twenties and early thirties, although George, Jinjur, and a few others were older. It took forty years for the laser-pushed lightsail to reach Barnard, and once there, the crew had decades of exploration work to carry out. The mission would literally take a lifetime, so no provision had been made to bring them back. During the trip out, the crew took the life-extending drug No-Die, which cut their aging rate by a factor of four, so that they aged only ten years during the forty-year journey.

During the long cruise phase, the mission had its first casualty. Nearly every member of the drugged crew came down with Hodgkin's Disease, an infectious form of cancer. The ship's doctor, William Wang, saved them with chemotherapy, but in order to properly care for the rest of the crew, Dr. Wang delayed his own treatment and died.

George himself came close to death during their first adventure on the double-planet Rocheworld. Here they had met the brightly colored flouwen, multiton shapeless collections of cells who surfed in the oceans of Rocheworld. Three of the flouwen had budded off human-sized portions of themselves so they could join the human explorers. During the second exploration visit to Rocheworld, the two species had explored the dry lobe of Rocheworld together. There, they found the gummies, distant genetic relatives of the flouwen, shaped like three-meter-diameter starfish. The three flouwen buds had also gone into space with the humans. Together they landed on Zulu, the innermost moon of Gargantua. Like Jupiter's moon Ganymede, Zulu was completely covered by an ocean capped with a thick layer of ice. Unlike Ganymede, however, Zulu had large hot-water geysers. Around those geysers there was life. On the surface lived the alien icerugs, with acre-sized bodies supporting a mobile and highly intelligent "node." Under the ocean the flouwen discovered the alien coelasharks, savage semi-intelligent fishlike animals.

On their most recent trip, using the last of their four rocket landers, the ten humans and three flouwen buds had attempted a landing on Zuni, the Earthlike second moon of Gargantua. Like the South Pacific, Zuni was mostly ocean, dotted with thousands of verdant volcanic islands. A rocket engine exploded during the final phases of the landing and they crashed. All were able to escape, but the rocket lander and the exploration airplane that it carried sank to the bottom of a deep lagoon.

Fortunately, the air on Zuni was breathable, the water drinkable, the native food edible, and the climate tropical. Both humans and flouwen soon found conditions quite pleasant. So much so, in fact, that the humans soon began to refer to their new home as "Eden." With no more landers available on *Prometheus*, however, they were stranded. Slowly the castaways adjusted to living in primitive conditions. Scientists all, these ten grounded astronauts turned their varied talents to understanding their new home.

It was soon apparent that theirs was not the only intelligence on the plant-covered island. They discovered an alien lifeform that had a six-legged treelike body, six free-flying birdlike "eyes," and six free-roving rodent-like "hands." Nicknamed the Jolly Blue-Green Giants, the tribe of four-meter-tall mobile trees welcomed the humans, and the two species shared the island while the flouwen explored the seas.

But, no matter how well life was suiting the stranded

astronauts, George still didn't understand their decision
to bear children. He guessed that it had probably started
with Carmen Cortez. As a last-minute replacement for
one of the original members of the crew, she had not
undergone surgical sterilization as the rest of them had.
The little señorita had long expressed her sadness at not
being able to have children in the limited space of
Prometheus. In George's mind, she had always been a bit
of a problem . . . first by her refusal to accept sterilization, and then that odd incident when John Kennedy's
exploration suit failed while surveying Rocheworld with
Carmen present.

George could only guess at the tensions that arose as
those in this idyllic "Eden" not only found time on their
hands but began to realize they would probably be spending the rest of their lives there . . . without leaving
descendants. There were six women and four men. The
sterilizations had been carefully done so that they could
be easily reversed, in case a crew member had to be taken
off the mission at the last moment. It took some effort
for the crew to devise a way to visit the still functioning
computer-operated sick bay in the airplane sunk in the
bottom of the lagoon, but they did, and now all six women
were pregnant!

That part was clear enough. When the idea was first
broached to the airplane's computer, Josephine, that the
sterilizations be reversed to allow them to have children,
Josephine misunderstood. During the operations, Josephine had used its motile not only to reverse the women's
tubal ligation, but had impregnated each one of them as
well, with sperm left over from the sperm count checks
made after the earlier vasectomy reversals on the men. The
women, having expected to proceed slowly through court-
ship, commitment, perhaps marriage, and finally—after
it had been determined safe to do so—procreation, found
instead they had already been fertilized . . . by computer!

George shook his head and turned back to the report,

listing the tools and devices those on the surface had requested in addition to the essential vitamin and mineral pills. All knew that space on the lander was at a premium and few personal items had been asked for. John Kennedy, trained as a nurse, was acting as doctor for the shipwrecked crew, and he desperately wanted a biochemical analyzer, but Caroline Tanaka was having difficulty designing one small enough. It would probably have to wait until next time they had contact, some six years in the future.

George turned his head slightly toward the imp on his shoulder. "Caroline?" he called. Instantly, James switched his message through the intercom links to the imp sitting on Caroline's shoulder. She was up on the workbench deck at the top of the cylindrical stack of decks that made up *Prometheus*. "Any breakthrough on that analyzer?"

"Sorry, George. What we need is a Star Trek tricorder, but the smallest version James and I can manufacture is one the size of a briefcase, and it masses fifteen kilos— way too much. I know it's important that John know more about the vitamin content of the foods they are eating, but so far, I can't help him much."

Caroline pushed her long dark hair away from her face and went back to the design. There had to be a way to reduce it! Driven by the desire to solve this nearly impossible engineering problem, her subconscious had come up with an idea during her sleep period, and she had risen early in order to try it out. She thought of the pictures of her stranded friends, passed up through the video link from the penetrator they had dropped near their camp. They all looked healthy and happy, but while the women looked round with pregnancy, the men looked too thin, their muscles strong but too clearly defined. What if there was something wrong with their diet and her analyzer could save them? If only she could make it small enough!

EDEN

"Our house, is a very very very fine house . . ."

Cinnamon Byrd was sitting in the shade, close enough to the fire at Council Rock to keep an eye on it, but away from the heat. The warm smell of wood smoke mingled with the heavy scent of Eden's spicy ocean. But, after all these months on the planet, Cinnamon hardly noticed it. In her lap, what was left of it, was what looked like a large shallow basket. Her nimble brown fingers were weaving long strips of dried seaweed tightly around the stiff ribs. She shifted position as she inspected her work, tugging the soft folds of her sarong around her, but there was no way anyone as pregnant as she could be truly comfortable. She smiled as Arielle Trudeau swayed up the beach and sank down into the shade next to her, dropping her load of firewood.

"Arielle," she scolded cheerfully, "I don't know how you do it! You are as far along as the rest of us and yet you manage to stay as graceful as ever!"

"Dancer's muscles," answered the Canadian beauty casually. "We gets lovely legs and ugly feet." With her back straight, she stretched her long legs out in front of her round belly in a pose Cinnamon hadn't been able to manage for months, and wiggled her long but admittedly knobby toes in the sun-warmed sand. "What you making?" she asked.

"I'm adding another room to my hut. This will be the roof, and I'll use sod bricks for the walls."

"Why so strong? So sturdy? Is no wild animals to break down door. You only trap the heat!"

Cinnamon smiled. In truth, the "town" that had sprung up around their campsite brought to mind the story of the Three Little Pigs, with each person or couple building homes to suit their own preferences. Her own round hut was as close as she could make in this tropical climate to the igloos she and her brothers had made in the Alaskan winters. Arielle had a fairy's bower, light and leafy, situated halfway up a tree. Jinjur and Shirley shared a hut made with a nod to General Jinjur Jones's military precision, all square-sided and right-angled, but Engineer Shirley Everett had added a pitched roof to shed the frequent rain. Carmen Cortez, the communications technician, had moved into a utilitarian pup tent made of peethoo saplings and feebook leaves next to the penetrator carrying the communicator that served as their link to those above. Richard Redwing had set up a tepee and moved Reiki LeRoux in with him after he learned that Josephine had chosen him to be the father of Reiki's child.

Only John Kennedy and Nels Larson still slept in the original lean-to the crew had used as their shelter during those early hectic days when they were first marooned, but the group still shared communal meals around the cooking fire. The hormonal "Leaps and Bounces" (as Arielle called it) of pregnancy had encouraged the women to seek privacy, but this tiny band of humans stranded on an alien world still gained strength and comfort from their nightly ritual of holding hands around the fire before the evening meal.

Now, as the glowing red globe of Barnard started to lower into the ruddy clouds of sunset, people were slowly straggling back up the beach from whatever explorations and experiments had occupied them for the day. Not that they didn't have domestic chores as well, but on this tropic paradise, they could divide things to suit personal preferences.

Arielle had been the pilot. Now that her wings had been clipped, she wandered the island gathering firewood and collecting small samples of the indigenous flora. She was making a map of their home marked with more practical aspects of the island than the photo surveys made by *Prometheus*.

Cinnamon had started out as the fire-builder ("Keeper of the Flame" according to Richard) and normally stayed close to it. Gradually, Cinnamon had taken over many of the humdrum chores that would have tied the others down. Now she dried the herbs and ground the grain at the little water mill. She also did much of the mending and laundering, and took care of a myriad of little household tasks that the others barely noticed. Shirley had become a Jack-of-all-trades, using her engineering skills to come up with solutions for problems that hindered the work of the others.

Reiki took her raft out every day and brought back whatever fish or sea plants the others had asked of her. Reiki also took care of the "chamber pots" that she emptied each morning into Necessity Beach. At first they had just gone to the distant beach whenever the need arose, but as the women's pregnancies progressed, the need for a closer nightly relief station became apparent. Fortunately, among the salvaged items from the lander were many large rectangular plastic containers with lip-locking lids. Originally designed for use in storing large mineral or biological samples, they had been pressed into more mundane use. The ammonia from the urine collected was crucial for the well-being of the flouwen, so not a drop was wasted. Indeed, Reiki was often greeted at the beach by the cheerful free-flowing blobs of color as they waited for their daily dose. The flouwen had quickly learned not to say anything to the prim Reiki about the load she carried.

Richard and Jinjur had taken over much of the hunting, managing to gather many different species of the local fauna, either with traps, slings, or Jinjur's longbow. The nightly ordeal of taste-testing each organ of each separate species for toxins was for the most part over. They had learned what they could eat and what they should avoid. At first, the humans had been afraid of interfering with the local ecology. But since the humans met the Jolly Blue-Green Giants, the intelligent plantlike aliens who lived on the island, they were reassured. Now, the castaways considered fair game those animals the Jollys also preyed upon. Indeed, the Jollys were thankful that the more agile humans were willing to help cut back on the small green-furred vermin that often nibbled at the roots of their protective thorn-wall hedges.

John was kept busy examining samples of the local foodstuffs with the biologists, Cinnamon Byrd and Nels Larson, trying to determine the nutritional values they contained. Now that the humans were reliant on the native food, it was vital that they learn just how well their diet would support them. The alien foods were mostly carbohydrates and seemed to be nutritious, but the proteins were different from Earth proteins, and with no equipment to analyze the food, or how well the humans were assimilating and utilizing it, the threat of severe malnutrition hung over them like a cloud.

There had been long debates about exactly what supplies they should include in the limited payload of the tiny crawler that would bring them true necessities from *Prometheus*. Anything they could get along without, anything the planet would supply, should be left out to make way for something else. Ironically, the equipment needed to analyze the content of their diet was still operative in the submerged airplane in the center of Crater Lagoon, but to get there involved a difficult and potentially dangerous journey in a jury-rigged "diving bell" and there were thousands of samples to test.

David Greystoke, a computer programmer of artistic temperament, was now spending most of his days with the slow-moving Jollys. At the moment he and Shirley were studying and recording the Jolly colony's day-to-day activities on one of the few pieces of their old technology left to them: a small pocket-sized electronic notebook that had been Reiki's personal diary. Each day, David and Shirley filled its electronic memory with notes and still-scan pictures, which Carmen transmitted back to the *Prometheus* at night. Carmen spent most of her time down on the beach monitoring their communications link to the life they had lost. Slowly she and the flouwen had managed to salvage pieces of communication equipment from the sunken lander. She was working to enlarge the original setup to include a flouwen taste-screen in the shallow waters. Now, the little señorita, so round with pregnancy that she was almost spherical, came bouncing up the beach. She was squeezing the water out of her long black curls.

"Finally, I really think I've done it!" Carmen said. "The Littles can now use their own taste-screen to make direct contact with the commsat net. They've even exchanged messages with their primary selves back on Rocheworld! The round-trip delay time was about three minutes, but that's nothing to the flouwen. From now on, the flouwen can talk to Rocheworld or *Prometheus* without me or someone else having to act as intermediary."

At the mention of the name of their former home, the two sitting on the ground automatically glanced up in the sky at the flat ellipse rising on the opposite side of the sky from the setting sun. The large multistory habitat that contained their nine companions was a mere speck in the three-hundred-kilometer-diameter aluminum moon reflecting the light from the setting sun. For the past few months, *Prometheus* had been off doing surveys from orbit of Gargantua's many moons. It was now on its way back for the first of the provision drops. After a pause, Arielle and Cinnamon returned their attention to Carmen, and she continued.

"Of course, trying to waterproof the connection from the taste-screen to the power umbilical was a challenge.

But you know those greens that John said must have latex in them?"

"Remember? It was me, tasted first!" said Arielle, spitting into the sand. "Can still taste it!"

"Well, they may taste awful," said Carmen, "but after I boiled up a lot of them, I skimmed off enough sticky stuff to waterproof the power leads. As long as the flouwen don't bump it too much, it should hold."

Jinjur and Richard had joined them quietly, dropping their crudely gutted game animals for Cinnamon to butcher with their one good knife—Shirley's Swiss Army Mech-All. "You expect the flouwen to be careful?" Jinjur asked incredulously.

While the flouwen had proved to be very intelligent, solving complicated mathematical theorems for fun, most of them seemed to have the temperaments of eight-year-olds. Of the three flouwen buds stranded here with them on Eden—Little Red, Little White, and Little Purple— only Little White acted maturely, although all three of them were many hundreds of years old. Little Purple was well over a thousand.

"Well, Little Red might accidentally break something, but frankly, I doubt he will be using it much. He is too busy surfing in the waves to talk to *Prometheus*, while Little Purple spends most of his time rocked up in the shallows, thinking. Little White, however, is always careful, and I'm certain he doesn't want to lose the opportunity to have talks with George." Carmen smiled. The milky-white flouwen had met his soul mate in the human physicist. The two of them could talk of science for hours, and Little White had been looking forward to renewing the contact.

"*Gracias a Dios*, I didn't have to rewire the taste-screen itself. . . . I'd never have been able to manage without any real tools. Ouch!" Carmen interrupted herself and clutched her belly. Then she laughed. "That must be an elbow. I know she is keeping her head buried deep against my bladder."

"Must we?" asked Reiki, arriving. The prim anthropologist was constantly trying to keep the rest of them civilized despite their primitive conditions. She had met David and Shirley on the way back to Council Rock, and now David was carrying her catch. He handed the carefully cleaned fish to Arielle, who impaled the fillets on sticks and began to sprinkle the pale pink flesh with spices prior to setting them before the fire to bake. Reiki and Shirley lowered themselves awkwardly into the sand with the other women.

"Yes, we must!" Carmen bridled. "As it happens, we need to talk about pee. While I was working on getting power to the flouwen's taste-screen, I wasn't about to go off and use Necessity Beach every time I felt the need. Besides, Little White was right there, so it wasn't wasted. John! Come here a minute! You need to hear this, too."

John and Nels were coming down the beach from the woods. At Carmen's call, John gave the tubers he was carrying to Nels and sprinted to her side and slipped his arm around her.

"Everything okay with Junior?" he asked, patting her stomach.

"Of course . . . or at least I suppose so. I was too busy to think about it much. It was Little White. He said that . . . well . . . that my urine tasted different. He used the taste-screen to communicate with James about it, and after a little discussion about how to discriminate between different tastes, they both agreed that it was glucose. That doesn't mean anything bad does it? He said there was only a tiny bit . . . ." Carmen trailed off, growing more and more alarmed as John just looked at her, eyes wide. In desperation she turned a stricken face to Cinnamon. "It's not too bad is it? Is there something wrong with the baby?"

"Oh, Carmen, it's nothing, really," said Cinnamon as she struggled to her feet. "A trace of glucose in the urine is sometimes a sign of diabetes."

"Diabetes! *Aye Dios Mio!* Diabetics aren't suppose to

have babies! How can we get insulin on this rock!?!"
Carmen was becoming hysterical.

"No, no," said Cinnamon soothingly. "Mild diabetes
during pregnancy is quite common. And we won't need
insulin; it can be easily controlled with diet. John? John!
Tell her!"

John had just been sitting there with a dazed look.
Then he took Carmen's face in his hands and kissed
her soundly.

"The flouwen detected glucose in Carmen's urine!" he
yelled and began dancing around the beach.

Reiki shook her head despairingly as John continued
yelling, chanting, and dancing up the beach toward Nels.
John shook Nels's shoulders as he repeated his cry. Nels
dropped the tubers and joined in, "The flouwen detected
glucose in Carmen's urine!"

"What are you doing? Have you no heart? I am sick!
Your baby is sick!" Carmen, furious after the scare, was
stomping over to the two men cavorting in the sand. The
rest of the group trailed along behind her.

"Don't you see?" said Nels, turning to her as she
approached. "The flouwen use taste to communicate
thoughts—even thoughts as complex as mathematical
theorems. In order to do that, they must have developed
a marvelously accurate sense of taste. Since they can detect
and identify large molecules like glucose in your urine,
then they should be able to detect the various other molecules in our foodstuffs. They can assure us that we are
getting all the vitamins and minerals we need to stay
healthy!"

"All these months!" crowed John. "All these months,
I've been trying to figure out what each thing we ate supplied to our bodies, and let me tell you folks, it has been
hell!" John laughed.

The spectators looked at each other amazed, and it
dawned on all of them just how long it had been since
any of them had heard John laugh.

"I was trying to figure out ways to test for these compounds while watching the reactions of our bodies as we ate various foods. I didn't want to worry the rest of you, but let's face it, I was guessing and hoping, terrified that I might be missing some little thing!" Relief colored his voice. "That, even if there was a vitamin present in some kind of food, it might not be in a form we could assimilate! Vitamins, minerals, amino acids, we may need only tiny amounts, but to be without them can be disastrous. How could I have been so stupid? Floating out in the water we have our own chemistry labs!"

"No taste-test for us tonight, then!" called out Jinjur. "Tonight we eat only our favorites and tomorrow we let the flouwen start doing the tasting!"

"We'll be able to figure exactly what vitamins the native food is giving us, and what vitamins we'll need to have supplements for, then tell James up on *Prometheus*," said Nels. "Just think of the savings in space, think of the tools we'll be able to bring down instead!" With a broad smile he reached out and took John's hand. Slowly, one by one, the little band of humans linked hands in a circle around the fire.

LOADING

Sam Houston was up on the top "workbench" deck of
Prometheus. The four-meter-diameter central shaft in front
of him was filled with a doughnut-shaped elevator platform that moved heavy items up and down the shaft. On
the platform was a robotic amphibious crawler with a boat-
like hull about one meter wide, two meters long, and a
half-meter high. Along each side of the crawler there were
treads with paddles built in, so the vehicle could operate equally well on land or on water. On the side of the
hull, near the front, the word "*Spritz*" had been written
in script on the crawler in bright blue. *Spritz* had video
camera eyes, long articulated arms folded up along its
topside that could reach any part of the crawler to effect
repairs, and numerous communication antennae, but its
commodious hull had been stripped of sensing and survey instruments, and its doors now were folded back as
it waited for the last of its cargo.

On the opposite side of the central shaft from Sam,
Caroline was operating the automated mechanical fabrication facility that took up one quarter of the twenty-
meter-diameter workbench deck. The machinery was
humming as it produced a complex part that Caroline had
just designed on its control console. The chemical analyses
that the flouwen had carried out on the native foods of
Eden had lessened the requirement for nutrition supplements, leaving a number of kilograms free on *Spritz* for

tools and other useful items. One versatile tool requested by those below had been more Swiss Army Mech-Alls. Caroline had modified the basic design by removing a number of screwdriver tips useful only for repairs of complex machinery and replacing them with a selection of knife blades, saws, awls, files, and cutters more suitable for the primitive environment of Eden.

Sam heard a rustle behind him and turned around as the Christmas Bush exited the chemical fabrication facility which took up that quarter of the workbench deck. The chemical facility was not designed for entry by humans. It consisted of racks and racks of molecular analyzing and synthesizing equipment which reached from floor to ceiling along a serpentine corridor ten centimeters wide.

The elongated Christmas Bush oozed from the narrow corridor like a glittering tongue of metallic ice crystals and reformed itself on the floor. Two of its branches grasped the looped carpeting and brought it erect, while one of its branches bushed out into a "head." The laser diodes built into the tips of the fine shoots and the joints of the thicker sticks flashed briefly as the Christmas Bush took in its surroundings. Blue lasers established communication links with similar lasers built into the corners and crevices of the room; yellow lasers determined the position and orientation of all moveable objects in the room; while red lasers carefully scanned the humans, noting every nuance of facial position and posture. A green laser from a ceiling fixture brightened as power was transferred from the ship to the main trunk of the Christmas Bush, where it was distributed by green beams down through the boughs, branches, twigs, sticks, and shoots, turning the metallic structure green with scattered light. It was during this recharging phase, with the red, yellow, and blue laser lights blinking out from its green branches, that the Christmas Bush looked most like its name. A portion of the head of the Bush vibrated, and James spoke from the Bush.

"This is the last packet of mineral supplements." The

Bush showed Sam the carefully wrapped package, walked to *Spritz*, and inserted it into the cargo hold with its one good arm appendage. The other two arms of the Bush consisted only of truncated main boughs, for their subdivisions were busy elsewhere on the ship as Christmas Branches, one in the galley preparing the next meal for the crew, and one on the hydroponics deck helping Deirdre O'Connor, now that the other two biologists who had made up the hydroponics deck crew, Nels Larson and Cinnamon Byrd, were trapped down on Eden.

Deirdre sighed, the small sound only accenting the silence of the hydroponics deck. For many years she had worked in these long racks of plants . . . here where a tiny piece of Earth was blossoming so far from home. Always before there had been, from somewhere else in the growing green or echoing down the rows of algae tanks, the sound of song. But Cinnamon was no longer here helping to tend the gardens, tanks, and tissue cultures, singing from her endless repertoire of old songs, and Deirdre missed her. Deirdre ran her fingers through the tiny dry seeds . . . grains, peas, beans, tomatoes, and other vegetables. They had been painstakingly gathered for the last several months and now would be sent down to the planet surface. The vitamins in these Earth crops could mean the difference between life and death to the castaways. Meticulously Deirdre and a Christmas Branch sorted each variety, choosing the best seeds and carefully labeling them. Two dozen little sacks, each filled with only a few grams of matter . . . it seemed almost wrong that they should be so important.

Deirdre handed the sacks to the child-sized Christmas Branch. The end of one of its six arms detached itself and reconfigured its shape into a miniature version of the Christmas Branch. It was now a Christmas Twig, no larger than a marmoset. The fine metal "toes" of the "feet" of the motile gripped the loops in the carpet that lined the floors and walls of the corridors and scurried off toward the central shaft.

Deirdre whispered into the pickup "hand" of her imp, reaching down from its position on top of her head, where it held her thick hair up out of the way. "The hydroponics deck contribution is on its way."

The voice of Sam came back through the imp. "Thanks Deirdre . . . we've got most everything tucked into the crawler now. Wanna come and see *Spritz* off?"

Deirdre didn't answer. The others were used to her retiring ways and wouldn't be bothered if she didn't join them. She had never been one for crowds, and these days it made her feel sad to see how small the crowd had become.

The Christmas Twig climbed rapidly up the shaft handholds, made its way along the bottom of the elevator platform, and came up through the hole next to *Spritz*. It placed the seeds in the compartment reserved for them, then leapt from the top of the crawler toward the larger Christmas Bush and reattached itself to one of the truncated limbs to form a second hand for the Bush.

"That does it for their essential daily requirement of vitamins and minerals," said Sam to *Spritz*. He looked into the voluminous cargo hold. There was plenty of room left, but the problem was not volume, but mass. If *Spritz* and its cargo massed too much, the aeroshell would overheat on reentry and everything would be lost in a literal flash.

"How much do they weigh? Do we have any mass left?"

Spritz activated its automatically adjustable suspension system and set itself to bouncing with the active damping system turned off. After timing a few bounces it announced, "Forty-three point one two seven kilograms. I can carry another seven kilograms. Are all essential supplies loaded?" asked *Spritz*.

"A few more things to come," said Sam, going over to the one-meter-diameter hole in the center of the central shaft elevator. He bent his two-meter-tall lanky frame over the hole and looked down the sixty-meter shaft. Way down at the bottom, swinging her way into the shaft column from the living area deck, he could see Katrina Kauffmann bringing a package from the sick bay. She climbed rapidly up the shaft in the low gravity, using only occasional pulls on the rungs with her free hand, her legs dangling.

Katrina shot up through the hole in the central shaft elevator, sure in the knowledge that James would have the Christmas Bush there beforehand to guide her body through. She was carrying some nonurgent medical instruments and medicines that would make life easier for the stranded crew. The small, no-nonsense nurse had packed everything efficiently into two remarkably small packages.

"This package contains the obstetrical forceps and child-sized medical instruments that James created in the mechanical fabrication facility," she said.

"For sure we didn't have those in sick bay stock," remarked Sam with a wry smile.

"I also included some nonrusting scalpels, forceps, drill bits, and other instruments useful for both surgery and general use. I've just finished sterilizing all of them down in the sick bay. I know we've been free of all regular diseases, including the common cold, for the last thirty years, but it could be that a cold germ or something worse is lurking somewhere on board, just waiting to be transported to an infant with a naive immune system. The other package contains pain killers, anesthetics, broad spectrum antibiotics, sleep inducers, muscle relaxants, tissue glue, bone epoxy, arthritis med—"

"Ar-thur-i-tis!" exclaimed Sam.

"They aren't getting any younger," retorted Katrina. Sam had to agree with her. He was the second oldest person on the crew after George. He had just turned ninety years old according to the Earth calendar, and his thinning gray hair and admittedly tender knee joints confirmed his biological age of sixty.

"I had James concentrate the medicines," she continued, "leaving out all the usual liquids and fillers. These drugs are very pure and very strong, but everything is labeled so that John can dilute them properly for dispensing."

"That's great, Katrina! Every ten grams saved means another rechargeable battery cell for the permalights and Reiki's recorder."

Katrina blushed. "Actually . . . I did have something else I thought would be useful. I know that they didn't ask, but I'm sure it's only because they forgot. . . ."

"What is it?" asked Sam resignedly. He had always figured that he wasn't going to be the only one slipping in a little something extra.

Katrina pulled out a long thin cylinder about the size of a cigar. "It's a sewing kit. A few dozen needles and safety pins, and some strong brightly colored thread. I know they are all wearing sarongs now, but when the little ones come . . ."

"Maybe you should include some diaper pins!" Sam said in a gruff tone. Then he smiled.

"Don't worry, love," he said. "I'll find room for the sewing kit." Sam tucked the various packages into the cargo hold of the crawler and it bounced up and down again.

"Forty-six point zero eight three grams," said *Spritz*.

"Good," said Sam, reaching into a pouch. Down on the surface was his best friend and fellow geologist, Richard Redwing. The tall gangly Texan and the Native American had worked together on many different planets, and it hurt to know that he would never be with his friend again. They enjoyed the sort of bickering camaraderie that did not translate easily to comm-link talks. Now, his buddy was about to become a father, and he couldn't even be there to tease him about it! Sam slipped into the cargo pod a pair of baby-sized moccasins cut from the leather of his boot tops. Richard would enjoy both the love and the teasing they represented.

On the opposite side of the deck, Caroline got up from the mechanical fabrication console, pleased. She held in her hand the first of the Mech-Alls produced, and she was taking the versatile tool through its paces. As she moved the control thumb-knob from indent to indent, the blob of complex memory metal alloy at the end of the tool reconfigured itself from scissors to saw to chisel to awl, through three screwdriver heads and six knife blades, to end with spoon and fork.

Just then a chime sounded throughout the ship and from each of their imps.

"Mealtime!" said Sam enthusiastically. He dove down through the hole in the elevator platform. Caroline smiled grimly over at Katrina and pinched at the slight roll of fat at her waist.

"It's not fair that the skinny ones can eat all they want. He eats tons of calories and fat and never gains a gram. All I have to do is look at a dish of algae ice cream and I put on ten kilos."

"He's almost as exasperating to watch at mealtime as Arielle was," Katrina agreed. The reminder of the beautiful birdlike aerospace pilot, now grounded on the moon below, brought a somber moment to both. Caroline and Katrina joined *Spritz* on the platform and took the elevator down the shaft to the living area deck where the crew were gathering for "mealtime," one of the three times of the day the whole crew got together. For a half-hour or so, James would be left in charge of the ship while the crew socialized.

Down on the upper of the two crew-quarters decks, Elizabeth Vengeance had risen and dressed early and was in the process of deciding how she would wear her imp today.

"Let's try the 'feather-hat' look, James," she said, looking at her reversed image in the view-wall that separated her living room from the bedroom. Her imp scrambled from her shoulder and formed itself into a spray of glittering metallic feathers that covered one side of her head, following the outlines of her short cap of bright red hair.

Her green eyes looked her reversed video image over critically. She was dressed in a bright green tailored shirt-and-slacks outfit that just matched her eyes in color and fit her slim body tightly. In the corner of one shirt pocket was a circular wear spot the size of a large coin.

"You're still in damn good shape for fifty-five," she remarked to herself with approval. She noticed a loose thread on her sleeve and muttered something to her imp. Instantly, a small mosquito-sized motile detached itself from the main imp, clambered down her sleeve to the offending thread, snipped it off, and carried it away. The thread would be saved, along with all the other green threads and worn out clothing made of the same synthetic fiber; ultimately to be dissolved, respun into thread, rewoven into fabric, and retailored into clothing for her to use in the distant future. She palmed the door open, and James, observing through her imp that she would be exiting at about the time the elevator would be reaching her level, brought it to a halt to pick her up.

In a room on the opposite side of the ten-apartment crew deck, Captain Thomas St. Thomas was running late. To hurry things along, he had started brushing his teeth while his imp was still shaving the left side of his face, its finest fingers pulling up on each black whisker in turn, pinching it off below the dark brown skin with another set of fingers, and passing the cut-off whisker to yet another set, which collected them all in a neat ball.

With half his face still covered by the glittering limbs of his imp, Thomas swung to his bedroom, grabbed a pair of coveralls out of the storage shelves, pulling them on and sealing them in one quick motion. As he was putting on his Velcro-bottomed corridor boots, the imp finished his shave and completed the morning toilet by rustling through his short Air Force-trim curly black hair, fluffing up the flat spots and sharpening up the edges. By the time Thomas reached the exit of his room and palmed the opening switch for the door, the imp had reformed itself into its normal six-armed tarantula shape on Thomas's left shoulder. As the door slid open, a wasp-sized motile detached itself from the imp and carried the ball of cut-off whiskers and loose hair up the central shaft to the organic material reprocessing unit that was part of the chemical facility on the workbench deck.

As the door slid shut behind Thomas, he saw that the elevator was there with Caroline and Katrina, picking up Elizabeth. Although Thomas normally didn't use the elevator for jumps between the lower decks, he joined the three women for the ride down. As he boarded, he looked in the cargo hold of the crawler.

"Still got lots of room, I see," he remarked.

Spritz bounced up and down slightly, then replied, "There remains zero point seven two cubic meters of volume, and three point nine one seven kilos of mass."

The elevator came to a stop at the living area deck, the "commons" for the crew of *Prometheus*. This deck contained the exercise area, sick bay, kitchen, dining area, lounge, and two small video theaters.

"I'm looking forward to this breakfast," announced Thomas as they left the elevator. "It's time for my real-meat ration for the week." As he passed by the counter between the kitchen and the dining area, the Galley Branch passed him a squeezer of coffee and a flip-top tray containing two pieces of algae-flour toast liberally loaded with algae-butter and pseudo-grape jelly, and an omelet packed with vegetables and real smoked-ham chunks cut from the pork tissue culture, Hamlet. Caroline contented herself with her squeezer of coffee and a small pastry. Katrina, being on the late shift, went to the smorgasbord the Galley Branch had set up in the lounge ahead of time. Sam was already there, a large slice of pumpernickel in one hand and spreading knife in the other, making a big dent in the liver spread made from Cinnamon's liver tissue culture, Pâté La Belle. It grew much faster than the other meat tissue cultures—Hamlet, Ferdinand, Lamb Chop, and Chicken Little—so there was always plenty of real liver for those who wanted it.

Resigned because her imp had informed her that the resonant frequency of her body indicated that she was now over forty-five kilos, Katrina limited herself to a piece of pickled 'ponics-trout and soured pseudo-cream on a half-slice of pumpernickel. The 'ponics-trout wasn't herring and the pumpernickel bread was really made from algae-flour and some chemicals from the synthesizers in James's chemical facility, but the Galley Branch had made it taste like the real thing.

The four newcomers joined the three who had just come off control deck duty. They had only been one deck down and were the first to arrive in the dining room after the mealtime chime. George, Linda, and Tony had already started, and were working on a large salad made with greens fresh from the hydroponics deck, topped with mushrooms and bell peppers. They had a main dish of linguine and algae-cream sauce with real clam meat chunks from Cinnamon's Blue Oyster Culture.

Deirdre dropped silently down the central shaft from the hydroponics deck and moved quietly over to the smorgasbord table. Picking up the half-slice of pumpernickel that Katrina had left, she raised it to her shoulder, where the bread was taken by her pet, Foxx, a rare marsupial somewhat like a flying squirrel. The creature nibbled on the bread, its long furry prehensile tail wrapped around Deirdre's neck, while she prepared herself a tray, tucking the delicacies under the tray lids before taking her place at the dining hall table. They all joined hands for a silent moment of companionship.

"*Spritz* said there was a little room left," Elizabeth remarked as they dropped hands and started eating.

"Even after I added my few needles and things," said

Katrina. "I just wish I could send much more. It's so hard, leaving them forever!"

Deirdre's rare chuckle broke the silence. "Aye, but it's living, they are, you know that, Katrina! And they expect us to be living, too. Reiki told me, in her last message, to 'use her laces,' but look you . . ." Deirdre's slender brown hands flipped a dainty wisp of lace around the plain collar of her wrinkled brown coverall, and she made an absurdly simpering face; the effect was as incongruous as ruffles on a gnome, and they laughed.

"There's almost no mass to the things at all, you see, so I'm returning most of them to Reiki. Except this one." She held up a fluffy confection of pure white and tucked it swiftly into Katrina's neckline. The snowy froth at Katrina's throat softened the stubborn line of jaw and brightened the blue of her eyes with a happy twinkle.

"I object!" blurted out Linda. Normally the little solar astrophysicist was cheerful and bouncy, but now her green eyes flashed. "How can you justify wasting even the tiniest bit of cargo mass in that crawler on trivia! Our people need tools, not frills!"

"I was going to fill up the last of the mass allotment with solar-rechargeable permalights and replacement cells for them," agreed Sam. "And maybe some pocket computers like the recorder that Reiki has, but with communication capability added."

"I would think that the sooner they get used to non-electronic technology, the better," said Caroline thoughtfully. "I'd vote for a few good pairs of nonrusting scissors."

"But morale is important, too," George reminded them. "We want them to know we care about them. The right kind of gifts are just as important as the right kind of tools."

"One gift, there is, that can come from us all," said Deirdre slowly. "And it be nearly weightless. A photograph of our own selves."

"Great idea!" said Thomas, getting up from the table. "I'll go get my best electroprint camera, and I'll have James laminate the print so it will last even in Eden's tropical climate."

In a short while he was back, followed close behind by the Christmas Bush. He settled the autofocus camera firmly in the Bush's grasp and joined the group, all the concerned and caring faces looking steadily at the lens.

"Say 'cheese'," said James through their imps. The trite phrase intoned in James's deep formal voice broke the tension and produced a picture full of smiles that would bring instant cheer to those who looked at it for years to come.

An hour later, *Spritz* was nearly full, and Sam and Deirdre had retired for their sleep shift. "Forty-nine point nine four five kilograms," *Spritz* announced, bouncing again. "There is mass allotment available for ten more sheets of permapaper and another stylus."

Linda counted out the ten sheets of untearable, waterproof, chemically-impregnated writing paper, and Tony added the thin metal stylus. The pointed end of the metal stylus catalytically produced marks on the chemically treated paper, while the rounded end reversed the chemical reaction, allowing the paper to be reused again and again. Caroline carefully closed and latched the internal lids on the storage compartments inside *Spritz*, then stepped back and watched critically as the winglike doors of the cargo hold folded themselves closed.

"Hold pressurized," announced *Spritz*. "No leakage detectable."

"Let's go up and get your ride," said Caroline. She turned to the Christmas Bush. With mealtime over, the Galley Branch had rejoined the main motile, and the Bush had six functional appendages again. "Please take us up to where *Charles* is stored, James."

The elevator platform came to a halt at level 22, where the door to one of the storage compartments was open. Inside, Caroline and Linda could see a Christmas Twig checking out a spacecraft, one end of which consisted of a large ceramic aeroshell, bigger than they were.

"Hello, *Charles*," said Caroline. "Are you ready?"

"All self-check routines have been double-checked by James. I am in perfect working order," said *Charles*. "I am ready to proceed with my mission."

"Let's get you out of there, then," said Caroline. The spacecraft, weighing more than a ton, was too massive for the relatively weak Christmas Bush to cope with, so it was up to the two humans to wrestle it out of its compartment. Muscles straining with the effort, Linda and Caroline got the massive spacecraft slowly moving, then let it drift slowly outward in the low gravity, occasionally giving it a hard push to keep one of its appendages from touching the sides of the door. Once it was free, they guided it to the center of the shaft, and after another bout of strenuous effort with their feet planted against the central shaft wall, they brought the massive vehicle to a halt, ceramic dome down. The two women held the spacecraft up over their heads with ease. Although it massed over a ton, its weight in the low acceleration of the lightship was only a few kilos.

"Release your dome, *Charles*," said Linda. The computer imp that resided inside the spacecraft eased out of an aperture and moved around the spacecraft, releasing the latches holding the ceramic aeroshell on. Unlike the Christmas Bush and its submotiles, which were remotely powered and directed by laser beams, this motile was connected to *Charles*'s central computer by an umbilical, which also served as a safety line.

Linda and Caroline each used one hand to lower the dome to the floor of the platform in front of the crawler, while continuing to hold the spacecraft overhead with their other hand.

"Do you see your attachment points, *Spritz*?" Caroline asked.

"All identified," replied *Spritz*, its video cameras active.

"Climb in," said Caroline. The two arms of the crawler grasped the rim on opposite sides of the dome, and while the humans held the dome steady, *Spritz* lifted itself into the dome like someone stepping into a small boat. There were some clanks from underneath as latches were secured, then *Spritz* folded its arms, lowered its video sensors, and pulled in its antenna.

"Ready," came *Spritz's* voice through their imps. The humans then guided the spacecraft down onto the dome and held it in position while the spacecraft imp secured the latches.

"Bottom floor, James," said Caroline, and the elevator started down, James letting it free-fall for a few minutes until it built up a reasonable velocity, then switching to constant speed.

When they got to the control deck at the bottom, they were met by George, Thomas, and Katrina. On the other side of the control deck, Elizabeth, at the navigation console, adjusted the lightsail trajectory for optimum orbital injection of the spacecraft. George and Thomas were in their spacesuits and Katrina checked George out by punching one code after another on his chestpack and comparing the suit response with a checklist. Katrina's punches, while solid, were far gentler than Shirley's had been, and George looked down at the head of straight brown hair, now streaked with gray.

"They've arrived," announced George as he saw the elevator coming down out of the central shaft hole in the ceiling. "Aren't you done yet?"

"Still got another page to go," said Katrina, deliberately punching in the next code. "And I'm not going to rush it or skip it. Shirley would never forgive me if we lost you due to a bad suit." Thomas went over to the elevator and helped Linda and Caroline with the massive spacecraft, which now massed almost two tons with its payload. The checklist was soon completed and Katrina floated over to the airlock control console as George joined Thomas and *Charles* in the airlock. Katrina activated the airlock control console and cycled them through.

Thomas and George looked out the open airlock door, *Charles* held between them. Off to one side was the small red ball that was Barnard, half as big as the Sun in the sky, looking like an aging charcoal briquette with all the ash blown off it. With the lightsail illuminated at that angle, it was possible to see almost all the way to its edge, a hundred and fifty kilometers away, rippling like an aluminum sea under the setting Sun as the slow rotation of the gigantic sail moved different portions of its stays and battens around.

George and Thomas, muscles straining, heaved the massive spacecraft with its precious cargo out the airlock door. It seemed to hang there, slowly rotating from the push they had given it, but the constant acceleration of *Prometheus* under the light pressure from Barnard soon flew them away from the spacecraft at ever-increasing velocity. Once it had reached a few hundred meters distance, George gave it a command.

"You may activate attitude control jets, *Charles*. Go into a low equatorial orbit around Eden and watch the weather patterns. At the first wide break in the storm fronts, drop *Spritz* as close as you can to St. Vincent Island. After dropping *Spritz*, join the rest of the commsat constellation we have there."

"Attitude jets activated," replied *Charles*, rotating itself into proper orientation. The main rocket fired and the semi-intelligent spacecraft set off on its assignment.

DELIVERY

A few hours later, *Charles* made one last burn and adjusted its elliptical orbit so the spacecraft would pass low over St. Vincent Island once each thirty-hour day—during the morning daylight period just before Barnard set behind Gargantua for the daily two-hour noonday eclipse. The weather on Eden was remarkably clear for once, so instead of having to wait days and days for a break in the rolling storm fronts, there was no need to wait at all.

"James?" Caroline murmured into her imp-mikes. "Is Carmen available?"

"She's sleeping in her tent shelter near the penetrator," replied James. "Shall I wake her?"

"I hate to do it, but we might not get this good a chance again for weeks if we don't take it now. What time is it there?"

"Four hours before dawn," replied James.

Caroline hesitated. "I don't know. Maybe we'd better wait. She's pregnant and needs her sleep. After all, the lander doesn't touch down until almost noon."

"Don't forget that the days are thirty point two hours long on Eden," James reminded her. "The nights there last fifteen hours, and there is little to do on the island after dark. From the snoring noises I have been picking up from the acoustic sensors on the penetrator, I would estimate that she has been asleep for nine hours or—"

"Nine hours!" exploded Caroline—who like all the others on the crew had been pulling continuous round-the-clock shifts on the shorthanded ship. "The most I ever manage to get on my eight-hour sleep period is seven! Wake her up!"

By midday, Jinjur had her troops deployed. Just in case the lander came down outside of the planned drop zone, two of the men had been sent east along the coast and the other two west, until all parts of the sky could be seen by one human or another, despite the nearby tall trees and the large volcano in the center of the island. The three flouwen were also watching, one near the island, and the other two east and west along the expected ground track.

Leaving Cinnamon to tend the fire, the other five women, not up to much hiking, went down to stand near the penetrator *Crash,* on the beach of Crater Lagoon, where they could easily look due west where they expected to see the reentry take place, while listening to Linda report the status of the deployment procedure through the communicator. High above them, over the northern hemisphere, hung the large circular sail of *Prometheus* in a position where it could see and communicate with the spacecraft and its deployed aeroshell at all points along their equatorial orbits around Eden.

"The aeroshell carrying *Spritz* was deployed earlier in the orbit by *Charles,*" Linda reported to the group. "It's now encountering a significant amount of drag. The trajectory is nominal—should drop right on you. The weather also looks good from here. How does it look from where you are?"

"Clouds building up in the west," reported Jinjur. "But they're still many kilometers away."

The light dimmed as Barnard started to pass behind the gigantic black circle overhead that was Gargantua.

"The midday eclipse has started," Jinjur reported. A few minutes later, the last bright spot of the tiny red sun dipped beneath the clouds of the gas giant and it became pitch-black. As their eyes adjusted to the darkness, they could see more and more stars, but they all were ignoring the constellations and looking west for a falling star.

"The aeroshell is experiencing significant heating," reported Linda. "We have a signal drop due to plasma buildup. You should start seeing it soon."

"It there!" cried the sharp-eyed pilot, Arielle, pointing. No one could see her arm in the darkness, but they didn't need to, for the streak rapidly grew brighter than any star.

"Seems to be right on target," Jinjur reported to Linda. "It's coming right out of the constellation Vela."

The bright streak ended almost overhead. Minutes later came a loud crack as the sonic boom hit them.

"Deceleration parachute deployed," came Linda's voice out of *Crash*. There was a long pause of many minutes. "Deceleration phase completed successfully. Main 'chute being deployed."

There was a cheer from the group as the skies above them were illuminated by a flare, swinging from side to side as it was slowly lowered down through the sky on its parachute.

"Good shot," said Jinjur to Linda. "Time for a celebration. Why don't you open a few bottles of James's Cabernet Sauvignon '66 for dinner tonight. We'll be joining you down here with a batch of vitamin-pill-enriched boobaa fruit brew."

By the time the parachute floated down from its initial deployment many kilometers high in the sky, Barnard had come out from behind Gargantua and the two-hour eclipse was over. The swift-swimming flouwen had seen the flare coming down and had swum to the spot where the aeroshell would be landing. There was a loud splash, and Little Red rushed to the spot.

☆Here it is! I've found it!☆

Roaring☆Hot☆Vermillion surged over the foaming

crests and dove to surround the object sinking slowly down through the water. ☆Yeow! Hot!☆

◊Of course it is hot, subset of Roaring☆Hot☆Vermillion,◊ chided Clear◊White◊Whistle. ◊That is the aeroshell that protected the crawler as it swam rapidly through the air high above the ocean. The rapid motion through the air caused the production of heat by friction. That is why it made a bright streak in the sky. The heat made it so hot, that you could not only feel the heat, you could look the . . . ◊

⬜Yes, yes, subset of Clear◊White◊Whistle. We know all about the heat built up by friction during rapid travel.⬜

Strong⬜Lavender⬜Crackle enjoyed hearing his own lectures, but not those of others. Especially not lectures by the subset of the much younger Clear◊White◊Whistle, only a few centuries old. The milky-colored flouwen might have embraced human technology and terminology more quickly than the rest of the flouwen, but this subset of Strong⬜Lavender⬜Crackle had also chosen to accompany the humans on this exploration trip and, as befitted an elder, had learned much about human technology himself. All of the human technology they had seen so far, could have easily been deduced by the pure mathematics and logic that the flouwen elders explored in the comfort of the shallow shorelines of the Islands of Thought at the Outer Pole of their homeworld Water—if they had desired to engage in such a trivial exercise. The large purple flouwen often wished he were back on Water. The major portion of himself was still there, living another life, discussing mathematical concepts with all the others in the pod, rocking up to think in the protected bays of the Islands of Thought, but he was trapped in this strange-tasting, too-warm sea.

The aeroshell finally cooled off enough so that Roaring☆Hot☆Vermillion could hold onto it. He engulfed it with his body, like a white blood cell surrounding a piece of soot, and brought it to the surface, where they all scanned it with their sonar.

☆Empty!☆

⎤Like a peekoo shell after you have eaten the delicious part inside.⎤

◊This is what humans call an aeroshell,◊ explained Clear◊White◊Whistle. ◊It protects the machine inside that carries the supplies. The machine—humans call lander— is still up in the air floating on large floppy thing like seaweed leaf—humans call parachute. Machine and parachute will be landing in water later. We are to take machine, parachute, and aeroshell to humans.◊

☆I will not wait!☆ said Roaring☆Hot☆Vermillion impatiently. ☆I will take aeroshell now!☆ The bulky aeroshell encased in his amorphous flame-colored body, Roaring☆Hot☆Vermillion formed into a manta-shaped wedge that was one of the shapes that allowed the flouwen to move quickly through the water, and headed off to the humans waiting on the shores of Crater Lagoon.

With Barnard now out from behind Gargantua, Clear◊White◊Whistle and Strong⎤Lavender⎤Crackle sensed the warmth and light coming down on top of their bodies as they floated on the surface of the water, their sonar sense seeing all around them, waiting for the return of one of the pings emitted by their bodies, or the splash of the machine hitting the water.

◊We should be able to look the machine now,◊ said Clear◊White◊Whistle. Each of them raised a pseudopod into the air. The end of each pseudopod developed a spherical lens shape, while at the same time, the colored liquid crystal nerve material that surrounded the cells in their amorphous bodies withdrew from the lens portion, leaving it clear. The light from above was focused by the lens onto their light-sensitive body, where it formed images. A few adjustments in the shapes of the lens and Barnard came into focus.

⎤I look a white circle, and hanging below it, held by long strands, is a silvery-colored rhomboid with appendages,⎤ said Strong⎤Lavender⎤Crackle.

◊The white circle and its strands are the parachute,◊ said Clear◊White◊Whistle. ◊While the silver rhomboid is the machine.◊

❑Machine hit waves,❑ reported Strong❑Lavender❑Crackle. Shortly they both heard the splash, followed by echo after echo as the sonar pulses their bodies had sent out reflected from the hard object. The returning echoes had complex side tones, as if parts of the machine were moving toward them while other parts were moving away, yet the main echo was definitely moving in their direction. They could also sense chirping pings being sent in their direction.

❑The machine is seeing us.❑

"Hello there!" called a familiar voice mixed with the pings.

◊It is James!◊ said Clear◊White◊Whistle. ◊It is talking to us through the machine. You get the parachute and take it to the humans in Crater Lagoon. I will go meet the machine and lead it there.◊

Late that afternoon, the happy group gathered for their evening meal. Nels had netted some fish from a lake nearby, while Reiki had gone to her favorite peekoo bed and brought home a large basket of the six-legged shellfish. As they gathered in a circle to eat, *Spritz* was there with them, its video eyes taking in the group and transmitting the image to a view-wall in the dining room of *Prometheus*, while perched in front of it, and connected by an infrared I/O link, the screen of Reiki's recorder presented a tiny video scene of the nine crew members up on *Prometheus*, who had also gathered together to share a meal with those stranded down below.

When the time came for the daily mealtime ritual of holding hands before dinner, Arielle, sitting next to *Spritz*, reached out her hand to the robotic crawler. James, understanding the gesture, had *Spritz* unstow its manipulators, and soon the circle was complete, the humans above included by mechanical proxy in the circle of friendship down below.

John started the meal by ceremoniously handing out the first of the vitamin and mineral supplement pills that *Spritz* had brought down, and watched as each person washed it down with a sip of boobaa fruit beer. Then dinner started, with the ten down below eating broiled fish and mashed vegetables from feebook leaf serving plates with their fingers, and the nine up above taking bites out of the compartments in their flip-top trays using civilized metal utensils.

The dinner ended with a dessert of the strawberrylike jookeejook fruits on the ground and real strawberries up above, followed by celebratory toasts and animated conversation.

"This crawler is going to be really useful as a communications link," exclaimed Carmen with obvious glee as she took another sip of beer. "With Reiki's recorder as a console, we can work with James just like we did in the good old days up on *Prometheus*. The recorder isn't a touchscreen, so we'll have to voice or key in all the commands, and the crawler isn't as versatile as an imp, but it will sure be better than having to work audio-only through *Crash*, stuck as it is down by the beach instead of up here in camp."

There was a general chorus of approval at the idea, but Jinjur remained silent, almost grim.

"I can check up on the status of all my hydroponics projects," agreed Nels. "And perhaps start some new ones."

"We can talk back and forth to our friends all we want," said Arielle. "And see them at the same time."

"And have more joint meals like this," suggested Tony from the tiny screen.

"And we can meet and see the Jollys," added George.

"I may even be able to get documented this sono-video composition that has been running around in my head since our first sunset here," added David.

"We'd love to be able to see and hear it," chirped Katrina, pleased at the thought.

"You're all forgetting something," growled Jinjur in a loud, slow, level tone. The conversation came to a halt, both on the ground and in the sky. Jinjur switched to her commander's voice and continued. "We are on a mission—to gather scientific data about the Barnard system and report it back to Earth—and we are going to continue that mission despite the recent setback we encountered on landing. Now that we have taken care of our primary concern—ensuring the future health of the portion of the crew down here—the mission will continue. With *Prometheus* many light-minutes away off on its mission of surveying the other moons, a video comm link through *Spritz* will be as useful as pity in a drill sergeant's heart."

She paused and laboriously got to her feet. Although she was rotund with pregnancy and clad only in a brightly decorated sarong, she still oozed the aura of command. You could almost see two stars glinting on each of her bare black shoulders as she squared them up. When Major General Virginia Jones continued speaking, she was giving orders.

"Shirley, Carmen, and David. I want you to check out *Spritz*. Make sure its navigation system is loaded with a map of Eden. Send it out to explore the neighboring islands and report back what it finds there."

"George. You and your crew will resume the planned detailed survey of the Gargantuan moon system. The first of the return sample rockets on the moons Zouave and Zapotec should be full before the year is out, so arrange for *Prometheus* to be there for pickup.

"Thomas, Red, and Sam. I want you to use the left-over Ascent Module vehicles to carry out surface exploration missions to the small airless moons of Gargantua, Zwingli, Zoroaster, Zeus; and, if James calculates that it is safe to do so, the asteroid-sized ones, Zen and Zion.

"Linda, Deirdre, Tony, Caroline, and Katrina. I want you to maintain daily contact with the flouwen on Eau, the gummies on Roche, and the icerugs on Zulu. I don't want them to forget us. That's in addition to your usual science and support duties, of course.

"The rest of us down here will continue collecting information about the Jollys and this island. Once we have preliminary reports back from *Spritz* on the neighboring islands, we'll build rafts for *Spritz* to tow, and explore them in more detail in person."

She paused to look around, pleased that she had things running smoothly again.

"That should keep us productively busy for a while." She picked up the small recorder and looked at the image of the nine people up on *Prometheus*, all sitting around a table, drinking the last drops of the Cabernet Sauvignon '66 from their squeezers.

"Don't sit there like a pack of pixilated poodles!" she exploded. "Get busy!"

George, taken aback, leaped to attention and almost floated away, but was brought back by the long arm of Sam.

"Yes, ma'am!" George replied, then turned to Tony. "Man the helm, Mr. Roma. Set sail for Zapotec." Tony left the table and the dinner was over.

"See you in six years for the second drop," said Jinjur. She turned to look expectantly at those around her. Shirley, knowing that look, immediately scrambled to her feet and went over to close the doors on *Spritz*, while the others, following her lead, finished dinner and started cleaning up.

"*Prometheus* will be in communication range for a day or so," said Jinjur. "After that, the round-trip delay time will make ordinary conversation impossible, although we can still transmit data and messages back and forth. So . . . make sure you say your 'good-byes' through the video link on *Spritz* soon. Any of you who have private messages for special friends can walk down to the beach and use the communicator on *Crash* where you'll have more privacy."

She looked around to make sure there were no questions, then headed down the beach toward *Crash* herself. It wouldn't do to have the troops see tears as she said her own good-byes. High above her in the sky, the gigantic aluminum-foil moon slowly tilted and *Prometheus* sailed away.

BIRTHS

When the first true contraction gripped Cinnamon, her reaction was one of anger. She didn't have time for this, not now. There was too much going on, and Junior would simply have to wait. For the last seventeen hours Cinnamon had been coaching Jinjur through her labor and the Marine was anything but stoic. Now, just as the General was going through transition, Arielle's water had broken.

When Shirley had first helped Jinjur into the "Shack" that John had set up as the clinic, John, acting as doctor, had allowed everyone to help, hoping for an easy delivery that would calm the women's fears about their own upcoming deliveries. As Jinjur's labor went on and on, the others had become only more anxious and frustrated. It was demoralizing to see their leader, usually so thoroughly in command of any situation, reduced by pain and exhaustion to a sweating shaking thing. Jinjur now had no strength left, able only to curse softly under her breath, and this was more than they could bear.

First Reiki, who knew that this was not a place for crowds, had slipped back to her tepee and Richard had joined her. Then, David, who had secretly harbored expectations of a beautiful natural celebration of life, had been brought rudely back to earth. Cinnamon could see the "You're Havin' My Baby" song being driven from his mind in the face of this new evidence. When Arielle announced that she was going back to her bed, David had gone with her. Carmen had tried to stay out of the way and had spent several hours in a far corner quietly whispering the rosary over and over, but after a time Jinjur became aware of what she was doing.

"Purple-pizzled Popes!" she swore in the bluest phrase Cinnamon had ever heard Jinjur use. "Carmen! Do your pestiferous praying somewhere where I can't hear it!"

John had left orders for them to wake him as soon as it was time for Jinjur to deliver, and for the last several hours now it had been just Cinnamon and Shirley talking the laboring woman through each contraction.

"I want to push!" Jinjur insisted.

"Jinjur? You have to listen to me," said Cinnamon soothingly. "I know it feels like you should push, but you're not fully dilated yet. If you push too soon, you'll only be pushing the baby against your cervix. You might tear yourself—"

"Peripatetic porcupines! That's why there are sutures! Just get this baby out of me!"

"The baby can't get past your cervix until . . ."

"He can if he tries! Come on little guy! Adapt! Overcome!" Jinjur was speaking through clenched teeth as she pushed with the contraction.

"No!" yelled Cinnamon, startling her into following orders. "Blow! Blow! Like this!" she said, blowing little puffs of breath into the General's face. Jinjur joined in and the straining stopped.

"You're in transition," said Cinnamon calmly, as Jinjur fought to regain herself in the few seconds she had between contractions. "Things are really moving along now and I promise . . . it won't be much longer. Three more contractions and I'll check your progress again." Cinnamon noticed that she was losing Jinjur's attention to a building contraction. "Try and stay limp . . . it's just like a wave . . . relax and glide over it . . . it won't be much longer . . . I'll even send for John. Shirley?"

"No!" Jinjur grabbed for her lover's hand. The movement cost her dearly as tension spread instantly throughout her body, and she was lost completely to the pain. "Don't leave me!" she sobbed.

"I'm right here . . . I'm not going anywhere . . ." crooned Shirley, stroking Jinjur's arms and shoulders, reminding her to relax again. She wiped the sweat from Jinjur's brow, pulling her back away from despair. "Go on, Cinnamon. I'll keep her from pushing," said Shirley quietly.

Cinnamon slipped out into the warm night air. Overhead, Gargantua was a huge pink ball filling much of the sky above her. A crescent of darkness had been taken out of one side, making the time well past midnight. Cinnamon's back twinged in protest as she stooped to get through the small door to her own cozy hut, where John was sleeping. She paused for a moment, letting her eyes adapt to the darkness. John had heard her enter and was sitting up.

"Jinjur ready for me?" he asked over a yawn.

"She feels the need to push and she's almost at ten centimeters, but I can feel the baby's head and it's really big. I know that you and the flouwen have been using their sonar to keep an eye on the babies' development . . ."

"Yeah, I knew Jinjur was carrying a pretty good-sized hero. But it shouldn't make that much difference . . ."

"Every centimeter counts! We both know that!"

"Hey! That's my son you're talking about! I know you're tired and I thank you for handling things up to now. But Jinjur's going to do fine." John moved away dismissively. "I don't want to argue in front of her. You just stay here and I'll handle things from now on."

"And just how many babies have you delivered!?"

John was taken aback, startled by Cinnamon's challenge. Usually she was the quietest person on the island.

"That baby is huge and the mother is about worn out! She still has hours of hard work ahead of her! She's going to need an episiotomy, maybe the forceps, and stitches regardless . . . I've delivered dozens of babies."

"And she's going to need you," agreed John, "but not like this. You can't help her unless you get a grip on yourself. Take a few minutes and pull yourself together. I'll be with Jinjur."

"It's not like you're the one in labor," he mumbled as he ducked out the doorway.

He's right, Cinnamon thought. *I'm no help to anyone if I can't keep my head.* She lit a fish-oil lamp made with an upside-down peekoo shell and sat down on her soft pallet, surrounded with the little comforts that made this her own home. The flickering light twinkled off the thin metal rods of the mobile imp that used to be her link with James. It had ridden on her hair like headphones for so many years, watching over her as it played old songs to her softly. Now it was just an intricate cascade of iciclelike strands sparkling over the doorway. In the highest curve of the roof hung drying herbs, giving the air a scent that was warm and personal. A quilt stitched from the ragged pieces left of their original clothes was spread on the bed beneath her, and coloring the walls were small squares of the Jolly's feltlike barkcloth that David had decorated with native dyes. These were rejects to him and she doubted he knew she had them, but she enjoyed these first efforts in his experiments with the local colors.

Cinnamon took a deep breath and felt herself come back into focus. She was just tired. Even without the stress factor, she had been working harder physically today than she had in months. And to top it all off, all the time she had been bending over Jinjur her back had been acting up. It had never bothered her before, and she resented it calling attention to itself now, sending sharp twinges from low down on her last vertebra, almost to her legs. She stretched, but nothing loosened. Just then she heard the gentle scratching that took the place of a doorbell here.

"Yes?" she called getting to her feet. She rubbed her belly. The pain in her back seemed to be reaching long fingers around to her groin.

"Is me, Arielle," said the thin blonde as she ducked through the doorway. "David, he put me out of the bed. I made everything wet."

"Your water broke?"

"Is wet, anyway."

"Are you having any pa— contractions?" Cinnamon asked, reaching out to stroke Arielle's belly. It felt hard as a rock beneath her fingers, and then gradually softened.

"Some squeezing," Arielle admitted with her usual aplomb, "but no pains . . ."

"Are you sure?" Cinnamon asked. "We had better get you over to the Shack anyway and let John check you out as soon as he can. Once the water breaks things can start moving quickly."

She slipped a supporting arm around the other woman's waist just in case a sudden pain caused the slender pilot to stumble. Instead, Cinnamon's own back spasms came back to bother her and she was glad of Arielle's support. Again Arielle's belly grew hard and Cinnamon counted silently. Thirty seconds later it was still as solid as a rock.

"It feels like you are contracting now," said Cinnamon puzzled. "Are you sure you don't feel that?"

"It is a bit squeeze, a little harder to breathe . . . it is contraction?"

"Usually there is no mistaking labor pains, but sometimes they can be deceptive. Some women have very little pain, some women have back labor . . ." As the words left her mouth, Cinnamon felt the back pain tighten into a strong pressure outward against the very bottom of her back and travel gradually around to her lower belly. They had reached the clinic and she clutched the doorframe reflexively.

"Go on in," Cinnamon said, striving to keep her voice even. "Tell John I'll be there in a second." From the doorway they could hear him telling Jinjur to push and the inhuman-sounding groan as Jinjur began to bear down.

"He sounds busy . . . " said Arielle doubtfully.

"Well, if those contractions aren't bothering you . . ." Cinnamon had to think about each word as her own pain slowly increased, "then you might as well just keep out of the way. But things could get worse quickly and it would be better if you at least were in the building." The pain passed and she straightened up. "Come on in and I'll get you a place to rest and wait."

Together they entered the Shack. It was lit up with the solar-rechargeable permalights that had come down in the first lander. Shirley was holding Jinjur's shoulder, curling her into a pushing position in the chairlike platform that they had designed for this months ago.

"Eight . . . nine . . . ten . . . take a quick breath and push again! One . . . two . . . three . . ." John was seated on the floor between Jinjur's legs, his eyes and light trained on the relevant area.

"Good, good, the head is crowning! Is the contraction over?"

Jinjur didn't answer, but slumped back in the chair, her dark face gray-brown with fatigue. Cinnamon stood behind John and handed him a scalpel. "Time for that episiotomy, John. She'll never stretch enough, and a straight cut will heal better."

Carefully John cut the taut tissue, blood welling up behind the knife. Jinjur paid no attention, looking inwardly to the building contraction. Shirley recognized her change in breathing and again gathered her up to push. "Come on, Jinjur, you can do this. Once more for the Corps!"

Cinnamon leaned against the wall, trying to relax and breathe her way through her own building contraction as Jinjur bore down. "One . . . two . . . three . . ." counted John and Shirley together. Then John broke off as his son's head was pushed clear and he gently wiped the mucus from the nose and mouth. Wet, dark hair curled all over the large head. Two pairs of blue eyes, linking these two

Kennedys to all those still on Earth, locked on each other, and for a moment John forgot where he was.

" . . . eight . . . nine . . . ten." Shirley's voice called him back.

"Deep breath and push again, while I turn him so you can deliver his shoulders," he said.

Jinjur felt herself rally. She was sore and tired, more tired than she had ever been, but the searing pain was gone and the pushing had given her focus. She could feel the otherness between her legs and the terrible stretching had been relieved with the passing of the head. She closed her eyes and pushed with everything she had.

"Eerrarrggg!"

John twisted the slippery person in his hands, easing out the broad rounded shoulders. Suddenly, the baby slipped free and John was holding his son in his lap. Jinjur flopped back, knowing her part was over. The baby, his lungs free of the constriction of the birth canal, drew in his first deep breath and sounded his challenge to the world.

John took the soft barkcloth towel Cinnamon handed him and gently wiped most of the wetness from the babe. Then he cut the cord and lay the still squalling baby in his mother's arms. Jinjur looked down at that angry red face, and all the aches and pains melted away. She nuzzled his warm damp curls, savoring the smell, even the taste of him.

"Good work," said John tenderly.

"You too." Jinjur looked from her baby's blue eyes to those of his father. Although they had never been lovers, each knew that they now shared a bond almost as great, because both had instantly and irrevocably fallen in love with the son they shared.

"Umm, Jinjur?" said Cinnamon quietly a few minutes later. "I hate to interrupt, but if you'll give just one more push, we can deliver the placenta and John can take care of these stitches."

"Can you do that, Cinnamon? I want to hold the baby, too," said John.

"Sorry, John, but my contractions are less than a minute apart now, and I might not sew straight. Jinjur, I don't want to rush you, but between Arielle and myself, your chair is needed!"

"Arielle?" John asked.

"Her waters have broken."

"Christ!" muttered John as he carefully pulled the placenta free and sutured swiftly. Then he and Shirley helped Jinjur into a soft bed near Arielle. The baby had stopped crying and was already trying to nurse. Jinjur grimaced as he latched on to her nipple.

"Well, you lead rest of us again," said Arielle. "You have firstborn. First man of Eden. What you name him?"

Shirley, John, and Jinjur looked at each other. "Adam!" they all said together.

When John looked back later on those hectic few days, although the feelings seemed to blur into a melange of joy, fear, frustration, and fatigue, each birth remained crystal clear, separate, and special.

Cinnamon delivered a daughter less than an hour after Adam's birth. The fast labor led to a bad tear in Cinnamon's cervix, and while John stitched her up carefully, he became aware that he was being watched. He had looked up to find himself staring into the baby's deep brown eyes as she lay on her mother's belly. Cinnamon was stroking the downy fuzz that covered her back while the baby looked around, her initial cry stilled almost instantly by her apparent curiosity. Named Eve, of course, Cinnamon and Nels's child seemed to be the quiet, watchful type; even her cries were more a gentle reminder than the furious demand for attention that sprang from his own son's lungs.

Shannon, the daughter of David and Arielle, slipped into the world in the easiest delivery John had ever seen. Arielle "labored" quietly while John got Cinnamon and

Eve tucked in together at home. Before he had even examined her, she said that she felt like she "need to shit" and he found her to be fully dilated. The blunt-spoken Canadian never evidenced any pain, while she calmly delivered a blue-eyed redhead. Tiny but healthy, the baby's good looks seemed more elfin than human. David had come in looking for his lover just in time to help cut the cord, and had taken over the baby completely. Arielle was given the baby only to nurse, but considering her rather haphazard approach to domestic chores, the arrangement seemed to suit the couple best.

John used the break in the action to get some sleep. He fell on his pallet exhausted. Richard woke him ten hours later with the news that Reiki needed him. Reiki, not wishing to disrupt the others with anything as simple and natural as childbirth, had quietly labored in the privacy of the tepee. Richard had left to go hunting without even knowing her labor had begun. When he returned for the noontime siesta, he discovered the prim anthropologist was unable to walk. He swept her up in his arms, where she almost vanished in his weight-lifter's muscles, and carried her into the Shack.

John had hardly rubbed the sleep out of his eyes when he was once again guiding another person into the world. The labor was complicated by the noontime darkness. As Eden slipped into the shadow cast by the huge planet above them, John had to expend again the jealously hoarded energy stored in the solar batteries. He had used the permalights too recklessly the night before, and nobody had remembered to take them out in the sunlight to recharge, so the beam from the flashlight was feeble. Fortunately, the darkness, although deep, was always short-lived. By the time the baby boy slipped into his arms, the first bright beams of reddish light were peeking around Gargantua, spilling into the open face of the Shack. John, surprised that the baby wasn't crying, quickly inverted him and gave him a smack. Still, the baby didn't cry, but in the growing light it was clear that he was breathing well and looking at John alertly and with what John could have sworn was reproach.

During the long bright afternoon, John was careful to see that the batteries for the permalights were recharged. That night Shirley delivered her son, a blond giant whom she named Dirk. This time the laboring mother had the coaching and support of one who had already been through a similar ordeal. Jinjur sympathized, cheered, and cajoled her lover throughout the night. John was hardly needed, except to care for Adam while his mother took care of the patient.

Nels, the father of this baby, thanks to the manipulations of Josephine, peeked in once or twice, but Shirley was too busy to notice. When the long night was over, and Dirk was hungrily nursing, Nels returned to see his second child. He stroked the soft round cheek, but Dirk was too engrossed in his meal to tolerate any disruption, and his tiny fist reached up to bat the tickling finger away. Nels didn't mind; he knew that this child would be primarily Shirley's to raise.

Carmen and John's daughter Maria was the last of the firstborn to make its appearance. For several days, John had followed Carmen around . . . it had been like waiting for the other shoe to drop. Carmen had wandered from home to home, visiting the new parents, playing with the babies, collecting tips and advice, and a few horror stories of labor. Warned that labor always lasted too long, Carmen had not been in a hurry to stop work. Besides, she was waist-deep in the warm waters of the bay, and the painful tightening seemed eased by the supportive water. It took a strong contraction to persuade her to leave the gentle waves. Fortunately, John had been watching for her and ran to meet her, helping her into the Shack. Cinnamon joined them to act as midwife while John observed from his place as father at Carmen's shoulder. Cinnamon caught the baby girl and presented her to them, and for once John was able to bask in the joy of the birth without the messy details of stitches and afterbirth. Together John and Carmen cuddled the baby as she suckled, and as she fell asleep, replete, her tiny fingers were clasped around his little finger. John was inordinately proud to be the father of this particular baby, for Maria was the only baby of the six that had been naturally conceived.

A few days later, Richard and Reiki took their baby boy to the warm freshwater lake above the camp for his daily bath. They supported the naked baby between them, holding him securely while washing him gently but thoroughly.

"Doesn't that feel nice, my poppet?" crooned Reiki, smoothing the warm lake water over the tiny feet. "Steady does it, my little one, let's get all those fat wrinkles rinsed off." The baby stared into the two hovering faces, its small face intent and solemn, but unafraid. Richard relinquished his hold and waded to shore for the soft barkcloth blanket; Reiki followed, and they wrapped the infant snugly.

"I'll take our catch up to the fire," said Richard. "You can come along when you're ready." Richard knew Reiki preferred to feed their son in privacy, and she smiled back at him before settling down to lean comfortably against a handy tree trunk. Richard stood, oddly irresolute, looking down on the two dark heads so close together.

"Umm. Carmen's baby's been named Maria, and Cinnamon calls her little girl Eve, so I guess that's her name. Have you thought of anything, besides 'poppet'? I don't really mind," he added hastily. "But maybe something . . . kind of . . . more like a boy? It'd be a good idea, I think, to get it settled."

He reached to stroke Reiki's breast, where the baby busily suckled, and then strode briskly down the beach. Reiki studied the little face dreamily, lost in contentment, until the noisy slurping slowed with satiation. She lifted the round little body to her shoulder to pat it until rewarded with an unselfconscious belch, and then laid the baby along the top of her legs to look into his round dark eyes. The baby gazed back at her quietly.

"We all talked about you, before you were born, you know. How we'd teach you all about everything on Earth, as well as everything we've learned here. We have such dreams for you and the other little ones, too! But we keep running up against problems.

"Why teach you Earthly things, even though they're your heritage? It's so doubtful you'll ever experience any of them—families, or countries, or beautiful scenes, or buildings—or even anything cold! All our own names come from that different world, and we can't even seem to make original names for the things we find here—Jolly Green Giants, for heaven's sake. But what to call *you*, my precious lambkin-love!"

Reiki stopped, and sifted again through the names she and Richard had considered. Japanese names, Indian names, names of powerful leaders—but all from the world of the past. Yet what could they be sure of in the future here? Names were important, of that Reiki was sure. They were a gift from society. In this fledgling society, how did Reiki and Richard wish their small son to be known? She looked around her, at the alien skies, the thick growth of strange blue-green plants, the sun whose red hue would probably be the only one they'd ever see again. She knew for a certainty that she would do everything in her power to ensure her son's survival, and was there anything more she would wish him? Reiki was wise enough to know that no one can make another happy—that was always up to oneself, if . . . Then thoughtfully, she decided.

"Your name is Freeman, my wee bairn—and free may you live, wherever you live." She bent forward to kiss the small nose and stood up.

The next day, as the ritual "bathing of the babies" time came to a close at the shallow end of the lake above their camp, Carmen called everyone to come together. John and she had discussed this beforehand, and had agreed to spring this surprise on the whole group rather than discussing it around Council Rock. At Carmen's insistence, everyone moved to form a loose circle.

Carmen handed little Maria to her father. She, like most of the freshly washed infants, was now tightly wrapped in soft white folds of pounded bark-fiber cloth. Carmen stooped, filling a pink peekoo shell with a bit of water from the lake. Then she stood and faced her baby.

"I baptize thee," she said, tracing the sign of the cross on Maria's forehead with a dampened thumb, "in the name of the Father, and the Son, and the Holy Ghost."

Then Carmen turned to Cinnamon, a question in her eyes. Cinnamon hesitated, but then held Eve out to her.

"I baptize thee . . ."

Jinjur leaned over to John and whispered furiously. "Perambulating pandas! I don't like this! I'm not Catholic!"

"She won't do Adam if you don't want her to, but after all, what harm is there in it? It's only a ceremony."

Carmen had moved on to Reiki and Richard, and a small cross was being traced between their baby's dark eyes.

Jinjur was not convinced. "It's a ceremony of an agreement to bring the child to God, to teach him to be a Catholic. I'm not going to promise to do that."

"It's also asking all those present to act as godparents; to look after the child."

"They will do that anyway!"

Shannon's red-blond curls darkened as the water dripped from her forehead.

John sighed. "Look, Carmen has become more interested in religion ever since she first found out she was pregnant. She wants to make sure that these kids have everything we had when we were growing up, even if we don't have the technology. Didn't your folks raise you with a religion? Weren't you baptized?"

"With us, baptizing came later. It was supposed to be a rebirth."

Shirley was holding Dirk out to Carmen. He did not even wake as her cool fingers touched his warm skin.

"This can symbolize whatever you want it to. Consider it a welcome to this life, to this planet."

Carmen was standing in front of them. Jinjur thought for a moment, and then slowly brought Adam down from his position on her shoulder. Carmen murmured the blessing softly, but as her cool wet fingers caressed the baby, Adam started awake and began to howl lustily.

"Humph," Jinjur snorted. "Be glad no one insisted on a bris!"

FLOUWEN

After a long strenuous afternoon of playing surf-tag, the flouwen were especially hungry, so instead of prying out some delicious pink peekoos from their hard-to-open shells, they went to a vent bed where there were plenty of ripe oosheesh. The oosheesh were nowhere near as tasty as the multieyed, six-legged peekoo, but they provided a filling meal for the flouwen's hungry cells.

The ocean grew warmer as they approached the site of the deep bed of hot water vents that squirted out from the side of the submerged slope of the island volcano. Around each major vent, spaced almost as if they had been deliberately planted there, were a number of large underwater plants that the Jolly fishermen called the oothoo. The oothoo had large leaves that floated up toward the weak sunlight filtering down from the surface, doing their best to supply the plant with nourishment from photosynthesis. Photosynthesis in the weak red light from Barnard was a meager source of energy, however, and the more successful plants on Eden had evolved additional sources of nourishment. For the oothoo plant, it was the oosheesh, or filter-fish, as the humans called them.

The oosheesh were mobile appendages or "mouths" of the oothoo plant, which swam through the water near the plant and filtered out the microscopic creatures that lived on the minerals and chemicals emitted by the hot water volcanic vents. Originally, the "mouths" of the oothoo plants were likely to have been leaves folded over to make a crude trap, with spines at the "lips" to prevent the escape of the prey—similar to a Venus Flytrap on Earth. But form ever follows function, and over the aeons, the leafy "mouths" had evolved until they looked more like a miniature baleen whale than a leaf.

☆Here is big one!☆ said Roaring☆Hot☆Vermillion, as he plucked an oosheesh from its plant with a tug. The oothoo plant reacted to the loss of its feeder appendage by causing its other five oosheesh to scurry home to shelter between the strong, thick roots of the large plant. It would now have to grow another feeder to replace the one that Roaring☆Hot☆Vermillion had eaten. The other two flouwen plucked their meals from adjoining plants.

◊Filling, but not much taste,◊ complained Clear◊White◊Whistle as he tore his oosheesh apart.

❑There is a strange fish over there seeing us,❑ said Strong❑Lavender❑Crackle, interrupting his meal of oosheesh to beam a focused sonar tone at the distant animal, so the echo would make the creature stand out for the others. In return, the strange fish was seeing at them with its own sonar pings.

◊Strange shape,◊ remarked Clear◊White◊Whistle, as he sent a complex chirp that would enable him to determine the details of the internal structure of the strange fish. When the echo came back, Clear◊White◊Whistle was puzzled. ◊It seems to be all eye and fins—no evidence of mouth or teeth.◊

☆Wonder if it tastes good?☆ said Roaring☆Hot☆Vermillion. He slipped into his hunting shape. The strange fish watched Roaring☆Hot☆Vermillion intently as he changed his shape, then attempted to flee. It soon was engulfed in red jelly, slowly being torn apart into digestible pieces. ☆You are right. One big eye in front—tasty part. Fins along side, and tail for swimming—tail part tasty, too. Much tastier than oosheesh.☆

▢What about inside parts?▢ asked Strong▢Lavender▢Crackle. ▢Sometimes those not taste good or are too hard.▢

☆No insides!☆ replied Roaring☆Hot☆Vermillion.

◊No insides?◊ repeated Clear◊White◊Whistle. He swam up close to Roaring☆Hot☆Vermillion and sent into the red body a series of chirps focused on the chunks of flesh rapidly being digested by the cells surrounding them. ◊No insides,◊ he confirmed. ◊Just an eye, six fins along the sides, and a tail. Very strange fish.◊

☆There is another one!☆ said Roaring☆Hot☆Vermillion, noticing another eyefish looking at him from beneath some seaweed fronds. This one was not emitting chirps to see at them, but it had obviously looked them with its single large eye and was keeping at a safe distance. Suddenly, it darted away at high speed toward the dark depths of the deep ocean.

Roaring☆Hot☆Vermillion considered chasing after it, but he still had a half-eaten oosheesh as well as the first eyefish to finish, so he settled down to digest them.

A little while later, the eyefish was back—with two others like it. One of them approached cautiously, seeing at them as it came, with sharp chirps generated by its body, while the other two stayed off in the seaweed cover, just looking at them. One of the lookers left, then the seer left, leaving just the other looker. Soon they both were back—or were they different ones? To Roaring☆Hot☆Vermillion, the return echo from one of them seemed larger than he remembered. In any case, he had finished digesting his first two catches and was still hungry, so he assumed his hunting shape and started toward the three tasty morsels. The eyefish turned and fled at high speed toward the dark depths. Roaring☆Hot☆Vermillion kept his prey in sight by ping after ping of direction-finding sonar. He caught one, who responded with panicked chirps that spurred the others to flee even faster. Suddenly, Roaring☆Hot☆Vermillion came to an abrupt halt by splaying out his red body into a sea anchor.

◊What is the matter?◊ asked Clear◊White◊Whistle, who had followed along to see if there were more of these tasty eyefish to be captured. Then his sonar pings came echoing back, carrying an ominous message. There was something coming up the slope from the dark depths! And it was HUGE!

Strong☐Lavender☐Crackle soon joined them, and the three of them illuminated the large distant object with focused sonar chirps.

☆That is BIG fish!☆

◊We not see that kind of fish before. I will have to tell human Cinnamon about it.◊ Clear◊White◊Whistle sent off another chirp designed to accurately measure the distant creature, then converted the echo into measurements that Cinnamon would understand. ◊Four meters long and a meter thick. Six fins along the side, and lots of large sharp teeth.◊

☐Like big coelashark, but with six fins instead of four legs, and soft furry skin instead of armored scales.☐

◊Something like what Cinnamon say Earth sharks look like.◊

☆Has six holes in head. One hole has eye in it. The rest are empty!☆ added Roaring☆Hot☆Vermillion, finally making sense of what he was seeing with his sonar. They all saw the two fleeing eyefish swim up to the monster shark and nestle into two of the empty holes, eye facing out. The monster shark now had three eyes.

◊Those holes are nests for the eyefish,◊ said Clear◊White◊Whistle. ◊Just like nests in fronds of Jollys are for their flying eyes. You are eating one of the eyes of that shark, subset of Roaring☆Hot☆Vermillion.◊

☆Tastes good,☆ said Roaring☆Hot☆Vermillion, unconcerned, as he ripped the eyefish apart until it stopped screaming and started to digest the pieces.

The giant shark opened its mouth, and out from holes

in the roof of its mouth came four strange fish with strong tails and six fins along the sides, but instead of mouths and eyes on the head portion, they bore a number of tentacles. The outside tentacles were long and thin. Inside those were muscular-looking grabbers with suckers on them, while the innermost ones were short and ended in vicious-looking pincers. One of the strange fish used its sharp pincers to detach a filter-fish from an oothoo plant. Then all four fish used their tentacles to herd the filter-fish into the shark's mouth, where it was dispatched with a snap of the toothed mouth and swallowed. The strange fish then reentered the shark's reopened mouth, but instead of being eaten, they passed over the sharp teeth unmolested and settled into cavities in the roof of the shark's cavernous maw.

⊓Those fish may be like the gatherers which the Jolly use to gather food.⊓

The shark reopened its mouth and one of the strange fish came out and headed toward them.

◊Maybe the gatherfish is coming to 'gather' us.◊

☆Wonder if a gatherfish tastes as good as an eyefish?☆ said Roaring☆Hot☆Vermillion as he headed downward to catch the approaching gatherfish. Off to one side, two eyefish were watching.

◊You shouldn't be eating that creature's eyes and gatherers,◊ said Clear◊White◊Whistle. ◊It will get mad at you and attack.◊

☆I'm not scared!☆

⊓The creature may be intelligent. If so, the humans would like to meet it and talk with it.⊓

This comment brought Roaring☆Hot☆Vermillion to a halt. The subset of Strong⊓Lavender⊓Crackle was right. They were here on an exploration mission to find new forms of life, not just to eat and enjoy themselves in the surf.

⊓The Jollys talk by using their gatherers to whistle sounds,⊓ remarked Strong⊓Lavender⊓Crackle. ⊓Perhaps we can attempt communication with this shark's gather-fish.◻

☆Hello!☆ said Roaring☆Hot☆Vermillion at the approaching gatherfish, making sure he said it loud enough that the distant shark could also hear it. Except for the continual string of sonar chirps from the shark and the gatherfish, there was no response.

Clear◊White◊Whistle started to count, thinking that if the shark were intelligent, it would recognize that the regular pattern of sounds were indications of an attempt to communicate. If the shark then counted back, they could build on that beginning.

◊One, t-t-wo-wo, th-th-th-r-r-r-e-e-e, f-f-f-f-o-o-o-o-u-u-u-u-r-r-r-r . . . ◊ counted Clear◊White◊Whistle, giving each number a multitoned voice and multitongued pattern that epitomized the number that it represented. When he got to the final number in the flouwen's octal base numbering system, the word was a seven-toned, seven-tongued, majestic wonder.

The flouwen waited, but no sounds were emitted by either the gatherfish or the shark except the simple repetitive sonar chirps. The gatherfish came near Roaring☆Hot☆Vermillion and released a squirt of milky substance from the tip of one of its longer tentacles.

☆What a terrible taste!☆ yelled Roaring☆Hot☆Vermillion, backing away as the gatherfish turned and retreated into the mouth of the shark. ☆It tried to poison me!☆

◻Very complex taste,◻ remarked Strong◻Lavender◻Crackle as a whiff of the diluted cloud wafted toward him.

Another gatherfish came toward Clear◊White◊Whistle and squirted another cloud of chemicals from one of its longer tentacles.

◊Terrible!!!◊ complained Clear◊White◊Whistle, backing away.

◻Terrible, yes, but this taste is different,◻ remarked

Strong☐Lavender☐Crackle. ☐I think the shark is trying different chemicals until it finds one that either poisons us, or tastes so bad we will leave.☐

◊Let me try communicating one more time,◊ said Clear◊White◊Whistle. He repeated the integers up to seven again, then tried simple arithmetic. ◊One plus one is t-t-wo-wo, t-t-wo-wo plus one is th-th-th-r-r-r-e-e-e . . . ◊

There was no response. Instead the shark released another gatherfish from inside its mouth and sent it toward them. This time, Roaring☆Hot☆Vermillion was ready for it. Just as the gatherfish brought forth one of its tentacles and squirted a third noxious cloud, a red pseudopod shot out from Roaring☆Hot☆Vermillion's body and grabbed the end of the tentacle, pinching off the orifice. This hold established, other red pseudopods quickly reached out from Roaring☆Hot☆Vermillion's body and grabbed the other long tentacles, preventing them from squirting their poisonous loads, while one large pseudopod seized the tail of the gatherfish. With a quick twist, Roaring☆Hot☆Vermillion wrung the tentacle-head loose from the tail, tossed the poison-loaded portion away, and proceeded to digest the tail.

☆Tasty!☆

The sonar chirps from the shark now increased in intensity as they were focused on Roaring☆Hot☆Vermillion. There was still no modulation in them—no indication of any attempt at communication.

☐The shark is seeing at you! It may attack!☐ warned Strong☐Lavender☐Crackle.

☆Let it attack. It is probably tasty, too!☆

The shark opened its mouth and the five remaining gatherfish emerged. They formed a circle in front of the shark, who advanced slowly toward them, its mouth open to show its rows of sharp teeth. As the ring of gatherfish approached Roaring☆Hot☆Vermillion, he was ready for them, with multiple arrays of red pseudopods deployed. The five gatherfish flashed forward to meet the red pseudopods, their tentacles stretched out before them . . .

☆AAAGGH!☆ screamed Roaring☆Hot☆Vermillion as high-voltage electrical currents burned their way through his flesh. The shark followed up on the attack of its gatherfish by swimming rapidly toward the now limp blob of red jelly. Clear◊White◊Whistle and Strong⃞Lavender⃞Crackle started forward to protect their injured comrade, but were driven back by warning jolts of electricity from the gatherfish. They were forced to stay back and watch as the shark took a big bite out of the large blob of flaccid red flesh that was Roaring☆Hot☆Vermillion, and then proceeded to stuff the bite into its gigantic maw with the help of its gatherfish.

☆Yeow!☆ came a muffled voice from inside the shark. Then the shark went into convulsions as red jelly started to ooze out through its gill slots and between its lips.

Strong⃞Lavender⃞Crackle and Clear◊White◊Whistle took advantage of the shark's distraction to rush in and wring off the dangerous heads of the gatherfish as they had seen Roaring☆Hot☆Vermillion do. They experienced some severe shocks in the process, but they were localized to the pseudopod used to grasp the stinging, poisonous head portion.

The shark was now in severe pain. Its mouth wide open, it was shaking its head, trying to eject the burning red flesh which was attempting to digest the inside of its mouth and its tender gill slots. Soon most of the "bite" the shark had taken of Roaring☆Hot☆Vermillion was free and quickly rejoined the main body, but a chunk of the fiercely fighting flesh of the flouwen remained in the shark's stomach, battling to digest the wall of its living prison at the same time the digestive juices of the shark were digesting it. Strong⃞Lavender⃞Crackle and Clear◊White◊Whistle rounded up the small blobs of red flesh shaken loose during the battle and added them to the rapidly recovering remainder of Roaring☆Hot☆Vermillion. Focused sonar bursts were aimed at the giant shark's remaining eyes, which burst under the intense sonic bombardment. Maimed and blind, with all of its eyefish and gatherfish either destroyed or eaten, the shark headed for the depths.

◊That was a fish we have never seen before. A very strange fish with free-swimming eyes and manipulators,◊ mused Clear◊White◊Whistle. ◊The humans will be interested in knowing about it. We must tell them, especially Cinnamon. Her research is the various types of fish and how they might be related.◊

⌐The shark is also big enough to eat one of the humans in a single bite!⌐ remarked Strong⌐Lavender⌐Crackle. ⌐They should *all* know how big and dangerous it is, so they will be careful when they are in the deep ocean!⌐

☆It wasn't big enough to eat me!☆ bragged Roaring☆Hot☆Vermillion.

◊If we had not been there to get rid of the gatherfish, they would have stung you again, harder this time, so the shark could eat you before you ate it,◊ chided Clear◊White◊Whistle.

Roaring☆Hot☆Vermillion had to admit to himself that he now massed somewhat less than he used to. Part of him was now inside the shark's stomach.

◊Let us swim back to the lagoon and find a human, so we can tell them all about the big fish.◊

Since the waves were going the wrong way to allow them to surf back, they formed themselves into the snake-like shape that they used for cruising long distances below the surface and sped off for Crater Lagoon.

Insightful Thinker had much time to think. She was on duty in the ventilation shaft of Mother's residence, Green Home. Her dorsal fin was wedged in the crevice that kept her body from moving forward, while she stolidly moved the three sets of fins alongside her body—fin pair after fin pair after fin pair—pulling in fresh water through the ventilation port, then sending it into Green

Home with a last powerful flip of her massive tail. She was supposed to be memorizing her multiplication tables, but her mind kept wandering, especially when one of her lookers or grabbers returned with interesting information about what was going on elsewhere in Green Home and outside its thick walls made of blocks of greenish-gray volcanic stone.

A grabber returned from its long journey to the undersea gravel bed that spilled from the mouth of the large river on the nearby island. Insightful Thinker had sent it there earlier in the tidal cycle with its usual instructions to look through all the pebbles until it found an oval pebble made of blackglass. The grabber had returned early with a candidate pebble in its claws. As the grabber entered her mouth and attached itself to its feeder inside, Insightful Thinker used the suckers on the middle tentacles of her grabber to taste the pebble . . . it was pure blackglass! There were no impurity overtones.

Insightful Thinker shivered her fur all down her body in pleasure. Mother's Jar of 59 contained 58 perfect natural blackglass oval pebbles and one flawed one. With this perfect pebble, Insightful Thinker would be able to complete Mother's set. Another of Insightful Thinker's grabbers returned from inside Green Home with views of the Altar Room. Mother Precise Talker was at the altar. She was Telling 29 while chanting honors to one of her ancestors. There were piles of oval red pebbles on the altar, containing one, three, five, and seven pebbles. One of Mother's grabbers was taking one red pebble after another out of a red jar on the altar and adding them to the last pile until the piles contained one, two, three, five, seven, and eleven red pebbles, the first six prime numbers. There were twenty-nine red pebbles in all—also a prime number.

Mother's grabbers swept up all the red pebbles from the six piles and put them back into the red jar, then she started Telling 29 again, as she switched her chant to honor another of her departed ancestors. She would do this twenty-nine times before she completed her devotions. The tastes of her chant swirled about them as they exited the altar room.

"Meticulous Observer, Great Mother of mine, who at great risk to herself, mouthed me into herself, and took me from the lake of ignorance, to the ocean of knowledge. . . ."

Insightful Thinker interrogated the memory of the grabber that had found the blackglass pebble. The grabber had traveled some distance away from Green Home, and many of its soundings would be valuable additions to her surroundview. The soundings the grabber had collected on the way to the gravel bed contained little new, except for a view of Steadfast Defender in her normal slow patrol of the many vent field beds around Green Home. The soundings of the gravel bed were equally ordinary, except for the occasion of the finding of the blackglass pebble. The soundings on the way back, however, contained some strange echoes, and Insightful Thinker extracted the memories from her grabber with care and studied them thoughtfully before placing them into her surroundview.

At a great distance from Green Home, up slope at the furthest vent bed fields, where the glaring light from the sky filtered down through the warm surface waters, the echoes back from the pings of the grabber had indicated the presence of three strange creatures. They were large and formless, like a cloud of smoky water emitted by an underwater vent—yet the clouds did not float with the currents, but swam purposefully. The echoes showed no signs of interior structure, either heavy bones or air-filled bladders. Despite their lack of structure, they were living creatures, since they not only swam against the currents but emitted chirps for sounding the water around them, as well as more complex noises. Steadfast Defender must have scanned them, too, for the grabber had seen Steadfast Defender swimming slowly up slope to examine the strange echoes, some of her lookers and grabbers spread out before her.

Intrigued now, Insightful Thinker sent out a looker to follow Steadfast Defender and to both scan and look at what was going on. After a while, she sent a second looker to replace the first. The two lookers, shuttling back and forth, would keep her surroundview updated, while she continued at her assigned task of ventilating Green Home.

When the first looker returned, Insightful Thinker pulled out the images, one after the other, and perused them. The light images obtained by the eye of the looker showed that each of the three creatures had a distinctly different color. One was a bright red, one a deep purple, and one a cloudy white—like the tastecloud of a complex multithought expression.

The looker had approached close to the three strange creatures somewhat behind the lookers that Steadfast Defender had deployed. One of Steadfast Defender's lookers was irradiating the blobby creatures with a directed chirp, and the other lookers collected the returned echoes to form sound images to augment their light images. As before, the echoes showed no signs of internal structure in the creatures—no bones, no air bladders, and no teeth. Since they had no teeth, they certainly couldn't be too dangerous, even if they did seem to be larger than Steadfast Defender. Yet despite their lack of teeth, the echoes returning from inside the red creature showed it had not only captured and torn apart a fishfruit from a ventplant, it had also captured one of Steadfast Defender's lookers and was tearing that apart, too!

Highly disturbed, Insightful Thinker sent out her looker again, with a caution to stay at a safe distance. Shortly her other looker returned with even more disturbing scenes for her surroundview. The red creature had quickly dissolved nearly all of the chunks of flesh from the fishfruit and Steadfast Defender's looker, then changed its shape and started after the other lookers observing it—including Insightful Thinker's looker. The red creature had caught another of Steadfast Defender's lookers.

The red creature finally sensed Steadfast Defender slowly rising up from the dark depths and came to a halt. Soon all three blobby creatures were floating next to each other, sending chirp after chirp in the direction of Steadfast Defender.

Since the three strange creatures were each larger than Steadfast Defender, and were able to capture and eat food without having teeth, Steadfast Defender approached them with caution and respect. She, true to her name, never thought of fleeing—for her job was to protect the ventplants Careful Harvester and the others had planted around Green Home. Instead of attacking immediately, however, she decided to act in a civilized manner and first attempt to communicate with the strange creatures—even though they had damaged her by eating two of her lookers. Steadfast Defender opened her mouth and tasted the incoming water with her grabbers. The strange creatures had a nasty smell like an air-room with a clogged waste pipe. There was no taste of any attempt to communicate on the part of the strange blobs.

The red creature made a noise. Although it was directed toward Steadfast Defender and her grabber, it was a strangely useless noise—containing much the wrong frequencies for accurate imaging. The white creature also made some noises. These started out simple, and became more complex—but again, certainly the wrong frequencies for scanning. Since the creatures didn't seem to want to talk, Steadfast Defender decided to attempt conversation herself. She inserted a thought into one of her grabbers and sent it out. The grabber dashed quickly up to the red creature, squirted the greeting out of one of its stingers, and dashed back.

"STOP! Attack-not. Peace, make we."

Steadfast Defender waited patiently for the creatures to emit their response, but the only taste in the water was the nasty smell of air-room waste. The creatures made more strange noises, only they were directed at each other instead of toward Steadfast Defender. They would have been useless for seeing her anyway.

She tried again to talk to the strangely uncommunicative creatures. Perhaps her first attempt at communication was too complicated for the simple creatures to understand. This time she sent her grabber to the white creature with a much simpler message.

"One, two, three, five, seven, eleven," she said, Telling 29.

It was no use. There was no response, no taste at all, except the terrible stench of their blobby bodies. The loathsome creatures gave off more noises, while Steadfast Defender had to watch her eye being dissolved inside the body of the red creature. Steadfast Defender tried one last time to make peace. She opened her mouth and sent out a grabber with an even simpler message. Even a baby straight from his Mother's mouth should be able to Tell 3.

"One, two," said the grabber of Steadfast Defender, as it squirted the cloud of two simple chemicals from its stinger. Instead of responding, the red creature shot out a tentacle and seized the stinger. Other tentacles suddenly appeared, grasping the grabber until it was helpless. Steadfast Defender watched in horror as her grabber had its head torn from its tail and the tail swallowed into the interior of the stinking body of the odious blob.

The time for attempting civilized discourse was over—it was time to fight! Steadfast Defender quickly inserted an attack plan into her five remaining grabbers, opened her mouth wide, and sent them out. They formed a circle in front of her as she advanced, her sharp-toothed mouth wide. As they approached the red creature, it grew a multiplicity of tentacles, which reached out to grab the stingers of her grabbers. Obviously, this creature had never encountered grabbers in attack formation before.

The red creature gave a scream of pain as the electric shocks from the grabbers coursed through its body. Then the red flesh went flaccid and the ocean stank as the internal fluids of the loathsome red monster leaked into the water. The other two creatures attempted to come to the rescue, but Steadfast Defender had anticipated this response and her grabber fish had assumed the defensive position she had set up beforehand. While they held off the other two, Steadfast Defender took a big bite of the red flesh, her grabbers assisting by pushing in the torn parts. Once the creature was in her belly, she wouldn't have to taste it.

Steadfast Defender was greatly surprised when the bite of red flesh recovered quickly from the electrical shock and started to yell and struggle inside her mouth. Creatures swallowed whole could be expected to struggle, but this was a bite torn out of a creature! Bites might twitch in your mouth, but they didn't struggle to get out like this one was doing. She mouthed the chunk of red flesh with her sharp teeth in order to kill it, but the more she snapped, the more active it became. Soon she could no longer breathe, as the red flesh forced its way through her gill slits to the outside, digestive acids burning her tender gill feathers as it passed through. Her tongue and lips were also burning, and Steadfast Defender went into convulsions as she opened her mouth and tried to shake the torturing red flesh free. Then, more pain came from a new direction as focused sonic shocks from the other two creatures hit her! She fled in panic.

The last views of the battle brought back to Insightful Thinker by her looker were appalling. The three monsters made short work of Steadfast Defender's five grabbers, ripping their heads from their tails—one after the other. Steadfast Defender was now maimed and dumb. She had no means of manipulating anything—or even talking. The monsters didn't stop there, but circled around their fleeing victim, subjecting her to blast after blast of focused sound that exploded the last few eyes of her lookers in their sockets, killing them and driving the now blind Steadfast Defender into the deep ocean.

Insightful Thinker quickly sent a grabber off to tell Mother Precise Talker what had happened, and another to Accurate Calculator calling for her assistance in rescuing Steadfast Defender. Abandoning her post in the ventilation shaft, Insightful Thinker swam off, lookers and grabbers viewing hard around her for any signs of the marauding monsters.

She was joined outside the walls of Green House by Accurate Calculator, where together they found the still-suffering Steadfast Defender, mouth empty of grabbers and eye sockets empty of lookers. Their sonar picked up noises from the burning red flesh of the odious attacker still within Steadfast Defender's belly, feeding like a fungus on her living flesh. Swimming on each side of her, like nursemaids guiding a baby, they led her back to Green Home and Mother. Mother's grabber shot a dense cloud from its stinger as they approached.

"Steadfast Defender! Baby mine! Speak to me!"

"Speak, she can not. Grabbers, she has not," said Insightful Thinker, adding tastes of sorrow and concern.

"Speak, she will-not, until new grabber grows," added Accurate Calculator.

"Command! Accurate Calculator! Take her to Tireless Worker to tend and to feed, along with Baby," said Mother, taking firm charge of her home again.

Mother, then, nervously Telling 3 with three of her grabbers while she did so, tasted carefully as Insightful Thinker reported what her lookers had seen during the battle of Steadfast Defender with the three foul-smelling monsters. She then had Insightful Thinker record her memories on a taste scroll and take the scroll around to all the other

Homes in the Schooling—first to Great Home of Mother of the Elders.

At Great Home, all the Elders read the taste scroll and were highly disturbed by the events described.

"Dangerous, are blobs from above," said one.

"Damaged, however, were blobs by shocks from grabbers," said another.

"Kill monsters, perhaps, with shocks from many grabbers," suggested a third.

"ATTACK MONSTERS! Strongtails from all Homes in Schooling all together," said one of the youngest of the Elders in a pungent cloud.

Mother of the Elders put an end to the warlike talk. "Precious, Schooling is to me. One, lose-not. Fishfruit, have we in plenty. Monsters, let eat."

Mother of the Elders used two of her grabbers to take out a blank taste-scroll from the ornately carved scroll case in the library room of Great House and unroll it. Another grabber, still attached to its umbilical leading from the inside of her mouth, extended its stingers, and Mother used them to write a warning to all in the Schooling.

"Proclamation! Monsters, foul-smelling, formless, blobby, colored, are dangerous. Away, stay you. Scan you, them let-not."

Insightful Thinker took the proclamation scroll, along with her own scroll of what had happened to Steadfast Defender, around to all the other Homes in the Schooling for all to taste.

Back at Green Home, Mother Precise Talker was nervously Telling 3 with her grabbers. Her sensitive sonar had shown that the red cancer was growing within the wounded Steadfast Defender. She reached a decision. Mother went herself to the nursery and took over the care of the mortally wounded Steadfast Defender, taking her back to Mother's large private resting room where they could stay in quiet and seclusion. She stroked her dying daughter with the soft caresses of a six-grabber embrace, bathing her in the tastes of comfort and love. The tides passed, and Steadfast Defender's suffering grew, until finally, as Mother had expected, the poisonous red blob finally ate its way into Steadfast Defender's brain. Mother felt her daughter go flaccid through the feelers of her grabber, and she knew that the spirit of one of her children had slipped into the Prime. Mother now allowed all the grief and anger she had been holding back to overwhelm her sensibilities. She sent shock after shock from her grabbers jolting though the lifeless body of Steadfast Defender, and kept it up long after she was certain that the horrible red fungus was dead. Whatever these odious blobs were, they killed with ease and there was nothing she or her children could do to fight an enemy so poisonous. This small piece of one she could blast out of existence, but Mother knew that the big ones must be avoided at all costs.

When the others in the Schooling tasted what the monsters had done to Steadfast Defender, they readily acquiesced to the proclamation of Mother of the Elders. Since the monsters created a great deal of noise while they traveled, they could be heard at a great distance and as a result could easily be avoided. Never again would anyone of the Schooling let themselves be seen by those abominable blobs from the waters above.

As the three flouwen approached the entrance to the lagoon, Roaring☆Hot☆Vermillion raced far ahead of the others. Once inside the lagoon, he could recognize the voices of the humans Jinjur and Reiki, and he pinged in their direction to see them better. They were crouching in the water and scrubbing cooking pots with sand. Even at this distance, the sensitive chemical senses of Roaring☆Hot☆Vermillion could taste the bitter molecules of burnt food.

☆Reiki must have tried to cook again.☆

He raised his voice and called out a greeting in human language.

"Hi! Hi! Hi! We've been fighting! I won!" He headed for the beach, with Strong☐Lavender☐Crackle and Clear◊White◊Whistle close behind him.

"Little Red is bragging," said Strong☐Lavender☐Crackle as they drew near the beach. "We found a large shark eating the filter-fish. It had six eyes that swam ahead of it, and six gatherers that herded the filter-fish into its mouth. It was quite large, with many sharp teeth in its mouth, and could have eaten enough of us in one bite to turn us into a youngling. But we attacked its eyes and gatherers with focused sonar bursts and drove it away."

"Big fight! Big shark!" bragged Roaring☆Hot☆Vermillion, loudly.

Clear◊White◊Whistle came up beside them. Reiki and Jinjur, half-scrubbed pots rolling on the sandy bottom at their feet, were soon surrounded by the three large blobs of flame-, milk-, and grape-colored jelly, which tickled their legs with their voices.

"Big, yes, and *very* carnivorous!" agreed Clear◊White◊Whistle. Realizing that the humans would want a description of the creature, he tried to describe it in as much detail as he could. "The shark was quite similar in design to a Jolly. Both have six freely moving eyes that return to the main body periodically to report their observations, and both use six freely moving gatherers as hands to gather in food. Perhaps they have a common ancestor despite that one is designed to operate on land and the other in water."

The human Reiki listened carefully, and then responded. "Humans and dolphins are similar in the same way. Despite one having legs and the other having fins, they are both mammals and have high intelligence. Since the Jollys are intelligent, perhaps these sharks are, too."

Clear◊White◊Whistle thought over the recent incident

carefully. "This shark did not have intelligence," he concluded.

"Shark dumb!" agreed Roaring☆Hot☆Vermillion.

Clear◊White◊Whistle continued by giving his reasons for his conclusion. "As we approached the shark, I listened carefully to the sounds it was making. The main body, the eyes, and the gatherers were emitting only simple clicks and chirps, sufficient only to see each other and their prey with sonar sight. There was no evidence of any complex sound variations such as would be needed to use sound for talking. Since they don't talk, they must not be intelligent."

The human Reiki made a humming sound. Clear◊White◊Whistle recognized that the sound indicated that the human was thinking. "You are probably correct in your observations. Although dolphins and whales use clicks and chirps for seeing underwater, they also are able to make other sounds that are for communication. We still don't understand the language, but we do know they are talking to each other."

"Tell us more about those sharp toothed monsters," said Jinjur. "How big are they? Are they dangerous?"

"Very dangerous," replied Strong☐Lavender☐Crackle.

"This one was about four meters long," started Clear◊White◊Whistle.

"Just a minute," said Reiki. "I want to turn on my recorder." Clear◊White◊Whistle could hear a rustle of cloth and finally heard a click coming through the air.

"The shark was four meters long and at least a meter thick . . ." began Clear◊White◊Whistle again. He wished the humans could pass memories by taste instead of talking. It took so much longer to pass on information this way. As he continued his lengthy description, Roaring☆Hot☆Vermillion and Strong☐Lavender☐Crackle became restless and wandered away to surf the waves coming up the beach at the entrance to the lagoon. Clear◊White◊Whistle wished he could join them, but the scientist in him kept him at the important task at hand.

He could hear the other two talking back and forth in the distance as they tried to surf the small waves.

☆Sand!!! I hate sand in my cells!☆ complained Roaring☆Hot☆Vermillion as the wave he was on dumped him onto the sandbar.

☐We are getting too large to surf well,☐ agreed Strong☐Lavender☐Crackle as he too ended up on the sandbar. ☐I must be as big as my primary self back on Water.☐

☆Bigger!☆ argued Roaring☆Hot☆Vermillion. ☆If we are too big, then there is an obvious way to lose weight—a lot of it all at once—without having to stop eating.☆

☐You are right,☐ agreed Strong☐Lavender☐Crackle. ☐The three of us are now certainly large enough.☐

Roaring☆Hot☆Vermillion beamed a call through the water to the distant Clear◊White◊Whistle, trying to hurry him up.

☆Come on!☆ He followed the call with one through the air in human language, so that the humans would know they were delaying them.

"Come on! Come on! I'm feeling too bulky, let's—" then he realized that there was no equivalent human word and had to finish with the flouwen word ☆ —'co-mingle'.☆

Within minutes, all three flouwen were once again out on the ocean, surfing along the rollers going up the coastline. They passed by the mouth of the river that led to the Jolly village and continued north. Clear◊White◊Whistle was delighted with Roaring☆Hot☆Vermillion's idea. He too had been feeling his bulk lately. Besides, life had become boring lately—except, of course, for the recent run-in with the large shark. It would be nice to have someone new to talk to—especially someone who would float enraptured and listen intently as he pontificated at him, instead of rocking up or swimming away as the subsets of Roaring☆Hot☆Vermillion and Strong☐Lavender☐Crackle did.

⬜We need a shallow place where we won't be disturbed.⬜

☆I know a good place!☆ said Roaring☆Hot☆Vermillion. ☆Follow me!☆

On the north side of the island Roaring☆Hot☆Vermillion led Clear◊White◊Whistle and Strong⬜Lavender⬜Crackle across a flooded beach into a shallow lake that lay in a marshy plain between the flanks of the central volcano and the shore.

☆Sand!☆ complained Roaring☆Hot☆Vermillion as he circulated his flesh around to the surface where the water could wash away the irritating particles. The others, not as bothered as he was, explored their new surroundings. The water was brackish, half salt and half fresh. There was a strong stream bringing fresh water into the lake from the slopes of the volcano.

◊Cool!◊ said Clear◊White◊Whistle.

⬜Reminds me a little of the ocean on Water,⬜ said Strong⬜Lavender⬜Crackle.

◊Needs to be much cooler for that.◊

A quick search around the small lake soon determined that they would not be disturbed. Their sonar spotted a number of fish, but they were small and the flouwen were large, so the fish were staying well hidden under logs and in the marshy parts of the shore. Roaring☆Hot☆Vermillion joined them near the center of the lake where the water was about eight meters deep. They floated about two meters above the bottom, each a colorful cloud a meter thick and almost ten meters in diameter.

⬜Everybody feeling bulky?⬜

☆It will feel good to be in surfing shape again.☆

Clear◊White◊Whistle reached out a milky-white pseudopod to the others and assumed a triangular shape.

◊Let us co-mingle.◊

The other two flouwen extended their pseudopods and grasped the milky-white one.

◊Hold on tight!◊

The tips of the three pseudopods entwined in a three-way grip. The three flouwen then flowed together until they formed a circle nearly twenty meters in diameter, each colored body filling up a one-third section of a circle. At places around the outer perimeters of their bodies, clumps of cells shed their water and became denser. The dense clumps fell down to the lake bottom trailing thick streamers, where they formed hard rocks that anchored the floating bodies in place.

☆Twirl!☆

The portion of their bodies near the center started to rotate, elongating the pseudopods and forming them into a spiral pattern of white, purple, and red.

◻Too fast! Slow. Enjoy.◻

The twirling slowed, but continued on and on, drawing the elongated ropes of flesh into thinner and thinner bands.

◊Ooooooooo.◊

☆Aaaaaaaa.☆

◻Sssssssss.◻

As the multicolored whirlpool in the center grew, the bodies of the flouwen slowly shrank in size.

◻Feeling younger already!◻

☆Feels good! I could do forever.☆

◊Slowly now . . . . Make it last . . . .◊

The bands in the large spiral were now so fine that they blended together into a creamy mauve color.

☆More?☆ There was a tug from Roaring☆Hot☆Vermillion to increase the spiral, but the tug was resisted by the others.

◻Is big enough.◻

◊Slow . . . and stop.◊

For long minutes the three remained motionless, enjoying the extreme sensual pleasure of so much of the surface of their flesh in intimate contact with the flesh of others.

◊I am ready to withdraw.◊

◻I too.◻

☆Pulling red!☆ announced Roaring☆Hot☆Vermillion. At the very center of the spiral, the red liquid-crystal genetic and nerve substance in one of the three inter-spiraling bands started to withdraw, leaving a clear band of transparent cells behind.

◊Wait for us!◊

The withdrawing of the nerve essence now started in the white and purple bands, leaving the center of the spiral a clear blob of jelly.

☆Nnnnnnnn.☆

◻Kkkkkkkk.◻

◊Mmmmmmmm.◊

As the liquid-crystal fluid was withdrawn from the spiral portion, the color-engorged flesh in each main body took on a richer and deeper color. Finally, the spiral blob in the center was completely clear of all genetic fluid and was connected by three fine clear strands to the three progenitors.

◊The youngling is clear.◊

◻Pinch off!◻

The connecting threads were broken, and the three adults stayed anchored in position, patiently watching the clear blob floating between them. Each had contributed about one-sixth of their initial mass, so it was about half as big as they were.

The transparent lens of spiral jelly merged into an amorphous blob. For a long while it remained trans-parent. Then, deep within it, a specialized enzyme interacted with the bits and pieces of the randomized genetic information from the three adults, encoded as patterns in the surface of the cells they had donated. Using the patterns on the cells as a guide, the enzyme synthesized a complex macromolecule of liquid-crystal nerve tissue. It was a viable pattern. Using that as a template, other enzymes built more and more copies. A wave of pink color spread out from the nucleation point, until it suffused throughout the entire multiton blob of floating jelly.

The newly formed youngling spoke. Its first tones were in a mixture of the varied speech patterns of its three progenitors.

⬚Where.◊Where!☆where?⬚WHERE!☆Where?◊

But it soon developed its own distinctive voice, a blend of three voices into a throaty chirring sound.

✱Wherre.✱Wherrrre!✱Wherrrrre?✱

☆Pink color! You can tell who helped make this youngling!☆

✱Pink colorrrrr,✱ repeated the small pink flouwen.

Strong⬚Lavender⬚Crackle moved to stroke the youngster, who responded by pushing up against the large purple flouwen.

⬚He also has a warm body like you, subset of Roaring☆Hot☆Vermillion.⬚

✱Warrrrrm body,✱ repeated the youngling.

◊Such a pretty chirr he makes when he talks,◊ added Clear◊White◊Whistle.

✱Pink colorrrr . . . . Warrrrrm body . . . . Prrrrretty chirrrrrrrr . . . . Pink colorrrr.✱

☆That's a good name for him!☆

⬚What?⬚

☆Warm✱Chirring✱Pink!☆

✱Warrrrrm✱Chirrrrrrrrrrrring✱Pink,✱ repeated the youngster.

◊It certainly is a good name. The center portion is a self-describing representation.◊

⬚Let's see how smart Warm✱Chirring✱Pink is,⬚ said Strong⬚Lavender⬚Crackle. ⬚One plus one is . . . ⬚

✱T-t-wo-wo,✱ responded the pink-colored youngling, expressing the number both figuratively and literally in the proper flouwen fashion, by switching to a double-toned voice and enunciating each syllable twice.

⬚T-t-wo-wo plus one is . . . ⬚

✱ Th-th-th-rrrrr-rrrrr-rrrrr-ee-ee-ee,✱ replied

Warm✳Chirring✳Pink, triple-tonguing the word in a triple-toned voice, but adding his own distinctive chirr.

◊I do believe he knows his addition!◊

☆Smart! Like me!☆

◻He is probably hungry. I go catch something for Warm✳Chirring✳Pink to eat.◻ Strong◻Lavender◻Crackle swam off into the lake to look along the shores for a hiding lake-fish.

☆I go get some peekoos!☆ said Roaring☆Hot☆Vermillion, heading at high speed for the sandbar that separated the lake from the ocean beaches. The tide had not peaked yet. ☆Sand!!!☆ he yelled in disgust as he oozed across the strip of beach and into the ocean.

Clear◊White◊Whistle was left in charge of Warm✳Chirring✳Pink, and the two swam around in slow circles, bodies closely touching along the sides, while Clear◊White◊Whistle continued the math lesson. The youngling had in his genetically transferred memory all of the fundamentals of number theory and higher mathematics. All he needed was a little practice and soon all that memory would be instantly recallable.

◊Th-th-th-r-r-r-ee-ee-ee plus one is . . . ◊ prompted Clear◊White◊Whistle.

✳F-f-f-f-o-o-o-o-u-u-u-u-rrrrr-rrrrr-rrrrr-rrrrr,✳ rolled Warm✳Chirring✳Pink in a chirring quadruple-tongued, quadruple-toned voice, then continued on with his addition tables.

Clear◊White◊Whistle was pleased with the youngster's fast progress. He obviously could now do addition automatically. It should take less than a day for him to master subtraction, multiplication, division, fractions, powers, squares, roots, geometry, algebra, and calculus. Then a few days after that, he would be able to ask some interesting questions. It was always the young ones, who still had that naive way of looking at things, who seemed to find interesting research topics in mathematics.

*   *   *

At the time of the next tidal pulse from the daily passage of Zulu in the skies overhead, the three adult flouwen took the youngster out of the lake and into the ocean, there to teach him how to "fish" for his own peekoo shellfish. After a boisterous session of surfing all night during a strong storm, the four made their way back around the island.

◊We will be meeting the humans soon,◊ said Clear◊White◊Whistle. ◊They do not speak like we do.◊

☆Humans DUMB!☆ complained Roaring☆Hot☆Vermillion. ☆Can only make one tone at a time.☆

◊But they are our friends, so we will speak the way they do.◊ Clear◊White◊Whistle extended out a pseudopod toward the pink youngster. ◊Here. Taste this. It will remind you how to speak like a human.◊

Warm✳Chirring✳Pink extended a pseudopod, and taste memories were passed from the adult to the youngster, to augment the memories about the human language which he had inherited from his three parents.

"Hello. I am verrrrry pleased to meet you," practiced Warm✳Chirring✳Pink.

⌐Sound like human Reiki.⌐

◊That was very good,◊ said Clear◊White◊Whistle encouragingly. ◊I believe we are ready to meet the humans.◊

☆I hear humans walking along shore and talking!☆

The four swam into the lagoon near the human camp and waited in the shallows. The three adults formed eyes and extended them up above the water to look onto the shore, and saw Reiki and Richard. Richard was carefully carrying a wrapped object.

He saw the colorful bodies of the flouwen in the surf and came down into the water until he was wading through the red jelly that made up Roaring☆Hot☆Vermillion's body.

"I've got something to show you, Little Red," said Richard. "Our baby." He unwrapped the baby and gently laid it on top of Roaring☆Hot☆Vermillion, who gave it a quick scan with his sonar. The baby gave a loud cry at the change in support.

"Make sure you keep his mouth and nose out of the water," warned Richard.

"Is that the noisy part?" asked Roaring☆Hot☆Vermillion, passing the squirming creature over to Clear◊White◊Whistle with a ripple-wave along his surface. "I could hear that from the outer edge of the lagoon!"

Clear◊White◊Whistle scanned the baby thoroughly. "It certainly is built like a miniature human." The vibrations from Clear◊White◊Whistle's sonar soothed the baby and it began to make soft oo-ing sounds. "Except the head is too big for the body, and some of the smaller sticks inside are still soft."

Warm✳Chirring✳Pink, intrigued by the sounds, pushed his pink body between Roaring☆Hot☆Vermillion and Clear◊White◊Whistle.

"Wherrre small noisy thing?" he said in a quite acceptable human voice.

Strong☐Lavender☐Crackle could see through his eye the response of the humans. Both of their heads turned quickly to look at Warm✳Chirring✳Pink, while Reiki's mouth gaped open and a gasp came out—very unlike her usual calm demeanor. "Reiki, Richard, this is our youngling!" Strong☐Lavender☐Crackle explained.

"Rrrrreiki, Rrrrricharrrd?" repeated Warm✳Chirring✳Pink.

The human Reiki responded with strange small sounds, quickly followed by the smile she used while other humans would be laughing.

Clear◊White◊Whistle explained. "It will learn better speech, but it does say that particular sound in a repetitive way. We call this youngling, Warm Chirring Pink."

"We all have younglings now," said Strong☐Lavender☐Crackle, as he carefully placed the tiny pink human child on top of the large pink flouwen youngster so he too could scan the baby.

"Our young bigger than your young!" bragged Roaring☆Hot☆Vermillion.

"Be quiet, Little Red!" chided Clear◊White◊Whistle in human. "That is not polite!"

Roaring☆Hot☆Vermillion ignored the reproof. "Our young can talk!" he said proudly. "Human young can't talk. Human young DUMB!"

Roaring☆Hot☆Vermillion glided the baby off Warm✳Chirring✳Pink and back into Richard's hands, then started moving off toward the mouth of the lagoon.

"Come on!! I feel a storm coming up . . . let's go SURF!!!!"

As the four swam away to the mouth of the lagoon, they could hear the human Reiki calling after them. "Watch out for the sharks!"

JOLLYS

After the arrival of their six babies, the human parents struggled to resume their normal routine. It soon became apparent, however, that things were never going to be the same. Throughout her pregnancy Reiki had continued fishing, spending hours all alone on her tiny boat, diving in the shallow water a few hundred feet from the shore for peekoo and other shellfish, or tossing weighted nets into the deeper waters for oosheesh. But, while Freeman was an extraordinarily quiet baby, Reiki could not leave him alone on the deck while she swam below the surface. Jinjur tried carrying young Adam on her back while she hunted, but if he managed to stay quiet enough for her to catch any game, she rapidly became overloaded and had to return to the camp. Domestic chores doubled, and it was some time before the scientists could once again devote some of their time to exploring the planet and getting to know its residents.

Eventually, arrangements were made for a visit to the Jollys' village. David and Arielle, Nels and Cinnamon, and Reiki and Richard, along with their children, planned to spend several days as guests of the chief of the Keejook Tribe, Seetoo. Shirley, Jinjur, Carmen, John, and the other three children stayed at their encampment near their crash site on Crater Lagoon. The human camp was some distance from the Keejook village on a nearby river, so it took a number of hours to get there. Halfway, there was a narrow ravine through which ran a constant flow of hot lava, blocking the path. When they first passed this way, they had built a bridge of vines and planks, strong enough to support the weight of an adult Jolly, but the vines did not last long in the baking heat rising from the lava flow below. The bridge had to be rebuilt each time a Jolly wanted to use it, but as the walking plants were timid about staking their lives on the swinging span, only the bravest were willing to take this route. Most of the Jollys, instead, took the long detour which allowed them to cross the lava flow down near the ocean, where it had spread out and cooled enough to form a firm but hot crust.

For their own use, the humans had strung two metal cables between boobaa trees on opposite sides of the ravine, the cable having being salvaged by the flouwen from the lowering winches of the submerged rocket lander. The humans slid down one of the cables riding on a wheeled seat, its wheel formerly the winch pulley. On the way back, they used the second cable, located a few meters above the first, which sloped in the other direction. Nels was the first across, his long hairy legs dangling from the T-bar of the swing. After he arrived at the far side, Richard pulled the swing back by its lanyard.

"What a ride!" called Nels across the ravine. Dutifully Cinnamon tightened the straps holding Eve to her back, fastened the safety line around her, and pushed off. She didn't look down, but kept her eyes on Nels as she slid swiftly across. Only a few seconds later she was in Nels's arms and he was helping her down.

"Is me next!" called Arielle, handing Shannon to David. The graceful pilot launched herself over the void. As she glided rapidly down the cable, she leaned far backward against the safety line, her arms spread out behind her like wings. "Wheee! Am flying!"

"Be careful, dear!" called David from the launching point.

"Oh, pooh!" Arielle called back as she came in for a

landing. "He worries only that he will have to feed Shannon hisself," she told Cinnamon. She turned and took the baby from David's arms as he completed a more sedate crossing, arms firmly gripping both Shannon and the T-bar.

Reiki was the next one over, with Freeman in a backboard similar to the one on Cinnamon's back. Both women had decided the best way to keep their children safe was to wrap them securely and fasten them to a stiff frame that they could carry with them. Diapered with absorbent peethoo leaves, the babies were comfortable and dry. The baby, frame and all, could be carried everywhere and propped up, so the child could watch its parents work. Eve and Freeman were quiet, watchful babies and enjoyed observing everything around them.

Reiki was uneasy on the high swing. She tried to relax, knowing that Richard would come to her rescue, hand-over-hand if necessary, should the unthinkable happen and her swing stopped halfway across, but still she held her breath until she was safely across. It wasn't the height as much as knowing how foolish she would feel, hanging there, if her swing should stall.

Richard came swooping over behind her, unconcerned as always about heights. Still, he knew that Reiki didn't like to cross, or even to watch him cross, so the instant he landed, he kissed her. The others ignored her startled squeak; they knew that Reiki felt more comfortable believing that the others hadn't noticed how much she and Richard were in love.

Now that they were across, they had another hour of hiking before they came to the Jolly village. The trail they were following weaved its circuitous way between large dense groves of trees on either side. The grove to the right of the trail consisted of a single peethoo tree, the banyan tree of Eden. Each large low tree covered many acres. The long, thick limbs from the main trunk at the center were supported along their lengths by "saplings" that grew down from the bottom of the limbs to the ground. Shirley had found that the long, thin, branchless saplings made excellent poles for her various construction projects. The leaves of the peethoo tree were large and spongy, and were spread out to form a multilayer canopy that absorbed not only all the sunlight and moonlight that fell on the area occupied by the tree, but also all the rainwater. The rainwater was loaded with hydrocarbon molecules, which had fallen in on Eden from the outskirts of the torus of smog surrounding Zouave's orbit. It was a major source of nourishment for the tree, and the leaf canopy had evolved an ability to block all the light and capture all the rain before it touched the ground.

No plant life could survive under a peethoo tree, but it was the home of many smaller animals and mobile plants that hid in the thicket of saplings to elude their larger predators, such as the Jollys and the humans.

On the opposite side of the trail was a tall stand of boobaa trees; the Eden equivalent of a coconut palm tree. The boobaa was very tall, with a bare trunk, large leafy crown, and large spongy tough fruits. The trees lived in interconnected "families." Their crowns met at their edges and they too covered acre-sized areas. Like most plant life on Eden, they lived on the energy-rich nutrients in the rainwater. When one of the boobaa trees was attacked by a climber vine, attempting to suck the tree dry of sap while climbing its trunk to take over the canopy area, the tree under attack would pass on its stored resources to its neighbors through their interconnected root system; then deliberately shrink in size to let the neighboring boobaa trees grow to shade it, killing off the vine. Like the peethoo tree, the clump of boobaa trees engaged in underground trench warfare with neighboring groves.

"It's remarkable how clear of vegetation 'no-man's-land' is, here between the groves," remarked Richard, looking down at the dirt trail which was bare of even grass or moss.

"Not completely clear," said David, as he stooped to look at the trail in front of him. "You must have stepped on a buried keekoo tree thread hidden in the trail. It's broken through the surface and is already starting to fatten up to catch whatever it was that disturbed it."

"It'll have to move faster than that to catch me," said Richard with disdain.

Arielle turned back to see what David had found. "It cute!" she said, looking at the slowly writhing root, now the size of a garden snake. "I feed it something." She went into the boobaa tree grove, brought back a fallen fruit, and dropped it in the coils of the blindly searching root. In response to the touch of the fruit, the distant keekoo tree pumped more resources through its long, thin thread, and the snakelike portion grew thicker. The root captured the fruit in its coils and started to move off up the trail— not by physically moving, but by shifting its swollen portion along the root thread, dragging the trapped fruit along with it. Bemused, the six humans watched the fruit pass through their group, then followed as it moved slowly along the trail. Behind them on the trail, other keekoo tree coils were erupting from the surface where they had stepped.

As they approached the Jolly village, an owl-like bird with blue-green feathers and one huge eye flew down the trail. When it spotted the group of humans, it circled around them.

"Don't forget to hold still while the eyebird is looking at us," David reminded them. "Seetoo and the others often complain that trying to make sense of a worldview with fast-moving humans moving around in it makes their brain-knots ache—we're often seen in two or three places at the same time."

Once the eyebird had obtained a view of the group from all sides, it came down close and hovered in front of each person, observing them. After looking at the adults, the bird also hovered in front of each baby. Eve was annoyed by the flapping noise and the large solemn eye. Her face crinkled up and she glowered at it from under dark brows.

The bird finally flew off down the trail in the direction of the Jolly village.

"That's probably one of Seetoo's eyes," said David. "He'll soon know we're almost there."

My last eye finally returned and joined the five others resting in their nests in my fronds. As it nourished itself from its nest teat, I extracted the images it had gathered for me. There were many images showing the group of humans coming along the trail. I looked up with one of my nested eyes at the Daylight God. It was approaching the thin illuminated edge of the Nightlight God, whose eye was nearly closed. The midday darkness would soon come. It was time for me to retire to my hut and have my eyes emulate the Nightlight God during the period of darkness, while I added the images my eyes had gathered for me to my worldview.

I opened my mouth and used my inside gatherer to whistle a return call to my other five gatherers. They had been busy mending my game net, carrying threads over and under and tying knots at the proper places. They left the net at the whistled command, clambered up my front limb and into my mouth, where each reattached itself to its mouth-teat. I fed three of them, then turned them off to let them rest, while sending two others out to bring back my midday meal. Soobeek, the herder, had butchered a jookeejook earlier in the day and had set aside two of the meaty limbs for me. Following the view map I had inserted into them, my two gatherers crossed the compound and soon returned, each one holding a jookeejook limb grasped firmly by the claws of its two front legs, while their other four legs trotted busily across the swept dirt, up my front limb, and into my mouth, where they placed the meat in my crop at the back. Before starting to eat, I reached up with two of my side limbs and lowered my mouth apron.

To assure that my appearance was befitting that of a

chief, I send out one of my eyes to look at me to make sure my apron properly covered my mouth. Upon its return, I viewed the image it had collected and was pleased. Daaveed had painted the soft thick cloth apron with a geometric pattern in bright colors. A trick of coloring made the pattern seem almost three dimensional. It made the others nervous to see something obviously flat appear to be made of cubes, but as chief, it pleased me that my mouth apron disturbed the others.

With my mouth properly covered, I contentedly ground away with my gizzard at the tough but tasty jookeejook meat, swallowing the juices and bits of flesh with pleasure, while my eyes and gatherers fed themselves from their teats and rested. Darkness came, and while my gizzard kneaded away, I closed up my fronds and retired into my mind to refresh my worldview with the new images my eyes had brought to me.

As tribal chief, my first concern was the safety of the village. I first viewed the periphery of the thook barrier around the tribal compound. All was secure. I viewed around the inside of the camp. The jookeejook were safe in their pens, eating greedily from the slop troughs and sprouting many ripe fruits between their fronds. The seedling beds along the river bank were doing nicely. One of the older seedlings had even succeeded in releasing an eye and nesting it again without help. Everyone in the tribe was contentedly busy with their tasks.

I replayed the exits and entrances of the members of the tribe through the three gates, then added the views that my eyes had gathered as they returned along the trails for their midday rest period. Along one trail, leading up the riverbank to Wide Pond, was the watermaster, Faafee, dredging the irrigation ditch that brought fresh water from Wide Pond down to the village and through the seedling beds and jookeejook pens. This was grimy work that could not be done with gatherers, and Faafee was in the ditch, limbs lifting rootfulls of mud out of the bottom of the ditches and depositing it along the sides. The second trail, leading down to the mouth of the river and the ocean beaches, was empty, except for a wild jookeejook crossing from one tree grove to another. Down on the beach, Beefoof and Haasee were using the ocean raft to harvest seaweed for fertilizing the seedling bed. Beefoof would pole the raft out into the seaweed beds and drop a length of thorny thook vines weighted at the ends, and Haasee would pull the vines ashore and unload the harvested seaweed into the two-wheeled cart that the human Shiirlee had made for us.

Along the third trail leading inland were the humans. They moved so rapidly that I had three views of them at almost the same time. One as they left their encampment, one as they crossed Lava Ravine—using their shiny unbreakable vines to fly across the ravine almost like eyes, and one as they approached the compound. They would probably be arriving at the thook barrier during the midday darkness, using their tiny light-Gods to illuminate their way along the trail.

I scanned through the views my eye had collected of the group of humans and consolidated them. The humans were hard to tell apart unless one looked carefully at the differences in their features. They had only four limbs, and instead of using three of them to maintain a secure balance while moving the fourth, they instead precariously staggered from one bottom limb to the next. They had only two eyes that were always nested in sockets just under their stringlike fronds. The fronds seemed to be purely decorative, since they were obviously of little use for collecting either sunlight or rainwater. The differences in eye and frond color, however, helped to distinguish one individual from the other.

Fortunately, they came in two different types, males and females, which cut the problem of identification in half. The females wore cloths around their whole trunk, while the males only wrapped the bottom portion. None

of them had the decency to cover their mouths. It was
not clear why the women covered the bulges on the front
of their trunks near their upper arm attachment points
while the men didn't. It certainly wasn't because of the
size of the bulges. Although most of the human females
had large bulges, the human males Reechaard and Naals
had bulges that were bigger than those of the human
females Aareeaal and Ceeneemaan.

The midday darkness was soon over, and the warm light
of the Daylight God flooded down from the sky on my
opening fronds. My eyes fluttered anxiously in their nests,
eager to resume their viewing. Keeping one eye in its nest
to serve me directly, I generated scanning paths for three
of my eyes that would take them along the three major
trails to update the views in those directions and check on
the distant workers. One by one, I fed a simplified version
of my updated worldview into their minds through their
teat, along with the scanning path they were to follow. I
had chosen these scanning paths to be high in the sky so
as to update as much of my worldview of the land around
us as possible. The fifth eye was set with its normal scan
pattern, circling the compound and bringing back its views
after each circuit in order to maintain my worldview of the
activities of my people as they worked at their assigned
tasks. The sixth eye I sent off with instructions to locate
the humans and report back with their present location.
This eye would be kept busy flying back and forth, as the
humans would be moving rapidly along the trail toward our
compound. My sixth eye was soon back. The humans had
moved even faster than I had expected and were now
outside the thook barrier, waiting for it to be opened.

I activated one of my gatherers, and it scampered out
of my mouth to my storage shed to obtain a tablet of moist
writing clay. After the gatherer had returned to its teat
and was connected back into me, I used its front claws
to impict a proclamation to the tribe concerning the
imminent visit of our human friends.

"I, Seetoo, Chief of all the Keejook, announce the arrival of six humans for a visit that will last several days. I command you to welcome them with spread fronds, since they will bring new knowledge with them that will benefit the Keejook in the future. I recognize the visit will be disturbing, since the humans have an annoying tendency to move themselves and other objects rapidly from place to place, making it difficult to assemble a proper worldview for directing your eyes and gatherers. They, however, have promised to try to move slowly and to remain still in front of an individual if they wish to be properly viewed."

My gatherer took the completed tablet to Proclamation Rock and whistled, calling an eye from every member of the tribe so that all would know of the human's arrival. Soon many curious eyes fluttered around, following me as I stumped slowly to the thook border to greet the humans waiting outside.

The humans had arrived at the thook hedge surrounding the Jolly village shortly before the midday darkness. This dense thicket of thorns was a living wall which protected the Jolly village. The Jollys provided the hedge with water and fertilizer, and in return the semiintelligent plants stood guard, rolling back their springy, thorn-covered looped branches to allow members of the Keejook tribe to pass safely, while closing against anyone else who tried to get through, the long thorns impaling any transgressors, such as prowling animals or marauding stronglimbs from warring neighboring tribes. While the humans could move quickly enough to pass through any gaps in the wall before the hydraulically operated branches of the plants could trap them, the scientists knew their arrival was expected and had stopped outside the hedge and waited patiently to be noticed. While they were waiting, they passed around a travel net containing feebook-leaf-wrapped jookeejook-meat sandwiches on sourdough bread. Although Nels was the baker for the human encampment, the sourdough was the invention of Reiki—when she accidentally let a pot of flour paste "spoil."

"Maybe we should give a holler and let them know we are here," suggested Richard after finishing his sandwich.

"Richard, dear," said Reiki. "The others are still eating."

David looked up through the tall tree branches. There was the sound of fluttering wings overhead. "Wouldn't do much good anyway. The noonday eclipse is about to start. The Jollys don't function well without sunlight and are probably pulling in their eyes and settling down for their daily siesta."

"That sounds like a good idea to me," said Nels, lying back on his blanket roll, half a sandwich in hand.

The dark came rapidly. As they relaxed in the cool blackness, lit only by the stars and moons, the women took the opportunity to nurse their babies while the men dozed in their accustomed after-lunch siesta.

Shortly after the nearly two-hour-long midday darkness lifted, an eyebird appeared overhead. As soon as the eye spotted the humans, it flew back over the fence to the inside.

"That must have been Seetoo's eye, looking for us," said Richard, getting up. "He should be here any minute now."

"You mean any hour now," said Nels, maintaining his relaxed position.

Although the thook hedge was impenetrable, it was possible to see through it by moving one's head back and forth while looking at a distant object. For a long time, the humans saw little moving in the village, just slowly swaying four-meter tall trees, each in front of a little hut, which were scattered in a seemingly random manner around the compound. Occasionally a gatherer would move from one place to another, or an eye would flutter to or from its nest in the fronds of one of the trees.

There was a whistle from a gatherer standing on top of a large flat rock in the center of the compound, and the amount of activity increased as a large flock of eyes gathered to flutter above the rock, then return to their nests. One of the trees started to move. The fronds of the tree had a ribbon woven through them with a bow hanging down the back. The ribbon was a bright red—a royal-red according to the Jollys—reserved for use only by the chief of the Keejook tribe. Dangling below each eye nest, like drop earrings, was a decorative cluster of beads made of colored shells and gold nuggets. At the "waist" where the six large rootlike limbs of the tree joined the main trunk, the tree wore a belt made from what looked like fish skin. Hanging from the belt, dangling down between the long legs, were various pouches and utensils, one of which was a long dirk with a blade made of a single piece of obsidian.

"Here comes Seetoo," reported Richard, "as fast as he can." Seetoo had not finished eating, so David's psychedelic mouth apron was still lowered over the chief's mouth. The trunk of the chieftain remained rigidly upright as Seetoo balanced firmly on a tripod formed of a back limb and two forward side limbs. The other three limbs—the front limb and the two rear side limbs—lifted from the ground. The limbs moved, not by bending at a joint, but by hydraulically contracting, somewhat like the trunk of an elephant. At the ends of each of the limbs was a stubby but prehensile root system that functioned as both hands and feet. Right now the fingerlike roots were splayed out as feet to provide maximum support to the limbs acting as legs. The leading triplet of legs now swung forward to take a step, then expanded to make contact with the ground. With all six limbs now firmly implanted, Seetoo's trunk shifted forward to transfer the weight of the body from the trailing triplet of legs to the leading triplet. During the whole process, the tall trunk remained steadily vertical, for if a Jolly fell over, getting up again was a major task. The stepping process now repeated, with the trailing triplet contracting, reaching forward, then extending and touching down to establish a firm tripod base under the center of mass, so the leading triplet could again take another step.

"He's practically running," remarked Nels as he watched the colorfully decorated Jolly moving across the compound. "He must be taking three steps a minute."

Knowing the human's regrettable tendency to haste, Seetoo whistled to the thook hedge long before arriving and the hedge opened before Seetoo reached it. The chief settled down on all six legs, and from behind the mouth apron one of the gatherers inside whistled a greeting to the humans over the grinding, gurgling noise coming from the gizzard in the rear. Like Reiki, the Jollys ignored any inconvenient noises emitted by the body.

"I, Seetoo, Chief of all the Keejook, welcome you to our Inner Sanctuary. I welcome you, Raakee, One Who Honors the Form, and you, Reechaard, One of Great Strength. I welcome you, Daaveed, One Who Spreads Color Like the Daylight God, and you, Aareeaal, One Who Moves like the Wind. I welcome you, Naals, One Who Studies Life, and you, Ceeneemaan, One who Sings. May your visit spread knowledge like pollen on the wind, fertilizing all who are sticky to receive it."

Reiki waited until Chief Seetoo finished the greeting and then stepped forward. "Greetings, Seetoo, Chief of all the Keejook. We have the honor to introduce to you the newest members of our tribe. This is Freeman, fruit of Richard and Reiki." She brought her son around so that the baby's face was close to the chief's nested eye. Then she indicated the other children in turn, "This is Eve, fruit of Cinnamon and Nels, and Shannon, fruit of David and Arielle."

Seetoo had been aware of the babies for many days; its eyes kept a regular but discreet surveillance of all that happened in the human tribe. But the chief was rather shocked to learn that the children all seemed to have different fathers! How could a race survive unless only the most dominant was allowed to do the fertilizing of seed? Seetoo mentally added this question to the long list of others it planned to ask of the humans during their stay.

"Welcome human seedlings," said Seetoo formally. "Welcome Shaaneen, of the fiery foliage. Welcome Freemaan of the watchful eyes. Welcome Eev . . ." For a moment, the Jolly paused. An eye fluttered briefly in front of the baby to take a good look at the peaceful sleeping face. The draft from its wings woke the child, who glared irritably back at the large single eye of the creature that had disturbed her. Her face wrinkled up and she squalled in complaint.

"Welcome Eev, of the wrinkled face."

Laughing, the humans crossed though the thook hedge and entered mainstream Jolly life. The Jolly village was bustling with activity. Each Jolly worked at its trade as decided by ability and desire . . . and, of course, as decreed by the chief. Just inside the thick thorn hedge along the riverbank at the lower end of the village were the pens of jookeejook. These miniature versions of the Jolly had eyes and gatherers that were tethered to the main body by permanent umbilical attachments. They were the Jolly equivalent of pigs, eating refuse while producing food in the form of delicious fruits and meat. While the similar form of the jookeejooks indicated they were distantly related to the Jollys, the kinship was hardly acknowledged. Jookeejook meant "person that is not a person," and the smaller plant showed almost no sign of intelligence. A herder was in the pen, harvesting the ripe fruits from the animals as they ate from the feebook-leaf-lined slop trenches. The herder sent forth an eye to watch the procession as Seetoo led the humans past the pens and deeper into the large Jolly village that lay between the river on one side and the slopes of the island's volcano on the other side.

Further up along the riverbank were the seedlings of the tribe, rooted in their carefully tended gravel bed. As the humans slow-stepped by the bed, keeping pace with their guide, they could see seedlings at various stages of development. Some were simple rooted plants, some had developed mouths and more complex root systems, and some had fully developed eyes and gatherers, but all of them were firmly rooted in the bed.

The Jollys didn't have much use for straight lines, so there were no "streets" in the village, but they did keep clear the winding paths between the structures. Most of the Jollys lived in the same buildings in which they worked, and the placement depended on function. Seetoo introduced the humans as they came to each hut. Weehoob the knifemaker had a hut high on the slope of the volcano, where there was a good supply of the clear black obsidian that made the sharpest edges. Pootee, the potter, had a hut close to the riverbank, where there was a patch of soft dark clay. In the middle of the village was the hut of the elders. These were Jollys whose age or injuries were such that they were excused from strenuous activity. One elder, fronds yellow-brown with age, was telling stories to a small group of young stronglimbs from the nearby Youngling School. The school was the largest building in town, as this had to house not only Teeloot, the teacher, but the young Jolly stronglimbs as well. As the humans passed this structure, a veritable blizzard of fluttering eyes came out of the hut and surrounded them.

"There seem to be many young ones studying at the school now," Reiki remarked to Seetoo.

"Oh, no. The two crops of seedlings in the school only numbers eight. But the younger crop has imperfect control over their eyes and sometimes many are sent to view the same thing."

Moving at Seetoo's slow pace, the procession completed their tour around the village and ended up at Seetoo's home in the center. Right beside Seetoo's home was a large round clearing. In the center of this clearing was Proclamation Rock, a flat-topped stone some ten feet in diameter. The field itself was clear of all pebbles and leaves and had been raked into a decorative pattern. It reminded David of a "swept lawn" in America's Deep South. It was here that the tribe gathered whenever it was necessary for everyone to be present with more than just their eyes.

Chief Seetoo had arranged to house the scientists for the several days they would be staying. Three huts were set up for them near the large Chief's Hut, one for each couple and their child. The frames of the huts were made of peethoo saplings lashed together with tough keekoo root threads, while the walls were made of the large tough waterproof leaves of the ground-ivy plant, the feebook.

As the evening fell and storm clouds rolled in, the humans unpacked the supplies they had carried with them, while Seetoo returned to the privacy of the Chief's Hut nearby. With the Daylight God vanished from the sky, and the light from the Nightlight God blocked by the clouds, the Jollys liked to be home. While an adult Jolly could still function during the night, if necessary, the creatures retained the urge to conserve energy by dropping into unconsciousness during darkness as they had done as seedlings. Inside their huts, they could rest without fear of being blown over by strong winds.

The huts set up for the humans were spare, an empty square about four meters on each side. In the middle rested a pottery bowl containing water. Alongside this was a bowl filled with various fruits, nuts, and roots.

The visitors unpacked the bedrolls they had carried with them and Cinnamon laid out some of the smoked "oosheesh," or ocean fish, which Reiki had caught in her nets two days before. The savory fish and the sweet fruits made a fine repast, seasoned as it was by appetites built by the long day's hike. Overhead the evening rain beat against the sloping leaf roof.

The next morning, Cinnamon was helping Nels unpack and arrange the empty plastic containers, vials, and pouches that they had brought along to store samples they would collect for later analysis by both the flouwen and Josephine. Seetoo had cleared off a shelf in a storage shed, and Cinnamon was going back and forth from the hut to the shed, Eve on her back in her backboard. Eve was keeping a suspicious eye on Seetoo, who was talking to Nels.

Nels and Seetoo were discussing genetics. It seemed that there was some similarity between the genetics of the two alien species, since they both had two sexes, even though the Jollys were bisexual and the humans monosexual.

"Chief Levibotanist Naals? Am I correct in assuming that some of your pollen was used in the creation of the seedling Eev?"

"Yes, that's right. Each parent generates a special sex cell that contains half of its normal genetic pattern. When the two cells merge, the two half-strands merge, and a new genetic pattern, the pattern of the child, is created."

"The question I was trying to formulate had to do with the actual fertilization process. Are parents selected for the most desirable characteristics?"

"Well, I know it does not seem logical, but the usual breeding process depends more on human emotions. The 'flower' that hides inside each women becomes fertile several times each year. If she has been exposed to a fertile man's 'pollen' then a child is begun. But while the sex act is very pleasurable, it is also very personal, and usually people will only perform it if they have strong feelings for each other."

"This fertilizing act . . . does it involve much writhing around and groaning noises?"

Nels snickered. "It can."

"Because one of my eyes has observed such action between two of the humans here at the village. Reechaard and Raakee were watering themselves last evening in the Wide Pond, when a root at Reechaard's mid-trunk began to behave most oddly."

"I just hope that Reiki didn't catch your eye peeking."

"My eye was at some distance."

"Actually, I am rather surprised that the two of them have resumed sex so soon after Reiki gave birth. Birth is hard on the human body and we have not yet made arrangements for birth control. . . ." He turned. "Cinnamon? Did you and John give the women the go-ahead to have sex?"

Cinnamon put down the rack of vials she was carrying and wiped sweat off her forehead. "Once the postpartum bleeding has stopped and the episiotomy healed there is no reason to avoid sexual intercourse. It is wise to practice some sort of birth control, but . . ."

"You mean you women are ready already?" Nels said, coming over to her. "Why wasn't I told?" He slipped his arm around Cinnamon's waist. "Seetoo was just asking about the human mating process. Why don't we give him an up-close demonstration?"

"Excuse me?" asked Cinnamon in her best Reiki manner.

"Would a demonstration be possible?" interjected Seetoo. "Raakee and Reechaard had the relevant portions of their anatomy under the water."

Cinnamon twisted away from Nels and glared at Seetoo. "Excuse me?" she repeated dangerously. Nels didn't pick up the clue.

"Think of it as spreading information about our species, Cinnamon. After all, it's not as if we have never had sex before. While I was growing new legs you were always most helpful when ever anything . . . arose. In fact you've been most welcoming before, and I thought I managed to see to it that you—"

"Yes," Cinnamon interrupted, "we've had good sex. And you're a good friend. Sometimes I am even in love with you. But that doesn't give you the right to assume that I am yours for the asking—that you can use me casually any time you like . . ."

"Then the woman can refuse your stamen?" asked Seetoo.

"You better believe it, buster!" snapped Cinnamon. "I don't use you casually! For God's sake, we have a child together!"

"I'm not the only one. You and Shirley have a baby, too. Why don't you go ask her to service your needs . . . scientific and otherwise."

"I did ask her," Nels grumbled.

"What!"

"I just thought," he said, trying to explain, "since the three of us were all linked by the children, when we get back from this visit it might be a good idea for the five of us all to move in together. She said she liked you too much to consider it. I still don't understand what she meant."

"You spoke to Shirley about the three of us living together?"

Emboldened by Cinnamon's calm tone, Nels felt free to air his grievance. "You women weren't the only ones upset by Josephine's mistake," he complained. "If I had wanted to be a father I would have done it the right way. Just when the courting started to get serious the computer pulled the rug out from under all of us. I would probably have settled with you—"

"Settled?"

The edge to her voice made him retreat. "Settled down with you, I mean. After all, we have so much in common and now we have Eve, but I love Dirk, too. Can you blame me for wanting to have it all?"

"So you spoke to Shirley."

"Yes, but . . ."

"But not to me."

"Oh, I knew that you'd go along with it—"

Nels didn't even see it coming. The roundhouse slap struck him across the face with enough force to propel him into the Jolly's roots, and when he regained his bearings, Cinnamon was gone.

"Does this mean her flowers aren't in bloom?" asked Seetoo as the Jolly chief gently extended a limb to help Nels return to his feet.

The humans spread out around the village to learn what they could about the Jolly culture and occasionally to pass on information if it would benefit the Jollys and they desired it. Arielle went to the weaver's hut to watch Waathoo at work, while David visited the potter, Pootee. Reiki went to observe Teeloot teaching at the Youngling school, while Richard left the village by the upper gate and headed upstream to watch Faafee working on the irrigation ditches. While Nels continued his conversation on genetics and culture with Seetoo, Cinnamon calmed herself by visiting the seedling bed, where the seedling trainer, Shoowhaa, welcomed her.

"I am honored by your presence, Assistant Levibotanist Ceeneemaan," said Shoowhaa. The Jolly was shuffling slowly through the gravel bed, its rootlike feet turning the stones while its gatherers quickly picked up any weed seeds or sprouts that were turned up and put them in a basket to feed the jookeejooks. The six seedlings that Shoowhaa was tending were mere sprouts. They were only a meter tall and consisted only of a single trunk topped with a canopy of blue-green fronds.

"These must be the youngest ones," said Cinnamon, pointing and making sure she held her position until her arm and finger had been seen by Shoowhaa's nested eye.

"They were planted shortly after you landed in your noise machine."

"That was about a year and a half ago," mused Cinnamon. She took out her recorder and did a calculation. "That's about five hundred Eden days ago. I notice that they all seem to be the same size."

"They would, of course," replied Shoowhaa. "They were planted all at the same time at the Plucking Ceremony. The fruits on their parents had ripened. The chief plucked the best of the fruits from each parent during the Plucking Ceremony, and with all in the tribe watching, planted them here."

"So all the fruits ripened at the same time," said Cinnamon, mildly puzzled, since the difference in seasons on Eden was not strong, and it was slightly unusual to have all six fruits ripen on the same day. There would have to be some other timing event for the fertilization of the fruit than just a seasonal change.

"Of course," replied Shoowhaa. "The parents were all fertilized at the same time in the Fertilization Ceremony—shortly after the last midday flood wave."

"Flood wave?" repeated Cinnamon.

"When the Nightlight God and Oceanraiser are above in the sky and the Daylight God and Groundshaker are halfway through their journey under the ground, the tide in the ocean rises into a wave that floods the valley. With the wave come the terrible . . ." the gatherer, speaking from Shoowhaa's mouth, didn't finish the sentence. Shoowhaa reattached that gatherer to load up the next sentence and released another gatherer, who dropped its teat and whistled softly the single terrible word: ". . . Aaeesheesh." At the same time the gatherer spoke, Shoowhaa's fronds trembled, and the Jolly's nested eyes fluttered nervously, while the rootlike feet raised up off the ground one after another, as if they were trying to avoid having to step on something unpleasant.

The Jolly was obviously in distress, so Cinnamon didn't continue that line of questioning. Besides, she didn't want to get into a discussion of the Fertilizing Ceremony with Shoowhaa. Nels would probably get that information in one of his frank discussions about genetics and sex with Seetoo—if not—she would. She switched the conversation back to the seedlings.

"How long do the seedlings stay in the bed?" she asked.

"Nearly four flood waves," replied Shoowhaa. "The seeds are fertilized after a midday flood wave, and after three more flood waves, a midnight, a midday, and a midnight, they mature a few sixdays before the fifth flood wave—a midday one. They pull up their roots and are led to Seedling School."

Cinnamon did some more calculations and mused to herself. "Hmmm. If the seedlings stay in their bed for nearly four maximum tides, then that's about twenty-five hundred Eden days—twenty-five Eden years, or more than eight human years. Sort of like being stuck at your desk through nursery school and primary school, then graduating and walking off to junior high."

They came to the next ragged row of seedlings in the bed. There was an obvious gap between two of the plants in the ragged row of five plants. These five had reached a height of about two and a half meters, taller than she was. The single root at the base of these older seedlings had divided into six main roots that raised the trunk "body" up out of the ground until the seedling looked somewhat like a small swamp cypress. A hole had developed in the trunk, just above the point where the roots joined onto the main trunk. From the hole came six tentaclelike prehensile mobile roots. The roots were swollen at the ends and the swollen ends each had six rootlets extending from them. The mobile root-tip "gatherers" were picking up pieces of food from a feeding trough with their two rootlet front "arms" and using the other four rootlet "legs" to carry them back into the hole "mouth." Hanging from the fronds were drooping "flowers" with centers that looked like translucent ping-pong balls. The one flower "eye" above the active root followed it as it returned from the feeding trough.

"Fascinating!" said Cinnamon as she set her recorder to capture single video frames and took some pictures of the immature gatherers and eyes. "Ontogeny recapitulates phylogeny. But here it does it right out in the open where you can see it, instead of being hidden inside a womb."

"Some of your words are new to me," said Shoowhaa.

"I should not have used such technical terms," Cinnamon apologized. "I merely meant to say that these fat mobile root tips with six rootlet legs are obviously the first stage of evolution that will ultimately lead to a freely moving gatherer, while the light-sensitive organs hanging from the fronds of the seedling are obviously the first stage of freely flying eyes with a clear lens, iris, and eyelids." She paused at the gap in the row. "I notice that there are only five seedlings in this planting."

"There were six originally," said Shoowhaa. "One, however, did not open its eyes when the others did. It was the fruit of Pootee, the potter."

Cinnamon didn't want to ask what happened to the body of the seedling that had been "thinned" out from the crop. *Probably fed to the jookeejooks,* she thought to herself. Out loud she asked, "I presume Pootee will be allowed to contribute another fruit next time?"

"Only six are allowed to dance in the Fertilization Ceremony with the chief," replied Shoowhaa. "Pootee will not be one of them for a long time, if ever."

"So the chief is the father," said Cinnamon, beginning to understand the workings of the sex life of the Jollys.

"Of all those in this bed," confirmed Shoowhaa, releasing an eye that encircled the seedling area and returned. "Only those that are the strongest and wisest are allowed to participate in the Fertilization Ceremony, and the chief, being the strongest and the wisest, is the one who spreads the pollen for the others."

"The seedling that didn't open its eyes had two parents then. Chief Seetoo and Pootee, the potter. How do you know that the failure was not due to Chief Seetoo?"

"The others did well," replied Shoowhaa. "So the failure was not due to the chief. If two failures occur in a crop, or the six dancers in the Fertilization Ceremony are not laden with fruit at the time of the Plucking Ceremony, then a new chief is chosen and the old chief retires to the Hut of the Elders."

Cinnamon resolved to talk to Seetoo about getting permission to come to observe the Fertilization and Plucking Ceremonies. There would have to be reciprocation, of course, as Nels had suggested. But not so blatantly—even she knew that the mere fact of observation usually changed behavior. She slow-walked along as Shoowhaa shuffled in its tripod motion to the last row of seedlings.

There were six in this row. The gatherers and the eyes of the seedlings were now fully formed and had functional limbs, wings and eyes, but they were still permanently attached to the seedlings. The gatherers were connected by flexible umbilicals, while the eyes were at the ends of wirelike supports about a meter long.

"These seedlings look very much like a large jookeejook," remarked Cinnamon, then instantly regretted the casual remark. The fronds on Shoowhaa rustled loudly as they shook violently in response, and all of the Jolly's eyes fluttered out of their nests, chirping and whistling in annoyance.

"No!" "Not at all!" "Very different!" loudly whistled three gatherers one after another from Shoowhaa's mouth. The behavior of Shoowhaa reminded Cinnamon of an old-fashioned creationist denying the similarities between an ape and a human. There were major differences, especially in intelligence levels, but it was also obvious that the jookeejook was a distant genetic relative of the Jollys. Even the name, jookeejook, which meant roughly "person who is not a person" in Jolly language, showed that the Jollys recognized the relationship, even as they denied it.

"The seedlings are doing well," remarked Cinnamon, trying to change the subject.

"The eyes are now fully formed on both their gatherers and eyes," said Shoowhaa. "The views coming into their brains have awakened them and they are now aware. It is time for training. I will show you."

Shoowhaa placed a tasty morsel of food just out of reach of the gatherer of one of the seedlings. The gatherer strained at the end of its umbilical cord attached to the inside of the seedling's mouth, but couldn't quite reach the food. The seedling swayed its trunk on its roots in a vain attempt to give its gatherer a little more leash.

"Let go. . . ." Shoowhaa urged the seedling. "Let go. . . ."

Finally the seedling let its gatherer go by disconnecting the umbilical at the point where it entered the back of the gatherer's head. The gatherer paused for a second, a little disoriented now that it was on its own. Then it remembered the desire and the plan that had been implanted in its sub-brain by the seedling. It scampered forward, grasped the food in its two front paws and backed up, until the searching umbilical, guided by the seedling's nested eyes, could reattach itself to the mouth-hole in the back of the gatherer's head.

Cinnamon watched and commented on the training session until Barnard was nearly overhead and about to go behind Gargantua for the midday eclipse. Eve was getting restless in her backboard. It was time for lunch and the midday siesta. She started to excuse herself when she noticed a fluttering of eyes along the lower portion of the thook barrier at the gate opening to the trail that led down the river to the beach. As she watched, the thorny loops of thook vine slowly contracted and pulled back. Through the opening stumped two tall Jolly stronglimbs. They moved even slower than normal for a Jolly since they were coming uphill under a load. Between them was the cart that Shirley had made as a gift for the Jollys a year ago. It was basically just a deep bin with two wheels in the back and two drawbars in front. The large spoked wheels had wide rims in order to move more easily over the rough ground. There was a belt between the drawbars that went around the waist of the Jolly pulling the cart so it could use all six limbs for walking. The Jollys had modified the cart, putting a crossbar in the rear so another Jolly could push. Cinnamon couldn't tell who the two stronglimbs were, since the Jollys looked so much alike, but she suspected, from the nets stacked on top of the seaweed, they were the tribal fishermen, Beefoof and Haasee.

"A load of seaweed fertilizer for the seedling bed," explained Shoowhaa. "Necessary for growing strong limbs and clear eyes. I must go."

Back at their group of huts, the humans gathered for lunch together. Cinnamon pointedly ignored Nels, and went off with Reiki and Arielle into Arielle's hut to nurse babies, while the men prepared the meal. Each spoke of what they had learned during their morning visits with the various Jolly workers.

Richard took a bite of a carrotlike root he was scraping clean and slicing up with an obsidian hand-knife. "This would sure taste better cooked."

"So would a lot of things," replied Nels, cutting up some fruit. "But with the Jollys' well-deserved fear of fire, we knew when we came that we would be eating cold food during our visit."

"There is one Jolly that is willing to experiment with fire," interjected David, cracking another nut and picking out the pieces. "Pootee the potter explained to me how the Jollys waterproof their water pots with sap from a feebook plant. It's not very satisfactory. The water tastes funny and after a while it penetrates the sap layer and the sun-dried clay turns to mud. I explained that firing the clay in a kiln would make it hard and waterproof. Pootee believed me—told me about finding hardened clay after a forest fire had passed. I drew a diagram of a kiln oven. Since the fire is completely enclosed, Pootee is willing to try it and is now building a kiln out of clay bricks. This afternoon, we'll load it with clay pots and wood and I'll light the fire with Cinnamon's bow and tinder while Pootee watches."

"I don't think Pootee's gatherers are up to handling the bow at the speeds that are needed," said Nels dubiously.

"Doesn't matter," replied David. "Pootee will only be doing a firing every couple of weeks, and once the kiln is loaded and ready, I can come and light it."

"Speaking of forest fires heating up clay banks," said Richard, changing the subject, "this riverbank was pretty hot itself once."

"How's that?" asked Nels.

"As I was walking upstream to help Faafee work on the irrigation ditch, I noticed evidence in the riverbed of a collapsed lava tube. Sometime in the distant past, a large flow of lava came down this river valley, and the outer crust formed a stone tube while most of the liquid lava flowed down the inside until it reached the sea. Must have been a spectacular sight at the time."

"That sounds dangerous," remarked David. "Even if the lava didn't overflow the riverbanks, it would have been close enough to the Jolly village that the heat would have baked the Jollys or set them on fire."

"Especially the seedlings," said Nels. "They're right by the riverbank so the used irrigation water can drain off back into the river. I'm concerned."

"I wouldn't be," said Richard. "I can't tell for sure without an isotopic dating analysis, but I would suspect that lava flow occurred thousands of years ago. If it had happened in recent Jolly memory, they wouldn't be settled here now."

After a vegetarian lunch of root slices, nuts, and fruit, and a long rest during the midday eclipse, the humans scattered to resume their observations of Jolly daily life. Nels decided to follow the two fishermen as they set off upstream to the distant Sulphur Lake at the other end of a wide valley with a meandering stream, one of the many streams feeding the main river that flowed by the Jolly village.

"I have some questions to ask Seetoo about some

ceremonies connected with the seedlings," said Cinnamon, heading off to Seetoo's hut.

"Let me have your bow and tinder before you go," said David. "I've got a fire to light."

That evening, when Nels returned to the hut assigned to him and Cinnamon, he was relieved to see that Cinnamon was there. He entered slowly, uncertain of his welcome. A permalight was hanging from a ceiling pole and focused into a spot in the center of the hut. Off in one corner, Eve, hanging in her backboard, slept quietly in the shadows. The evening was clear, and a slight breeze flowed in through the door and out a vent flap that had been opened in the back of the tall hut, up in the dark recesses under the roof-line. Through the vent hole, Nels could hear the breeze quietly rustling through the fronds of a nearby tree. In the pool of light, Cinnamon was lying on her sleeping pallet, entering figures in her recorder. She laid the recorder down and moved over slightly as Nels approached, giving him room to sit beside her.

"Cinnamon," said Nels after a long pause. "I am so sorry. I didn't realize how much I was hurting you by taking you for granted. And I *was* taking advantage. We've always gotten along so well that I didn't think anything needed to be said. I didn't even think about it, or try to understand it, and I was complacent. But when you lost your temper earlier . . . in all the years I've known you, I've never seen you so angry. For a moment I was afraid. I thought that you might never want to be with me again and the idea terrified me. You've just quietly become such a big part of my life, I didn't realize how much I need you, how much I love you. I never meant to hurt you, if that helps, and I just wanted you to know how much the thought of losing you hurt me."

Cinnamon rose to her knees and kissed him strongly. Nels allowed her to push him back onto the bed. "Foolish man," she said, looking at him, her long unbound hair cascading down to tickle his bare chest. "This is a very small island. Where did you think I would go?"

"But . . ."

She silenced him with another kiss.

"Darling, if we are going to try to work this out, there is a phrase that you are going to have to learn. What you say now is: 'Yes, dear.'"

"Yes, dear."

She pulled off her loosened sarong and sat back, straddling his hips. "When we get back to camp, you are going to move into the hut with Eve and me."

"Yes, dear."

She pulled off his loincloth. "And as much as we love Dirk, we are going to leave Shirley to Jinjur."

"Yes, dear."

"See? That wasn't too hard. But this is, isn't it?"

"Yes, dear," said Nels, shuddering at her touch. He looked up at the permalight. "Don't you think we ought to turn off the light?"

"Let's not bother about that now. We've got other things to do."

"Yes, dear."

Seetoo moved away from the back of the hut as quietly as he could, although he was not likely to awaken the sleeping lovers. Cinnamon had been right, not only about Nels coming back to her, but that Seetoo would find the resulting exchange interesting. Human beings were so interesting . . . odd . . . repulsive and yet intriguing. Seetoo would have to replay the views many times in order to make sense of it all. Seetoo wished he could talk the event over with Nels, but Seetoo had promised Cinnamon not to let Nels know that he had managed to educate the Jolly Chief after all.

The next day, Nels went upstream to watch Beefoof and Haasee fishing in Sulphur Lake. That afternoon, he returned carrying a heavy bundle wrapped in soaking-wet peethoo leaves on the inside and waterproof feebook leaves on the outside. Behind him, like mice following the Pied Piper of Hamelin, were six gatherers, each carrying a smaller bundle in their two front limbs. The gatherers all gave a whistle at about the same distance from the upper entrance in the thook wall, and the procession entered the slowly opening gate. The gatherers immediately took their loads to a large shaded tank built into the ground near the irrigation ditch, where they unwrapped six live medium-sized fish and put them into the water. They then headed back to their masters, still fishing on Sulphur Lake. Nels brought his catch to the human camp.

"Come and see this beauty!" he cried out. "Come on, Cinnamon. I bet you've never seen a fish like this before!"

Around the village, the humans left the Jollys they had been visiting, and with a haste that unsettled more than one Jolly worldview, they gathered to see what Nels had brought.

"Did you catch yourself?" asked Arielle dubiously.

"Sort of," said Nels. "The two Jolly fishermen had it in their net, but it was too heavy for them to get onto their raft, so they hauled it to shore, and I waded in and grabbed it. It must mass over fifty kilos—good thing the gee level here on Eden is only twenty-eight percent, or I couldn't have carried it this far." He unwrapped the large fish. It had not survived the journey as well as the smaller ones and was motionless. "The Jollys call it a 'poosheesh,' or lake-fish."

"Six eyes!" exclaimed Cinnamon, poking at the two rows of three bulging eyes along each side of the head. "I can understand the six fins along the side; everything on Eden has six legs. But two eyes is all you really need for binocular vision."

"It's soft to hold, not scaly like most fish," said Nels. "It's got fur like a seal, but the shape of a shark."

"This furry shark have sharp teeth!" exclaimed Arielle, who was examining the creature's mouth.

"The better to eat you with," joked David, pinching her in the rear.

"I eat *it*!" exclaimed Arielle. "I tired of veggies. I want meat."

"Raw?" exclaimed Richard, his nose wrinkling.

"Sashimi is good," Reiki reminded him. "You know that we mustn't have fires—flames frighten the Jollys."

"Pootee's kiln has just finished its run and is cooling down," said David. "We could sweep out the fire chamber and roast a slab of fish inside that."

"It's going to be tough getting a good fillet off that monster with only this," said Richard, holding up the five-centimeter-long blade of his Swiss Army Mech-All. Arielle slipped away from the group.

"I want to do an autopsy on it first," objected Cinnamon, taking the Mech-All. While Richard laid the fish out on a shelf of the storage shed, Nels started getting out sample bags.

"You autopsy insides and other side," said Arielle, quickly returning. She had somehow talked Seetoo out of his long, sharp obsidian dirk. She grabbed the furry shark by the gill slot and started to remove a large fillet. "I have this side cooked by time you are done."

Shortly thereafter, Arielle found herself the center of a large collection of gatherers, their molelike noses twitching at the enticing smells coming from the bottom of Pootee's kiln. She gave each gatherer a small bite from around the edges. Soon they were back, whistling, "Taste good!" "More!" Some even said "Please!"

MORE ROOM

Months after the visit to introduce the children to the Jollys, the humans finally located an ideal location for a safe, stable site for their settlement. After surveying where the flood level had reached during the most recent quadruple conjunction extreme high tide, they found a meandering stream in a valley upriver from the Jolly village. The stream in "Meander Valley" came from Sulphur Lake, which was filled with many delicious lake-fish, while the water flow in the stream was large enough to supply plenty of water for drinking, washing, and irrigation. In fact, the humans wondered why the Jollys did not settle this area themselves. On their next trip to the Jolly village to help the Jollys clean up after the recent flood, they asked Chief Seetoo and were surprised to see the branches of the chief shivering in fright in response.

"That is the valley of the . . ." the dreaded word was finally forced out of a trembling gatherer, " . . . Aaeesheesh."

"Aaeesheesh?" asked Jinjur. "What are they?" She then regretted her question, as the branches of the chief started to shake once again, and it took some minutes before they were once again under control.

"Demons . . ." whispered Chief Seetoo finally, " . . . in the shape of fish. It is taboo to speak of them."

"Then we will not," said Jinjur firmly, knowing that it was more important to keep the friendship of the Jollys than to press them for more information about these so-called Demonfish—which were probably just a tribal superstition anyway. She changed the subject to other things the humans could do to help the Jolly village.

Nearby, Shirley was working side-by-side with John helping to repair a Jolly irrigation ditch. "I wonder what these Demonfish are that have Seetoo so scared?" she asked him.

"Well, the Jollys use gods and demons to explain the natural world around them. We have been trying not to interfere in their lives too much, and we certainly don't want to abuse their sensibilities, so none of us have talked much with them about their religious beliefs."

"Yes, I know." Shirley sighed. "In fact, Jinjur and Carmen have gotten into several arguments about it. Carmen wants to convert them."

John frowned. "You have to look at the Jolly beliefs from their point of view. These imaginary Demonfish must be attempts to explain the bad things that happen to them during the darkness, such as these midday eclipse floods. The Jollys slow down when they are in the dark. Even a cloudy day can make them sluggish. So imagine falling asleep and waking to find your whole world drastically changed by a flood. It might seem as if while you slept, demons had been roaming the island. Look at this mess. . . . Would you immediately believe that all this damage could have been caused by a little water?"

Shirley looked around. Branches, rocks, torn-up plants, and the bodies of unlucky animals lay in piles scattered by the receding water. Strange currents formed twisting paths between the piles, giving the destruction a planned, almost calculated look. It was as if a giant child had abandoned the sandbox in the middle of play.

"I guess I might blame it on demons. But wouldn't it be a good idea for us to educate the Jollys? We could show them how to better prepare for the floods, and that there are no Demonfish."

"Who are we to say what is best for them?" asked John. "We may think that our way is best, but their ways have been working for them for thousands of years."

"Of course. You're right. If we can accept Carmen's religion without trying to change her, I guess we can accept the Jollys' Demonfish."

The stream in Meander Valley was shallow enough to ford with ease, but deep enough that the flouwen could come upstream to the settlement for conversation and their daily doses of urine. The humans could clear small flat fields on the treeless midstream islands for their essential Earth crops, while the groves of trees along the stream supplied building materials and firewood. Their first responsibilities were to care for the children, but as scientists on a mission, they also had a responsibility to increase their own knowledge of the planetoid around them for periodic report back to James on *Prometheus*, and for later transmission to Earth. Farming was not the most constructive use of their time here, and these highly fertile, easily irrigated fields would practically tend themselves.

John hated the thought of moving so far away from the submerged lander and the computer-run sick bay that could do so much more for his patients than he could. But since the dangerous jury-rigged diving bell was the only way to get to the inhuman aid, getting rapid emergency help from Josephine was almost impossible. If the patient was well enough for an unassisted underwater trip in a cramped sealed capsule, then the extra walk from the new settlement to the beach wouldn't make any significant difference.

It had taken months to construct the new settlement. The building had gone slowly because other responsibilities came first. They had agreed that each would help the others build their homes, and all would move in at the same time. Their two years on the planet had taken them through more than six of the wet-dry seasons on Eden, which gave them sound ideas for the best architecture for the climate. The constant rain during the rainy season made sloped roofs a must, while the occasional earth temblors called for light flexible frames. Although the new location would not be affected by the flood waves at the extreme high tides, the occasional heavy rains and the resultant flooding of the stream over its banks would soon have made low floors soggy. The best sort of home for each of the individual families seemed to take a little from each of their original buildings. The woven rush-covered sapling floors were supported between the trunks of three boobaa trees. Part of this deck was left open, while a rounded roof covered an area large enough to protect the family from the rain. The lower walls of the dome were made of waterproof feebook leaves that could be removed to let the air flow through when the weather was warm. Light feebook screens divided the enclosure to give an illusion of privacy.

While each family wanted a separate dwelling, they all agreed that they needed a larger gathering place where they could continue their communal dinners. They chose a site where a climbing vine had attacked one of the boobaa trees. The infected tree had allowed itself to shrink far below the canopy of its neighbors, which were still growing strongly around it. They had cut off the dying tree some six meters from the ground and removed the soft inner core from the stump. An opening was cut into the side, and after lining the inside with clay, the tree was used as a fireplace and chimney. The fire, in turn, was protected and could easily be kept alive to revive the small fire of each home. With its deep-seated roots intact, the chimney was also a strong support for the roof of the meeting hall. The plank floor was two feet from the ground, supported by a layer of river rock rolled from the nearby streambed and painstakingly leveled. Inside, the tables and benches were large enough to accommodate them all at one time.

Finally the Settlement was ready. The Meeting Hall was closest to the main stream and in the center of the cluster of huts. John's own home was directly behind the Meeting Hall. As this home was also the sick bay, he planned to use the Meeting Hall for a hospital if necessary. Cinnamon, as his assistant, wanted also to be near, so she and Nels had their home against the base of the nearby ridge, about fifty meters downstream from John and the Meeting Hall.

Jinjur and Shirley made their hut about a hundred meters above the Meeting Hall and well away from the riverbank. A conduit made from hollowed-out peethoo saplings and flexible tubing salvaged from the crashed lander brought a thin trickle of water from the ridge creek into the house itself, enough for drinking and household use. Carmen's home for herself and Maria was near the top of the ridge. An antenna at the top of one of the trees that supported her home provided a line-of-sight link to the comm unit in the penetrator sitting on the beach.

On the other side of the stream, Richard and Reiki, with Freeman, settled in a home directly across from the Meeting Hall. Cinnamon's warning to Reiki to use birth control came too late and the prim anthropologist was again swollen with pregnancy. A vine bridge gave them direct access to the Hall when the stream was too deep to ford safely. Upstream, where the stream narrowed down and the tree groves grew close together, Arielle and David lived with their Shannon. Originally it was intended that they would also use the bridge, but David had come up with an idea, and for the last five days he and John and Richard had been working on it in secret. Arielle had grumbled when they hadn't brought home any game and was in a surly mood when David finally took her to see their handiwork.

"Is what?"

"It's a surprise," David repeated. "Go on up."

Arielle peered up the tall thin boobaa trunk. The bottom

of a small platform was just visible against the foliage. She, like most of the others, found it easy to climb the polelike trees in the low gravity of Eden, but David had made it even easier by adding a vine, so one could "walk" up or down the tree at an easy angle without having to grasp the rough bark with one's knees.

"You want me go up there?" she asked "Why?" She looked at him suspiciously. "You want to make love where baby not see, I bet. But she not care . . . and up there is too small!"

"Just go, woman!" David said. Arielle began to climb, with David right behind her. At the top they stepped off onto the small platform. It was not quite two meters on a side and had no railing.

Arielle looked around. Trees surrounded them on all sides, so there was not much of a view. "Is nice . . . is pretty. But there is not much room." She began to take off her sarong.

"No," said David. "That's not why we're here. Look, didn't you ever see a Tarzan video?"

"Sure. Is monkey boy," she said dismissively. "And good swimmer," she conceded.

David took one of the woven vines that had been fastened to the trunk above her head. "See that other platform over there?" he said, pointing through the trees. "Watch." He tightened his hold on the vine and leapt.

"AAAAAeeeaaaaeeeAAAAeeeaaaaaeeeAAAAAA," he yelled in the prescribed manner. He had hardly landed on the opposing platform before he heard a "Wheeeeeee!" coming up behind him, and Arielle was beside him again.

"Is wonderful!!"

"I've set up a whole string of them," said David, internally apologizing to the others for taking the credit. "We can swing all the way to the stream and across if you like."

"Like? I love! Where is next landing?" She was peering through the trees.

"If you need to go to a higher platform, you have to

jump up to push off, and if you get stuck, the vines are long enough for you to crawl down and safely jump!" he called out after her as he tried to follow her flight through the trees. The sound of her laughter helped him keep track of her progress, as did the occasional squawk of startled birds. Then he looked up to see her swinging back toward him and she landed in his arms, breathless with delight.

"Oh, David! You let me fly again!" She sighed.

The platform was big enough after all.

Reiki floated in the warm water of the bay, the familiar underwater landscape spread out below her. Shirley had finally managed to make the mask watertight around Reiki's small face, and long practice let her breathe through the snorkel easily. Now it felt as if she were a natural part of the life in the bay, soaring like a hawk over the submerged hills and valleys. A few leisurely kicks of her flippered feet took her far from where her little raft held her earlier catch of filter-fish.

Reiki enjoyed fishing more than any of her other chores. Now that she was more than eight months pregnant, the water gave her welcome support. The two pregnancies had come so close together it seemed to Reiki that she had spent years adjusting to her own rapidly changing body. In the water of the ocean, she once again felt graceful and in control.

Working slowly, with no sense of urgency, Reiki moved in behind a large pink peekoo. Taking care that she not let her shadow fall on the peekoo's eyes to warn it of her approach, Reiki dove and slid the obsidian blade of her knife under the flat bottom shell before the peekoo could use its six tiny legs to secure itself to the rocks beneath it. If taken by surprise, the peekoos were helpless, but once they managed to get a firm grip on the rocks, and especially if they were able to establish suction between their domed upper shell and the rock beneath, they were almost impossible to remove. Here in the deeper water the peekoos grew larger, some to over a foot across. It still took patience and care to collect enough of the crustaceans to feed everyone, but the work wasn't arduous.

Reiki carefully placed the clumsy creature into a net. Then, treading water, she inflated one of the envelopes Shirley had made for her out of feebook leaves. Tied to this float, the peekoo would be kept away from the safety of the ocean floor until Reiki came to collect it on her way back to the raft. As the afternoon wore on, Reiki left in her wake more and more of these little floats. Once in a while a balloon would fail and allow the tasty morsel to escape, but the method still worked better than constantly ferrying the take back to the raft or carrying the struggling prey with her while she hunted. Also, this way, the peekoos remained fresh until ready to eat, either raw on the half-shell or cooked into chowder.

The shadows lengthened, and Reiki finally decided that she had enough to make the chowder the group loved. She tucked her last catch into a large net and prepared to collect all the little caches she had left between herself and her raft. Suddenly she felt a snap, exactly as if a rubber band had popped inside her.

Puzzled, Reiki tread water and took an internal inventory. Whatever had happened, didn't happen again, and nothing seemed out of sorts. But when she started to swim back to the raft, a contraction gripped her so powerfully that she could hardly breathe, much less swim. Forcing herself to relax, she floated on the surface. Slowly, with long deep breaths, she waited out the pain. Finally it eased. When she had delivered Freeman, the labor pains had been mild and had slowly increased in intensity. This time, her womb seemed to know exactly what it was doing. Rather than cramping, the huge muscle was squeezing, pushing, insisting. Reiki knew that this labor was going to go quickly.

Catching her breath, she began to head toward her raft.

The contractions came again and again, forcing her to stop, slowing her progress. With each one, Reiki could feel her body responding and the baby moved lower. The tiny raft seemed even further away and the distance she covered between each contraction became smaller as they came closer together.

Breathe, breathe, breathe, thought Reiki to herself as she tried to stay limp enough to keep afloat while her womb worked. She was trying not to worry about how she would get on board once she reached the raft, and about how she would get the raft back to the camp. She stilled her rising panic by reciting a calming litany she had discovered in an old science fiction novel about a desert world:

I must not fear. Fear is the mind killer. Fear is the little death that brings total obliteration. I will face my fear. I will allow it to pass over and through me. Only I will remain.

The contraction eased. Reiki sculled forward cautiously, using only her wrists and forearms to move her along. The rest of her body remained limp and relaxed, resting. *Face my fear,* she thought. If the baby crowned before she reached the boat, or she reached it and was unable to climb aboard, what then? Babies had been born underwater before. Back in the eighties lots of babies were purposely delivered in warm water. Of course the women had not been alone, but those women were not as self-reliant. Reiki knew that babies didn't need to breathe until the placenta, which provided them with oxygen, was detached. This baby had spent the last nine months with its lungs filled with embryonic fluid; it would survive a few moments more. Finally Reiki identified the initial snapping pain. It had been her water breaking. She could count herself lucky, Reiki thought as a new contraction built. Lucky in that this had happened on Eden rather than Earth. The blood would have drawn sharks in Earthly tropical waters, but here on Eden there were no dangerous lifeforms.

"Hello . . . hello . . . hello!" called Little Purple as his huge lavender body rose up to surround her. "Are you aware that you are leaking sodium chloride and iron compounds?"

Reiki was concentrating deeply trying to get through the contraction and ignored the question.

"You are not seeing her properly! See how the youngling is deep in her trunk? She is subdividing!" Little Red surged around them, his sonar pulses allowing him to see through both Little Purple and Reiki's bodies.

"Why are you breathing like that? Is birth imminent?" asked Little Purple.

"Can we watch?" asked Little Red, curious as always.

Slowly Reiki regained control. "Yes," she said. "I am about to give birth. But I need help. I need human help."

"Do you want us to carry you into shore?" asked Little Purple.

Reiki thought about struggling through the surf. "No, just take me to the raft. But I do need for one of you to bring a human here."

"You are faster, subset of Roaring☆Hot☆Vermillion. Go and bring back one of the humans."

Little Red wanted to argue. He would have preferred to stay and watch. But his vanity had been touched by Little Purple's praise of his speed and he raced off to the beach camp. Meanwhile, Little Purple cradled Reiki in his dark mass, supporting her neck and shoulders above the water. She had no sensation of motion as he eased her alongside the raft.

"Do you want to climb on raft?"

"I don't think I can," Reiki said quietly. "Besides, you are too comfortable."

Little Purple tried to accommodate her as best he could. Using the chemical-separation capabilities of his body, he extracted the salt from the ocean water around him and created a pocket of fresh water for Reiki to lie in.

As Little Red approached the shore, he met Richard

swimming out. Richard had been hunting along the shore—checking on Reiki occasionally. He had become concerned when Reiki's usual swim and dive routine stopped, and he was swimming out to see what was the matter. He climbed aboard the flouwen and Little Red took him back to the raft far swifter than Richard could have swum alone.

When they reached the raft, Richard was in time to lift his daughter from between Reiki's thighs to the surface of the raft.

Richard tied and cut the cord, and gently wrapped the baby in his cape. Then he lifted Reiki herself on to the raft beside the baby. Reiki lay back on the raft with the baby alongside her, quiet. She trailed her fingers in the water, gently caressing Little Purple.

"Thank you for helping me and my daughter," she said.

"What will you call her?" asked Little Purple. Loud Wiggling Pink would have been his suggestion.

"I'll name her after you," said Reiki.

"Violet?" asked Richard.

"Lavender," said Reiki firmly.

SPAWNING

Two more years passed, and it was time for the next quadruple conjunction extreme high tide. This one would occur at midnight, when the shadows of all three moons would join together in the center of Gargantua's illuminated face. Reiki settled Lavender on her hip, and picking up her plate of sliced jookeejook fruit, she followed Richard out of the hut. Once outside, Richard swung Freeman up onto his shoulders while the small boy giggled. It was late, but the children had been given naps so they could all stay up to see the event that came only once every five years. They walked down the moonlit paths to join the other families gathering in the Meeting Hall.

"Do you think any of the flood water will reach us?" Reiki asked casually.

"Don't worry, pumpkin," said Richard. "If the water didn't reach this valley last time, it won't bother us this time. That's why we picked this spot, remember?"

"Surely. Of course." Reiki wasn't really concerned. After all, even if they did get a little water, it was not like they minded getting wet. But the time for the flood wave just seemed to have come around so fast. Everything seemed to be happening so quickly. Freeman was almost three, Lavender was walking, the seasons had come and gone, and the moons were lining up again for the big tide, and yet on Earth they still had not learned of their crash landing. The children were growing up fast, and Reiki didn't

129

need any more reminders of how quickly time was moving.

The Meeting Hall was lit with candles and fire, and it was warm with people and laughter. Although they all still met for their evening meal, this particular midnight gathering had a festive air and everyone was smiling. The firstborn chased each other, laughing and squealing, around the outer edges of the room where the ceiling was too low to allow adult interference, while the grown-ups drank cool wine and tasted each other's offerings. Reiki added her tray of fruit to the table. She knew better than to try to cook something for a party. While some of her attempts at cooking had led to important discoveries, they weren't always appetizing. The adults had plenty to talk about, even though they saw each other every day. Each was working on their own observations as they studied the island, and if they ran out of scientific topics to discuss, there was always the children.

Why is it that each parent seems to think that the latest observation of their own youngsters was wonderful, thought Reiki, *when it seems obvious that their children are not nearly as bright as mine?* Reiki kissed Lavender and let her down to toddle off to play with the others, and called to Freeman to keep an eye on his sister. The little boy nodded to her solemnly. He took his responsibility seriously. He took everything seriously. *Such a wonderful boy. So much more obedient than Dirk and Adam.* Shirley and Jinjur's boys were wrestling again. Reiki marveled that they didn't hurt each other and that their mothers didn't do anything to stop them. Maybe she should say something.

"Hello, Jinjur, Shirley," said Reiki. "The boys certainly are growing, aren't they? And so are you, Shirley!"

Shirley rubbed her tummy ruefully. Now in the last trimester of her second pregnancy, she had taken over the village's child care while the rest of the adults did the more strenuous chores. As Richard had been the one taking

Freeman and Lavender over to Shirley's hut, Reiki had not seen much of the engineer for several weeks.

"You're not kidding," agreed Shirley. "I must admit it's good to see you, so slim and trim, and know that you've had two children, too. It's a relief to know that there's hope that I can get my figure back. I can't tell you how nice it is to talk with grown-ups for a change. After a full day of nothing but three-year-olds I feel as if my vocabulary has been reduced to one word: 'No'."

"Then why don't you ever come up to dinner? I haven't seen you for weeks," asked Reiki.

"Once all the kids go back to their parents, all I want is a little peace and quiet. Jinjur fills me in on the gossip."

"Yes, I guess having all the children together is a real handful," agreed Reiki, looking pointedly at Dirk, who was punching Maria's doll as she screamed in protest.

Shirley followed her eyes. *That Maria, always crying about something.* Then Adam tackled Dirk and the two boys rolled on the floor, Dirk using Maria's doll to wale away at his "brother." *Those two have so much energy! They are such strong, active boys! Not like some*, Shirley thought as Freeman picked up the now abandoned doll and returned it to Maria. What a relief to know that no matter what the children did tonight, she was only responsible for her own.

"Have you tried the wine?" she asked. "Jinjur brought some that she made last winter. Not that I can drink it, but I hear that it's pretty good."

"Wine?" asked Reiki. *I will not check on Richard,* she thought to herself.

"She Who Must Be Obeyed!" said Richard, slipping an arm around Reiki's slim waist. With a flourish he presented her with a clear bulb filled with the deep pink wine. Nuzzling her neck, he whispered in her ear, "You know, I never thought I would lose my craving for alcohol, but if I had to choose between a drink or a Coca-Cola, the Coke would win hands down."

"You'll just have to find a way to make it with Eden ingredients," said Reiki.

"Maybe you'll have one of those miraculous cooking accidents and come up with something," he said, backing away from her as he spoke. "You're looking lovely today, Shirley," he added, turning to Shirley and trying to change the subject.

"Thank you. I don't know how you can say that to a woman my size, but I thank you."

"The conjunction is starting!" called John from the door. "The shadow of Zouave is almost at the center of Gargantua, and Zulu's shadow just appeared and is catching up with our shadow." They picked up all the children and went outside.

Thick clouds were gathering overhead, but through the breaks in their dark curtain the humans could see Gargantua in "full-moon" phase, filling the sky above them. Because this was a quadruple conjunction, the innermost moon Zulu was between Gargantua and Eden and was fully illuminated, a white spot on the reddish Gargantua. Zouave was now behind Eden, but its shadow showed up on Gargantua along with the shadows of Zulu and Eden. As the three shadows moved across Gargantua's face, the high tide would start. When the three shadows all reached the center of Gargantua's illuminated face at the same time, the tide would be at its peak.

Reiki tried to get back into the mood of the celebration, but part of her was still alert, listening for any sign that the gravitational pull of all those planets might affect them. Richard had said that there might be quakes, even a reaction from the volcano, but if anything, the night seemed more quiet than usual. The expected rain began to fall, slowly and gently, and its soft patter on the thatched roof was soothing. With the rain clouds blocking the view, everyone came back inside out of the rain to finish off the food. Reiki would remember later it was just as she truly relaxed that disaster struck.

With no warning, something huge broke through the back wall of the Meeting Hall. There was no noise other than the protest of splintering wood, and the beast was in their midst, bringing with it the stench of ocean and rot. The size of a rhino, the ferocious animal was covered with long ropelike hair the color of congealed blood. Its neckless hair-covered head swung from side to side, questing blindly as the beast pulled itself forward with its two powerful front legs, its long black claws digging and destroying the planks beneath it. The monster uttered no sound, but the room was filled with the screams of the children and their parents.

Reiki froze. Her children! She had to get to them. How would she find them in all this chaos? Even as the fear crystallized inside her, she felt two solid thumps on her legs as her small children latched on to her. Scooping the children up in her arms, Reiki ducked under the low edge by the wall and made her way to the doorway. Outside, the terror continued. The entire valley seemed filled with the ugly, stinking giants. Their familiar settlement had become a nightmare of rain, darkness, and fear as numberless monsters slowly made their way up the valley, destroying everything in their path. The silent destruction was eerie, the only sound the rasp of the beasts' claws against the stones lining the streambed and the hiss of the falling rain. Behind her, she could hear shouts and screams. Richard found her in the darkness and picked up both her and the children in his strong brown arms. He was hesitating, trying to decide which way to go, when he heard a commanding voice.

"To me! To me!" Jinjur ordered. She was above them on the trail they had carved out of the rock face leading up to Carmen's perch. He ran easily, despite his load, toward the sound. Richard's sure feet brought them quickly to the bottom of the trail where Jinjur waited with one of the permalights. Adam and Dirk clung to Jinjur's neck, and Reiki could see some of the others and their children further up the side of the mountain. The monsters didn't seem interested in traveling up the ridges.

"Where are the rest?" Reiki asked as Richard set her on her feet.

"Shirley's been hurt," said Jinjur flatly. "John and Cinnamon stayed to help her. They've taken her to John's sick bay."

"How badly?" asked Reiki.

"I don't know. It didn't look good." Jinjur was a general and a combat veteran, but the pain she was controlling showed in her eyes.

"If it's bad they'll need more help," Reiki decided. "I'm going back."

"No!" said Richard and Jinjur together. "And that's an order!" Jinjur added. Just then Dirk screamed. It was a high keening that seemed to reach right into their hearts and Jinjur looked stricken, staring back toward the reddish glow that marked the fireplace in the meeting hut, now visible through the destroyed walls. With the general distracted, Reiki moved to slip away.

"No!" Richard whispered. "If you really think someone should go, it must be me. I'm stronger."

"I know you're stronger, that's why I'm being selfish and I'm asking you to stay here and use your strength to keep our children safe." She put the wet and whimpering Lavender into his arms and tried again to slip off, but his rough hand reached out and encircled her wrist.

"Wait," he said, "take this with you," and he unholstered his geologist's All-Tool from his belt. With a twist of his wrist he set the memory-metal head to a wickedly sharp pick. The permalight built into the handle would help light the way. He smiled grimly. "I would have used it before, but I was carrying my life in my hands."

The light from the pick barely illuminated the ground right in front of her feet, but Reiki tried to hurry over the rough terrain. The rain was falling heavier now and her wet sarong dragged against her legs. Odd shadows and trees seemed to menace her, and the stench of the monsters filled her nostrils as she moved toward the fire's glow. A flash of lightning threw the entire valley into sharp relief for a second. Then the darkness returned, deeper than ever to Reiki's flash-blinded eyes. The swift-following thunder rolled over her, and for a moment Reiki was completely disoriented. Suddenly, a black shape detached itself from the darkness and reared up, towering over her. Reiki could see the long sharp teeth that filled the monster's mouth as it turned toward her feeble light, its jaws gaping in a silent roar.

Without thought, Reiki swung her weapon upward just as the brute's head dropped toward her. Lightning streaked the sky overhead as the sharp pick was driven up behind the animal's teeth and deep into its skull, the light from the tool handle drowned in a warm gout of blood. Sobbing with fear, Reiki tugged and tugged on the slippery handle of the weapon, refusing to release it, as thunder rolled all about her. The monster heaved and the blade pulled free. Reiki ran to escape. She bumped into a large flat form and stifled a scream, but then an illuminating flash showed her she had run into the side of John's home. She had reached the sick bay. Reiki could hear voices inside the hut and she felt her way along the walls to the covered door. As she slipped inside, John called out.

"Cover the door! The light seems to attract them!"

Shirley was lying on the table, her clothes gone and the top of her head covered with a blood-soaked cloth. Cinnamon was working steadily, alternately breathing into Shirley's open mouth and applying cardiac massage to her chest, as John stood over his patient's swollen belly.

"Get up there and give Cinnamon a hand. If we are going to save the baby, we have to work quickly," he ordered.

Still shaken from the fight, Reiki silently stood across from Cinnamon, slipping her hand below Shirley's neck and pinching her nose closed. Outside the storm raged,

but inside the hut, under the steady glow of the permalights, they moved with purpose. Gently Reiki blew air
into her friend's lungs and turned her head to feel the
soft exhalation on her cheek. *Breathe, listen . . . breathe,
listen . . .*

"Smooth . . . even . . . breaths," Cinnamon said approv-
ingly. "Don't hyperventilate and get dizzy." She had moved
back to her place at the patient's chest and continued the
steady pressure pulses to Shirley's chest. Adrenaline had
left Reiki in a dreamlike state and it seemed perfectly
sensible that Cinnamon was pacing her efforts by singing almost silently to herself, "We had *joy*, we had *fun*,
we had *seasons* in the *sun* . . ." while Reiki continued with
her task. *Breathe, listen . . . breathe, listen . . .*

John was making quick work. He sliced deeply into
Shirley's belly and blood welled up around his knife. He
then moved more slowly, the small permalight held in his
mouth so that he could see into the incision. The knife
clattered onto the floor as John reached in with both hands
and pulled the baby free, lying still in his hands. Reiki
kept at her task. *Breathe, listen . . . breathe, listen . . .*

John quickly turned the child over, draining the fluid
from its nose and mouth. He was rubbing its chest and
breathing into its blue lips. His breathing was a staccato
counterpoint to her own breathing with its mother.
*Breathe, listen . . . puff, puff, puff . . . breathe, listen . . .
puff, puff, puff . . .*

Then the baby coughed. John straightened and smiled
grimly as the baby began to cry raggedly. Cinnamon
touched Reiki on the shoulder. "You can stop now," she
said gently.

"But . . ." said Reiki. "Why are you stopping? Now that
the baby is safe, can't John use the drugs, the paddles . . ."

Slowly Reiki realized that John had not done anything
for Shirley, no attempt to clamp the bleeding, no concern with the size of the wound, nothing. She pushed up
the makeshift blood-soaked turban that covered Shirley's

eyes and head, and was appalled at what she saw. Gently, Reiki reached out and closed the soft blue eyes that stared blankly at nothing and replaced the cloth to cover the devastation. She didn't ask what had caused such a vicious wound. It didn't matter if it had been falling wood, or the swipe of a bearlike claw, or the bite of a sharklike mouth, all that mattered was that one of them—one of her family—had died. She used some sarongs to shroud the rest of the body.

Cinnamon had wrapped up the baby and was quieting it. "You have another son, John."

"Yes, and my last, if I have anything to say about it. It hurts too much. I want to grieve for the loss of a friend, but I am too busy cutting her up trying to save my son. . . ." He began to sob and retch. Frantically he stepped out into the darkness. Outside, the thunder and lightning had continued inland. The rain still fell heavily, but the main body of the storm had moved on. Reiki rubbed John's neck while he emptied himself of his despair.

"What kind of man am I? How did I ever manage to end up at this point in my life? What could I have done?" he whispered.

"You are just a man, John. Violence and sudden death can happen anywhere," replied Reiki soothingly.

"What were those monsters? Why didn't we know about them? Why weren't we prepared?"

"No one could have been prepared for that. We all just do the best we can. But burying yourself in self-pity and 'whys' and 'what ifs' is not going to help that young child in there. You have a young Caesar, and he is going to need all of us."

"All of us. We *all* need all of us. And now one of us is gone."

"Yes," said Cinnamon, joining them. She placed the baby in his arms. "But now there is a new one of us."

John couldn't see the baby's face, but he could feel the warmth and the wiggle as the baby turned its head toward him looking for a breast. "Poor lamb. I have nothing to feed you. Reiki? I know you were trying to wean your daughter but . . ."

"Not to worry. Between us we can wet-nurse this little one."

"Thank you. But not Caesar, I think. We needn't be reminded of his mother's death every time we call his name. Let him carry his mother's name. We'll call him Everett."

Together they made their way up to Carmen's cliff-top home. Inside the small hut, all the children were sitting, wide eyed and silent, watching.

"Nels?" asked Cinnamon, looking around.

"He and David and Jinjur have gone to see where those beasts are going," said Richard. "And to find out where they came from."

"And to see the Jollys. To warn them," said Carmen. Maria was tugging on her mother's curly hair, trying to get her attention. She wanted permission to see the baby.

"Somehow I doubt the Jollys need warning. They have been hinting for months that there are Demonfish, now I guess we will remember to take what they say more literally."

The next two hours passed in silence. Even the children were subdued as they clung to their parents. The rain had stopped and dawn was just breaking when Jinjur burst into the hut.

"Piscatorial pickerels! That was some battle!" said Jinjur grimly as she entered the room. Even in the weak light it was clear that she was covered in blood.

"My God, Jinjur!" said John, passing the baby to Carmen and Maria. "Are you all right? Where are you wounded?"

"Oh, I might have a few scratches, but most of this blood isn't mine. Nels and David are following me up and they are okay, too. Nels sprained his ankle, so David is helping him. . . . Cinnamon if you want to go . . ." She looked around the hut.

"She left the minute you walked in," John said.

"Yeah, she always knows where she's needed." She sat down heavily. "Pontifical penguins, I'm beat. I just wanted to report that the Demonfish are gone and they won't be back. At least not for another five years. Why don't we all just take a few hours to clean up and to settle the children? Then we can go back to what's left of the Meeting Hall and tell each other our stories."

There was a long silence. Then John said, "Jinjur, come on outside. There is something I need to tell you."

Reiki sank down in Richard's lap and pulled her children tightly around her. She was shaking uncontrollably as the fear-fed energy of the terror-filled night drained away, leaving only emptiness. Outside she knew that the sky was growing brighter and a woman's heart was breaking.

When the time for the midday meal came the next day, Jinjur did not join the others. She had decided that she wanted to be the one to feed Everett and had gone down into the submerged lander to get the necessary hormone shots to replenish her milk. Adam had only been weaned a few months ago, so her milk would be easy to reestablish. Besides, the long walk to the beach and the time she spent away from the others would give the general a chance to grieve privately. Nels, too, stayed away from the gathering. His ankle was badly sprained and he was staying home.

All things considered, the damage to the village was minimal. The carcass of one of the monsters filled the shadows by the sick bay where John would dissect it later in the day. The Meeting Hall was razed, but the central chimney was still standing and the stones that supported the flooring were still in place. They had three months until the daily rains returned and by then they would have the roof restored. Reiki and Richard's home had been completely destroyed, as had the bridge that crossed the stream, but the rest of the dwellings had not been touched.

Some of the Earth crops were lost, but Shirley was the only loss that they took to heart.

Instead of meeting at the wreckage of the Meeting Hall, the rest of the castaways gathered at Carmen's home on the hill. David wanted to tell them all what had happened after they followed the attacking Demonfish, and he wanted everyone, even those on board *Prometheus*, to hear his tale. Carmen set up three-way contact between the settlement, the spaceship, and the underwater console used by the flouwen. Those aboard *Prometheus* would have to cope with a delay of several minutes, but as the questions would wait until the end, this shouldn't affect them too much.

After such a shocking experience, none of the parents wanted the children to be out of reach, but they didn't necessarily want them to hear about the violence. Arielle volunteered to watch the children as they played outside the hut. Carmen passed around bulbs of juice that she spiked with wine. After the sleepless night she thought that they all needed to relax. Once everyone was settled, David took the floor.

"Once I knew that Arielle and Shannon were safely here on the hill, I looked around to see who else followed Jinjur's voice. She let me know that everyone was accounted for, although she didn't say anything at the time about Shirley . . . well. She had taken one of the permalights that Carmen had been charging up here in the sunlight and was using short bursts of light to illuminate the valley. It was obvious that the beasts, whatever they were, had some sense of the light. If she held the beam still for any length of time, they would definitely turn toward it. The lightning seemed to confuse them.

"The main body of the herd had already moved upstream before she and Nels and I were ready to move. Jinjur had her bow and the heavy arrows, and the three of us each took the sharpest mattocks we could find from the farm implement shed. One of the smaller beasts seemed to have lost its sense of direction and was thrashing around in the middle of the village for quite some time. Later we learned that was the beast Reiki tackled. The sounds of its dying made it easy to avoid.

"God knows the creatures were easy enough to follow even in the rain. The smell alone, like a dead whale in the sun, would have led us to them if they hadn't left so clear a trail. They have no rear legs, just their long fat bodies that they drag over the ground behind them. If the tail helps them move at all, I didn't see any sign of it. Instead of galomphing along like a seal on a beach, these animals moved their front legs one at a time, digging their long black claws into the ground and pulling themselves forward."

Here David held up his own two hands imitating the creatures claws and pawed at the air slowly, methodically. "Scrunch, scrunch, the sounds of their claws on the rocks as they marched up the riverbed could be heard above the sounds of the storm.

"It was clear that they were heading for the upland lakes.

"When we got to the lakes, we found the Jollys there. They were all painted with streaks of white reflective paint marking each trunk with long vertical strokes that made them easy to see even in the feeble light All the stronglimb warriors were there, and all of them were quiet, staring down at the churning lake.

"Jinjur greeted Seetoo. 'We have met your Demonfish,' she said. 'We feared you would,' Seetoo replied. 'But you didn't heed us. I hoped that as time passed you would understand us better, but you have no eye nipples. You can not absorb the proper information. The Demonfish are indeed fearsome, but now is the time for warriors to bravely face the fearsome ones.' Seetoo gestured toward the lake. The normally clear lake seemed polluted as if by the noxious odor of the creatures. The lake's water was clouded with mud and foam as the huge beasts thrashed in the depths. The placid lake-fish were struggling to escape the frenzied feeding of the Demonfish. During a flash of lightning I watched as one of the monsters opened its mouth and swallowed one of the lake-fish whole. I swear, it was one of the largest lake-fish I have ever seen and it swallowed that fish whole! Then Seetoo said, 'These Demonfish have always been the enemies of my people. They come into our land, uprooting seedlings, destroying anything that stands in their way. They kill the fish in the lake, gorging themselves on our food. It is only fitting that the flesh of the Demonfish should be used to feed our young.' Seetoo went on to tell of how the monsters had killed many of his ancestors. Every generation had lost stronglimbs to the Demonfish attacks. The creatures would blindly destroy the Jolly's strongest buildings, and they would eat so many of the lake-fish that it was common to find still-living lake-fish in the mouths of slaughtered Demonfish. Over the generations the Jollys were forced to abandon their best lands to the ravages of the Demonfish, like this very valley we are now in. But the Jollys don't allow the monsters free rein. They cannot prevent the creatures from reaching the lake, but once the beasts are glutted on their kill, they become sluggish. As they try to leave the lake and get back to the sea, they have to pass back through this valley and here they take their vengeance.

"Jinjur asked if we humans could help in the battle. 'I am a warrior among my people and have fought many battles. These Demonfish have hurt my lifemate. They have hurt me. I would deem it an honor if you let me fight at your side.' 'It is we who would be honored,' Seetoo replied. For a moment I wondered if it really *was* our fight—if we should be getting involved in a battle where we didn't even know the rules. It's not our planet . . . why should we get into the middle of a war that goes five years between battles? But then I realized that, like it or not, this *is* our planet. My daughter is a native of Eden. The

Jollys are kind and intelligent, and if they believe there is a need to fight off these ugly stinking beasts, then I was willing to trust their assessment of the situation.

"It was the weirdest battle I have ever witnessed. The Demonfish pulled themselves out of the water and marched slowly back down toward us. They now moved noticeably slower and their huge heads were kept low to the ground. Water streamed from the long rank ropes of hair covering them and the run-off stank as badly as the creatures themselves. If they have eyes at all under that disgusting mop, they didn't seem to use them, but just moved steadily downstream toward the sea.

"The Jollys' method of attack was equally methodical. The stronglimbs attacked in their slow ponderous way, carefully judging the approach of the Demonfish with their intercepting advance. A sharp spear would be planted just in front of a monster. If the stronglimb lost courage and moved away too soon, the spear would fall harmlessly and the Demonfish would crawl right over it. If the Jolly stayed too long, he risked being mauled by the beasts' savage claws. But I saw Seetoo, with perfect timing, impale several of the giant creatures, stepping carefully just out of range of the frenzied thrashing of the wounded beast.

"Once wounded, the Demonfish could not escape the wrath of the Jollys. Several of the animals escaped without harm, but those that were pierced with the initial spears had no hope of survival. Once the wounded creature was slowed by pain and exhaustion, the entire village fell upon it. Sharp blackglass dirks held in a firm root-foot allowed the Jolly to keep its balance while still striking down on its victim with its full weight. By the time they were through with a Demonfish, it was a punctured and slashed hulk.

"Jinjur watched how the Jollys fought for a moment, and then started in on the Demonfish with her bow. The long moplike hair stopped most of her arrows, and even the heaviest arrows did little damage. Her wet sarong stuck to her skin and she pulled it off and threw it into the mud. Then she snatched up one of the spears lying on the ground and dashed into the melee. Nels and I followed our valiant leader into the thick of the battle. My memory after this point is not as clear. I don't remember feeling afraid, although the thought scares me now. I don't remember thinking clearly, although my body acted sensibly. I only know that things were happening all around me, and that I acted and reacted.

"I remember seeing Jinjur plant a spear and hold it as a Demonfish bore down on her. At the last second she ducked and rolled away as it came down hard on the spear. It rolled away from the pain of the wound, still maintaining that alien silence, right toward me. I planted my own spear and it rolled directly onto it. I remember the hot sticky blood and the rotting smell of the rough wet hair. The Jollys, white streaks making them look more threatening in the flashes of lightning, surrounded me and I ducked out from between their legs, as afraid of an accidental sweep of their blackglass dirks as I was of the claws of the Demonfish.

"I risked shining the light of my torch into the chaos around me, looking for Nels and Jinjur. The General had climbed up onto the back of one of the monsters, and as I watched she plunged a blackglass dirk she had found deep into the back of the monster's head. The huge creature reared and opened its mouth in a silent scream and, I swear, I saw one of the lake-fish in its mouth. The fish fell free and thrashed out the rest of its life on the stones at my feet.

"The mortally wounded Demonfish was still bucking and rolling. Jinjur judged its wild tossing like a rodeo cowboy and jumped free just as it rolled completely over onto its back. She landed like a dancer on the slippery wet stones, but the Demonfish kept on rolling, its huge body about to crush her in its death throes. Then Nels came out of nowhere, covered in Demonfish blood and screaming a warning. He tackled Jinjur and the two of them went down beside a large river rock. The Demonfish continued its roll right over them and for a moment I thought they both had been lost. Then they stood and I realized that the stone had sheltered them from the monster's crushing weight, except for Nels's ankle.

"By now the bulk of the Demonfish had left the lake. The Jollys had brought down more than a dozen of them and were finishing them off with daggers and stones. Filled with battle lust they were almost as frightening as the Demonfish. Nels was limping, making his way up the hill and away from the slaughter. I moved to help him and then I looked back after Jinjur. She was wiping clean the grip of her dirk and moving purposefully after the next Demonfish. I called to her. 'Jinjur! Come on! The Jollys aren't chasing them any farther!' 'That's because the Jollys can't chase them downstream into the surf!' she called back, blood lust and determination making her voice sound deep and hoarse. 'You can't fight them in the ocean!' I called, appalled at the thought of these huge creatures fighting in the freedom of their own element. 'Not I,' she called back. 'The flouwen!'

"Nels and I made our way to the Kcejook village to see if the Jollys needed any help with the wounded and then we came back home. On the way back we met Jinjur and we all came in together, Jinjur cursing the flouwen the whole way back. Apparently, they had been off surfing and never saw the Demonfish at all."

David sat back and drank deeply from his glass. Visions of the battle still filled his head. Soon, soon, he would be able to get back to his hut, back to where he could surround himself with the love and safety of his wife and daughter. Then he would be able to exorcise the Demonfish with his paintbrush, freeing his mind by trapping the visions on canvas.

HEARING

GNASA Administrator Fred Ross was dropped off at the elevator in the Rayburn House Office Building parking garage by his robocar. He was running late and was relieved to see that Chairman John "Hooter" Ootah was in the robocar behind him. The meeting wouldn't start until the chairman got there.

Congressman Ootah had a chauffeur, who got out of the front of the robocar, opened the rear door for the congressman, then ordered the vehicle to park itself while he went to the coffee shop to wait for the congressman to return. Fred shook his head at the thought of what a boring life the chauffeur must have, since no one was allowed to touch the controls on a robocar inside the D.C. limits. Still, it was a job, and those were hard to find now that robots did nearly everything.

Ootah came bustling up to Fred and gave him a hearty two-handed congressional-candidate handshake. "Hooter" had played linebacker for the Saskatchewan Elks before running for Congress, and Fred's hand was swallowed by the massive paws.

"Hello, Fred! I hear you have some exciting news for the subcommittee."

"Nothing that you haven't already heard on the TV."

"But now it'll be official. Nothing really counts until it gets into the Congressional Record."

They entered the elevator. The person sitting in the

chair next to the audio pickup for the automatic elevator controller was obviously another of Congressman Ootah's appointees, for he greeted him warmly and inquired about his ailing mother.

"Second floor," said the operator to the elevator, and they were whisked upward, bypassing the first floor even though the floor indicator had a blinking white light flashing in back of the number 1.

They walked down the corridor together and entered hearing room 2318. Fred was relieved to see that Dr. Philipson from Cornell had made it—the weather was usually bad in Ithaca in January—and went to sit next to him in the front row of spectator seats. The hearing room was packed with a number of reporters and space buffs, Fred recognizing many of them. The congressman, meanwhile, made his way to his chair at the front as the room clerk announced the start of the meeting.

"There will now be a hearing before the Subcommittee on Space, Communication, Power, and Extraterrestrial Mining, of the Committee of Science and Technology, of the Greater United States House of Representatives, One-Hundred-and-Forty-Fourth Congress, second session. The chairman of the subcommittee, the Honorable John Ootah, State of Saskatchewan, presiding!"

Ootah banged his gavel. "The subcommittee will be in order. Without objection, permission will be granted for radio, video, and holophotography during the course of the hearing. During the next two days, on Tuesday and Wednesday, the fourteenth and fifteenth of January 2076, the subcommittee will review the reports recently received from the brave crew of interstellar explorers visiting the Barnard system nearly six lightyears distant—the first ambassadors of the Greater United States to the worlds across the great void of interstellar space."

"Our first witness this morning is Dr. Morris Philipson, Professor of Astronomy at Cornell University, who will brief us about Barnard and its unusual planetary system.

Then the Honorable Frederick Ross, Chief Administrator for the Greater National Aeronautics and Space Agency, will describe the mission and the vehicles used in carrying it out. We will ask the witnesses to present their testimony first. Then we will have questions after all of the testimony is completed. The House is going into session at eleven o'clock. There will be a series of votes, then a lengthy recess which will allow adequate time for more testimony. We hope in this process the delays in the testimony will be held to a minimum. Dr. Philipson, if you will proceed?"

Dr. Philipson stepped forward to the presentation table, notes in one hand and some videochips in the other. "Mr. Chairman and members of the Subcommittee on Space, Communication, Power, and Extraterrestrial Mining, I appreciate this opportunity to testify before you about the Barnard system. I have some color holoslides of a few figures that I would like to project during my testimony." He handed the chips to a projectionist seated on one side of the table, who turned and gave them to a motile, who scampered off and put them into the holoprojector that took up one corner of the room. Dr. Philipson then pulled out an envelope from his stack of notes and passed them to the clerk sitting at the other side of the table.

"I brought along black-and-white flatview versions of some of the holoslides that can be included in the committee minutes at the appropriate places."

Congressman Ootah nodded. "Thank you for your foresight, Dr. Philipson. Would the Guardian of the Committee Room Door please ask the room robots to dim the lights so we may better view the holoslides?" The door guard spoke into an audio pickup in the wall by the door and the room lights dimmed. "Thank you," said Ootah to the guard. "You may proceed, Dr. Philipson."

"Thank you, Mr. Chairman. I will read from a personally proofed printout. With your permission, we can relieve the clerk from having to transcribe manually the robotic record and just insert the printout into the committee robotic reader." He passed his notes to the clerk, who looked at the chairman for permission first.

"That will be fine, Dr. Philipson."

The clerk dropped the sheets of paper into the input tray, and when they reappeared in the output tray, handed them back to the speaker. Dr. Philipson took back the notes and started to read from them.

"Barnard is a red dwarf star that is the second closest star to the solar system after the three-star Alpha Centauri system. Barnard can be found in the southern skies of Earth, but it's so dim it requires a telescope to see it. A 3D computer-animated view of the Barnard planetary system can be seen on the holoview screen in the corner."

The holoprojector went through its brief "audience attention focusing" mode, which started out with the floor-to-ceiling quarter-cylinder screen brightly lit with white light. The light seemed to lift from the curved surface and collect into a white ball floating in front of the screen, while at the same time a quadraphonic audio whistle added cues by focusing sound at the same point as the floating ball. With the audience's eyes and attention now focused in front of the screen instead of on the surface of the screen, the white ball faded and its place was taken by a three-dimensional image of a small glowing red ball, a slightly larger mottled red globe surrounded by a number of smaller balls of various colors, and a small whirling double planet. The large planet circled majestically at a fixed distance from the central star, while the double-planet moved in a smaller and highly elliptical orbit.

"The Barnard planetary system consists of the red dwarf star Barnard, the giant planet Gargantua and its retinue of moons, and a corotating double planet called Rocheworld. Gargantua is in a standard near-circular planetary orbit around Barnard, while Rocheworld is in a highly elliptical orbit that takes it in very close to Barnard once

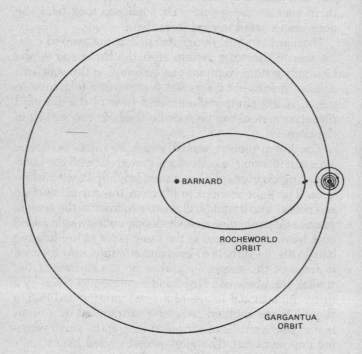

BARNARD

ROCHEWORLD
ORBIT

GARGANTUA
ORBIT

Barnard Planetary System

every orbit, and very close to Gargantua once every three orbits. It has been suggested that one lobe of Rocheworld was once an outer large moon of Gargantua, while the other lobe was a stray planetoid that interacted with the outer Gargantuan moon to form Rocheworld in its present orbit.

"Rocheworld consists of two moon-sized rocky bodies that whirl about each other with a rotation period of six hours. The two lobes of Rocheworld are so close that they are almost touching, but their spin speed is high enough that they maintain a separation of about eighty kilometers. There are exactly one hundred and sixty rotations of Rocheworld around its common center, or a Rocheworld 'day,' to one rotation of Rocheworld in its elliptical orbit around Barnard, or a Rocheworld 'year.' There are also exactly three orbits of Rocheworld around Barnard to one rotation of Gargantua around Barnard. This locking of Rocheworld's rotation period and orbital period to the orbital period of Gargantua keeps Rocheworld fixed in its highly elliptical orbit and keeps the double-lobed planet rotating fast enough to prevent its two lobes from touching each other. The energy input needed to compensate for the energy losses in the system due to tidal friction comes from the gravitational tug of Gargantua on Rocheworld during Rocheworld's close passage every third orbit."

The holoimage faded and the room lights came back on. Congressman Ootah turned and looked at the presenter.

"Thank you very much, Dr. Philipson. That's quite a spectacular planetary system there. If your schedule permits, we will proceed with the other witnesses and then have the questions and answers. The next witness will be the Honorable Frederick Ross, Chief Administrator for the Greater National Aeronautics and Space Administration. We want to welcome you here and congratulate you for one of GNASA's most successful missions."

Fred took Dr. Philipson's place at the presenter's table.

"Thank you very much, Mr. Chairman, and members of the committee. I hope you remember your congratulations when you are working on our budget for the coming year." A ripple of laughter passed through the audience and the chairman smiled.

"We most certainly will, Administrator. I personally will recommend a major new start to send a follow-on expedition."

"Thank you, Mr. Chairman. I will be glad to work with your staff on the details of the bill. Some of my engineering staff have been busy with their plans for the follow-on mission vehicles and will present them at the session tomorrow morning. Now, having been in office only five years, I can take credit for only one-tenth of this fifty-year long mission."

Fred bent forward and passed some papers and videochips to the clerk and projectionist.

"The vehicles used on the Barnard expedition were unusual because of the unusual nature of the target. I will go through their structure and function in some detail. The first component was the interstellar laser propulsion system. The payload sent to the Barnard system consisted of the crew of twenty persons and their consumables, totalling about 300 metric tons; four landing rockets for the various planets and moons at 500 tons each; four nuclear powered VTOL exploration airplanes at 80 tons each; and the interstellar habitat for the crew that made up the remainder of the 3500 tons that needed to be transported to the star system. This payload was carried by a large light sail 300 kilometers in diameter. The sail was of very light construction, a thin film of finely perforated metal, stretched over a lightweight frame. The payload sail was not only used to decelerate the payload at the Barnard system, but also for propulsion within the Barnard system. The 300-kilometer payload sail was surrounded by a larger ring sail, 1000 kilometers in diameter, with a hole in the center where the payload sail was attached during launch from the solar system. The ring sail had a total mass of 71,500 tons, giving a total launch weight of the sails and the payload of over 82,000 tons.

"The laser power needed to accelerate the 82,000-ton interstellar vehicle at one percent of earth gravity was just over 1300 terawatts. This was obtained from an array of 1000 solar-pumped laser generators orbiting around Mercury.

"The final transmitter lens for the laser propulsion system was a thin film of plastic net, initially 100 kilometers in diameter. Called a Fresnel zone lens, it had alternating circular zones that either were empty or covered with a thin film of plastic that caused a half-wavelength phase delay in the laser light. Such a Fresnel zone lens can transmit a laser beam many lightyears without the beam spreading significantly. The configuration of the lasers, lens, and sail during the launch phase can be seen in the top part of the diagram.

"The accelerating lasers were left on for eighteen years while the spacecraft continued to gain speed. The lasers were turned off, back in the solar system, in 2044. The last of the light from the lasers traveled for two more years before it finally reached the interstellar spacecraft. Thrust at the spacecraft stopped in 2046, just short of twenty years after launch. The spacecraft was now at two lightyears distance from the Sun and four lightyears from Barnard, and was traveling at twenty percent of the speed of light. The mission now entered the coast phase. For the next twenty years the spacecraft and its drugged crew coasted through interstellar space, covering a lightyear every five years. Back in the solar system, the laser array was used to launch another manned interstellar expedition. During this period, the Barnard Fresnel zone lens was increased in diameter to 300 kilometers. Then, in 2060, the laser array was turned on again at a power level of 1500 terawatts and a tripled frequency. The combined

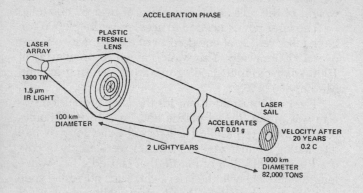

ACCELERATION PHASE

LASER
ARRAY

1300 TW

1.5 μm
IR LIGHT

PLASTIC
FRESNEL
LENS

100 km
DIAMETER

2 LIGHTYEARS

ACCELERATES
AT 0.01 g

LASER
SAIL

VELOCITY AFTER
20 YEARS
0.2 C

1000 km
DIAMETER
82,000 TONS

DECELERATION PHASE

LASER
ARRAY

1500 TW

0.5 μm
GREEN
LIGHT

300 km
DIAMETER

6 LIGHTYEARS

300 KM DIAMETER
10,000 TON
PAYLOAD STAGE

DECELERATES AT 0 1 g

STOPS IN 2 YEARS
AT BARNARD

1000 km DIAMETER
72,000 TON
DECEL STAGE

ACCELERATES AT 0.01 g

FLYS BY BARNARD

Laser-Pushed Lightsail Propulsion System.
[*J. Spacecraft*, Vol. 21, No. 2, pp. 187-195 (1984)]

beams from the lasers filled the 300-kilometer diameter Fresnel zone lens and beamed out toward the distant star. After two years, the lasers were turned off, and used elsewhere. The two-lightyear long pulse of high energy laser light traveled across the six lightyears to the Barnard system, where it caught up with the spacecraft as it was 0.2 lightyears away from its destination.

"Before the pulse of laser light had reached the interstellar vehicle, the vehicle was separated into two pieces. The inner 300-kilometer payload sail was detached and turned around to face the ring-shaped sail. The ring sail had computer-controlled actuators to give it the proper optical curvature. When the laser beam from the distant solar system arrived at the spacecraft, the beam struck the large 1000-kilometer ring sail, bounced off the mirrored surface, and was focused onto the smaller 300-kilometer payload sail as shown in the lower portion of the diagram. The laser light accelerated the massive ring sail at 1.2 percent of Earth gravity and during the two-year period the ring sail increased its velocity slightly. The same laser power reflecting back on the much lighter payload sail, however, decelerated the smaller sail and the exploration crew at nearly ten percent of Earth gravity. In the two years that the laser beam was on, the payload sail slowed from its interstellar velocity of twenty percent of the speed of light to come to rest in the Barnard system. Meanwhile, the ring sail sped on into deep space, its job done."

Fred then went on to describe in more detail the construction of the starship's habitat, the landing rockets and the exploration airplanes. He finally concluded. "Well, those are the vehicles that the exploration crew used to travel to and in the Barnard system. It's now time to hear about what they found there. For that, I would like to utilize the scientific expertise of my capable assistant, Dr. Joel Winners. Thank you for your time, Mr. Chairman."

"Your complete statement will be part of the record,

Mr. Ross," said Congressman Ootah. "We thank you. Our next witness is Dr. Joel Winners, Associate Administrator for Space Sciences of the Greater National Aeronautics and Space Administration."

Fred got up from the presentation table. He knew what Joel would be presenting, since he had sat through the dry run the previous day. Instead of staying to hear again about the flouwen, the intelligent aliens found on Rocheworld, he excused himself so he could get ready for the next day's session—the plans for the follow-on mission.

The following day, Fred Ross was in the meeting room early when Congressman Ootah arrived and started the second day of the Barnard Star hearings.

"The subcommittee will be in order. Without objection, permission will be granted for radio, video, and holophotography during the course of the hearing. Today we will hear from the GNASA Administrator about the plans for the follow-on expedition to Barnard. Mr. Ross?"

Fred Ross came to the presentation table.

"As you know, the news from the exploration crew at Barnard about the discovery of intelligent alien lifeforms on Rocheworld only arrived back at Earth a few weeks ago. Until that discovery, there had been no serious plans for follow-on missions. The teams of explorers we have already sent to Alpha Centauri, Barnard, Lelande, Sirius, UV Ceti, Epsilon Eridani, and the other star systems further out, were all volunteers on one-way missions designed to last for an entire human lifetime. Each team was given the equipment to carry out a complete and thorough exploration, not only of the stars, but the major planets and moons of each system. Once they had completed their survey and transmitted their images and data back to Earth, there would be no need for further scientific exploration of that particular system until all the other nearby star systems had been visited in a similar manner.

"The discovery of intelligent and friendly alien lifeforms

on Rocheworld, however, has completely changed the picture. Although the exploration crew there will do their best to learn as much from these creatures as possible, and will arrange to provide them with communication equipment so that they may exchange messages with scientists on Earth, this leaves much to be desired. The human crew are now in their forties and fifties, and although some of them will live for many more decades, they all must die eventually, ending direct interaction between humans and aliens. The communication links back to Earth will help, but with Barnard six lightyears away, there will be a twelve-year time lag between a question and its answer—hardly suitable for proper communication between species. We need to replace the exploration crew with a suitably chosen team of scientists, and we need to get them to Barnard as fast as possible, and bring them and some aliens back. I have queried my propulsion engineering experts, and they have come up with two possible concepts to achieve rapid roundtrip interstellar travel."

Here, Fred Ross handed a videochip to the projectionist, who handed it to a motile, who put it into the holoscreen projector.

"This first figure will look familiar to those that were here yesterday. But something new has been added. This is a design for a laser-pushed lightsail interstellar propulsion system, like the one used in the present Barnard mission, but this one has an extra sail stage, cut out of the middle, this gives it a round-trip mission capability. Since we may want to use this design on other missions than the Barnard mission, it was sized to go to star systems further out, such as Epsilon Eridani, almost eleven lightyears distant."

"Amazingly enough, we do not need to make any major changes to the design of the interstellar spacecraft itself, except to add the third stage. We do, however, need to upgrade the laser driver system here in the solar system, by increasing the laser power and increasing the size of

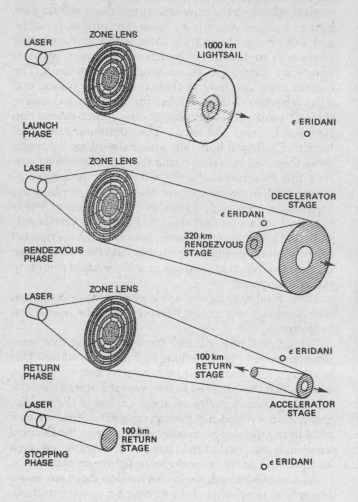

LASER   ZONE LENS   1000 km
LIGHTSAIL

LAUNCH
PHASE   ε ERIDANI

LASER   ZONE LENS   DECELERATOR
STAGE

320 km
RENDEZVOUS
STAGE   ε ERIDANI

RENDEZVOUS
PHASE

LASER   ZONE LENS

100 km
RETURN
STAGE   ε ERIDANI

RETURN
PHASE   ACCELERATOR
STAGE

LASER

100 km
RETURN
STAGE

STOPPING
PHASE   ε ERIDANI

Round-Trip Laser-Pushed Lightsail Propulsion System
[J. Spacecraft, Vol. 21, No. 2, pp. 187-195 (1984)]

the Fresnel zone lens from its present 300 kilometers to 1000 kilometers. As you can see in the figure, the lightsail on the spacecraft itself has now been divided into three stages. The outer ringsail is the same as before, 1000 kilometers in diameter with a 320-kilometer diameter hole, while the inner sail has been divided into two pieces, a rendezvous stage consisting of a sail 320 kilometers in diameter, and a return stage consisting of the inner 100-kilometer portion of the sail that carries the payload at its center.

"We want to get to Barnard as fast as possible, so we will use more laser power to push the sail while at the same time keeping it below its melting point. This will require boosting the power of the laser generators by a factor of thirty. The lightsail will accelerate at thirty percent of Earth gravity and reach half the speed of light in less than two years. At this speed, the time dilation factor is thirteen percent. We could continue to accelerate to higher coast velocities, but the radiation generated from hitting dust grains and hydrogen atoms starts to become hazardous. As before, as the lightsail approaches the target star, the inner rendezvous stage separates from the decelerator stage, the laser light from the solar system strikes the decelerator stage and reflects back on the rendezvous stage, bringing it to a halt in the target star system. The crew can then use the rendezvous stage as a solar sail for transport within the target star system. When the crew is ready to go home, they separate out the return stage from the remainder of the rendezvous stage, which now becomes the accelerator stage. The laser light from the solar system reflects off the accelerator stage onto the return stage, and it again accelerates at thirty percent of Earth gravity to half the speed of light. One final burst of laser light will then bring them safely to rest in the solar system. Assuming a coast velocity of half the speed of light, the roundtrip travel time to Barnard is about twenty-seven years. We can cut that some by continuing to accelerate to higher coast velocities and adding more radiation shielding."

"Twenty-seven years!" exclaimed Congressman Farquar from the end of the subcommittee table. "Isn't there a better and faster method of getting there?"

"Yes. Antimatter propulsion," replied Ross. "What is desired is a spacecraft that can accelerate at one to three Earth gravities in order to reach speeds closer to the speed of light more quickly, can provide rapid transport around the target star system once it arrives there, can land on and take off from all but the largest planets in that system, and can head for home the instant the crew is ready to do so. An antimatter rocket provides that capability—if we can build it."

"Are we going to be able to afford it?" asked Congresswoman Polk at the other end of the subcommittee table. "I was under the impression that antimatter cost billions of dollars a gram."

"It used to," replied the administrator. "And if that were still true, I wouldn't be suggesting its use. But some recent experiments in particle physics have discovered a Higgs-mediated charge-exchange resonance in the near collision of protons with electrons. The resonance was so narrow that it was missed up until now. But being very narrow, it is also very strong. If a beam of polarized electrons at *just* the right speed is shot at a beam of polarized protons at *just* the right speed, and the two polarizations are set at *just* the right angle, then the protons and the electrons exchange charges. The electron becomes a positron or antielectron, while the proton becomes an antiproton. The two types of antimatter are easily separated from the normal matter in the beams, decelerated to a stop, put together to make antihydrogen, and the antihydrogen stored without loss in electromagnetic traps until you are ready to use it—in our case for space propulsion. Amazingly enough, essentially no energy is required, since you can get back most of the particle beam energy during the deceleration process. My engineers inform me that within a few years, we could have antimatter factories producing literally tons of antimatter a year—more than enough for an interstellar mission, *if* we can build an engine robust enough to utilize the antimatter at its full potential. Let me show you an idealized picture of an antimatter powered interstellar rocket."

The holoscreen went through its "audience attention focusing" routine, and the focusing ball faded away and was replaced by a long, thin spacecraft that reached from nearly floor to ceiling in the corner of the hearing room. It looked like a fire-arrow, with glowing red feathers on its tail, and a purplish-blue flame coming out of its rear.

"This is pretty much what an antimatter rocket would look like. The antimatter engine is at the rear, emitting a high temperature plasma made of energetic particles moving at almost the speed of light. To keep the engine from melting, it must be cooled, and the liquid-drop radiators for the cooling are the three bright red triangular 'tail-feather' structures at the rear. In front of the radiators is a heavy tungsten radiation shield that blocks most of the gamma rays being emitted by the engine. In front of that are the storage tanks for the propellant that will be heated by the antimatter, and in front of that are the storage bottles for the antimatter itself. Way at the front, at the end of a very long boom, is the crew compartment, far away from the gamma rays emitted by the engine during its operation, and shielded by the mass of the tungsten shield and the mass of the propellant. The critical part in the entire design is not the container that holds the antimatter, but the engine that uses the antimatter. We're going to have a tough time making it. Let me show you roughly what it must do."

The three-dimensional image of the antimatter rocket disappeared from the holoscreen, and a black-and-white drawing showed up on the flatview screen to the left.

"This is an idealized schematic of what happens inside

an antimatter rocket engine. The antihydrogen is injected into the reaction chamber along with a stream of regular hydrogen. The positrons in the antihydrogen immediately annihilate with the electrons in the hydrogen, producing weak gamma rays and releasing the antiprotons which then immediately annihilate with the protons from the hydrogen. Unlike the annihilation of electrons and positrons, which always produces gamma rays, the annihilation of protons with antiprotons always produces between three and seven subatomic particles called pions. They are roughly equally divided into three types, uncharged, positively charged and negatively charged. The uncharged pions almost instantly produce highly energetic gamma rays, which is why antimatter engines are dangerous to be near when they are operating and need shielding.

"The other two thirds of the pions, which are moving at ninety-four percent of the speed of light, contain twothirds of the annihilation energy, are charged, and can be contained and directed by a magnetic field—if it is

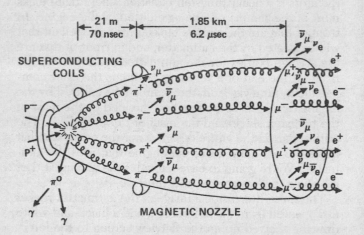

Antimatter Rocket Engine

strong enough. These charged particles will travel a spiral path that is twenty-one meters long before they decay. During that travel, they not only push against the magnetic field of the engine, providing rocket thrust, they also will heat up the excess hydrogen atoms that were not annihilated, and that hot plasma will also provide additional thrust. The charged pions decay into other charged subatomic particles called muons, which also will be trapped and directed by the magnetic field, providing further push to the magnetic field and additional heating of the hydrogen gas. These muons travel over a mile before they decay into electrons and positrons. By this time they will have left the engine, having used up most of their energy pushing the rocket. It is easy to make an antimatter rocket engine that is good enough for missions in the solar system—you just accept poor performance out of the engine and put a little more antimatter in the fuel tanks. But for fast interstellar missions, we are going to have to get nearly all the energy out of those charged pions and muons before they leave the engine nozzle, and to do that we are going to need superstrong magnetic fields. We can make superstrong magnetic fields with the new 'room temperature' superconductors, but although they are called 'room temperature,' they really are not. The superconducting coils require cooling to dry ice temperatures, and that is next to impossible to obtain in a coil built into an antimatter engine that is emitting high energy gamma rays. What we need is not a 'room temperature' superconductor, or even a 'high temperature' superconductor, but a superconductor that can carry high currents with no loss when it is red hot."

"What are the chances of that?" asked Chairman Ootah.

"Not good," admitted Ross. "In the next year or so I will have my materials scientists working on coming up with a true 'high temperature' superconductor. If they are successful, then we can design and build an antimatter rocket that will provide fast, convenient transport back and forth to Barnard. If they are not successful, then we will be stuck with the slower round-trip laser lightsail system."

"We all hope you *will* be successful," said Chairman Ootah. "That concludes our testimony for today. The subcommittee is adjourned until the next call for a meeting."

TEACHERS

"Doesn't it remind you of Christmas?" Jinjur said as they set up a picnic on the beach around the old Council Rock. Time and tides had washed away all signs of the beach camp that they had deserted four years earlier, but the shape of the shoreline was still welcoming and familiar. The whole colony had come down to meet the second drop of supplies from *Prometheus*, and the thought of new and better tools had everyone in a good mood.

"I know what I am looking forward to most," said Cinnamon wryly.

"Don't forget, the birth control pills will take several days to reach full effectiveness," John warned.

The medical staff and the computers on board the lightsail craft had decided that the best way to control the population on Eden would be with oral contraceptives for the men. For the last five years, the men and women on the planet had had to avoid actual intercourse, or risk pregnancy. After decades of indulging freely on board *Prometheus*, the restriction had seemed severe. Indeed there were several small children to attest to their lack of restraint. But while some of the children had not been planned, all were wanted and loved, raised as they were with the cooperation and help of the whole community.

The six-year-old firstborns were working intently down by the edge of the surf constructing an elaborate sand castle. Adam, insisting that as the oldest, he was in charge, was ordering the others around, and thanks to the support of his "brothers" Dirk and Everett, the children fell in line with his grand plans. Freeman, Lavender, and their little brother Justin were slowly canvassing the beach looking for shells to decorate the structure. Eve and her two little sisters, Rebecca and Sarah, hauled sand from Dirk's moat to Adam and Everett's tower, and Shannon carefully added flourishes and tiny details.

The adults had learned long ago that, usually, the best thing for their bright and opinionated progeny was to leave them alone, and so they were sitting comfortably in the spot that had once been the center of camp. David and Nels were setting out the festive food that the men had made for this special occasion, and Arielle was, as usual, eating it.

"Don't eat too much, Arielle," John cautioned. "You are setting yourself up for heartburn." The petite blonde was at the end of her second pregnancy—the flouwen had informed them it was a boy—and the former beauty queen never seemed to stop eating.

"Ha! I have stomach like horse! You only want more food for yourself." Arielle snickered, her mouth full of fruit.

"Don't worry about it," said David to the others. "I've grown used to my woman's appetite. I brought along plenty."

"But Nels had us work so hard getting each recipe just right, arranging everything so fancy. . . ." John muttered. "And no one gets to see how beautiful it is, if you eat it before it's even put on the table."

"Relax, John," Nels said. "I think you've been living alone too long. People eating the food with pleasure is the best compliment a cook can have. I like watching people eat." He looked toward Cinnamon, nursing their fourth daughter. The baby's downy blond hair looked golden against Cinnamon's tan breast.

"That's right," said John. He was used to the kidding he received as the only bachelor. "I'm getting old and crotchety and set in my ways. Humph. I like my ways. Good ways." John had offered to live with Jinjur and his children after Shirley had died, but she had declined. Carmen rejected his offer, too. *Maybe . . .* he thought for the millionth time, *maybe I should have asked instead of offered.*

Just as the midday eclipse was half over, the children called out, "There it is! There it is!", and a shooting star flared across the sky. A moment later, there was the distinctive "boom" as the aeroshell's shock wave reached them.

"Hurray! Hurray!" The children were all dancing on the sand at the edge of the water. The adults knew that it would take a while for the flouwen to find the crawler and bring it to them, but the sense of excitement continued to grow.

"Hello!" Little Red finally called from the surf. "Little Pink is bringing the crawler!" The flouwen had decided to let the youngling do the honors now that it had gained enough bulk to hold the crawler. Little White and Little Purple were escorting the youngling, and Little Red had gone on ahead to tell the humans they had found the package from the skies.

Nels, Richard, and Jinjur headed into the water and together they wrestled the heavy metal box onto the sand. "Crawler" was a misnomer, as the motor that ran the treads had been removed to allow more mass for precious cargo. The outer hatch was carefully removed, and each item was unpacked gently as they enjoyed the touch of civilization sent to them by their friends aloft. The time they had spent aboard *Prometheus* seemed as distant as a dream now. Except for the occasional conversation over the comm-links, the Edenites had little contact with their past. Even Josephine, the computer in the ship trapped below the lagoon, was visited only in extreme emergences . . .

just a few of the children had made the risky underwater trip.

Most of the cargo space was filled with vitamin pills. Data fed to the *Prometheus* from the flouwen concerning the nutritional content of the local foodstuffs had led to a weekly supplement about the size of bird shot, but with years between drops and the growing population, the vitamins were precious indeed.

Also included in this drop were "Teachers" for the children; small handheld computers filled with educational software. Each of the almost indestructible, light-powered Teachers had been specifically programmed for each child. Shannon's, for instance, had an animated dragon to explain each lesson, and the explanations themselves were be tailored to appeal to her joy of art and drawing. Eve, who had inherited her mother's musical sense, would find that her computer would use songs to teach her spelling, math, and the periodic table, while Freeman's curiosity would be rewarded with more and more complicated explanations as he requested them. The firstborn took the teachers reverently amid the *oohs* and *ahs* of their siblings, and each vowed to work diligently. The parents, more realistically, had agreed to rotate the chore of supervising the children's learning so that none would return to Earth with an incomplete education.

For the adults there were spare communicators and battery packs, as the older batteries slowly lost their ability to recharge fully. There were tools to replace those that had been lost, and new multipurpose tools that Caroline had fabricated to order in the automated machine shop on *Prometheus*. There was also an updated picture of the crew up above. They were getting older and grayer, and Sam was missing, having died ten months ago.

Each treasure was lovingly bundled up for safe transport back to the village, where it would be used and valued. Technology that they had once taken for granted now seemed as magical as gifts from the gods, and no tool would be lost or mistreated even by a child. Heartened that their everyday chores would be made a little lighter by these aids sent down by their family overhead, the party on the beach lasted far into the afternoon. Then, as Barnard slipped into the ocean, the weary but happy humans straggled back to the homes they had carved out for themselves on this alien world.

FOLLOW ON

The three astronauts met in person for the first time on the bridge of the antimatter-powered rescue ship *Succor*. Their mission was to get help to the explorers stranded on Zuni as quickly as possible. Their high-speed spacecraft would be followed within the next few years by a larger exploration and development fleet that would include contingents of scientists and engineers, along with their accompanying flocks of robots. While the three astronauts had all conversed at length over the solnet in the process of helping to design and program the spacecraft, they had been too busy getting ready to spend the next thirty years away from home to get together physically before.

Laura Brooks was the last to arrive. She had taken a well-deserved lunar-day-long vacation at her home in Mare Imbrium on Luna before selling off the house and taking the daily Lunavator capsule between Imbrium and the space station Goddard. The station robots brought her out in a Goddard flitter to the kilometers-long interstellar spacecraft, which was floating in space a safe distance away from the station. First making sure that she was securely tethered, the robots led her through a temporary shielded passway they had erected across the short gap between the small flitter and the airlock entrance to the human quarters portion of *Succor*. The airlock cycled and she pulled her off her helmet. Her long blond hair was pinned into a crown on her head, exposing the implant set into the top of her spine. She had been upgraded for this mission, and the soft down of her back hairline was still stubble from the preoperative shaving. Laura patted her hair and licked her lips nervously. It had been weeks since she had even talked to another human being face-to-face, and these men would be her sole living companions for more than six years.

She stepped from the lock, and with an expert push with her foot, she floated into the *Succor*'s central deck. Two men floated before her in the room, looking as nervous as she felt. Laura smiled and nodded a greeting.

"Laura Brooks, logging on," she said.

The shorter and younger of the two men formally returned the nod. He gestured to the slender black man standing beside him. "May I present Orson Pratchette of Valkyrie, Mars?" Orson bowed at the introduction, somehow managing to do the full Japanese business-bow in free-fall without looking ridiculous. He was bald, and his slender frame and smooth dark skin called attention to the beauty of his well-shaped head. The shorter man continued. "And I am Beauregard Darlington Winthrop the Sixth," he said. Then his face broke into a broad friendly grin. "Just call me Win. Welcome aboard."

Laura knew the name, of course. Playboys and politicians, the various Winthrops had made the name both famous and infamous. But the face was familiar, too; hadn't she seen him attending classes at Lunar University? The smile changed his entire face, and he looked young and handsome. He was small for a Lunie, just over two meters. Laura realized that if they were standing against pull he would only come up to her chin. She looked down curiously at his extended hand and slowly put out her own. She jumped at his touch as he gently gripped her fingers, but she remembered that this greeting was still rather common on Earth. His hand was warm and smooth, and for a moment Laura wondered just when she had last felt the touch of another person.

"Are you from Luna or the planet?" she asked, and then wished she could withdraw the words. How could she ask so personal a question?

"I grew up on 'Mud.' Stunted my growth," said Win with a smile. "After graduation from the Space Academy, and getting my commission, I was scheduled to spend the rest of my life deep in the Pentagon. Thankfully my father managed to pull a few strings and save me from that fate. Got sent to Space Exploration grad school at Lunar U."

It was Orson's turn to be surprised. "You actually relocated just for grad school? Why didn't you take the classes by holovision?" He had a heavy accent that Laura couldn't identify; it hadn't been apparent during their discussions over the solnet.

"Yes," said Win, "my folks were pretty old-fashioned. My dad and granddad were both alumni, and they said college was better experienced with more than just your brain. Besides, my mom wanted me out of the house."

"Well, you are surely out of the house now," said Orson. "Shall I introduce you to the ship, Commander?"

Although officially Win was in command of this mission, he was known to be a relic of the old boy network that was still operative, even though it had lost most of its influence over the newly scientific military community. After decades of science being warped toward military ends, scientists had gradually moved up the military ranks and changed it from within. Now the armed services were filled with the cream of the college crops, graduate school had replaced boot camp, and military missions were now undertaken for the purposes of exploration, utilization, and colonization rather than destruction. But there remained ingrained remnants of families with long-standing political influence. Win had done much of the work on the design of the many exploration and resource identification systems that they would be leaving deep inside the Barnard system and had worked with the team that had perfected the terraforming programs, but up until a month ago Win was to be just another member of the team of scientists and engineers that would come along later. Suddenly, the original commander of the *Succor* had been given a promotion he couldn't refuse, Win had been promoted to brigadier general, and put in charge of the mission. It would be some time before he grew to fill the label of Mission Commander that had been applied to him.

Orson's rank of colonel reflected the fact that he had designed most of the hardware on the spaceship *Succor*, including its super-intelligent computer, "Mike." Laura, the software expert, was the civilian on the mission. She and Orson had spent much virtual connect-time together "inside" Mike as they tuned Mike's hardware and software to optimum performance, then slowly "woke" the computer up and turned it into a nearly sentient being. Since she and Orson had participated in being Mike's "parents," she knew Orson well, but she and Win had only met on the solnet occasionally.

"They told me in flight school, 'Always do a walk-around inspection before you take her up,'" said Win, "so please do show me around."

"Virtual or real?" asked Orson.

"Real," replied Win.

"You're not going outside, are you?" exclaimed Laura. "That's dangerous—even in a hardsuit."

"Not *real* real," Orson assured her as he led them to the three compchairs on the central deck that would connect them to the main computer. "But instead of visiting a computer simulation to view what *should* be there, we will use roboproxies to physically inspect what is *actually* there."

The three soon were in the compchairs that connected them to Mike—arms connected through virtual gloves, eyes connected through virtual goggles, and brain connected via an infrared link from their spine implants to a receiver in the compchair headrest. Soon, all three were outside the ship in their roboproxy bodies as Orson showed them around.

Space seemed harsh and unpleasant. The sky was jet-black while all the pieces of hardware around them seemed either too bright with sunlight or too dark with shadow. But that was reality, exactly what Win wanted. As he listened to Orson, he kept the eyes of the roboproxy flickering across panels and struts, looking for something out of place—a panel with a puncture, or a strut with a weak point—some little thing that might kill them if he didn't find it first. Win looked hard and was almost disappointed when he couldn't find anything wrong with Orson's spacecraft.

Orson started them at the tail end of the ship. "This is the antimatter engine," he said, "where the antimatter meets the matter to generate a high energy plasma that is exhausted out the rear to provide thrust."

"Not much to it," remarked Laura. "Looks somewhat like a gigantic butterfly net. You would think that the plasma would leak out of all the holes between the cables in the net."

"It's the part you can't see that makes it work," said Win. "The magnetic fields generated by the electrical currents flowing in the cables turns the net into a solid wall for the plasma. Let's go down and look at it from the inside." He started his roboproxy down, but it slowed. "Something wrong with this goddamn robot, Orson," Win complained. "It's balking, and red lights are flashing in my peripheral view."

"Safety feature, Commander," said Orson. "Even though the magnetic fields generated by the superconducting polycables in the engine are only set at the minimum level needed to maintain the shape of the engine, they are still much greater than can be tolerated by the superconducting metal shielding around the roboproxy's electronics. If you force the 'proxy any closer, its metal shield will go normal, the magnetic fields from the rocket engine will penetrate its electronics, and the Hall effect will shut its gates down."

"Goddamn it! Why don't they build 'proxies with better shields? I want to go inside!"

"It's got the best superconductor that was available at the time—a metal-oxide multilayered compound that holds off tens of Tesla at room temperature. It's just that the polycable in the rocket engine is better. The compound in the polycable is brand-new, and the entire output of the first production run all went into building our engine. It came from the stars and it's going back to the stars."

"Came from the stars?" asked Laura, puzzled.

"The cables in the net are made from a new flexible metal-organic polymer that is superconducting up to a temperature of almost a thousand degrees, just below the temperature where the polymer itself starts to melt. The compound was found in the nerve tissue of the alien icerugs on the moon Zulu around the planet Gargantua in the Barnard system. The icerug nervous system uses it for transmitting electrical signals in the icerug's acre-sized bodies. The compound is not only superconducting at a very high temperature, it is also a very strong polymer with a high melting point. Without the discovery of this compound by the Barnard system explorers, we would not be able to build this magnetic nozzle, and without this magnetic nozzle, we would not be able to build a high-speed interstellar antimatter rocket. We would have had to send a slow lightsail ship instead, which would delay the rescue of the stranded explorers by decades."

"So the discoverers are going to be the first beneficiaries of their discovery," remarked Laura. "How fitting!"

"Well," said Win, still slightly annoyed at his roboproxy, "if we can't go inside in reality, let's switch to virtual and go in that way."

"Very well, Commander," said Orson, and their views

all changed subtly. Instead of the harsh shadows and glaring brightness of real sunlight on real objects, and occasional annoying glints from sunlight reflecting off "anti-reflective" surfaces on real optics, the scene before them was now perfectly illuminated. Orson led the way to the inside of the rocket nozzle, then up the antimatter injector and into the antimatter fuel tank, with its myriad snow-flakes of antihydrogen, while at the same time discussing the technical features of each piece of apparatus as they passed by or through it, until they got to the leading end of the arrow-shaped ship.

The only part of the ship designed for human occupation was at the very tip of the barbed "head" of the arrow, as far away as possible from the flood of gamma rays that were emitted by the matter-antimatter reaction.

" . . . and here we are," said Orson, as he led them into the virtual control deck, where they could see their bodies lying in the compchairs. Win and Laura could see that Orson was taking off his helmet in the virtual scene, so they followed suit.

"That was a long afternoon sit," said Win, getting out of the chair. "I think I'll go to my quarters and have dinner." He looked at Laura questioningly. "Like to join me for dinner?" he asked. "And perhaps get to know each other better?"

Laura was tired. "Some other time, maybe," she replied, and they all three headed for the doors to their quarters.

The tip of the *Succor* was slowly spinning to provide artificial gravity to the crew quarters. Each crew member resided in a multistoried "penthouse" that made up the three barbs on the arrowlike head. The positions of the living quarters could be adjusted further or closer to the axis of spin, allowing each person to regulate the "gravity" within their personal living quarters to their liking. Orson, from Mars, could mimic the 38% Martian gravity in his quarters, while Win could live at the standard gravity of his childhood or the 16% of his college years.

Laura had never experienced anything stronger than the gentle Lunar pull, and had set her quarters at the 28% gravity of Eden in order to strengthen herself so she would be able to investigate the new world in comfort.

Laura entered with relief into her three-story stateroom, where she was warmly greeted by her attentive masculine "personal servant." Although she knew consciously that the body of the android was just a copy of the loving and caring android that took care of her in her mansion on Luna, the soft, ready smile and the twinkle in his eye as he tenderly enveloped her in his strong arms and greeted her with a big hug, let her know that the same wonderful "John" was inside.

"What a lovely new place you have found for us, Laura," said John appreciatively. "A little more compact than our place in Imbrium, but that means that I won't have to spend as much time keeping the place clean and will have more time to spend on you."

As he was giving her one last squeeze before releasing her, he noticed a speck of lint on the front of her uniform. As he reached his hand up to her breast and removed the offending speck, the feedback link from her brain through her implant connection reported an unusually strong emotional response to his touch.

She must have been aroused by meeting real men, thought John. *I must respond to her romantically this evening and be prepared in case she needs me.*

"How about a bath before dinner?" he asked her with a smile. "If you would like, I could follow it with a massage."

"I would like that very much, John," said Laura, pleased once again how thoughtful John was, always anticipating her every mood. Still, after spending the day with two real men, John's solicitousness rang a little false. Sure, it was relaxing to not have to worry about John's feelings after spending the whole day striving to behave as diplomatically as possible with her new crewmates, but was that really what she wanted? To spend so much of her time with a being who merely made her comfortable? Maybe she should have his programming updated, modified slightly so that she would be more challenged, more stimulated. Then John began to rub her back with soft, almost tickling strokes. As he peeled off her uniform, Laura sighed. In his own way, John was stimulating enough.

When Win entered his stateroom, "Doll" was there, looking gorgeous as usual. "Hi, Handsome," she said brightly, her perky little nose wrinkling upwards in greeting as she raised her face for his welcoming peck. Win felt his hackles relax as he realized that he no longer had to deal with uncertain and emotional responses from unpredictable humans and was back again with Doll, who always anticipated his every need. Although the accommodation he would have on *Succor* was a small three-floor stateroom, instead of commodious Winthrop Mansion on the banks of the Cooper in South Carolina, as long as Doll was here, this was home. As he took off his jacket with the bright new stars on it, he took an envelope and a small box from an inner pocket. The envelope was old-looking and had the embossed imprint of Senator Beauregard Darlington Winthrop III on the upper left corner. The name "George G. Gudunov" was written in fading black ink on the front.

"Put this in my safe, will you?" Win asked, handing it to Doll.

"Certainly, dear," she said, as she commanded a distant minibot to come out of storage. She would have the minibot do the task while she concentrated on taking care of Win. She looked at the letter carefully so she would be better prepared to retrieve it if Win asked for it. "Isn't George Gudunov the commander of the Barnard Star expedition?"

"Yes," said Win, "that letter is for him. It goes with the box, which contains George's brigadier general stars. When my father gave it to me, he said that I should give it to him personally, or, if he's dead, to set it on his grave." Win chuckled. "You know, I was listening the day my great-grandfather, the senator, first passed this note down and gave it to my grandfather. I was only a kid, but the way I remember it, Gramps didn't say 'set it' he said 'spit.' Odd how the memory can play tricks on you."

The minibot came scuttling into the room, took the letter and box from Doll, and hurried downstairs to the study.

"What would you like for dinner?" asked Doll, pulling Win by the hand toward the large, comfortable sofa before the large living-room window displaying the view over the veranda as seen from Winthrop Mansion in June. A tall mint julep was sitting on the table beside the sofa and Win picked it up as he sat down.

"I can have the cook be starting on it, while you tell me all about the meeting with your crew." Doll sat down on the sofa next to Win and snuggled up under his outstretched arm as he took his first sip of the strong drink. She could smell the strong perfume of the woman Laura on Win's clothing, and through her feedback link, she could sense that he too was smelling it, although subconsciously, and the lingering smell was having a strong emotional effect on him. Win liked to think that all women desired him at first sight.

"*Especially* that Laura woman!" added Doll, picking her words and emphasis carefully to produce a response from Win that would make him feel better.

Win grinned at her remark and laughed loudly. He was amused and pleased that the android seemed to be jealous of the human.

"Don't you worry, Doll," he said, giving her a hug. "Nobody will ever replace *you!*"

Orson entered his quarters and shook off his tension from the long afternoon as he shucked off his coat. After some hours in free-fall on the central deck, his reflexes had not yet readjusted to gravity, so the coat dropped onto the floor. He shrugged and kicked it into the corner, then called out cheerfully as he headed to the kitchen.

"Hey, Mom, I'm home! What's for dinner?"

After a few weeks of checkout, it was time to go. Laura made herself comfortable in the compchair in her apartment so that the infrared link had adequate signal-to-noise through her hair. Once fully connected into Mike, she felt herself lift free of her own awkward body as Mike's neurnet spread out before her. She danced over neurons like a butterfly, sensing rather than seeing any loops or glitches in the programs. The commnet of *Succor* was sparkling and supportive, and she enjoyed the beauty of the implied landscape. An electric blue spark appeared beside her. Laura knew Orson better in this guise, and she moved within the glow of his personality. Their minds merged and Laura tried to match the deeply personal warmth of the connection with the formal reserve of the man she had met personally earlier that week. They had not met personally since. Each preferred the custom compchairs in their own suites to the ones on the free-fall central deck, and with the quality of the virtual links it made little difference where they were physically.

Together Laura and Orson spent the morning taking Mike through the final prelaunch check. But with no glitches to fix, after that there was really nothing left to be done but admire their own work. The actual firing of the antimatter rockets would be done by Goddard Station. They would be accelerating at three gees for a number of months to get up to speed in a hurry, so the human crew would have to be in their suspended animation tanks and under before ignition.

Reluctantly Laura pulled out of the link. She got out of the chair and stretched, her arms and legs stiff from the inactivity. Time spent in the ship's neurnet always seemed short until she logged off.

If a few hours of sitting still can make me stiff, thought

Laura to herself, *I wonder how I'll feel after fifteen years*. John was waiting by the side of her chair to help her out of her clothing and into the narrow bed of the deepsleeper. He stood by as the tiny metal fingers of the med unit inside the deepsleeper painlessly microneedled the improved deepsleep version of the life-extending drug No-Die into the vein at her collarbone, and Laura felt herself slipping into sleep. After a few minutes, John tenderly lowered the lid on the deepsleeper. A moment later foam filled the interior, surrounding her body with a strong soft cocoon. The room grew dark and quiet except for the soft glow from the tell-tale lights of the medical monitor and the simulated breathing noises of the ever-loyal John, waiting patiently beside the coffinlike box for his sleeping beauty to awake.

TOOLS

It was time for the third drop of supplies, and once again the whole settlement had turned out to sit on the beach. The party atmosphere had been muted with the news from George that Katrina Kauffmann, the efficient, no-nonsense nurse, had passed away at the adjusted age of 68. Jinjur, who was a year older, was taking the loss particularly hard.

"I just don't understand it!" Jinjur said again. She had been going over it with John for hours. "She had James and the Christmas bush monitoring her health round the clock! There is no way that she could just die!"

"Jinjur," said John patiently. "Whether you understand it or not, whether it makes sense or not, Katherine is gone. Eventually the human body wears out."

"But with the facilities on *Prometheus* . . ."

"Facilities that Katrina was in charge of," John reminded her. He had been monitoring the read-outs on Katrina's health through his communicator link to the commsats and *Prometheus*, and he had suspicions of his own, suspicions that it would do no good to share. If Katrina didn't want to face a slow decline, if she overrode James and resisted treatment, that was her choice. "Facilities that were designed to deal with occasional illness and accidents, not to rebuild an aging human body that had worn out."

Jinjur looked down the beach to her own three boys.

She had given birth to only one of them, but she had been mother to them all. *Katrina had died. Died because she was old. Am I old?* Jinjur wondered to herself. *I don't feel old. I suppose that my hair is getting rather gray, but surely . . .* Her thoughts slipped back on to a more familiar path. *Shirley. Gods, I miss you. Look at your sons, at our sons. They are getting so big, but they are still just children. I can't be old. I won't allow it. They need me.*

"John?" she said quietly. She wasn't arguing now. John had been watching the boys, too, especially their son, Adam, and had followed her thoughts.

"We have time, Jinjur." he said. "Rescue is coming. And when they get here, you and I are going to be here to greet them." *If only in the person of our son,* he finished to himself. A cheer rose up from the surf as the children caught sight of the fiery tail of the incoming aeroshell as it met the Eden atmosphere. The light-hearted fun of playing with the flouwen in the shallow water vanished as the giant fluid bodies tensed, eager to get a bearing on the crawler's splashdown.

"Come on, Little Red! You can give me a ride!" called Adam. Tall and strong for his twelve years, his long brown body cut through the water until he broke the surface in the middle of the large red alien. He shook some of Red's mass out of his thick black ringlets. Jinjur had given up trying to keep her boy's hair combed and now resorted to simply cutting out the larger tangles. As a result, the soft sausage curls stayed close to his scalp, and while the cut had little style, it was practical.

"I'm coming, too!" called Shannon as she splashed into the middle of the pink flouwen youngling. The redhead had inherited her mother's beauty and grace, but she took pride in being able to keep up with the boys, and they accepted her company on most of their adventures without complaint.

"Come on, Lavender," said Little Purple, who had grown

deeply attached to the child he had helped deliver. "If we go fast we can beat them to it!"

Lavender's blue eyes sparkled as she giggled with excitement. The little girl had spent so much time playing in the water with her godparent that her fair skin had tanned golden brown and her long dark hair had sun-bleached streaks. She knew the flouwen's vibrating voice had been pitched too quietly to be picked up by the grownups on the beach. If they moved quickly enough, they would not only catch up with the smaller Warm Chirring Pink, but be well underway before the adults missed them.

"Adam!"

That was Jinjur. Lavender lowered her head to leave as small a profile as possible against the water. Little Purple was moving quickly, but her face was well away from the front of him and the "bow-wave" didn't splash her. She loved the feeling of moving so quickly while floating in water that was perfectly still.

"ADAM! Come back here!"

"Aww, Mom!" Adam moaned.

"Aww, Mom!" Little Red joined in.

Lavender lowered her head still further. If her ears were under the water and she couldn't hear her parents call, she could hardly be blamed if she didn't come.

Adam waded back up the beach to where Jinjur stood hip deep in the surf. Gently she took his shoulders and walked back up the slope to the others on the shore, propelling Adam along in front of her.

"Come on, Mom! I just want to go along. I won't get into trouble, I promise!"

"Oh. And you weren't going to get into trouble last month when you just wanted to 'watch' the Demonfish. If Seetoo hadn't spared an eye to come and get me, I would never have known you had left the hut."

"Dirk went, too," Adam mumbled.

"And was it all his idea?"

Adam scowled. Dirk was bigger and stronger than Adam; the stocky blond was growing so fast that even Reiki didn't try and make him wear more than a loincloth. But Dirk was not as clever as Adam, and while Dirk made a good ally, Adam had always been the leader. Adam would never let Dirk take the blame. He was stung by the suggestion that he was trying to get his brother into trouble, but he knew better than to argue with the General. *At least she didn't find the Demonfish spears we had made*, thought Adam rebelliously. *We just wanted to see if they'd work. We wouldn't have been hurt. Grownups just don't understand.*

"This is different," Adam said, swallowing his anger and trying his most winning smile. "The flouwen are just going to fetch the crawler. It's not dangerous at all. Even the girls are going."

"No," Jinjur agreed, "it's not the same. But you are grounded, as grounded as much as anyone can be in this pulchritudinous place, and you may not go. Not even if the girls are going."

"Girls?" asked Reiki. She looked up from where she was spooning mushed jookeejook fruit into little Ernest's mouth. She could see her boys, Freeman and Justin, playing with Cinnamon's girls. "Adam? Where's Lavender?"

"She's riding Little Purple," Adam answered, a trifle jealous that Lavender had managed to sneak off.

Reiki was at first alarmed, then she relaxed. Little Purple might be one of the more irresponsible flouwen, but she knew that he loved her daughter with all his . . . mass. Little Purple would never let any harm come to his charge.

Little Red, seeing that Adam was inexplicably in trouble, lingered for a few moments to see if the boy would win a reprieve. When it became clear he would not, the flouwen took a moment to be thankful that Jinjur had not been a flouwen elder when he was a youngling. Then he cheered up. Unencumbered with passengers, he would have no trouble reaching the crawler before the others.

He settled into his most streamlined shape and raced off through the deep green water.

As the minutes passed, the adults moved closer to the water and searched offshore for signs of the flouwens' return. Although they had adjusted well to life without the conveniences of technology, their quality of life improved with each drop. This time the fifty-plus kilo payload would be filled with larger tools like axe-heads, hoes, saws, and files, as well as more Teachers and more powerful communicators.

Fortunately, it was no longer necessary to devote any of the payload mass to the vitamin supplements which had filled so much of the earlier crawlers. It had taken thousands of samples and hundreds of days of work, but with the aid of the flouwen's excellent taste sense, John had managed to find all the vitamins and minerals they needed either in native plants and animals, or in the village's Earth crops. Josephine's chemical analyzer had confirmed the results, and while not all of the necessary foods were palatable, all were readily available.

"Here they come!" called David. His fatherly eyes had picked up the blush of his daughter's hair as she rode high in the water. Shannon was riding much higher than usual; indeed, she appeared to be sitting on something. Lavender, following close behind, was also seated. Had they sent two landers?

"Look what we found!" called Shannon. "It was all over! It covered the whole ocean!"

Little Pink and Little White surfed over the waves with their passengers, pulling back only at the last moment to deposit the girls at the waterline. The waves worked with them as they pulled two huge sodden bundles up onto the beach.

"What is it?" asked Reiki, "And where is the crawler?"

"Little Red is bringing it in, Mom," answered Lavender. "Little Purple didn't want us out there because there might be Demonfish."

"Demonfish!?" Reiki was horrified and relieved at the same time. Thank goodness her trust in Little Purple had not been misplaced! She took her daughter in her arms and hugged her tight. The wet girl wiggled, too excited to be held.

"Demonfish!" said Jinjur. "Did you see any? Was there sign?" The Demonfish had always been a mystery. They came from deep beneath the ocean whenever there was a quadruple conjunction, and then they disappeared for another five years until the next midnight quadruple conjunction. Their thick fur seemed to absorb the flouwens' sonar pings and the flouwen found them almost impossible to track. Where the vicious creatures went, and how they spent the years between their coming ashore had never been discovered.

"If this isn't sign," said Shannon, "I don't know what is." She indicated the sodden mass she had dragged up behind her. The General looked more closely.

"Pussyfooting Percherons! It's Demonfish hair!" The long, dark red locks of hair taken from the bodies of the Demonfish had turned out to be extremely useful. Washed and carded, it could be spun into soft yarn and knitted into luxurious fabric much prized by the humans and the Jollys.

"It was amazing!" said Shannon. Her eyes glazed as she recalled the scene. She was itching to get to her Teacher where she could put the fantastic sight into her sketch-pad program. "The green waves were flat, too heavy with the crimson hair to rise. The sky was purple with pink clouds, the rose glow from Gargantua overhead, and all around us the waves looked like . . . like . . . the waves had texture, from the curling ropes of hair, dark and deep. . . ."

David smiled and put his arm around his daughter's shoulders. He understood how the words wouldn't come, how the hand longed to get to a medium that would let her recreate the vision trapped just behind her eyelids. He led her from the shore, knowing how easy it was to stumble when the eyes were too busy looking inward and could not be spared to see the way. He handed her Teacher to her and she sat down immediately with it, trying to capture the images before they drifted away.

"It was reekee, Mom," said Lavender, taking over. "The whole sea seemed full of the stuff. I know how you like to weave with it, so I had Little Purple bring you some, but he thought the Demonfish might still be around, so he sent me home on Little Pink while he stayed to guard."

"Come on Richard," said Jinjur. "Let's go see if we can find out more about this!"

"Are you sure you should go after the Demonfish in their own element? Sounds like bearding a lion in its den," cautioned Reiki.

"We won't fight them, just see if there is any sign of where they might have gone," Richard assured her. The two of them rode off on the flouwen, back the way they had come.

Little Red arrived moments later, carrying the crawler, but he didn't stay to see it unpacked. He, too, wanted to see if the strange tide of Demonfish fur would lead to the discovery of the elusive beasts' hiding place. But when Jinjur and Richard returned they had only more loads of the dark red fur. There was no sign of the terrible Demonfish.

DAM

It had taken many weeks of work, but at last they were ready to detonate the charge. At first, the little human settlement had needed only the water from the stream flowing through Meander Valley to fill all their needs, including the irrigation of the vital Earth crops. The last year an extreme dry season had forced them to ration the fresh water to their fields, and they wanted to ensure that this would never again be necessary. It was decided to dam one of the feeder streams to make another lake. The dam would be upstream from the village, but not in line with the normal paths the Demonfish took to the upland lakes. No one wanted to risk its being damaged by their rampage. Once the spot was selected, the long work of building a dam began. The stream's normal run-off was left unrestricted during the construction. Several sturdy boobaa trunks bridged the stream and the construction grew over and around them. Rocks had to be brought in, loaded by hand into a wheelbarrow, walked to the stream, and then piled around the site. Each stone had to be fitted and mortared into place, and as the final dam would be a meter thick and several meters high, the work took months.

There had been a great deal of discussion on how to collapse the remaining hole that allowed the water to escape beneath the growing wall of the dam. They had considered simply covering the entrance with planks and stones by hand, with the larger men working in shifts in the slowly rising water. Jinjur had wanted to prop a large load of stone over the opening and then pull the prop away to allow the stones to fall and block the water, but a prop strong enough to hold the load of stones would be too strong to be easily shifted. It was Adam who suggested using gunpowder.

"Gunpowder!" said Jinjur. "Of course!"

"What do you mean, 'of course'?" said Reiki. "One thing we don't need on this planet is something as destructive as gunpowder!"

"Gunpowder is a tool, Reiki," said Jinjur, "nothing more. It's only destructive if it's used destructively. Engineers have used explosives in construction for hundreds of years."

"Can we make gunpowder?" asked Carmen.

"I don't see why not," said John. "Let me think. You need carbon . . ."

"That's easy enough," said Jinjur. "The charred wood from a fire."

"And sulfur . . ."

"There is sulfur leaching out of the volcano by the lava bed," said Richard.

"And saltpeter," John concluded.

There was a moment of silence. Then Adam cleared his throat.

"We've found some," he said. "There is a lot of the stuff on the walls in the caves on the dry side of the volcano."

The growing youngsters had enjoyed the run of the island all their lives and none of the adults were surprised that the children knew the island better than they did themselves. But the fact that Adam had not only found a concentration of saltpeter, but had identified it, told his mother even more.

"Adam . . ." she said dangerously. "You have already made some gunpowder, haven't you?"

The tall boy looked down at his bare feet. "Yes, Mom,"

he admitted. Towering over his mother, the teenager hung his head and tried to hide his blue eyes under his long dark curls.

Everett stepped forward. "It was my idea," he said, trying to get the heat off his brother. "I was reading about it on my Teacher and it sounded . . . interesting." The wiry blond boy smiled ingratiatingly. His cheerful smile had won over their mother's objections in the past, and Jinjur had struggled to keep from spoiling the boy.

"It should have sounded dangerous," said Jinjur, sounding pretty dangerous herself. "It should have sounded like something that you should have left alone."

"We just wanted to see if we could do it," said Dirk, joining his brothers. Dirk was not as tall as Adam, but he was heavier and seemed to put on muscle daily. To see Jinjur berating her boys was like seeing a mockingbird scolding three young eagles.

"And could you?" asked John, getting back to the central issue. Jinjur could punish the boys later.

"Yes," said Adam. "At least we made something that went bang when we hit it with a rock."

"If they can make a small bang, we can make a large one," said John with conviction. His sparkling blue eyes all but disappeared when he smiled.

"Yeah," said Richard enthusiastically. "We could make a great *big* bang. We could blow off part of the valley walls over the stream. Then we wouldn't have to go as far to get more rocks for the dam."

"I bet there is a lot of things we could blow . . . I mean, use the powder for," said Nels.

"I hope you're happy," Reiki grumbled to Jinjur. "Now they are going to go about just looking for something to blow up. Next thing you know they'll be building a cannon!"

"Don't be ridiculous, Reiki," Jinjur said reassuringly. She patted the sociologist on the back. "I won't let them build a cannon." The General watched the other woman walk away and then looked speculatively at the old men talking to the boys. "Not a cannon. But maybe . . . if we could get a strong enough barrel . . . melt river gold into bullets . . . snazzier than the Lone Ranger!" She joined the men.

Amazingly, they managed to make and test the gun-powder without anyone getting seriously hurt. John assured Reiki that Richard's eyebrows would grow back, and to make her feel better, Richard agreed not to go along when they set the charge. In fact, most of the others would be waiting in the village while the last section of the dam was filled. It was only John and Nels who placed the bag of black powder beneath the supports and reeled the fuse up to where Jinjur waited.

"All clear?" Jinjur called.

Carmen was up at her home and had all the children, even the teenagers, corralled inside. All the parents agreed that they weren't to light the fuse until they were absolutely sure that the children were nowhere near the site. Carmen's voice answered the General over the weak comm-link in one of the communicators.

"Don't worry, Jinjur. I'm looking at all three of your boys even as we speak."

"Nels?" Jinjur held out her hand, and Nels handed her the lit taper. She held it to the fuse for a moment until the end began to smoke and spark. She set the burning fuse on the ground and moved away. If they had calcu-lated the charge correctly, the results would be unspec-tacular, but the crude grinding process had made the power of the black powder erratic.

The bright sparkle of the fuse was hard to look at directly with eyes that had long been used to the dim glow of Barnard, but the dark smoke marked the burn's progress. It dribbled down the side of the hill and dis-appeared into the pile of rocks below. They waited long moments for the fire to work its way below the stones to the support and the bag of black powder beneath. They waited. It was taking too long.

"Should we go a set a new fuse?" asked John.

"No . . ." Just then they heard a loud *thump*, and the precariously balanced pile of stones tumbled down, splashing into the fast-flowing water.

"Hurray!" They all cheered and ran to the other side of the dam. The water began to drop dramatically and only a thin trickle leaked from the stone-filled hole at its base.

"A few days of silt and debris will fill up the fine cracks," said Jinjur, smiling with approval. "Come on, men, let's set the wheel!"

Together they eased the heavy wheel onto the wooden axle. Even now, the water level was creeping up the sides of the ravine, and up the rocky face of the dam itself. Once the water level reached the top of the dam and began to spill over, the wheel would begin to turn. A system of gears would transfer the turning power of the wheel into the energy they needed to grind wheat, and turn the lathe and potter's wheel.

"Jinjur?" came Carmen's voice from the Teacher. "The water in the stream has dropped. Is it all clear?"

"Yes!" called the General, panting with exertion. "All is wonderfully clear!"

The children didn't wait for permission, but burst from Carmen's hut like the seeds from a peethoo pod. The long-legged teens ran with the ease of youth down to the water and up the wet and empty streambed. Several of them stopped to gather up the bewildered fish that had not found safety in the deeper pools.

Adam, Everett and Shannon were the first to reach the area near the dam. Warned by their parents that they weren't to get near the edifice until the adults had judged it sound, they moved away from the waterline. They pushed on up the hill and ran through the woods where the going was slower. Finally they came to a stop in a quiet glade, struggling to catch their breath. The three of them were almost surrounded by the tall green trees, but here there was a break in the greenery. They sank down to rest in the shade where they could watch the rising level on one side of the dam and see the water's first fall over to the other.

"Say, Shannon, I wanted to thank you for not saying anything about our own experiments with the black powder," said Everett with a smile.

"Experiments? You mean the gourd rockets you were exploding in the lava flow? Terrifying all the game in miles?" Shannon chuckled.

Shannon had watched entranced as the boys had dropped the powder-filled gourds into the trench filled with smoldering red lava. They had exploded in bright flashes as they reached the terrible heat that rose from the molten rock. It had taken the deepest reds of her palette to recreate the glowing background to the brilliant bursts of light. She had been further entranced at their cavorting in the stream later when they washed off the telltale smell of the gunpowder. Especially on the one occasion when they had taken Maria to watch their "experiments."

"Don't worry. I'll keep your secrets." said Shannon "I'll even keep the one about Maria," she said teasingly.

"What about Maria?" asked Everett nervously.

"You know," she said mysteriously.

"Don't pay any attention to her," said Adam contemptuously. "She doesn't know anything."

"Oh? I don't know anything?" Shannon smirked. "I know enough to know that your back wasn't the only thing Maria was scrubbing the gunpowder smoke off of."

Everett paled. "We were only playing." He smiled wanly. "You should know. You've gone swimming with us before."

"Yes, but I've never done *that* before," said Shannon, enjoying his discomfort.

"Oh, pay her no mind, Everett." said Adam. "She's just a kid. She doesn't understand about such things."

At that Shannon's temper flared. "Just a kid! I'm only a few hours younger than you, Adam Kennedy, and I do so know what you and Maria were doing. I just think it's awful that she would do it with both of you . . . as if you were all three married or something. And you just better watch out. I won't have to tell if you make her get a baby."

"You can't make a baby unless you take those pills the men take," said Adam contemptuously.

Shannon laughed. "The pills make babies *not* come. Didn't your mom tell you anything about sex?"

Adam just glowered.

"She told us something," Everett stammered, "but it was all about Jolly's pollinating and flouwen merging and how babies come after people merge."

"Yes," said Shannon. Her temper had improved with the chance to prove that she knew more than the boys did. "Babies come after people 'merge' unless the men take their pill. If they don't take a pill, sometimes babies come, sometimes they don't."

"Oh, God!" said Everett. "I only did it that once!"

"Then what are you worrying for?" Shannon got back to her feet. "Maria had her period last week."

Realizing that he had been had, Everett lunged at her. "Why you . . . !"

The slender redhead had no trouble keeping away from him. Her laughter lingered in the glade as she ran down the hill to the rapidly filling lake.

"Adam?" said Everett quietly. He didn't want to assume that Shannon had really gone. "*I* only did it that once . . . but you . . ."

Adam sighed. "I'll talk to Dad about it. There has to be some advantage to having the doctor for a dad."

"But what if he tells Mom?" Everett asked.

"Everett," said Adam, "I don't even want to think about it." The two of them followed Shannon down the rocky path to the river, but even the first slow turning of the wheel did little to lighten their mood.

RESCUE

"Okay, okay! *Damas y señores!* Everyone settle down!" Carmen called the group to order. She had asked that all of the scientists and most of the fourteen-year-old first-born attend this meeting. Now they all settled quietly onto the benches she had set up outside her hut as the comm expert turned up the volume of the link to *Prometheus* so that they all could hear.

"Okay, George, go ahead," said the little señorita as she took her seat. Time had turned her black curls the color of iron as her generous curves settled into a more matronly silhouette, but her dark eyes still sparkled flirtatiously. "We are all awaiting your slightest word."

"Wonderful, wonderful," came the reply from George. The view of his face on a Teacher hooked up to the comm-link widened to show that all the remaining crew, Red, Thomas, Linda, Tony and Deirdre, were standing around their commander. Caroline had passed away only a few days ago, but the scientist's faces were wreathed in smiles. "I wanted us all to be together when I brought you this news," said the eldest member of the crew. Time had been kind to him and his thick white hair framed the face of a cherub.

"When we set out from Earth, we all expected that this was going to be a one-way mission of discovery and exploration. None of us ever expected to see Earth again. But this system that has been our home for so long has proven to be full of wonders. We have discovered the flouwen, the gummies, the icerugs, and the Jollys . . . life, intelligent life . . . beyond all Earth's expectation."

"We know all this!" Adam grumbled.

"Shh!" said Cinnamon. "He's having fun."

"Just wish the old man would get on with it."

"Earth has come to realize, as we all have, how important it is that the Barnard system be fully explored and studied, and it seems that they are not willing to leave it to us old folks . . . or to our descendants," said George, with a nod to the firstborn. The youngsters had grown up with observation and scientific method as their watch-words, and with the help of the computer Teachers, most of them were budding scientists themselves. "My friends . . . truly, my family, I am pleased to inform you that the follow-up mission is underway. Six years ago, Earth launched the rocket ship *Succor* to bring us displaced Earthlings back home. Following behind them is a major scientific exploration team to further study Barnard and its planets, and maintain contact with the intelligent races we have found."

The cheerful rumblings that had started at the first mention of a follow-up mission gave way to enthusiastic applause. The old folks cheered and hugged their spouses and children, thrilled at the confirmation that their offspring would be able to rejoin the rest of the human race.

"The advances in space propulsion that have occurred since we left, means that the *Succor* will have a shorter trip than the one we took on *Prometheus*, and we can expect company in about nine years," George continued, although he had lost most of his audience. All formality had disappeared and questions flew back and forth, slowed only by the slight delay as the signal bounced from the ship to the planet and back.

Carmen brought out the wine and the newest astronauts were toasted. Even the firstborn were allowed small sips of the fruity beverage. The youngsters, however, were not as excited at the thought of rescue as their parents. They had learned about Earth and its technology from their Teachers, but Eden was all they had ever known, and the thought of leaving it all behind forever seemed intimidating. Still, the ship was still nine years away and they would be twenty-three before they had to worry about it. They would be old by then.

Finally the mood settled. Rescue would mean that the children's futures were assured, but nine years was a long time. Arielle took Eve, Shannon, and Maria and they left the gathering. The comm-link with the ship was cut and John moved the discussion on to more serious matters.

"Okay!" he called, holding his hands up to call for silence. "I know that we all are overjoyed with this news, but there are a couple of things, not quite so pleasant, that have to be discussed." All eyes turned toward him.

"The sad news is that not all of us will be here to greet the follow-up mission. I am saddened to tell you this, but Arielle has cancer."

There was a shocked silence.

"Is there anything you can do?" Jinjur asked.

"I'm afraid it has spread too far. I'm not even sure what I would have done had I caught it earlier, but now there is simply nothing I can do."

David interrupted. He and Arielle had wanted all of the others to be aware of the situation, and wanted to be sure that John would not have to shoulder any blame. "Arielle has already been down to visit Josephine in the submerged lander. Even with everything aboard the sick bay there is nothing we can do for Arielle except keep her as comfortable as possible for as long as she has with us. We wanted John to let you know so that you would understand that neither Arielle or myself will be available for assignments."

"No," said Jinjur sympathetically, "of course not. From now on your only assignment is let us know if there is anything we can do . . . anything at all . . ." Jinjur knew how painful loss could be, but the right words just wouldn't come. David had a long hard journey ahead of him, and all of them would do all they could to lighten his load.

"Thank you," said David simply, and he left to follow his wife home.

"Oh, John!" said Carmen. "How . . . how long?"

"It's hard to say. It looks like it might be related to the cancer that attacked all of us on the trip out." John sighed. Hodgkin's disease had cost them their original medical doctor, Dr. William Wang, who had not lived to reach the Barnard system. Now it was claiming another victim. "She is not in pain now, but that will probably change. Josephine has made me a supply of painkiller, and . . . if Arielle fights . . . she may have a year, maybe more."

"Now," he said, standing with his arm around Carmen, "there is one more rather difficult thing we have to discuss. Carmen?"

Carmen straightened. Behind her back, she gripped John's hand for support. "I'm sorry . . . I regret . . . Oh, hell. The fact is . . . Maria is pregnant."

The meeting exploded.

"What!"

"She's only fourteen!"

"She's just a child!"

"Who's the father?"

"ADAM!" said Jinjur, turning on her son.

"Dad!?" beseeched Adam as he backed away from his mother.

"Jinjur," said John, coming to his boy's aid, "this is one thing you can't blame Adam for, although it apparently wasn't for lack of opportunity. Adam came to me months ago, and while I gave him quite a lecture about having sex with his half-sister, I also gave him a dose of our birth control pills. God knows I haven't needed to dose myself for years now. I also called Everett in for a talk as well. Rest assured that this baby will not be a product of incest."

"Who does Maria say the father is?" asked Cinnamon.

"She will not say," Carmen confessed. "She says that it could be any of the older boys. She says that the baby is only hers and it does not matter who the father is. She says that if I was willing to break the rules to be a mother then I should not fault her if she does the same.

"Suddenly I don't know her. Half the time she doesn't talk to me and then when she does, what she says makes no *sense*."

"I know," said Cinnamon reassuringly. "We all know. We all have teenagers. I find myself wishing my parents were still alive so that I could thank them for letting me live though my own adolescence."

"The fact remains that she freely admits sleeping with all of the boys, and if Adam and Everett were using protection that leaves . . ."

"It was not me," said Freeman, crossing his arms over his chest. "I would not sleep with her."

"Freeman," said Richard severely, "I know that Maria was hanging about, following you around. If you have done anything, if you might be responsible . . . well, I want you to tell the truth about it. Right now."

"Maria *did* want to do it, but I did not. I would not." The boys implacable black eyes met his father's directly.

"You turned her down?" asked John incredulously. "Why?"

Freeman turned to face the rest of the group. He took a moment to choose the right words but when he spoke it was with conviction, forcing all of them to see the truth of his word. "I would not sleep with Maria because that would hurt Eve. I love Eve. I will make love only with her."

"Oh . . . my . . . God . . ." whispered Cinnamon. Eve's mother closed her eyes and rubbed the bridge of her nose. Nels slipped his arm around her.

Reiki looked up at her son's face. He looked so much like his father that she looked in vain to see any sign of her solemn little baby in his face. "You are only a child," she implored, wishing that it were still true. "What do you know of love?"

"I know that it is love for Eve that keeps me from wanting Maria," Freeman answered his mother simply. "When I am ready, when *she* is ready, I will share such things only with Eve."

Cinnamon had been watching Freeman closely, and now she nodded. "Thank you," she said to Reiki, who was looking at her son with loss and pride battling in her eyes. Then Cinnamon turned to her mate. "Well, Nels, I think the next move is up to you." Pointedly, she took Jinjur's arm and the two of them left the room.

One by one the rest of them filed out until Nels was left alone with his only son, Dirk. Throughout the discussion Dirk had stood sullen and withdrawn. The heavy blond youth was handsome and well muscled; like all the children of Eden, he had grown up tall and healthy. The look of the man he would become had already marked his features. His blue eyes watched this father of his warily.

"I know it's a little late for me to play much of a role as your parent," said Nels, wishing that those blue eyes, so much like his own, would soften. "You know the facts of your conception."

Like all the firstborn, Dirk's parentage had been decided by a computer. Shirley had been delighted that Nels had been matched with her but had also made it clear that the baby was to be hers alone to raise. After her death, Jinjur had clung to her lover's sons as if their existence were all that kept Shirley's memory alive. The General had jealously taken over every part of the boys' lives and Nels had been relieved. Cinnamon had become so important to him that Nels was grateful to Jinjur that she considered Dirk's parentage a trivial technicality.

"I have never been much of a father to you," he conceded. "But it looks like you are about to be a father yourself. You'll find out for yourself that it's not easy, and God knows I haven't given you much of an example to follow.

But I have learned a great deal about parenthood in the last fourteen years. I have been able to be deeply involved in the raising of my daughters, and I loved every minute of it. If I had known what I was giving up when I agreed to let Shirley and Jinjur have the privilege of raising you, I'm not sure I'd have made the same decision. Children are wonderful, rewarding, and a huge responsibility. Maria is not Shirley or Jinjur. She's no more an adult than you are. She's going to *need* your help, and you are going to need mine. If you'll take it." Nels held out his hand.

"Thank you, sir." Slowly Dirk reached out and grasped the offered hand. A shy smile softened the strong young face. "I want to do the right thing . . . I hope you'll help me figure out exactly what that means." They might never have lived in the past as father and son, but they were prepared to deal with the future, supporting each other, man to man.

WAVE

Ruth's golden hair shone in the rosy sunlight as the ten-year-old splashed about in the tiny warm waves of the ocean, which were lapping up against the shoreline, sounding like a kitten drinking milk. Cinnamon straightened up from her task and rubbed the small of her back as she kept an eye on her fourth and youngest daughter playing on the distant ocean beach. The small baby peekoo "crabs," which Cinnamon, Eve, and Freeman had been stalking so diligently, were tricky to catch, and bending over to see them crawling on the muddy bottom of the brackish marsh was hard on Cinnamon's stiff back.

The baby peekoos had gathered in the sheltered marshy delta of a small stream that fed into Crater Lagoon, only a few hundred meters from the original Council Rock. The stream ran by the large grove of boobaa trees that occupied a high knoll not far from the beach. The tree-covered knoll was like a blue-green island in a sea of yellow-green grass-covered dunes. The tall boobaas in the grove supported a platform that had been built long ago as a lookout to keep track of those out on the water fishing. The firstborn had occasionally used the platform for a clubhouse since then and had kept it in good repair. The little girl had wandered around the lagoon and down onto the main ocean beach, where the sand was toasting redly in the morning sun.

Cinnamon had taken the children on a long-promised

"trip to the beach," which had culminated with the routine "monthly" harvest of the six-legged baby peekoo crabs. Every eighteen Eden days, just prior to the triple conjunction caused by the lineup of Eden between Zulu and Zouave, the mature peekoo shellfish would release their eggs and sperm into the ocean waters. The fertilized eggs would then be washed up into the fresh-water streambeds during the high tidal pulse caused by the triple conjunction. The resulting young peekoo would thrive and grow in the fresh water of the stream, and at the time of the next triple conjunction, the more mature of them would congregate in the brackish lower reaches of the stream, ready to ride the tidal backwash out into the deep ocean, to join their elders in the rock beds. Although two or three of the adult peekoo pried up from the rock beds in the deeper parts of the ocean were enough for a meal, it took dozens of the tiny but delicious soft-shelled babies to make a decent pot of peekoo chowder.

"Mom?" said Eve, who had been working quietly a few meters from her mother, trapping the tiny creatures in a cup made from the hollowed-out joint of a peethoo sapling. "Why don't you rest? Freeman and I will be able to finish filling the bucket."

Eve and Freeman did work well together, Cinnamon admitted to herself. *Just like her father and I,* thought Cinnamon. When she and Nels had worked together on the hydroponics deck of *Prometheus,* they hardly needed to speak; each one's work naturally complemented the other. Cinnamon smiled, waded out of the marsh, and sat down tiredly on a hummocky dune.

It was a beautiful day, but then it was so often beautiful on Eden. Cinnamon watched Eve and Freeman washing the sand and mud from the little crabs before putting them in the "bucket"—a plastic box originally designed to hold frozen food on the now submerged lander. The box's snaptop lid had been lost over time, and now it had a makeshift handle of tough keekoo tentacle roots threaded through holes poked through the corners just under the lip.

Eve had inherited her mother's straight black hair and it fell in a long curtain to her waist. Cinnamon looked wryly out of the corner of her eye at a strand of her own hair. It had once looked like that, but now it was gray and frazzled and hardly reached below her shoulders. Eve was willowy and thin, her slender arms and legs softly curved with muscle. The simple white sarong flattered the golden brown of her skin. Freeman looked at her with adoration in his eyes, adoration that Eve returned with gentle trust.

He will be a good match for her, thought Cinnamon, not for the first time. Freeman had finally stopped growing and was losing his adolescent clumsiness as he got used to the size of his own body. Freeman might not be as tall as the other boys, but like all the Eden children, good health gave him grace and beauty. Cinnamon sighed again and rubbed her legs.

These are old woman's legs, she thought to herself. She looked at her old hands. *Rubbed with old woman's hands. When did I get old?* she wondered. She looked again at the two young people, both so intent on their work and yet so aware of each other. *Do they really appreciate the beauty of each other?* she wondered. *Do they appreciate their own youth and grace?* She thought about it for a while. *Youth is wasted on the young,* she finally decided.

"Mommy!" sang Ruth as she ran up the beach. "Come see!" The little girl grabbed her mother's hand and dragged her down to the main beach where they were clear of the trees. "Look! I can see Daddy!"

Cinnamon shaded her eyes. On the horizon she could just make out the profile of the tiny flotilla. Jinjur, Nels, John, and David had taken the big raft and the dugout canoe, and were fishing just beyond the shelter of Crater Lagoon. They had originally planned on just Nels and Jinjur going out to catch the saltwater filter-fish, but at the last moment John had suggested that he and David join them in the dugout.

John had felt that David needed to get out of the house and spend a day with his friends; he needed to take a break from his self-imposed vigil of sitting beside Arielle in her sickbed. Arielle spent most of her time sleeping these days and would not even know he had left. The disease that was taking her life had first stolen her strength and beauty. Gaunt and haggard, the free-spirited pilot had been trapped on her sleeping pad for more than a month now.

"Can they see us, do you think?" asked Ruth. "Daddy!" she called, waving enthusiastically. "Daddy! Here I am!"

Cinnamon waved, too. *Who knows?* she thought. *Maybe he can see us. . . .* She was reaching to take her communicator out from the pocket in her sarong, to let Ruth talk to her daddy, when the ground moved under her and she was thrown off her feet. Instinctively she rolled across the quivering sand and caught Ruth into her arms. Covering her daughter's body with her own, she remained on all fours as the beach shook and trembled beneath her.

"Mommy?" Ruth whimpered.

"It's okay, sugar, it's just an earthquake. It will be over soon." As suddenly as it started, the shaking ended.

Eve! thought Cinnamon. *I've got to make sure she's all right.* She got to her feet and took Ruth by the hand.

"Mother! Are you all right?" Eve called as she came running toward them, Freeman running along behind her.

How long has she been taking care of me? Cinnamon wondered as she brushed the sand off her legs.

"I'm just fine," she answered calmly. "It was a big quake, but it's all over now. Let's just get back . . ." Cinnamon's voice faltered as she caught sight of the ocean.

The tiny waves were no longer lapping innocently onto the sand. Slowly, ominously, the ocean was retreating. Rocks and plants that had never been exposed before were lying in shallow puddles, the sunlight sparkling on their wet surfaces.

Run! screamed a voice in Cinnamon's mind, while another voice said, *Think!*

I mustn't scare the children. They might freeze if they are frightened, thought Cinnamon, struggling to control her own panic. "Come on," she said, walking rapidly up the shore toward the nearby knoll with the clump of tall boobaa trees. "I want you all to go up the boobaa to the clubhouse."

The girls didn't know what the problem was, but they obeyed Cinnamon without question. When Freeman tried to hang back and help her, she shot him a look of pure fury. Startled, Freeman climbed rapidly up the trunk. Pushing the youngsters ahead of her, Cinnamon forced her tired old bones up the slender rungs of the child-sized ladder. By the time Cinnamon had pulled herself, panting, onto the small platform, the youngsters had found time to look back toward the ocean. Their eyes were now wide with apprehension.

The horizon had changed. The small boats that had been out on the ocean had disappeared. Most of the lagoon had also disappeared. The bar of sand at the entrance to the lagoon was rapidly eroding away, as the water in the lagoon poured out and down the still-emptying shore. In the ocean beyond, a gigantic wall of water was moving inexorably toward the shore, growing larger as it came.

"Quick!" shouted Cinnamon, trying to break the thrall of horror the looming danger had cast on the children. "Take off your sarongs!" Cinnamon had removed the long white cloth that she used to cover her own withered flesh and was pulling off Ruth's. Her communicator fell from her sarong pocket onto the platform and clattered off down to the ground below.

"Why?" asked Eve, even as she moved to emulate her mother.

Cinnamon didn't waste time trying to explain as she started to tie Ruth's sarong to hers. Eve quickly understood and added her sarong to the other end, Freeman lending his strong muscles to tighten the knot, then adding his loincloth to the end. Cinnamon pushed Ruth's bare body up against the trunk of the tree, then placed her meager body so it would protect the small body of her youngest child, as Eve and Freeman positioned themselves around the smooth trunk on either side of her. Cinnamon wrapped the knotted length of clothing around them all, so that it fastened them to the tree, and held it taut against their bodies while Freeman, facing out, tied the loose ends together—Cinnamon watching the knot critically. Freeman then twisted around until his back was to the oncoming wave and his face was looking at Eve's. He reached out and took Eve's hand. They waited. . . .

A deep rumble from the burdened ground vibrated the trunk beneath their bellies as the base of the massive tsunami climbed up onto the shore. At the same time, through the air, came the sound of the aerated water in the rapidly rising crest, hissing like a menacing cobra that was about to strike. It grew dark as the top of the cresting wave blocked the afternoon sun. . . .

In that last moment, before the whole world came crashing down, there was a moment of calm. Cinnamon could see Eve and Freeman looking at each other, their eyes filled with love and trust.

All that matters to them is that they are together, thought Cinnamon—just as all thought was knocked out of her head.

Cinnamon could feel the strain as the tree bent beneath the wave's assault and she was shoved violently against the tree and her daughter beneath her. She was surrounded by a chaos of green and white and water and foam; the breath was knocked out of her lungs and there was nothing to breathe except water. She lost all feeling in her body, all sense of direction, all awareness of the child so close to her. She was trapped in an endless swirling of water as it surged against her, pulling at the bonds, sucking at her limbs, trying to rip her free so that she could be tossed about along with the sand and debris that the wave had picked up and was now beating against her back.

Then all was still. The water surrounding them lifted strands of Cinnamon's long white hair so that they floated before her face like exotic seaweed. Cinnamon felt her lungs scream with the need to breathe, and she opened her mouth to let the seawater rush in and out, a child's trick to beat the craving to draw the water in more deeply.

We weren't high enough, she thought calmly. *I have tied them to a tree just so they could drown. I wanted to protect them, and all I have done is make them attractive corpses.*

Then, the surface broke over her head. With her first breath, Cinnamon ducked her head back under the water and exhaled the air into the startled but eager mouth of Ruth. It took two such breaths until the water fell far enough for the little girl to breathe for herself. Out of the corner of her eye, Cinnamon saw Freeman sharing breaths with Eve. At least their lips were pressed together and Cinnamon figured that whatever they were doing, they were alive.

It took almost fifteen minutes for the water to drain back down from the dense jungle of trees and allow the beach to reappear, so that they could climb down from the tree and cross the scoured dunes from the knoll to the safety of higher ground. They spent the waiting time in silence. Cinnamon tried to keep her thoughts empty of speculation, empty of the fear for the safety of all the others. Without the communicator, there was no way to know what had happened to them.

All along their three-hour walk back to the settlement, they could see where the landscape had been changed by the wave's passage. Trees had snapped, rocks had been shifted, destruction was everywhere. When they finally reached the entrance to their usually sheltered valley, they almost didn't recognize it. New stream channels now made shortcuts across some of the meander bends of the old stream, some of the new channels cutting right through what used to be fields of grain. Huts were shifted from their foundations, and the Meeting Hall was full of mud and rubble. Only Carmen's hut, high on the ridge, was untouched, although several rock slides marred the normally smooth sides of the ravine. When they called up to her, Carmen answered.

"Gracias a Dios!" she called down to them. "Thank God you are safe! All the children are here and all are well. After the quake I had Maria bring them all here, so they could call their parents through the comm-links. Just as they had all come up the mountain . . . the water filled the valley."

"And Arielle?" called Cinnamon.

"She is okay. The water level didn't reach her bower."

"What about Richard and Reiki?"

"They're in the Jolly village. Things there are a real mess, with most of the Jollys washed off their feet and some of the seedlings uprooted, but they are okay, too. They are staying to help the stronglimbs get things back in order. Are the others with you? I thought if their boats were far enough away from the shoreline the wave would hardly have bothered them."

"I haven't seen them," said Cinnamon evenly. She knew that the boats were much too close to the shore to have escaped the tsunami, but bad news could wait.

"Well, the Jollys have their eyes out searching for any sign of them," Carmen finished. "We'll learn soon enough."

"I'm going to see if I can help the Jollys," said Cinnamon, moving off. *And to see if they have any word of Nels,* she thought to herself.

"We're coming, too!" called Adam, Dirk, Everett, and Shannon as they piled down the stairs from Carmen's.

"What about us?" called the younger kids.

"Yeah! We're not babies!"

"Anyone over thirteen can go as long as you stay within

sight of a grownup. And that's within *their* sight, not them within yours," compromised Carmen.

Ernest, Sarah, and Christopher groaned as they went back into the shelter while their siblings ran joyfully down the hill.

The whole island had been affected by the giant wave. The Jollys' buildings had never been designed to withstand such an assault, and the entire village had been razed. Richard attempted to save the youngest seedlings with some quick replanting work with a spade they had made from a piece of scrap metal from the lander. But as the Jollys predicted, the effort was in vain. The seedlings would wilt from root shock before the end of the day.

Cinnamon had just reached the village with her pack of young reinforcements, when one of the Jolly's free-flying eyes brought word of one of the humans. She was able to follow the owl-like eye through the forest and found Nels, battered and unconscious where he had washed up in a nearby valley. He was bleeding heavily from a wound in the leg. If they had not found him when they did, he would probably have died. Of the others on that ill-fated fishing trip, John, Jinjur, and David, there was never any sign.

With John gone, Cinnamon was now their doctor. As Cinnamon tended Nels, she started teaching Eve about medical care by using her as an apprentice—for one day she too might be gone and they would need someone trained as a doctor to take her place.

Over the next several days, they all struggled to come to grips with the loss of their loved ones—and the devastation that had happened so quickly and with so little warning. The grain crops that had been so close to harvesting were gone, and many of the younger fruit trees would not survive to bear fruit. Game was easy to catch, as it too had been made homeless with the loss of so much underbrush, but that meant lean times later. Rubble cluttered the beaches and daily they searched in vain for signs of their lost ones.

As Arielle watched the rest of them try to get on with their lives, she reached a decision of her own. She waited until she was sure that all of them were busy. Then she took a large drink of the bottle of painkiller medicine that John had prepared for her. After leaving a note on her recorder she pulled herself out of bed and left the settlement.

Arielle moved slowly, searching the unfamiliar flood-reworked landscape for signs of the trail she had taken so many times in the past. Finally she came to the deep chasm spanned with tight cables. She looked down. The surface of the lava was now back at its normal red-gray, heated from within by the slow but constant flow of liquid rock down the gigantic tube of hardened lava rock that filled the canyon floor from wall to wall. She had seen the pictures Shannon had made of the gourd bombs the boys had dropped here. She remembered how they had exploded from the extreme heat before they even reached the glowing surface of the molten rock.

Arielle knew in her heart that David was dead, but she didn't grieve for him. *Grief comes from knowing that you have to live without someone,* she thought. *I don't have to live without David, and now I can be happy that he never had to live without me.*

The children would be cared for. The rescue ship was only a few years away, and the children would be safely taken back to Earth. She had done all that she could do in this life. Now, she only wanted to be free, free of the pain, free of this body that disease had turned into a prison. She opened the medicine bottle and drank down the last of the painkiller. It was a big dose. Shortly afterward, she could feel her body growing numb. Before the numbness went too far, she unfastened the small wheeled swing and adjusted it on the end of the taut cable. The grace that had been a part of her all her life did not fail her now as she launched herself over the chasm. As the swing reached the middle of the ravine, Arielle let go, spreading her wings in her final flight.

TABLET

A few weeks later, while hunting game with Adam along the shore on the other side of the river from the Jolly village, Dirk came upon a long, thin, rectangular slab of stone which had been washed far up the beach. It was the beginning of the rainy season, and the heavy rains had washed the sand from the stone slab and had left it glittering in the grass. The stone had strange markings on it. Dirk picked it up and took it to Adam.

"Look what I found," Dirk said, handing it over. They both stood looking at it, rainwater dripping from their noses. "What do you make of it?"

Adam looked at the markings on the stone carefully, having to tilt it slightly in order to see them in the dim red light of Barnard filtering through the drizzling gray overcast sky. One side of the stone slab was rough, like the surface of an ordinary lava mound. The side with the markings was highly polished.

"Looks like a drawing of something. On a pictotablet like the Jollys use. But this tablet is made of stone instead of clay. Hmm . . . All the lines are so straight they must have been made with a ruler. These two house-shaped things at the ends must be end views, while the rectangle with one sloping side must be a side view. With the sloping roofs, it looks like a drawing of some sort of a shelter to me."

"What are the crosses and bars next to the lines?" asked Dirk.

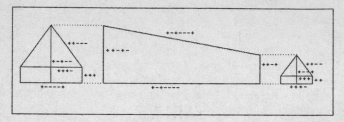

The Stone Tablet

"Must be the measurements of the thing . . . you know . . . a number telling how many meters or centimeters long that part is."

"They don't look like numbers to me," said Dirk.

"Of course, they wouldn't, jookeejook brain," said Adam. "These must be Jolly numbers, and this must a drawing of a Jolly hut. I bet it got washed away from the village by the tsunami. I'll take it to Chief Seetoo and see if it's important. I doubt it, though. Probably an ordinary pictotablet." He added the tablet to his hunting net and then forgot about it as the two continued their hunt.

As the day drew to a close, Adam and Dirk crossed back over the river by swimming across the rain-sprinkled Wide Pond where the river currents were not as strong, towing their sodden catch on a small makeshift wooden raft behind them. It seemed to Adam that the catch got wetter from being in the heavy downpour than the hunters did from being in the pond. Adam sent Dirk up the muddy trails of Meander Valley with their catch, while he headed down to the Jolly village with the stone tablet.

As Adam approached the thook barrier, he gave a whistle and the thorns obediently rolled away to let him through, showering the ground with water droplets as they twisted themselves back from the entrance. As he walked through the Jolly village, he took time to look around carefully at the shapes of all the huts and storage sheds, even though he knew the general arrangement of the village well, having been in it many times. Not one of the structures looked like the drawing on the tablet. The sloped roofs of the Jolly huts were all flat, so that the constant rain dripped off down the back of the hut, while the houselike drawings on the tablet had a peaked roof like the humans' Meeting Hall. Also, the Jolly huts were tall and narrow, to fit the Jollys, while the houselike things in the tablet were short and squat.

He went to the chief's hut. Seetoo was settled just inside the opening, out of the wind, resting on four limbs while two other limbs were working away slowly at the task of attaching one of Weehoob's blackglass spear points onto a long shaft. The chief had two nested eyes watching the work of the strong root fingers carefully braiding the complicated knot.

Adam came to a halt in front of Seetoo and waited patiently in the warm rain—water dripping off his thick black ringlets and down his dusky shoulders—until his presence was finally noticed. One of Seetoo's long root-limbs ponderously lowered the partially finished spear to the ground. At the same time, the chief's mouth opened and a gatherer inside whistled a greeting.

"Welcome! Aadaam of the curly black fronds; seed of Jeenjuur and pollen of Jhaan."

Adam had no problem understanding and talking with the Jollys, for like all human children, his parents had made sure he had been exposed to the Jolly language at that critical portion in a child's life when learning languages came easily, even to the point of boarding each of the children for a few months in the Jolly village as fast-moving, intelligent, "gatherers" for the tribe as a whole. As a result, Adam and all the other children were bilingual. The Jollys in turn, found it much easier to communicate with the younger generation of humans than their elders, since the children and Jollys had rapidly evolved a pidgin mixture of human and Jolly languages that they both were comfortable with. Often, the children were called upon as interpreters when complex concepts needed to be exchanged between a Jolly and an adult.

"Dirk found this pictotablet," said Adam, putting the stone slab down on the muddy ground in front of the hut entrance so it would not move while Seetoo's eye fluttered down to take a close look at it. Seetoo added the image to the worldview in its mind and then examined the image closely as Adam continued talking. "It is a drawing of something. But it is made of scratches on a stone tablet instead of indentations on a clay pictotablet. We thought it might be important, so I brought it here for you to look at."

Seetoo ponderously stretched out a forelimb into the rain outside and ran sensitive root tips over the polished stone tablet, feeling the scratches carefully.

"This is not a stone of this tribe," said the chief. "My worldview does not contain any tribe on this island or any other island that would make this stone."

"I think those crosses and bars might be numbers. I know how to count in Jolly language—" Adam knew that the Jollys used a base six number system and knew how to count all the way up to 216, the Jolly equivalent of 1000 "—but these don't look like Jolly numbers. Your numbers are all circles, with line patterns inside indicating the numbers from zero to five. This tablet has only two symbols, like your symbols for one and four, but they don't have circles around them."

"You are correct. Those are not Jolly numbers. This is not a Jolly tablet."

"I guessed as much. Since there are only two symbols, it must be a binary number system," said Adam, who had gone farther than most of the firstborn in his mathematical studies program on his Teacher.

"Binary number system?" repeated Seetoo, showing interest in learning something new.

"Never mind," said Adam, bending over to pick up the tablet. He knew that the Jollys—unlike the flouwen—were mathematically illiterate. They used mathematics solely for counting; things like the number of days between high tides, and the number of fish they had caught. They didn't own plots of land that needed surveying, and they didn't build massive structures that needed precise construction, so they had yet to learn multiplication in order to calculate areas. They were also ignorant of geometry, including the Pythagorean theorem for calculating the length of the long side of a right-angled triangle from the lengths of the two shorter sides. They even thought that pi was three. It would have taken Adam seasons to explain to Chief Seetoo what the base-two binary numbering system was.

Adam rose and put the tablet into his hunting net, then held himself still again in front of Seetoo until he was sure that his new position had been recorded into Seetoo's worldview.

"I, Adam, seed of Jinjur and pollen of John, bid farewell to his friend, Seetoo, Chief of all the Keejook." He turned and trotted away through the rain. It was getting toward evening, and he didn't want to travel the slippery muddy trails in the weak light that Gargantua would supply under the heavy overcast sky.

With the clouds pouring rain down in a steady torrent, after the communal meal everyone settled in together for the long evening in the refurbished Meeting Hall. The children got out their Teachers, which had been charging all day with their ultraefficient wide-spectrum photoelectric converters facing toward the blazing cooking fire, and most of them played games.

Adam, his heart still heavy over the recent loss of both of his birth-parents, and beginning to feel the weight of responsibility of being an adult, couldn't get in the mood to play games. Instead, he opened up the mathematics studies program on his Teacher and started in on the puzzle of the numbers on the tablet. When Shannon heard the distinctive chime that the math program used to announce itself, she stopped playing chess with her Teacher and came over to see what Adam was doing. In the past, Adam had always treated the tom-boyish Shannon as just another guy, but now, primarily because they spent a great deal of time together, and especially now, as she snuggled up beside him, he and his body were beginning to notice the softness of her curves. Shannon went into her artistic mode as Adam showed her the tablet. Her long fingers brushed appreciatively over the polished surface of the stone.

"It's beautiful," she said, admiring its simplicity.

"Just a drawing," said Adam, as he ran the scanner edge of his Teacher across the tablet. Instantly, a replica of the tablet was on the screen of his Teacher. He looked at the image critically, and using the bit-map expander feature, touched it up by erasing extraneous dots caused by dirt specks and filling in missing portions of the lines. "Looks like a hut, but it's not like any Jolly hut. I was going to try to see if I could figure out what the marks mean. It only uses two symbols, cross and bar. Sure complicates things that they are just like our plus and minus signs, but since there are only two symbols, it's obviously written using a binary number system. It should be simple."

"Splendorious! Let me help!" exclaimed Shannon with excitement, switching from artistic mode to scientist mode. Adam was glad she was helping, for of all the firstborn, she was farthest along in the Teacher's math program. Shannon looked at the tablet itself in the firelight, turning it around and around, first one way, then the other.

"That's the first thing we need to figure out," said Adam. "Which way is 'up' on that diagram? That should help us figure out which way the numbers go."

"We don't need to know which way is up to determine that," said Shannon. "Besides, it could be that whoever wrote the numbers wrote them from right to left, instead of from left to right . . . could even have been written from bottom to top. But, to figure out which way the numbers go, all you need to do is look at the numbers themselves. One end of all the numbers is always a cross, while the other end can be either a cross or a bar. That means the cross is one, while the bar is a zero—you don't put leading zeros in a number."

Adam felt stupid. He should have thought of that.

"Well, that makes it easy," he said. "Let me list the numbers that we have, leading cross first. Lessee, the smallest is a two-digit number consisting of two crosses, then three crosses—no other three-digit numbers . . ."

"But three crosses occur twice," said Shannon. "Once in the 'cross-beam' of the diagram of the small house, and once in the 'wall' of the big house diagram."

Adam paused and put the Teacher in measurement mode. "Let me check that—to see if jookfruit are jookfruit." After a few seconds, he grunted. "Yeppa. The two lines that have the three crosses next to them are the same length."

"Lemme try something," said Shannon, her brain racing faster than Adam's, her fingers twitching as she reached for the screen. Adam stretched his long arms out to keep the Teacher away from her and she backed off.

"Measure the height of the two houses," said Shannon. "It looks like the big one is exactly twice the size of the little one." Adam quickly applied the measurement program to the diagram. Sure enough, the dimensions of the smaller one were exactly half that of the larger one.

"Good," said Adam. "That means that the numbers on the large house are twice those of the numbers on the small house. That gives us five equations to work with. Plus, we have two right-angled triangles that we can apply the Pythagorean theorem to."

"Don't forget, there's another right angle triangle in the slope of that long thing," Shannon reminded him. "We just have to subtract the short end from the long end to get the third side."

By now, Adam had listed the twelve numbers on the diagram in order of increasing length and started converting them. "If it is straight binary, and a cross is a one, then two crosses is one plus two, or three, while three crosses is one plus two plus four, or seven . . ." he paused. "Hmm."

"That kills that idea, doesn't it," remarked Shannon. "In the small house, one side is marked with two crosses, while in the big house, that same side, which is supposed to be exactly twice the size, is marked with three crosses. If two crosses is three, and three crosses is twice as large, then three crosses is six—not seven. It must not be a binary numbering system."

"But only two symbols are used," replied Adam, bewildered. "It *has* to be a binary system."

"The facts are . . . that it isn't," said Shannon, taking the Teacher away from him and nestling into his lap as her long slender fingers played over the touchscreen. Adam, his arms now full of well-filled sarong, didn't mind this time.

The puzzle, however, wasn't easy to solve, even by the nimble brain of Shannon backed up by the calculational abilities of the Teacher, and late that evening the Teacher was turned off and the stone tablet placed on a storage shelf, its mystery still intact.

The next evening, after their usual communal dinner in the Meeting Hall, instead of gathering with the adults for some evening conversation, Richard went to the children's corner with Freeman to look over the mineral samples that the fifteen-year-old had brought home from his latest expedition. Freeman had them lined up on a shelf, and as Richard picked them up and examined them with his permalight, Freeman explained where he had found them and what he thought they were. The youth was usually right, and even Richard had to call up a color image from Freeman's Teacher to categorize one unfamiliar rock sample.

"Some of these are unusual enough that they should go into the sample return box," said Richard, picking out three of the rock samples. Freeman felt quietly proud that some of his findings would someday be taken up for analysis on *Prometheus*, and perhaps even be taken back to Earth.

"What's this rock?" asked Richard, reaching down to the shelf below.

"That's something that Adam and Dirk found on the beach," said Freeman. "Just an ordinary piece of hardened lava. Looks just like any other lava sample that you'd get anywhere else on this island. Only thing that makes it interesting is that one side has been cut and polished and marks made on it."

"Hmm," said Richard, taking out a pocket microscope from his carrying pouch and looking carefully at the polished portion of the stone. "But this lava sample is different."

"It is?" said Freeman as his father handed him the stone and the microscope.

"Look how smooth it is," said Richard. "What is the biggest vesicle that you can see?"

"I can't see any," said Freeman initially, then after looking for a while longer, he added, "now I see them, but they're real tiny." He looked up in partial understanding and partial puzzlement. "This lava sample has the same color and has the same crystal inclusions as the other lava samples I've looked at, so it came from the same volcano, but the vesicle bubbles are really tiny in this sample. How come?"

"It solidified while it was under high pressure," explained Richard. "The gas and steam emitted by the lava couldn't expand into the big bubbles you normally see in lava samples from Hoolkoor. This uncut side is obviously the original surface of the pillow of lava after it hardened, so there wasn't any pressure from the weight of the lava itself, so the lava pillow must have formed in the deep ocean under high water pressure."

Richard, being a geologist, had looked at the material in the stone tablet first. Now, he began to look at the diagram itself. "Where did this drawing come from?" he asked.

"Nobody knows," answered Adam, joining them. "At first I thought it was a Jolly pictotablet. But Chief Seetoo said it wasn't produced by any Jolly tribe known. Besides, the numbering system is wrong. It's obviously binary, while the Jollys use a base six numbering system. On every island we, *Spritz*, and the stronglimbs have visited, the local Jollys may speak and write differently, but they all use the same base six counting system."

"It's not binary, either," said Shannon with surety. "In fact, I don't think it has a base."

"A number system *has* to have a base," said Adam.

"The Roman number system doesn't have a base," retorted Shannon. "Each symbol represents a different number weight; 'I' equals one, 'V' equals five, 'X' equals ten, 'L' equals fifty, and so on. But the weights alternate from base five to base ten. In a base number system, the symbols are usually ordered according to weight, but that's not always true for the Roman number system. For example 'I' usually comes after 'V' but not when you write 'IV' for four. In fact there are two ways to write some numbers. Four can be either 'IV' or four 'I's. The Romans showed that you don't need a base to make a useable number system."

Richard, trying to get back to the subject, interrupted. "But what's really important, is: who made this drawing?"

"Don't know," replied Adam. "But whoever did it made the lines very straight. They are precisely made, as if guided by a straight edge. I hardly had to do anything to the image after it had been scanned into my Teacher."

"Let me see those lines again," said Freeman, taking the tablet from his father and looking at them with his pocket microscope. "The lines *are* very straight, while the symbols have a slight bit of waver, and vary slightly in length, like they were drawn free-hand. . . ." He paused while he scanned all the lines carefully. "This is interesting! The bottoms of the lines are rounded and smooth, while the edges are relatively sharp. If the marks were scratched into the surface with a sharp tool, you would expect scratch lines on the bottom, and rough edges where pieces of stone broke away. These marks look like they were etched by a powerful chemical."

"Well, if no Jolly tribe made this drawing, then who did?" said Richard. "Is there another intelligent species on this moon that we don't know about?" Reiki, hearing the discussion going on between Richard and the children, left the last of the after-dinner pot scrubbing to Everett and Sarah and came over to see what they were talking about.

"Another intelligent species?" repeated Reiki. Freeman handed her the stone tablet and she looked at it carefully as Adam and Shannon explained what they had learned and not learned about the diagram.

"So . . ." concluded Shannon " . . . it's not a binary-base number system, and I have yet to make any logical sense of the symbols as numbers, even though there are lots of right-angle triangles that allow me to check different guesses for the different strings of symbols."

"I'm intrigued by the fact that Richard said this lava had formed in the deep ocean," said Reiki. "Could there be an intelligent creature that lives in the ocean that we have yet to meet?"

"An intelligent creature that has the technology to cut, polish, and etch stone—which the Jollys *can't* do," added Richard.

"And that need sloped roofs on their buildings to shed the rain . . ." added Adam " . . . under water," he continued.

"Which probably indicates that this diagram is not of a building," said Shannon.

"But it *is* a diagram," Reiki reminded them. "And it

does have symbols that seem to be related to parts of the diagram—although whether the symbols are numbers or words or something else has yet to be determined. Whoever made this diagram certainly shows signs of intelligence, and it is important that we find them, meet them, and learn more about them."

"If they really live underwater, then we have the right allies to find them," said Richard.

"I'm sure the flouwen would have already told us if they had discovered another intelligent lifeform on the planet," said Reiki.

"I'm not so sure of that," said Richard. "If it had been Little Red that discovered them, he might have dismissed them as being unworthy of reporting if they didn't know how to surf. But to be sure, I'll show the tablet to the flouwen tomorrow morning at P—" He looked at Reiki and modified his language. "Necessity Beach. At the very least, it will inspire them to look harder and deeper."

The next morning, on the men's bend of the stream below the village, Richard unwrapped his loincloth and joined the boys in the bow-shaped pool. Little Red and Little White were at the men's bend, while Little Purple had taken Warm Chirring Pink and Cool Blue Trill to the women's bend. As Richard waded into the thick red jelly of Little Red's body, carrying the stone tablet in one hand, the water around him spoke.

"Pee!" it demanded, and Richard let loose. After he had finished, he spoke.

"I have something to show you," he said, putting the tablet into the water. The red jelly around his hand firmed up and took the tablet from him. "It's a diagram, with numbers next to some of the lines. It looks like a binary numbering system, because it only uses two symbols, cross and bar. But it *isn't* binary, since if you use a binary base to assign weights to the various places in the numbers, the numbers don't add up right. If it isn't a binary base system, what is it?"

"Too easy!" replied Little Red, almost instantly. "It not 'bi'-nary base, it 'prime'-nary base!" He passed the tablet to Little White with disdain, then slithered downstream toward the ocean, muttering, "Humans dumb!"

"Prime-nary base?" repeated Richard at the disappearing red spot in the stream, not understanding at all. Adam, seeing the tablet supported in the water by Little White, came wading over to hear what Richard was learning about his strange find.

Little White patiently stayed behind to explain. "Numbers on tablet make sense if position weight is prime number—one, two, three, seven, thirteen, twenty-three, and forty-seven."

"I see!" said Adam, understanding instantly. "That means that two crosses are one plus two, or three; while three crosses are one plus two plus three, or six—twice two crosses! Just what it needs to be!"

"That doesn't make sense," said Richard. "Why didn't they use something easier, like the binary sequence of one, two four, eight, sixteen and so on?"

"Maybe they just like prime numbers," Adam suggested.

"Prime numbers very interesting," Little White added.

"But why those particular prime numbers?" asked Richard.

"They are first prime equal or smaller than sum of previous primes plus one," replied Little White.

"Sounds very inefficient and complicated to me," protested Richard. "Even simple things like addition and subtraction are going to be complicated, while multiplication and division is going to be nearly impossible. There is even more than one way to write the same number. Three can either be two crosses or one cross followed by two bars."

"The Romans built an empire, constructed temples, calculated taxes, and figured out gambling odds using *their* crazy system," said Adam, who had listened to a long lecture on the subject by Shannon.

"So what we are looking for is an intelligent underwater creature that likes prime numbers—to the point of stupidity!" concluded Richard. "Little White . . . have you or the others seen any strange creature in the ocean that might have been intelligent enough to have made this drawing?"

"No," replied Little White. "Only creature we see in ocean that is big enough to have large brain is big sharks that live in deep ocean. But they do not talk, so they not smart."

"Have you ever seen the sharks with artifacts, like this stone tablet?" asked Richard.

"Not see sharks much," replied Little White. "They run away and hide in rocks in deep ocean when we come near. We not go after them. They too dangerous. Ate some of Little Red."

"You're both forgetting the Demonfish," Adam reminded them. "They live in the ocean and are big enough to have a large brain."

"Those mindless destroyers?" replied Richard. "Impossible!" He strode to the shore, wrapped himself in his loincloth, and he and Adam picked up their slings and set off on their morning hunt. As they walked into the jungle, Richard's mind was busy with the puzzle of the missing intelligent species that had etched the diagram into the stone tablet. Tonight at dinner, he would have to tell everyone about Little Red figuring out the solution to the puzzle of the tablet.

They should now encourage the flouwen to look harder for unknown creatures in the ocean. Maybe the flouwen would find the Eden equivalent of an octopus or squid—or something with an even more bizarre body shape. Something that had a large intelligent brain, used a crazy number system, and built underwater houses from stone blueprints.

DEMONFISH

Precise Talker hated herself.

Her last looker had finally worked its way back through her thick mat of red hair and settled down in its socket, blinking to wipe the stray hair strands from its eyeball. Through its feeding teat, the looker fed into Precise Talker's surroundview the most recent views it had gathered with its eye and chirper. They showed Precise Talker meditating in the Green House altar room.

Precise Talker looked at herself in her surroundview and hated the way she looked. She hated the way she felt. She hated the way she smelled. She hated everything. Irritably, she sent off a grabber to spit a complaint to Insightful Thinker about the lack of water flow. Then, shortly after the grabber had left, she hated herself for having done so, since there was probably plenty of fresh water circulating in Green House—it was just her thick mat of hair that was making her feel too warm.

It was only fivesix tides ago that she had beseeched her ancestors that she be freed of this burden of the flesh. But, even back then, as she was going through the devotion of Telling 101 to her ancestor, Exceptional Mathematician, the Great Mother of Tides, she had felt the presentient tingling at the tips of her front fins. Those tingles had been the first indication of what were now hideous sharp claws on the ends of grotesque stubby leg-fins. Her other two sets of fins were now unobservable under the

227

ugly mat of curly red hair that now replaced what formerly had been her beautiful pelt of smooth gray fur.

With her six lookers now hidden beneath the stinking ropy strands drooping down her face, she looked like the monster she felt like. A monster of the flesh, whose belly was painfully swollen with eggs, and whose mouth itched to hold a baby. She almost wished that she would be killed this spawning by the blackglass-pointed spears of the Demontrees, or the sharp shining weapons of their new allies, the Swiftmovers. At least death would release her from this horrendous, loathsome transformation she was subjected to every Great Tide.

She finally got herself calmed herself down by Telling 11 with her jar of red coral stones. She reminded herself that death was not the only way to obtain release. She had survived many, many Great Tides and was growing older and wiser with each one. If she would but continue her meditations to her ancestors, and especially if she would continue to find new large prime numbers, then she was sure the pure spiritual effort expended in those praiseworthy tasks would allow her to raise herself up from the mundane muck of the flesh into the blessed nirvana of the spirit. Those who lived in the Great Home of the Elders had done so, and she knew that if she persevered with her meditations, then she too could join the Elders in Great Home—free from the trials of the flesh.

But now she was *of* the flesh—and hating every moment of it. Fortunately it would not be for long, for the Great Tide would soon be on them, and she would ride the Smooth Wave up the river with the others to complete her mission and bring back her new Baby.

The thought of the new Baby quieted her, and by the time she had finished Telling 11, she hated herself a little less. Precise Talker was now prepared in her mind for what she must do at the time of the Great Tide—which would arrive exactly at the middle of the coming night.

* * *

Reiki led a delegation of humans down Meander Valley through the morning sunlight to Wide Pond for a meeting with the Jolly Elders. Tonight, at midnight, there would be a nearly perfect quadruple conjunction and a maximum high tide. Riding in on the bore wave caused by the tide would come the swarming Demonfish. The night before, the humans had come to a joint conclusion on how best to deal with the expected invaders, but they would need the cooperation of the Keejook Tribe. Reiki was sure that the process would involve much discussion, so she was prepared to spend the whole day if necessary. The flouwen, who had already paid their usual early morning visit to the human encampment just after daybreak, followed the humans down the meandering stream, each of them giving one or more children a ride. By the time the humans and flouwen arrived at the meeting dock that the humans had constructed at Wide Pond, the dock was already crowded with the tall, long-fronded bodies of Chief Seetoo, Assistant Chief Tookee, and the Elders of the Keejook Tribe, so the human adults stood in the shallows around the dock, surrounded by the colorful bodies of the flouwen. On the shore, where they could hear what was being discussed, were gathered many of the stronglimb warriors of the tribe and the firstborn of the humans, now almost seventeen. On the periphery of the gathering, the younger members of each group played, the second-born slow-jousting with some of the younger stronglimbs using blunt spears, while the young flouwen, Warm Chirring Pink and Cool Blue Trill, quietly played "tug-stick" with the younger humans that weren't required to stay back at the nursery with Maria.

Little White started the discussion. "We have searched the ocean, but we found no sign of the Demonfish. They must be gathering for the swarming, for the time is near, but with their thick fur they are almost impossible for us to see, unless we are close enough to look."

"We not see them until they are almost here," admitted Little Purple. "Even if we see them, we cannot stop them. All three of us must fight to kill even one of the monsters."

"Taste terrible!" grumbled Little Red. "Fur all fluffy."

"They are no real threat to you anyway," said Cinnamon.

"They are a threat to us," said Chief Seetoo. "They come ashore to steal our lake-fish even though the ocean is full of food. They trample the jungle. They can crawl faster than we can walk, and they bite and crush anyone standing in their way."

"They can't be *too* much of a threat to you, since you know exactly when they are coming," said Reiki.

"And, from what I have seen in past swarmings, you can at least move fast enough to stay out of their way," said Richard. "You do nothing to stop their incoming rampage, but then you attack them when they try to leave."

"That is how all wars are fought," explained Chief Seetoo. "When an aggressor attacks he must move into an unsecured position. A good warrior chief waits and defends against the advancing enemy. It is then that they are most vulnerable."

"All your battles are fought like that?" asked Reiki, the sociologist in her intrigued.

"Yes. First one side attacks. If the defenders prove that they have the bravery and strength, the attackers know that they will not be beaten into submission and so withdraw. Then it is the turn of the other side to show its valor."

"Doesn't it seem odd to you that the Demonfish are only dangerous on their way inland? You must have noticed that they don't bite on their way back to the ocean, even when you are attacking them," said Richard. He had been in his share of battles, both as a combatant and as an observer, but he had never seen as formal and as ritualized a battle as that fought by Jollys and the Demonfish.

The distinctive whistlelike laugh of the Keejook chief

echoed over the water. "You speak as if the Aaeesheesh were thinking creatures! They are only animals! They follow only the laws of nature! When the Flame-Demons in a forest fire advance on the peethoo trees, the plant must suffer the advance. The peethoo suffers the terrible agony of having its supporting saplings burned into ashes. Then, once the Flame-Demons have advanced far enough, the peethoo's green canopy falls upon them, smothering and quenching them. The main trunk is saved by the sacrifice of the saplings. All of Nature moves in waves this way."

The humans were silent. Maybe the Jollys were right. Maybe it was the nature of Eden wildlife to fight in this slow dance, with each side attacking in turn. The creatures of Earth might deal with their competitors in a more forthright manner, but then Earth didn't have trees that walked. Reiki shook her head.

"That just doesn't make sense to me," she said. "I just don't believe that an animal which will fight when it's not being attacked will then retreat without defending itself. There must be something more."

"But we have all seen it happen," Richard reminded her.

"We *have* seen the Demonfish behave this way," Reiki agreed. "But, the question remains whether or not they are mere animals, or whether they are acting in a more subtle manner. That is one of the reasons why we must observe their behavior more closely."

"Why is this?" said Tookee. "The Aaeesheesh are fearsome but honorable enemies that have battled us bravely since time began, but they are only beasts. That is why, each time, they lose."

"But do they lose? Or do they accomplish what they came for?" asked Cinnamon. "We know from the evidence of the tablet that there is another intelligence on the planet, one that lives under the water. The Demonfish are the largest predators we have encountered, even larger than you are. Since they are at the top of the underwater food chain, it makes sense that they might be the intelligent beings we are looking for."

All the Jollys were laughing now. "Aaeesheesh intelligent? You might as well say that flouwen are polite! You have seen for yourself the uncontrolled rage with which the Demonfish attack humans, Jollys, even trees and rocks, on their way up to Sulfur Lake," said Seetoo.

"They are mindless animals!" insisted Tookee. "They obey the laws of nature! If they were intelligent, they would learn from their failures of the past and would not repeat the same line of attack season after season."

"Yes," insisted Seetoo. "How can you claim that the proof of their intelligence is that they behave stupidly?"

"Intelligent beings do stupid things all the time," insisted Reiki. "At least, they do things that appear stupid until the reasons behind their actions become clear. All I am saying is that the reasons for the strange behavior of the Demonfish have not been properly studied. We humans have discussed the actions of the Demonfish during the swarming and realize that we don't know enough about what is happening during that time. We would like to request that this time, the Keejook Tribe take no action when the Demonfish come ashore, so we humans can study their behavior."

"You ask us to hold back from the fight?" said Chief Seetoo, shocked.

"But the glory! The joy of the battle! We can't give that up," Tookee insisted.

"But what if it isn't a battle at all? What if the Demonfish have a reason for coming up to Sulfur Lake and then are only trying to return to the sea as quickly as possible?" said Cinnamon, slowly building her argument so the Jollys would follow her reasoning. "What if the glorious battle you speak of is simply an ambush you are springing against terrified animals that do not want to fight? A gauntlet of terror that you are forcing the poor creatures to pass through as they seek only to escape back to the ocean?"

There was a long moment of silence as the Jollys considered this perspective.

"It would be a battle without honor," Tookee finally conceded.

"There would be no glory," admitted Seetoo, "but there would still be plenty of meat."

Reiki sighed. "Whatever you decide, the humans have decided not to participate in the slaughter this year. We have lost too many of our elders, and we have convinced everyone, even the firstborn, to only observe this time." Reiki smiled wryly. It had taken a good deal of arguing to get the hot-blooded firstborn to agree to stay out of the fight. She had finally had to agree to lower the voting age on Eden to sixteen. The few remaining adults had agreed that it would be worth enfranchising the children to keep them safely away from this—possibly the last attack of the Demonfish they would have to face—before they returned to Earth.

"You have managed to convince Adam that it is better not to fight?" Seetoo was impressed. The chief had rooted for long periods with the strong-minded human teenager. If the arguments of Reiki and Cinnamon had managed to persuade Adam that the Demonfish should be watched rather than hunted, then perhaps he should allow himself to be dissuaded.

"You wish us to let the Aaeesheesh return to the sea without fighting them?" he asked.

"Yes," said Reiki.

"We want to observe closely everything the Demonfish do while they are on land," said Cinnamon.

"They must accomplish something," Reiki explained, "or they wouldn't keep coming back."

"We bend to the force of your wind," said Seetoo, tilting his fronds away from them. "As a sign of the friendship between the Keejook Tribe and the human tribe, when the Daylight God is beneath the sea, and the shadows of the lesser gods merge on the Eye of the Nightlight God, the Aaeesheesh will be allowed to pass unharmed."

There was only an occasional cloud passing overhead that night as the humans and the Jollys gathered to watch the streambeds from positions at higher elevations. A contingent of stronglimbs, blackglass-pointed spears at the ready, guarded the banks of the river along the seedling beds in case a Demonfish tried to crawl up the steep bank. As the shadow of Zulu approached the nearly merged shadows of Eden and Zouave in the center of the fully illuminated face of Gargantua, both humans and Jollys could hear the whispering rush of the tidal bore making its way up the river valley, getting taller as the streambed narrowed. Some of the humans flicked on their permalights to add their white illumination to the red moonlight beaming down from Gargantua, while others took pictures with their recorders of the sight—dozens of gigantic red-mopped fish riding the bore upstream. The wave expended itself on the cluster of rocks at the base of the natural dam that formed Wide Pond, then retreated, leaving the Demonfish to proceed on their own. The humans and Jollys watched silently from the banks as the massive brutes pulled their sodden bodies through the shallow waters. The long claws in their strong front feet dug into the sand and pulled on the rocks as they marched forward, dragging their long tails uselessly behind them. The matted ropy strands of dripping hair covered their entire bodies, and hid everything but the shuffling feet, although there were glints from underneath the sodden fur at the front of the head—reflections from eyes peering out from underneath the waterlogged shaggy covering. The strobing illumination of the permalights mixed with the eerie shuffling noise of the monsters, combined with the rotting stench of their fur, gave all of them the terrifying feeling that they were living in a nightmare.

How easy it would be to give in to the fear and disgust; to attack these loathsome beasts and force them back into the concealment of the waves, Cinnamon thought. She did her best to stay in her ichthyologist mode, forcing herself to look in a detached manner at the Demonfish, not as murdering monsters, but as simple animals— strange, crawling, hair-covered fish that she had been called upon to observe and classify. Standing by her side, Reiki was looking for more. She was looking for a sign— any sign at all—of intelligent behavior.

"They are moving quickly," noted Reiki. "And although they are destructive, they all seem to move along the same course together. They are not fighting with each other."

"You're right," agreed Cinnamon. "Although they do attack any vegetation that is in their way. They are moving pretty much straight upstream toward the upper lake, but they do make shortcuts through the jungle when they come to a meander in the river." Together the two old women followed the massive, stinking creatures, helping each other over the rocky moon-shadowed hillside trails that paralleled the valley floor, now full of danger. The humans had learned their lessons after the first swarming, and now their dwellings were built safely out of the path of the marauding Demonfish.

When the Demonfish finally reached Sulfur Lake and entered the water, their heavy tail muscles took over. Reiki and Cinnamon joined the others who had been waiting around the shoreline of the lake. Cinnamon looked clinically at the swarming Demonfish. With their thick matted coats of streaming red hair, the Demonfish could hardly be called graceful, but in their natural element they showed a strength and agility that was almost beautiful.

The torches that the humans had cached at positions around the lake were now taken out and lit. Flowers of light bloomed all around the lake shore, illuminating the scene taking place in the roiling waters. Even some of the Keejook stronglimbs held burning brands in the root-fingers of a well-extended limb, their fronds pulled well back from the flames. They knew that the distinction they would gain by being so close to fire would take the place of the battle honors they could have earned this night.

"With so many large fish in the lake, they are stirring up the mud," said Reiki, disappointed. "I can't see much of anything."

"They are thrashing their tails around in the pebble beds of the streams that lead into the lake," said Cinnamon slowly, "and it looks like some of the larger lake-fish are doing the same thing in the same places. It's almost—" she paused as what she was seeing began to make some sense "—it's almost as if they were both engaging in spawning behavior. . . ." She let the implications sink in.

"Spawning?" asked Reiki. "But we have seen no Demon-fish young in the lake."

"No," said Cinnamon, "but there are lake-fish in the lake." Her thoughts were jumbled as various possibilities filled her mind.

"Lake-fish aren't anything like Demonfish," Reiki objected. "Besides the great difference in size, the lake-fish have six small fins along the side, while Demonfish have only two large legs at the front—legs with long sharp claws!"

"Besides that, the Demonfish have thick ugly red hair," added Richard, "while the lake-fish have a soft gray pelt. I agree with Reiki, they don't look anything alike."

"Well," replied Cinnamon. "Salmon fry look nothing like their parents either. The spawning male salmon develop huge jaws and sharp teeth . . ." Her voice trailed off, for she wasn't sure either.

"I've been watching them carefully," interjected Nels. "The lake-fish always seem to visit a spot that a Demonfish has just left—just like a male fertilizing the eggs of a female. Maybe the lake-fish is the male and the Demonfish the female of the same species, even if they don't look anything alike."

"We've seen weirder pairs of mismatched mates," remarked Reiki. "Remember the icerugs and the coelasharks on Zulu?"

"There's one little problem," said Richard. "I can see how the baby male lake-fish get to Sulfur Lake—they are born here. But how do the baby female Demonfish get to the ocean? I've seen lots of fish in the river, but none that look like either a lake-fish or a Demonfish."

"Maybe they go downstream as small fry," suggested Nels.

"Wouldn't stand a chance," said Richard. "Either the fish in the river or the fish in the ocean would eat them up."

"How many would have to get to the ocean and survive, Cinnamon?" asked Reiki as she stared down at the swirling waters of the lake.

"Not many," Cinnamon conceded. "Only as many as come back upstream to spawn, I would guess."

"Look!" said Reiki, pointing. "Look at what they're doing now! That Demonfish is taking one of the larger lake-fish in its mouth!"

"It's not unusual for mating animals to devour each other after the eggs are fertilized," said Cinnamon.

"But they're not eating them—they're taking them into their mouths—being very careful not to bite them in the process."

"When we kill Demonfish," said the stronglimb Peebeek, "we find lake-fish inside mouth. Lake-fish is alive. Needs to be killed too."

"The Demonfish must be trying to take the lake-fish back to the ocean!" exclaimed Reiki.

"That would explain why they are willing to fight and bite on their way up to the lake, and yet never even open their mouths while the Jollys are attacking them on their way back!" said Cinnamon. "But that still sounds more like an animal following its breeding instincts than a thinking creature. I have *yet* to see any signs of intelligent behavior."

Reiki's spirits fell as she looked in vain for any evidence of Demonfish intelligence. As they watched, the ugly stinking creatures hauled themselves out of the lake and began the long slow march back to the ocean. With no danger of attack from the closed-mouthed Demonfish, the observers looked on with the professional detachment of scientists. It was clear that the attitude of the Demonfish had changed after their short swim in the freshwater lake. They had lost their frenzied purposefulness and were now moving off in a straight line, marching along the shortest route to the safety of the sea, each Demonfish keeping its mouth tightly closed. The deadly rage that had given the huge fish the veneer of cunning was gone, and they now moved like slow-witted farm animals seeking the shelter of the barn.

Precise Talker was feeling calmer now, although extremely tired, for the climb up the riverbed to the lake had been exhausting. Her belly, relieved of its burden of eggs, no longer had that bloated, stretched feeling. All over her body, her hair was itching. As she crawled over the sharper rocks in the streambed, she felt chunks of matted hair coming loose and staying behind. But her mind hardly noticed these external bodily feelings, for glowing deep within her came an intense pleasure from having Baby in her mouth.

As she started down the streambed, she alerted her lookers to keep a close watch in all directions, for she must protect Baby at all costs! This was now the dangerous time, when the Demontrees attacked with their impaling spears, and the Swiftmovers struck fiercely with their sharp, brain-piercing weapons. Her lookers reported many Demontrees nearby, but they were staying at a distance instead of laying traps with pointed spears ahead of her. The lookers also reported the close approach of some agile Swiftmovers—

but they too didn't attack. Precise Talker was bewildered
by this behavior. Because she had been on many swarmings
before, and was familiar with the hormonal feelings that
were driving her body back to the ocean to assure the
safety of Baby, she was able to temporarily shunt aside
those bodily feelings and look objectively with her mind
at the surroundview her lookers were building up.

The Swiftmovers were very strange creatures indeed.
They only had four limbs and walked about rapidly on
two limbs while carrying tools and weapons in their other
two limbs, since they had no grabbers for that task. One
tool gave off light, somewhat like a glowworm cage, but
much brighter. Since the Swiftmovers could control light,
they must be extremely intelligent, unlike the Demontrees,
who were mere savages. Each Swiftmover had two lookers,
but the lookers stayed in their heads instead of flying
around like the lookers on the Demontrees. This meant
that to look at things up close, the Swiftmovers had to
bring their bodies near to what they were looking at. The
Swiftmovers seemed very interested in Precise Talker and
the others, and followed them closely as they went downstream.

Most importantly, however, the Swiftmovers were not
attacking them this time. The Swiftmovers also must have
used their superior intelligence to keep the Demontree
savages from attacking. Previously, the Demontrees had
always engaged in a bloody killing frenzy at the end of
the swarming. Precise Talker was most grateful to the
Swiftmovers. For once, the dreadful carnage that ensued
during each swarming would not be inflicted on the Swimming. For once, the joy of new Babies being brought home
would not be dimmed by the sorrow of the ones who had
been lost—slaughtered—along with their helpless Babies,
by the terrible six-legged Demontrees.

Precise Talker wanted to thank the Swiftmovers—to
tell them how much she appreciated their kindness—but
she couldn't think of a way to do it. The Swiftmovers lived

on the land while she lived in the ocean. There was no way that she could communicate with them. Even if she could understand the language of the smells they used for communication, she couldn't smell what they were saying because the smellers on her grabbers were inside her mouth, and she couldn't open her mouth without fear of losing Baby.

It was some time later, while crawling over a band of pebbles on the upper slopes of the ocean beach, that it finally occurred to Precise Talker how she might be able to communicate with the Swiftmovers. She wouldn't be able to say much to them this time, for her primary concern was to get Baby safely home. She hoped, however, to let the Swiftmovers know that she recognized them as beings with intelligence and perhaps even a soul, not single-minded animalistic butchers like the Demontrees. Perhaps, later, she would attempt to communicate with them again. She was bemused by the thought. It would be intellectually stimulating—trying to compile a new smell dictionary of how the Swiftmovers talked. It would be almost as mentally and spiritually challenging as finding a new prime number.

As Precise Talker slid into the welcoming waves at the shoreline, her lookers reported that two of the Swiftmovers had followed her down the beach and were watching her closely. So, instead of slipping off into the safety of the ocean depths, she turned around in the shallow water. Opening her mouth just slightly, so as to keep Baby safe inside, she sent out a grabber with instructions. The task she had given the grabber was complicated, but the grabber had carried out that task countless times before. As the next wave moved up the beach and over the band of pebbles, the grabber followed the wave in, picked up a number of pebbles in its suction tentacles, and returned on the backwash with the load of pebbles. Then, on a clear band of sand in the shallow water, it proceeded to Tell 29.

* * *

The humans followed the contingent of returning Demonfish as they swam down the river and crossed the broad delta of sand and pebbles to get to the ocean, where most of the Demonfish quickly vanished into deep water. The flouwen, who had been waiting offshore, followed the Demonfish down into the ocean depths in an attempt to see where they were going.

Reiki and Cinnamon, who were tracking the path of the largest Demonfish, were surprised to see that this Demonfish didn't leave immediately like the others did. Instead, it floated for a while in the shallows of the ebbing tide, as if looking at them out from under the matted hair that covered its head. As Cinnamon and Reiki kept an expectant eye on the Demonfish, wondering what it would do next, Cinnamon noticed a small fish dart about briefly in the waves. The small fish disappeared in the direction of the Demonfish and the Demonfish finally left.

"Well, that's that," said Cinnamon. "We've observed the Demonfish, and we've managed to learn something about them and their breeding habits, but we still haven't found the mysterious authors of that stone tablet. The Demonfish are certainly not the authors—they didn't show a single sign of intelligence." She paused and sighed. "I guess it shouldn't really surprise me. On Earth, the great white sharks are at the top of their food chain, but they are nothing but eating machines—no intelligence at all. It must be one of the prey animals of the Demonfish that are the intelligent ones that wrote the tablet. I wonder if we will ever find out who they are?"

Reiki sighed. "I suppose that there is no reason to stop the Keejook from hunting the Demonfish at the next spawning. I only hope that I haven't spoiled all the nobility the Keejook Elders managed to generate about what was really only a formalized gathering of a local crop."

"Yeah," agreed Cinnamon. "The Jollys have managed

to build up practically an entire religion over the ritual-ized slaughter of a bunch of love-crazed fish." Suddenly, she spotted something in the water. She walked quickly down over the wet sand to where the final Demonfish had lingered. The extreme high tide was still retreating. As it pulled back, it revealed six small piles of pebbles, lying side-by-side on a clear band of sand. Cinnamon fell on her knees and pushed the smooth stones with one finger. Then she laughed out loud.

"Loved-crazed fish, did I say?!" she sang. "Since when have mere fish done something like this? Look, Reiki!" She counted the stones in each pile, and as the pattern built, Reiki started counting along. "One. Two. Three. Five. Seven. Eleven. . . . The first six prime numbers!"

Reiki thought for a moment, calculating in her head, then added her conclusion. " And their sum is twenty-nine! Another prime number!"

INTERPRETERS

The next day, the flouwen, Jollys, and humans met again at the dock on Wide Pond to discuss what they had learned about the Demonfish during the previous night. There was a light rain, so Cinnamon, Reiki, Shannon, and Eve came in under the sheltering fronds of Chief Seetoo and Assistant Chief Tookee and sat on the "knee" bends of the giant trees, leaving Nels, Richard, Adam, Dirk, and Freeman standing outside in the drizzle. Some of the second-born were also there, riding on the Littles, who had their eyes up on colored pseudopods. On the opposite shore of the pond, Cool Blue Trill and Warm Chirring Pink, their bodies busily converting their morning dose of pee into pure ammonia, were playing a noisy game of "keep-away" with some of the other human youngsters.

Little White was explaining to the assemblage what he and Little Red had observed as they had tracked the Demonfish back into the depths of the ocean.

" . . . and as they swam through the sea, huge chunks of hair came off in the water."

"Hard to see them!" said Little Red. "Fluffy stuff eat up echoes!"

"But Demonfish continued down, deep into ocean, shedding hair as they swam. Soon they were nearly hairless. We could now see, in addition to the two large crawling legs up front, two smaller swimming fins along each side. When the Demonfish reach bottom, they were met by many deep-ocean sharks, similar to one that nearly ate Little Red . . . ."

"I nearly eat IT!" protested Little Red.

"I expect fight to start between deep-ocean sharks and Demonfish. Instead, each sent out gatherfish and eyefish that touched and looked at each other without fighting. The Demonfish then opened their mouths and the lake-fish swam out. All then merged into a big group swimming along together, the small lake-fish at the center, the larger deep-ocean sharks around them, and the very large Demonfish following along behind. Except for larger size and longer front legs, Demonfish look very much like deep-ocean sharks."

"Insides see same, too!" added Little Red. "Same bones. Same nothing-holes."

"See insides?" queried Tookee, fronds shaking in puzzlement. The motion sent a small shower of drops down on Eve and Reiki.

"The flouwen use sound to see with," Reiki explained to the Jolly. "They can see the bones and air holes inside a creature in the sea. If both species have similar internal as well as external arrangements, then they must be closely related, if not the same species."

"Hmm," said Cinnamon. "If you saw the Demonfish losing their hair after the swarming was over, then the hair is probably a temporary attribute that aids them during the spawning period."

"Thick hair would help keep their skin and eyes moist during their trek over dry land," suggested Nels.

"I wonder if the large front legs and the long claws are also temporary," added Cinnamon, "and that after the spawning period, the Demonfish revert to being deep-ocean sharks."

"This is beginning to sound like a Dr. Jekyll and Mr. Hyde movie," remarked Richard. "During the day we have the mild-mannered deep-ocean sharks that stay in caves at the bottom of the ocean and avoid contact. But when it is midnight, and the moon is full, they grow long hair, sprout claws, and swarm to the attack. Maybe they're not ordinary sharks, but were-sharks!"

A gatherer appeared in Tookee's opening mouth.

"That is a human term for an imaginary monster," Reiki whispered to the gatherer before it could ask its question.

"Little Red can make loudest noise," continued Little White. "So he makes noise good for looking inside something, while I make noise good for tracking movement. We both see both echoes. Learn many things. The deep-ocean sharks and Demonfish not only have same insides, they each have six gatherfish and six eyefish nested in same places in mouth and on head. Demonfish and sharks built much like Jolly."

"The Aaeesheesh are like us?" exclaimed Tookee in surprise. A nested eye fluttered from beneath Tookee's fronds and circled down to look at the clear eye-lens held up above Little White's body on a white pseudopod. The eye-lens tracked the flying eye as it circled, with the white pseudopod twisting around on its base four times before the eye returned to its nest.

"They have six free-swimming eyefish that live in sockets in their heads, just like the six free-flying eyebirds that nest in your fronds," said Little White. "And they have six free-swimming fish with grabbing tentacles that live in their mouths, like the six gatherers that live in your mouths."

"Gatherfish of deep-ocean sharks not talk, though," Little Red reminded them.

"What part do the lake-fish play in this?" asked Freeman, intrigued.

"The lake-fish are much smaller than the other two, so they probably are the young," suggested Cinnamon.

"That smells of the truth," said Chief Seetoo. "The lake-fish have six eyes, like the Demonfish, but their eyes stay in their head sockets, just like the eyes of our seedlings stay in their nests when the seedlings are young. I have eaten many lake-fish. I know that the largest of them also have six strange knobs in the roof of their mouths, behind their teeth. These are like the buds in the roof of the mouths of our seedlings—that later turn into gathering roots and then gatherers. The lake-fish also have six fins along their sides. I would agree the lake-fish are probably the seedlings of the Aaeesheesh."

"That must be why they take the largest of the lake-fish back with them when they return to their homes in the ocean," said Nels.

"I remember something else!" said Little Red suddenly. "Insides of lake-fish same as insides of sharks, which same as insides of Demonfish!"

"That makes it pretty certain then," said Nels. "The deep-ocean sharks, the Demonfish, and the lake-fish are all different versions of the same species."

"The 'wereshark' species!" said Richard. Reiki protested, but the name stuck.

"This is beginning to make some sense," said Cinnamon, obviously thinking hard. "Like many fish on Earth, the weresharks have to leave the salty and dangerous ocean and go up into the freshwater streams and lakes to lay their eggs, where the hatchlings have a better chance of surviving. To make it easier to travel up the streambeds during the spawning period, the weresharks grow long hair to keep their bodies wet, and their front fins grow into strong, clawed legs to pull them upstream. They turn from ordinary deep-ocean sharks into Demonfish. They lay their eggs in the upland lakes, where they grow into lake-fish—the wereshark young. The Demonfish then brings one of the larger lake-fish back into the ocean, where it then grows up to be a wereshark."

"Then . . ." said Richard, using a scary voice " . . . the next time the moon is full . . . and the midnight hour strikes . . . the mild-looking wereshark turns into a Demonfish and ravishes the countryside once again!"

"Gag, Dad!" said Freeman in disgust at his father's clowning around. "Grow up."

"Freeman . . ." warned Reiki, and Freeman muttered an apology.

"That still doesn't explain the spawning behavior that we observed in Sulfur Lake. There, the lake-fish acted more like breeding males than young," Nels reminded them.

"Yes. That is a puzzle," Cinnamon admitted.

"Another puzzle remains," said Little White. "Cinnamon tell us that Demonfish know prime numbers."

"And because of that, they must be the ones that made the tablet with the drawing on it and the numbers written in a prime number base," continued Cinnamon.

"Prime number?" whistled a gatherer from inside Tookee's mouth.

"Root with you later," promised Adam in an aside to Tookee, and Tookee pulled back the gatherer and shut his mouth. Adam was one of the few humans with the patience and language skills needed to explain complex human concepts to the Jollys. He could "root" motionless in front of a Jolly for a whole half-day at a time until he made sure that a concept was clear in the Jolly's worldview.

"If Demonfish know prime numbers, then Demonfish are smart," said Little White, starting a logical syllogism. "If sharks are Demonfish, then sharks smart. If sharks are smart, why sharks not talk?"

"Sharks DUMB!" Little Red agreed.

"Literally," muttered Nels.

"Just because weresharks don't talk doesn't mean that they aren't intelligent," said Cinnamon. "It may be that they just don't have the sound-generating mechanisms that are needed. Look at the larger ocean animals on Earth. Whales and dolphins talk, since they are mammals and breathe air, while sharks, which are similar in size, but breathe water instead of air, don't talk. Sharks don't even use sonar to track their prey, but rely on their sense of smell."

"But Earth sharks aren't intelligent," objected Nels. "While the weresharks evidently are."

"The weresharks must have developed further than Earth sharks," suggested Cinnamon. "If they have intelligence, then they probably communicate with each other in some manner. Perhaps they are using some other method than sound for communication, like body positions, electrical signals, patterns of gatherfish, or something else we haven't thought of yet, like smell or taste. Of course, to an animal that inhales through its mouth, smell and taste are practically the same."

"Could the weresharks be communicating with taste?" Nels asked the flouwen.

"When we first meet wereshark, its gatherfish squirted cloud of terrible-tasting stuff at us," remarked Little Purple.

"Try to POISON me!" exclaimed Little Red.

"Perhaps not," said Little White. "Let me think . . . and recall the exact tastes. . . ." The large white blob pulled down its eye-lens into its fluid body and started to shrink visibly.

"What is White Swimmer doing?" asked Chief Seetoo, two eyes fluttering out to better observe the process.

"Rocking up to think better," explained Freeman. They all watched as Little White became a dense milky-white boulder on the bottom of Wide Pond, looking like an alabaster pedestal left on the shores of the Aegean Sea, worn smooth after years of pounding by the surf.

"If it turns out the weresharks communicate by smell, the flouwen are well suited for that," remarked Nels, as he watched Little White shrink in thought. "They are floating chemical analysis labs."

The humans took the opportunity to eat the lunch they had brought with them. They gathered some distance away and kept their backs turned so the Jollys would not be distressed by seeing them eat without mouth-aprons. It wasn't long before Little White dissolved back into his normal jellylike blobby shape. By the time he had reformed his eye-lens, the humans had gathered back at the dock.

"When we first met a wereshark, its gatherfish emitted three clouds of taste," reported Little White. "Many different tastes in each cloud. The first cloud was very complex, the second was simpler, and the third simpler still. The tastes in the third cloud were also tastes in the second cloud. It is as if the third cloud was a repeat of the second cloud, but simpler."

"As if the wereshark was repeating something that wasn't understood the first time," remarked Nels.

"Littles?" said Reiki to the flouwen. "Would you be willing to pay a visit to the caves of the deep-ocean sharks and attempt to talk with them? It would be most important to know if they are as intelligent as the tablet seems to indicate they are."

"We can certainly taste what they emit, and can probably make enough different tastes so we can talk back," said Little White, thinking. "But we are enemies. Little Red has eaten some of their eyefish and gatherfish, and a wereshark has eaten a piece of Little Red in return. It may be dangerous."

"I not afraid!" boasted Little Red.

"At least try . . ." pleaded Reiki. "Please?"

☆Rather be surfing!☆ complained Roaring☆Hot☆Vermillion to Clear◊White◊Whistle as they headed down the river toward the ocean.

◊We came to this world to explore and learn, not to play all the time,◊ Clear◊White◊Whistle reminded him. ◊Besides, the human Reiki said, 'Please,' so it must be important to her.◊

☆How are we going to start talking with them, when we know nothing about how they speak?☆ asked Roaring☆Hot☆Vermillion.

◊We do know something,◊ Clear◊White◊Whistle reminded him. ◊The wereshark we met sent gatherfish out to emit three clouds of taste. We can start by repeating one of those—the simplest one first.◊

☆Stop for a while so I can rock up and recall the taste,☆ said Roaring☆Hot☆Vermillion.

◊There is no need,◊ said Clear◊White◊Whistle, extending a white pseudopod to the red snakelike blob swimming alongside of him. ◊Taste the taste.◊ Memory juices were exchanged, and instantly Roaring☆Hot☆Vermillion recalled the complex flavors that the gatherfish had emitted. They still tasted something like poison to him. Perhaps there was another way that they could start out the conversation—something even simpler—that both species could instantly agree on the meaning of.

☆Of course!☆ he said when they came to the beach where the river met the ocean. Instead of heading out to sea, Little Red dove down to the gravel bar beneath them.

◊Where are you going?◊ asked Clear◊White◊Whistle, coming to a halt.

☆Be right back!☆ Roaring☆Hot☆Vermillion shouted back through the water. Clear◊White◊Whistle waited patiently until his impetuous comrade returned. A quick sonar scan of Roaring☆Hot☆Vermillion's body revealed the reason for the short disappearance. He was now carrying a load of pebbles, 101 of them to be exact. Clear◊White◊Whistle was chagrined that he had not thought of that method of communicating. The Demonfish on the beach had communicated with the humans using twenty-nine pebbles. The pebbles that Roaring☆Hot☆Vermillion was carrying would certainly get them off to a good start in learning how to use taste to communicate with the weresharks. If they and the weresharks could establish a common taste language that could handle numbers and mathematical logic, then they could build on that to develop a common language that could handle more complex logical concepts. As the two flouwen approached the cave entrances where they had last seen the weresharks, Clear◊White◊Whistle felt much more confident than he had at the beginning of their journey. Now that they had the pebbles to get them started, it shouldn't be too long before he and Roaring☆Hot☆Vermillion were speaking like weresharks.

It *wasn't* that easy. When the flouwen first approached the region where they had last seen the weresharks, the echoes from their sonar initially showed a number of creatures moving about among the rocks and caves. By the time they arrived, however, all the creatures were gone. Not only that, but some of the larger entrances to the rock caves now seemed to be blocked by piles of large stones. Roaring☆Hot☆Vermillion and Clear◊White◊Whistle came to a halt some distance away.

☆They are afraid of us!☆ bragged Roaring☆Hot☆Vermillion.

◊They have good reason to be,◊ replied Clear◊White◊Whistle. ◊The last time we were here, you left one of them blind and crippled.◊

☆Tried to eat me . . . ☆

◊Not until you had eaten some of its eyes.◊

Roaring☆Hot☆Vermillion, not wanting to admit that he had done something wrong, headed for a patch of sand outside one of the cave entrances. Soon there were ten piles before the cave, containing one, two, three, five, seven, eleven, thirteen, seventeen, nineteen, and twenty-three pebbles, 101 in all.

◊Now let us move back, so they will not be afraid to come out and see what we have done.◊

☆One last thing!☆ Roaring☆Hot☆Vermillion sent his red pseudo-gatherfish back to the piles of pebbles, where it made marks in the mud next to each pile.

◊Excellent idea!◊ said Clear◊White◊Whistle, understanding instantly. ◊By writing their symbols for the number next to the pile, that will speed up the learning process.◊

☆I wrote our number symbols, too.☆

Clear◊White◊Whistle wished he had thought of that.

The two flouwen waited off at a distance for a long time, occasionally seeing at the cave entrance with a weak chirp. Finally they received a doppler-shifted signal back, indicating something was moving.

☆An eyefish is looking out!☆

◊Quiet! We must not scare it.◊

The two halted their chirps, trying to see only with the noise from the ocean waves high above. For a while they could detect small objects moving around near their pebbles. After a while things were quiet again. Starting their sonar chirps again to announce their approach, they returned.

☆Stinks!☆ complained Roaring☆Hot☆Vermillion.

◊Many strange tastes,◊ agreed Clear◊White◊Whistle. Soon the two realized that the strong tastes were concentrated near each pile, as if the pebbles had been sprayed with scent. The smell for each pile was different, with the larger piles having more complex flavors.

☆Tastes for piles 1 and 2 same as poison that shark squirted at me!☆

◊That means the shark was not trying to poison you,◊ replied Clear◊White◊Whistle. ◊It was simply trying to teach you how to count in its language.◊

☆I teach it to count in *my* language!☆ said Roaring☆Hot☆Vermillion, taking apart the piles containing prime numbers of pebbles and rearranging the number of pebbles in each pile so that they were in ascending order, from 1 to 13. There were ten pebbles left over that he put to one side. Beside each pile, he wrote in the mud the flouwen symbol in their octal base numbering system, while on the piles themselves he squirted chemicals in the wereshark's "prime-nary" base system. The flouwen left. It didn't take long this time for the hidden wereshark's gatherfish to come out and smell what they had left.

When they returned, the gatherfish was waiting for them outside the cave entrance. It had the ten spare pebbles in the suction grip of its grabbing tentacles. The gatherfish moved cautiously forward—both flouwen not twitching a cell—and squirted a tiny cloud at them, at the same time dropping one pebble.

☆One!☆ said Roaring☆Hot☆Vermillion, sensing the taste and responding with the flouwen verbal equivalent.

Clear◊White◊Whistle knew, however, that in the long run it would be better for the flouwen to learn to speak the wereshark language, than for the weresharks to attempt to learn the flouwen language. The flouwen could generate chemicals to communicate with, while the weresharks might not be able to make complex sounds. So, instead of talking, he squirted back the proper chemical taste for "1."

Next, the gatherfish squirted a more complex taste that was not the taste of any of the prime numbers used in counting, followed immediately by another "1" taste, while at the same time dropping another pebble.

☆Must be doing addition!☆ ventured Roaring☆Hot☆Vermillion. ☆Next logical thing to do after counting. The strange taste must mean plus.☆

"1 'plus' 1," squirted Clear◊White◊Whistle. So far his chemical synthesizers had proved up to the task. The gatherfish left and was replaced by another one. The new gatherfish swooped down on the two pebbles, emitting a strange smell as it did so. It pushed the two pebbles together, while at the same time it emitted the smell of the number 2.

"1 plus 1 equals 2!" squirted both Roaring☆Hot☆Vermillion and Clear◊White◊Whistle at the gatherfish. The gatherfish disappeared with their reply and was soon replaced by another one.

☆Let me do!☆ said Roaring☆Hot☆Vermillion, picking up some pebbles. While the new gatherfish watched with its sonar, Roaring☆Hot☆Vermillion put down a pile containing two pebbles, then one containing three pebbles, then pushed them together to make a pile of five pebbles, while at the same time squirting, "2 plus 3 equals 5."

The gatherfish went off to report what it had observed, and was soon back again. It went directly up to Roaring☆Hot☆Vermillion and squirted a clear liquid at him. Instead of the intense and sometimes unpleasant flavors that he had been expecting, Roaring☆Hot☆Vermillion was surprised to find that the liquid was very pleasant tasting.

☆Glucose!☆ said Roaring☆Hot☆Vermillion in surprise.

◊Your reward for good performance!◊ said Clear◊White◊Whistle. ◊Even a brand-new wereshark youngling could understand the meaning of that flavor.◊

☆Rather have ammonia!☆ grumbled Roaring☆Hot☆Vermillion.

The gatherfish wasn't done with them yet. It picked up two pebbles and went through the routine of dropping one pebble, dropping the other pebble, then pushing them together into a pile of two pebbles.

☆Why you doing that?☆ roared Roaring☆Hot☆Vermillion at the gatherfish. ☆We already know how to say that!☆

◊Not so loud, subset of Roaring☆Hot☆Vermillion. There must be some reason why we are having to go over it again.◊

As the gatherfish finished pushing the two pebbles together, it emitted a single burst of chemicals, containing the scents for 1, 2, plus, and equals. Now slightly confused, the two flouwen attempted to repeat the sequence of tastes.

"1 plus 1 equals 2," they both squirted back, emitting the tastes in sequence. The gatherfish took their reply off to its master, still hidden behind the rock barrier at the entrance to the cave. It was soon back. It went to a point between the two flouwen and emitted the tiniest jet of scent that either had seen. It was dense, and dark, and *stunk*!

☆Worst smell I ever tasted!☆ complained Roaring☆Hot☆Vermillion, using his body to generate a jet to squirt the offending smell off into the distance.

◊I don't think we did that right.◊

The gatherfish repeated the performance. Without emitting another smell, it first put down one pebble, then another pebble, then pushed them together into a pile of two. Only *after* it had completed the action did it emit the complex flavor containing the scents for 1, 2, plus, and equals.

◊They seem to speak in whole phrases. All squirted out at the same time in one complex flavor,◊ said Clear◊White◊Whistle. ◊This is not going to be an easy language to learn!◊

☆This will take forever!☆ grumbled Roaring☆Hot☆Vermillion. ☆Rather be surfing.☆

It didn't take forever, or even too long a time, thanks to the excellent memories of the flouwen and their exquisite sense of taste. During the seasons-long process of teaching the flouwen their language, the weresharks eventually overcame their fear and hatred of the "Slimedevils," as they called the flouwen, and even ended up inviting them into their homes.

Precise Talker was showing Roaring☆Hot☆Vermillion around Green Home. Roaring☆Hot☆Vermillion was very impressed with the ornate stonework that filled the interior of the multiroomed house. What looked like a pile of greenish rocks from the outside was a majestic mansion inside.

They entered a complex of rooms through a sliding door made with a green stone frame and white coral slats carved in an intricate interwoven pattern. There were three rooms, one small, one medium, and one large. In the small room was a lake-fish, its eyes still embedded in sockets in its head. In the next largest room was a small wereshark. A number of its eyefish and gatherfish came over to look and taste Roaring☆Hot☆Vermillion. The mobile appendages, however, all remained connected to the main body of the young wereshark through umbilicals. Taking care of the two young ones was a much larger wereshark.

"Tireless Worker is this person. Youngster is this person," squirted Precise Talker at Roaring☆Hot☆Vermillion. "Baby is resting in next room. Grabbers of Baby are still budding, so Baby talk-not yet."

"Do Baby and Youngster have names?" asked Roaring☆Hot☆Vermillion.

"Names given after third Homebringing, when new-Baby is brought home at Homebringing. Old-Baby becomes new-Youngster. Old-Youngster leaves nursery and is apprenticed to another Home. Old-Youngster is given name by Mother of new-Home."

Precise Talker sent out a gatherfish to squirt at one of the tethered gatherfish of Youngster. "Meet new-friend Loud-Hot-Red."

The eyefish and gatherfish of Youngster had been looking and tasting Roaring☆Hot☆Vermillion during the discussion.

"Stinks!" said Youngster, its gatherfish withdrawing to avoid the strong ammonia odor which Roaring☆Hot☆Vermillion emitted.

A gatherfish darted from the mouth of Tireless Worker and zoomed to the dorsal fin of Youngster, where its stingers gave the young wereshark an electrical shock that even Roaring☆Hot☆Vermillion could feel. There was a chirp of pain from the main body of Youngster as all of her appendages pulled back rapidly into their sockets in the head and mouth.

"Youngster say greeting properly and politely!" warned

Tireless Worker with a squirt at Youngster from another gatherfish.

Youngster opened its mouth and a gatherfish exited slowly, dragging an umbilical behind it.

"Release grabber . . ." warned Tireless Worker.

The gatherfish reluctantly released the umbilical and swam up to Roaring☆Hot☆Vermillion, where it released a small jet of taste, then darted quickly back inside Youngster's mouth.

"Welcome to Green Home, new-friend Loud-Hot-Red," said the taste cloud.

Both Precise Talker and Tireless Worker sent out gatherfish to squirt some glucose of praise at Youngster.

Just then, the nursery door slid open, and Careful Harvester came in, her gatherfish herding two small filterfish in front of her. The smallest filter-fish was herded into the small room. Baby awoke, immediately gobbled the fish up in one bite, then closed its eyes again.

"Baby seems to spend lot of time with its eyes shut and doing nothing!" said Roaring☆Hot☆Vermillion. "Just like humans!"

"Baby has growing and changing to do," explained Precise Talker. "Baby must grow grabbers in mouth so it can talk, and Baby must change insides so it can lay eggs."

Roaring☆Hot☆Vermillion had been specifically warned by Cinnamon and Reiki not to ask any questions about the sex life of the weresharks, so he didn't comment on Precise Talker's last statement. He knew, however, that the humans would be very interested to know that Baby was changing sexes. During their language lessons, the flouwen had learned that all the weresharks were females, and that all of them expected, in time, to participate in the swarming that occurred during the extreme midnight tide, in the hopes of bringing home a baby in their mouths. The humans had guessed that the lake-fish were not only the babies, but the males of the species, and this statement now showed that they were probably right, but the males changed into females as they grew older.

Back in the other room, Careful Harvester was feeding the other filter-fish to Youngster. Roaring☆Hot☆Vermillion could taste her conversation with the young wereshark.

"Play-not with fishfruit!"

"Fishfruit gone," said Youngster a short while later. "More?"

"More-fishfruit I get you," said Careful Harvester, to Youngster, then sent another gatherfish over to squirt a comment to Tireless Worker. The amount of scent used in the phrase was small, but the flavors were so strong that Precise Talker and Roaring☆Hot☆Vermillion had no problem tasting it. "More-ventplants I must set out. Demontrees, Swiftmovers, and Slimedevils steal most of ripe-fishfruit."

The scents for "Demontrees," "Swiftmovers," "Slimedevils" and "stealing," with their odious overtones, dominated the taste of the phrase that Careful Harvester had squirted, and the unpleasant scent hung in the room. Careful Harvester knew that she shouldn't have used such words within tasting of Loud-Hot-Red, but although the others in the Swimming had managed to do so, she had never forgiven the red-colored alien Slimedevil for killing her fellow vent-field worker, Steadfast Defender.

"You set out ventplants on purpose?!?" exclaimed Roaring☆Hot☆Vermillion. "I did not know! Jollys did not know! Humans did not know! We thought they grew by themselves and were free for anyone to take! We did not know they were yours!"

It was hard for Roaring☆Hot☆Vermillion to bring himself to apologize, but when he did, he did it thoroughly, carefully making sure that he emitted the same odious tastenames that Careful Harvester had used.

"I apologize for the terrible behavior of myself and my fellow Slimedevils in stealing your fishfruit. I apologize also for the stealing of your fishfruit by my friends the Demontrees and the Swiftmovers. When I return, I will inform them all that the fishfruit are yours, and are not for anyone to take. It will not happen again." Roaring☆Hot☆Vermillion knew that the flouwen and the humans would keep that promise, but he had doubts about the Jollys.

Precise Talker then took Roaring☆Hot☆Vermillion to the next room. It was a large one in the center of Green Home. On one long side of the rectangular room was a high table. At each end of the table was an ornate open-work cage made of carved stone, and in each cage were some fat worms, their bodies glowing dimly in the blue-green. At one end of the table were a number of small stone jars with lids, each jar a different size and a different color. From what he had learned about the wereshark culture during the language lessons, Roaring☆Hot☆Vermillion knew this was the Home Altar, and these were the Telling Jars that held the prime number of pebbles for the various levels of honor chants to the Home ancestors. Along the back of the altar were a number of statues of mature weresharks. Roaring☆Hot☆Vermillion was intrigued that the statues were designed to be seen with sound as well as looked at with light, since there were density differences inside that added an internal dimension to the surface features. Most of the statues were merely heads, but one was of a Demonfish with three lake-fish inside its mouth. Roaring☆Hot☆Vermillion wondered what sort of story went with that one.

Along the wall opposite the altar was a long stone rack holding a large number of scrolls. On top of the scroll-rack was another cage of glowgrubs and a number of other statues. Unlike the ones on the altar, which were repre-sentations of deceased weresharks, these had freeform or geometrical shapes. Roaring☆Hot☆Vermillion was intrigued with one that consisted of all the regular solids, a dense tetrahedron, inside a less dense square . . . all the way up to a low-density twenty-sided icosahedron.

Precise Talker sent a gatherfish to each of the light-cages and soon all the glowgrubs were giving off a bright bluish light. Since the wereshark obviously wanted to have him look at something, and not just see it, Roaring☆Hot☆Vermillion quickly formed an eye-lens. Precise Talker then proudly displayed her collection of carved stone Telling Jars and the prime number of colored pebbles in each one, holding each pebble up in front of the light-cage to show its color and flawlessness and commenting on how well the colors of the pebbles matched.

Roaring☆Hot☆Vermillion was politely complimentary about each pebble collection, although his cells itched to ask the obvious. If the wereshark masons were so capable of cutting, grinding, carving, and etching stone, then why did Precise Talker take so much pride in the fact that the not-quite-similar stones in each jar were formed naturally, when it would have been very simple for the masons to make identical pebbles for each Telling Jar. Reiki, having heard from the flouwen that the weresharks had homehold altars, had warned the flouwen that to ask questions about religion was even worse than asking questions about sex, so Roaring☆Hot☆Vermillion kept his questions to himself.

Now that the light in the room was brighter, Roaring☆Hot☆Vermillion could look with his eye and confirm what the chirps from his body had been seeing about one of the statues on the altar. Unlike the others, that showed a normal wereshark head with its mobile appendages in their sockets, this one showed the open-mouthed head of a wereshark with no eyefish and no gatherfish. The gills on the head were also spread painfully wide, as if the wereshark was in panic or agony.

"Who is that?" asked Roaring☆Hot☆Vermillion, using a pseudopod to point.

"Statue is reminder of Steadfast Defender," said Precise

Talker. The chemicals she squirted were low in intensity and did not have any overtones of anger. "Steadfast Defender was only person in recent-memory of Swimming to die defending her home . . ." There was a long pause, and then another gatherfish appeared from inside Precise Talker's mouth. " . . . from you."

Roaring☆Hot☆Vermillion resolved right there to collect his own Telling Jar of colored pebbles. When he had done so, he would bring them here to this altar and Tell his own apology to the memory of Steadfast Defender. The only question in his mind was whether to make the number 59 or 101.

Precise Talker led the way out of the Altar Room into the next one. The walls of the room were lined from floor to ceiling with stone racks containing rolled up scrolls. In the center of the room was a younger wereshark hovering over a simple machine that held two scrolls side-by-side. The mouth of the apprentice was open, and two of its gatherfish were outside the mouth on umbilical connections, hovering over the flattened open portion of the two scrolls.

"Copy Room is this place," she said. "Apprentice Faithful Transcriber is this person."

Faithful Transcriber sent out a freely swimming gatherfish which squirted them both a greeting. Meanwhile, its two captive gatherfish continued with their tasks. One of the gatherfish was moving along one scroll, tasting the surface with its inner set of sucking tentacles, while the other gatherfish matched its motion along the surface of the other scroll. This gatherfish, however, was using its outer stinger tentacles to squirt complex tastes into the finely woven, linenlike scroll material.

"What is Faithful Transcriber doing?" asked Roaring☆Hot☆Vermillion.

"Copying old-scroll to new-scroll," replied Precise Talker through a gatherfish. "Tastes fade with time, so scrolls must be recopied."

"You waste much time doing that!" objected Roaring☆Hot☆Vermillion. "You need a method of making permanent records."

"Permanent-records we can make," said Precise Talker. "Ancients used strong chemicals emitted by their grabbers to etch pictographs and numbers on stone tablets. Etching symbols takes much time. Pictographs suitable-not for complex ideas. Writing tastes on scrolls much faster and better. Stone tablets now used by masons for permanent drawings only. Masons use-not anymore pictograph symbols. Masons use-now only number symbols for dimensions in drawings."

They swam out of the Copy Room. As they were leaving, Precise Talker added a comment, keeping the amount squirted low, so Faithful Transcriber wouldn't be able to taste what she said.

"Copying of scrolls is good method of impressing knowledge of ancients on unwilling brains of apprentices."

"What is in this room?" asked Roaring☆Hot☆Vermillion, curious, as they passed by a sliding door with an unusual yet somehow familiar-looking peaked top. Most of the sliding doors in Green Home were rectangles. This door had a square bottom but a triangular top.

"Air Room is this place," said Precise Talker, swimming on.

"Can I see inside?" said Roaring☆Hot☆Vermillion, curious.

"Important to you is request, then yes," said Precise Talker, the rapid motions of her gatherfish and eyefish showing her annoyance.

Roaring☆Hot☆Vermillion slid open the door to reveal the smallest room in the home. The room was long and narrow, with a triangular peaked ceiling which tapered down and inward toward the back. It would just fit the body of a wereshark if the wereshark backed into the room. On the floor, at the rear of the room, was a carved receptacle shaped something like a bowl, with a hole in the bottom of it that went into the floor. The back wall of the Air Room had the same odd shape as the door, a rectangular bottom portion and a triangular top portion. In the middle of the wall was a lever.

"What is Air Room for?" asked Roaring☆Hot☆Vermillion. There was a long silence as gatherfish after gatherfish appeared between the lips of Precise Talker, then withdrew back into her mouth without speaking.

"What does this lever do?" asked Roaring☆Hot☆Vermillion, pushing down on it. Immediately there was a hissing sound, and through the back wall could be heard bubble after bubble of air making its way upwards, as if moving through a narrow channel. Water started to flow out through the hole in the bottom of the basin. Curious, Roaring☆Hot☆Vermillion formed a red pseudopod and stuck it into the basin, allowing it to be dragged down into the hole by the rapidly flowing water. At this point, Precise Talker closed all six eyes and left with her mouth tightly shut, unable to speak. Roaring☆Hot☆Vermillion let his pseudopod be dragged through the piping until it finally came to an exit. He issued a sonar chirp from the end of the pseudopod and looked around. His pseudopod had exited up at the top of the large pile of rocks under which Green Home lay. The exit point was high above the vent fields, where the prevailing ocean currents provided a constant flow of fresh water.

In the process of pulling back his pseudopod, Roaring☆Hot☆Vermillion figured out how the mechanism in the Air Room worked. Below the room was a chamber full of air—no doubt kept full by some apprentice to Precise Talker. The air was released into the venting shaft by the lever that Roaring☆Hot☆Vermillion had pushed. The air lifted the water in the shaft, pulling the water in from the basin, along with anything that had been deposited in the water.

Suddenly Roaring☆Hot☆Vermillion realized why the door to the Air Room had looked so familiar when he first saw it. The Air Room was shaped like the diagram on the tablet. The mysterious tablet that had been tossed up on the shore was nothing more than a mason's working drawing for what Richard would call a shit house!

Roaring☆Hot☆Vermillion caught up with Precise Talker as she entered the next room. Reiki had also warned the flouwen that after religion and sex, excretion was the next worst topic to bring up in polite conversation between alien species, so although Roaring☆Hot☆Vermillion had questions about the operation of the Air Room, he kept them to himself.

The next room had a large floor with a large number of short grooves in the floor. In each groove were two large pebbles, one rough and one polished smooth. These pebbles were perfectly round, unlike the subtly oval pebbles that the weresharks preferred for their Telling Jars. Moving over the grooves was an apprentice, gatherfish out in front of her, pushing stones back and forth in the grooves. Precise Talker waited until the apprentice came to the end of her task. All the grooves now had their rough pebbles set at one end of the groove, while the smooth pebbles were either in the middle or at the other end of the groove. Once the apprentice marked the results in a scroll, Precise Talker introduced her.

"Accurate Calculator, this is Loud-Hot-Red."

"Tasted, I have, that you know some mathematics," squirted Accurate Calculator.

"I know lots of mathematics!" bragged Roaring☆Hot☆Vermillion, returning to his boasting manner now that he was in more familiar territory. "That must be a calculating machine. What are you calculating?"

"Factoring, I am, a number Precise Talker gave me. If factor I find-not, then Precise Talker a new prime number has found. Return to my task I must." With that, Accurate Calculator swam back to the end of the grooves and started moving pebbles again. Precise Talker and

Roaring☆Hot☆Vermillion left the room so that Accurate Calculator would not be disturbed.

"Is finding new prime numbers important to you?" asked Roaring☆Hot☆Vermillion.

"Yes," replied Precise Talker. "Finding of new-primes is one way a person can leave wretched state of bodily desires and reach exalted state of spiritual purity."

With both sex and religion now suddenly topics of conversation, Roaring☆Hot☆Vermillion moved quickly back to the safer subject of mathematics.

"Fortunately, there are many prime numbers to be found."

"Concern we have, that primes come to end," said Precise Talker.

"Primes not come to end," replied Roaring☆Hot☆Vermillion, with surety. "I prove to you. Take set of prime numbers. Any set. Even set you think contains all prime numbers. Multiply all primes in set together. Add one to get new number. Primes in set now cannot be factors of new number. New number either prime or not. If prime, it bigger than all primes in set, so it new prime. If new number not a prime, then it has prime factors. Prime factors not members of set you think contains all primes. Prime factors are then new primes. Either way, you get a new prime. Add new prime to set and repeat. You will repeat forever. Primes not come to end," he concluded.

Precise Talker was glad to hear that. She would be sure to include Roaring☆Hot☆Vermillion's proof as her contribution to the news-scroll that circulated from Home to Home in the Swimming.

"Exists there method which will always generate a prime?"

"Yes."

"Tell me!"

"You not understand method."

"Teach me!"

"I teach you how to surf instead. Easier. More fun, too."

Roaring☆Hot☆Vermillion changed shape and headed out
the exit door of Green Home, heading for the surface of
the ocean and leaving behind a large pungent cloud.
   "LET'S SURF!!!"

LAVA

Richard, at the lead of the work crew, paused at the top of the low ridge that separated Meander Valley from the narrower river valley that contained the Jolly village. A flood during the past rainy season had damaged the meeting dock at Wide Pond, and the humans were coming to reseat some pilings and replace a few missing planks. He glanced up at the red ball of Barnard as it began to slip slowly behind the planet Gargantua.

"The midday eclipse is about to start, boys," Richard said to the others. "Sit down and take it easy."

Nels, Dirk, Adam, and Freeman lay down their tools and planks and made themselves comfortable. Freeman started a small fire that would provide them some illumination for the upcoming two-hour eclipse period, while the others started unpacking their lunches wrapped in feebook leaves. Shannon remained aloof and standing, not joining the others.

"Oh!" said Richard, finally noticing her. "Sorry. I meant people."

Shannon smiled, accepting his apology. In a society with little technology, simple physical strength had separated many of the daily tasks along gender lines. The women, as the majority, had been aware of this problem and had done their best to make the men feel that their physical labor was just as valued as the more complex intellectual tasks of the women. They quietly conspired to be sure that one of them would go along for the more mind-numbing and back-breaking physical chores—a token female would show the men they weren't being treated as mere muscle. Still, if she was willing to go along to help muck about in Wide Pond, Shannon insisted she be acknowledged.

Shannon shifted her brightly painted sarong into a more modest position as she settled cross-legged onto the ground with the others, and straightened her back so that her long tangle of red curls wouldn't quite touch the ground. She had found that thin braid tips made from her auburn tresses worked quite well as paint brushes to apply her natural dye paints to the soft white paperlike fabric that the humans and Jollys used for clothing. Several long slender braids now snaked down her shoulders, ending in a wisp of bright green or red or blue where the paints had permanently stained her hair. The rest of the unruly mass had been gathered into a thick loose braid that hung down her back. While Shannon rarely brushed it, she was careful to keep it clean enough that she could gather up a new braid-brush as needed.

As the light started to fade for the midday eclipse, Shannon studied the group of men around her. Nels and his son Dirk, both blond and tall, sat together quietly. The two had grown much closer since Dirk's daughter Mirth had been born to Maria and Dirk had assumed the responsibility of fatherhood. Maria had made it clear that having Dirk's daughter did not tie her to Dirk, however, and that she was not ready to settle down. Once Mirth was weaned, she left her in the care of Dirk and Carmen. At first Carmen tried to take over completely, but Nels had talked with her, and now Dirk was the little girl's main parent. Dirk made a surprisingly good parent, and Mirth was now the only "woman" in his life. Carmen accepted the lesser role of grandmother, baby-sitting her grand-daughter whenever Dirk had to leave her behind. Nels and Cinnamon also took care of the little girl on occasion, for Dirk had become part of their larger family after Jinjur's death.

Richard and his son were also sitting together in silence. Freeman was smaller than his muscular father, but his slender body was agile and strong. Years of following Richard on his long trips exploring the geological makeup of the island had honed his young body into a fine-tuned machine. Shannon, looking wistfully at Freeman, felt a twinge of jealousy that Eve had so captured the heart of this darkly handsome man.

Adam was the odd man out. Blue eyes sparkled mischievously out of the dark face, and Shannon realized that while she had been watching the other men, Adam had been watching her. Shannon fought down her irritation. Adam was smart and strong, but despite their occasional flirtations, Shannon had always considered him to be too arrogant. He deferred only to the parents. As the "eldest" of the firstborn, even though it was only by a few hours, Adam assumed the lead in all their joint endeavors. The worst thing about all his plans, Shannon thought, was that they usually worked. She wished he had experienced more failures. If he could only be taken down a peg or two, he would be a nicer person.

All of them were lounging on the ground in the darkness, lit only by the tiny fire, when the first vibrating tremor rippled beneath them. They each looked around, searching in each others' faces for confirmation of what they felt.

"What was that?" Adam asked the two older men.

"An earthquake?" hazarded Nels.

"I don't think so," said Richard, puzzled. "It's too gentle and it's lasting too long." A deep, quiet grumble echoed through the valley. "It feels more like the volcano is rumbling inside."

"What?" Shannon squealed, leaping to her feet.

"I've got to get to Mirth," said Dirk determinedly, also getting up.

"Calm down, everybody," said Richard, holding up his

hands. "There is no need to panic. Look at the Jollys. They have been living on the sides of this volcano ever since it made topsoil. They aren't panicking."

"How could you tell if they were?" demanded Dirk. "They move so slowly."

"That's just the point," said Richard. "They move very slowly, and yet for years they have been safe living on the side of a volcano. It isn't like living on a huge bomb or something; it only means that the magma is closer to the surface."

As he was speaking, the tremors underfoot were growing stronger.

"Any lava that comes out is going to follow the channels already followed by the previous flows," Richard continued calmly. "Lava from the main caldera travels to the sea through the lava valley to the west of our settlement, and there is a high ridge between it and home." The initial fear had faded, and Richard felt the group calming down. "Even if the lava should break through somewhere else, lava moves rather slowly. It's not hard to escape."

"Tell that to the people of Pompeii," muttered Nels, although he knew that Pompeii had been buried by a choking ash flow, not lava, and this volcano didn't emit much ash.

"Our primary duty is to our own settlement," said Dirk solidly. "Not fixing a dock. I say we head back home now. The rest of them might need us."

"It's an hour's walk back to the village," said Adam.

"All the more reason we get started now," insisted his brother. "If there is a lava flow and if it threatens the village . . ."

"Those are pretty big ifs," said Nels. "Besides, the rest of the camp is perfectly capable of taking care of themselves and all the little ones—including Mirth."

Dirk didn't feel convinced, but the rest of the work gang relaxed a bit. It was more likely that the others back home would be worrying about them, rather than needing their help.

Shannon took her Teacher out of the pouch on her belt and activated the screen. She didn't use the computer much as a "Teacher" anymore, for she was now almost nineteen and had finished her compulsory school lessons long ago, but she kept it around because of its special sketch-pad screen and its art programs. The versatile mini-computer had other functions, however, including being a two-way radio. Her long fingers danced over the touchscreen as she set up the comm program, and the speaker squeaked to life.

" . . . men to Shannon. Shannon do you read me?" Carmen's voice sounded tinny through the small speaker.

"Yes, Carmen, I hear you. We're all fine. How are things there?"

"And how's Mirth?" Dirk called over.

"Mirth is fine," replied Carmen soothingly. "We are *all* fine. But as a precaution, we're going to leave the forest area and go down to the cleared areas near the stream."

Richard took the Teacher from Shannon. "That's a good idea," he said. "Even a little eruption can send out embers or hot ash that might start a forest fire—even though Eden's plants are all pretty flame resistant." He smiled. They had all experienced how difficult it was to light the damp green wood found on Eden. Except during the driest seasons, wood had to be keep under cover from the daily rains or it wouldn't burn.

"Mirth?" called Dirk. "Take your Teacher with you so you can talk to Daddy."

"Dirk . . ." Carmen replied with a patient tone. "The Teachers aren't strong enough to communicate directly with each other over that distance. The only reason I can reach you now is that I'm using the main comm unit. But . . . don't worry. While the others will be heading out of the forest, I am going to stay here and will relay any messages."

"Will you be safe there?" asked Nels.

"Safe? This house has always been the safest. I'll be fine. But that Teacher doesn't have much reserve. Turn it off now and only use it for emergencies. Also, don't forget there's a comm unit in the center of the Jolly village. It should be powerful enough to contact the Teachers of the others directly. If you do talk to the others, however, don't forget to keep me up to date, too. I worry. Carmen out."

Shannon broke the connection and switched the unit to standby. Carmen was right. The little handheld unit was light-powered, and now that the eclipse had started, its small batteries would be drained rapidly by long transmissions. They would have to use the Teacher only if they had a serious problem, not just if Dirk was worried about his daughter.

The ground beneath their feet was still trembling, but after so many minutes, they had almost gotten used to the vibration. Still, the attitude of the human work crew had changed to one of wariness. Instead of closing their eyes and resting in the darkness, their eyes now scanned the distant primary caldera of the volcano Hoolkoor in the west for any sign of lava. The first indications of lava, however, did not come from the distant caldera, but a place much closer.

"Look!" cried Shannon. "Over to the east!"

There, almost directly up the mountainside rising above them, they could see pinpoints of glowing orange.

"But that's not where the mouth of the volcano is," objected Dirk.

"No . . ." said Richard, slowly. "But there's a smaller secondary caldera up there. Freeman and I have explored that region."

"It looks like that caldera wasn't as dormant as we thought it was," replied Freeman.

The two of them had often gone hunting near the mouth of the small crater. There had been little plant life inside the crater, since the warm ground emitted toxic fumes, but the birds enjoyed riding the thermals generated by the heat. They had experienced good luck with a sling as long as the prey didn't fall into the middle of the crater where the fumes were the heaviest.

"Is that light caused by lava or a forest fire?" asked Nels.

"Hard to tell," said Richard. In the darkness the orange glow on the hillside seemed to merge with his retina's afterimages. The shape, and even the position of the flickering light, seemed unstable.

Shannon had inherited the excellent color sense of her father, David, and her younger eye had less trouble focusing on the apparition. "It's moving slowly," she said. "But I can't be sure if it is molten rock or burning trees."

"Up or down?"

"What?" asked Shannon puzzled. Freeman rarely said much, but he usually made more sense than that.

"A forest fire burns uphill, lava moves down," Freeman explained.

Shannon looked again, concentrating. The golden-red glimmer was almost directly overhead, making it hard to judge its direction. "Both," she said finally. "There is a lava flow coming down, and forest fires spreading out from it—going up."

"It doesn't sound good," said Adam.

"I'm not exactly sure," mused Richard, continuing to look up, "because in the darkness one ridge line looks like another, but it looks like the lava is coming out of a fissure in the side of the secondary caldera . . . and it's flowing down the river valley that leads right here . . . *and* goes on down by the Jolly village!"

"We need to warn the Jollys," said Adam.

"Won't they see it for themselves?" asked Nels.

"The Jollys' eyes are used to flying up close to things to see them," Adam reminded him. "Their long-range vision is almost nonexistent. And, since it is dark and all their eyes are in their nests resting, they can't see the distant danger like we can. While they may feel the vibrations and know that the volcano is causing them, they probably won't be able to add the threat of the lava to their worldview until it is right on top of them."

"We'd better go warn them, then," said Richard. Together they felt their way down the quaking slope toward the Jolly village, the beams from their permalights flickering across the rough path ahead of them.

When they got to the bottom of the ridge and reached the banks of the river above Wide Pond, they were able to look up through the gap between the ridges that formed the sides of the steep river valley. There was a menacing orange glow, high up near the top of the valley. It was moving slowly toward them. They stopped to look up in awe at the sight.

"Freeman?" said Richard. "Do you remember that remnant of a lava tube I pointed out to you in this valley? It looks like that old worn-down lava tube is about to be replaced with a fresh one."

"I can see more fires now," said Nels. "Although the plants along the river valley are as fireproof as most vegetation on Eden, they are burning like an Earth forest fire."

"The heat from the lava seems to be drying out the trees first, then setting the dried wood on fire from a distance," said Shannon.

By the time they reached the Jolly village, it was nearly the middle of the eclipse period. The Jollys were all standing at the doorways to their huts, their eyes in their nests, waiting out the darkness. Richard stood still in front of Seetoo and called loud greetings to the chief, while lighting his face with his permalight so that the Jolly's eyes would be able to see him. After a few moments, the chief awoke and whistled acknowledgment.

"Hoolkoor is hungry and is shaking his fronds!" the Jolly said. "Soon he will disgorge his digestive fluids and take a fiery taste of the vegetation in the valleys to the west!"

Richard didn't want to get into a theological debate, he just wanted the Jollys to be aware of the imminent danger. "The lava flow to the west is not the only one! There is a new lava flow. It's coming right down this river valley and is setting fire to the vegetation all along the banks. You must get your people away from the river to a safe place, far from anything that might catch on fire."

"We will redirect the water in the irrigation channel to water the thook hedge. Once the thook has drunk its fill, it will not allow the Flame-Demons to overcome it."

"A well-watered thook hedge might be safe from flying embers," said Richard, "but that lava flow is so hot it will ignite anything near it, watered or not. And that includes you and your people."

"We will defend our village," replied Seetoo. "And if Hoolkoor decides to take us into his mouth, we will accept his judgment," said the Jolly chief fatalistically.

While they talked, Seetoo used a gatherer to fetch a pictotablet of soft clay and was now painstakingly writing out instructions for the defense of the village. As the first light of Barnard appeared from behind Gargantua, the chief sent the gatherer to Proclamation Rock with the pictotablet. The gatherer gave a whistle and soon eyes from all of the tribe came to Proclamation Rock for guidance

Although the Jollys moved slowly by human standards, their thick legs were strong and their independent gatherers were nimble. The stronglimbs moved to protect the village, while coping with the trembling ground and the fear of falling it produced in them. Soon the gentle flow of water from Wide Pond that was normally used to irrigate the seedling fields and the jookeejook pens had been increased in flow. Some of the water now flowed into a shallow ditch that ran along the thook hedge. The leading thook plants greedily absorbed the first of the flow, and it was several moments before the water moved on to quench the thirst of the next plants. Richard guessed that it would take almost an hour for the entire perimeter hedge to be replete.

"Seetoo!" insisted Richard, trying to make the Jolly understand. "Even if this water protects the village from the forest fires started by the lava, it is not going to save the seedlings! The seedling bed lies right alongside the river. The fronds on your seedlings will burst into flames from the heat!"

"We will soak the seedling bed and sprinkle their fronds with water," replied Seetoo.

"Getting them wet will only 'boil' them instead of burning them!" shouted Shannon, now highly concerned. Chief Seetoo didn't understand what the human word "boil" meant, but it sounded deadly.

"We've got shovels," Nels said to Richard. "Let's dig up the seedlings and transplant them at a safe distance."

"Seedlings cannot be moved," replied Seetoo. "Their roots are tender. If the roots of a seedling are ever disturbed, the seedling always dies."

"We've got to think of something!" cried Shannon. "We can't just let them stay there and die!"

"If they die," said Seetoo, "then I will die with them."

"What do you mean?" The humans were aghast.

"The fruits from my pollen are being threatened. I must stay and fight for them. Even if there is no defense against the fiery bile of Hoolkoor, I will not desert them." Seetoo, who had eyes and gatherers roaming over the entire village—making sure that all was in readiness—now started moving slowly and steadily toward the riverbank that bordered the seedling bed. Once there, the chief settled into a position along the bank between the seedlings and the oncoming lava stream that threatened them.

"Richard!" insisted Shannon. "There has to be *something* we can do."

"Like what, Shannon?" yelled Richard irritably. "Look, I don't like this any better than you do, but lava is one of those irresistible forces. We can't just erect an immovable object to meet it."

"What about a dam?" asked Freeman. "If we went upriver and built a barrier in that narrow cleft just below where the water from our stream comes into the valley, we could divert the lava flow eastward into the next ravine. If you remember, when we were surveying that region, I mentioned there is only about five meters elevation separating this valley from the next at that point."

"Build a dam with what?" responded his father angrily, not wanting to admit defeat. "If we had a week or two, we might be able to move in enough dirt and rock to divert the lava enough to save the seedlings. But we have an hour—maybe two. How are we going to build anything large enough to make the slightest bit of difference?"

"We could use the black powder we have stored back at home," suggested Adam. "We could blow rocks off the walls of the valley to block—"

"Gunpowder would just bring rock down," said Nels. "We would still have to pile it up."

"If we got all the Jollys to help . . ."

"As slowly as the Jollys move . . ."

Nels and Adam continued arguing, but Richard had stopped listening. Without asking, he had taken the Teacher from Shannon's belt pouch and was searching through its massive reference files. Shannon looked over his shoulder as he called up various aerial views of the island and compared them to the maps that he and Arielle had surveyed in their early days on the island. The argument ground to a halt as they realized that Richard was definitely working on something.

"It only has to divert . . . but the stream wanders . . . and it's been dry lately. . . ." Richard was mumbling under his breath as he finished his calculations. "Hmmm. We have the Teacher to give a signal . . . could Carmen do it? No . . . we need her at the comm." He switched the Teacher back to comm mode.

"Richard to Carmen. Carmen? Has everybody left but you?" he asked.

"Carmen here. No, Everett stayed here to help me. He's outside watching for any sign of flames."

"Everett? He's perfect. Go get him!" cried Richard.

"What's up?" said Nels.

"I think I have a way to build up a wall of rock, and we won't have to lift a pebble," Richard replied while waiting. "What we need to do is deflect the lava at the point where the stream from Meander Valley joins the big river valley. If we can get enough water on the face of the lava flow at just the right time, we can cool the face enough for it to harden and form our immovable object. Then, the frozen lava face will divert the rest of the lava behind it in a new direction, just as Freeman suggested. I think we have enough water to do that, but at the moment it is ten kilometers away, sitting behind our dam—" He was interrupted by a voice from the Teacher.

"Everett here."

"Everett? Listen here, m'lad, I have an important job for you." He then quickly outlined the plan. Ten minutes later, Everett was on his way out of the village, a Teacher bumping against his hip. The heavy pack on his back made him awkward, but the agile blond had spent his life running up and down these trails. It was a long run, and when the trail grew steep, Everett switched to a brisk walk. Barnard was now completely out from behind Gargantua, and the midday darkness was over, but the air itself was now growing thick and dark with smoke. When Everett first smelled the burning vegetation, he tried to speed back up to a jog, but the hill was too steep and soon he was gasping in the stinging smoke. Trying to regain his breath, he slowed back down at a straight portion of the steep trail and turned around to take a few steps backward in order to rest the aching muscles in his thighs.

Although the wind was blowing away from the fires, the ridge above the secondary caldera was now fully involved. Everett could see through the trees to the next ridge where long tongues of flame leapt into the air and then curled back away. Thick brown smoke billowed up in long plumes along the horizon. Everett tried not to think about what would happen if a stray ember should land on his loaded backpack, but more than that, Everett hated the smell of the burning forest. Wood smoke was not pleasant when some of your best friends were trees.

After what seemed like years of climbing over the quivering earth, Everett reached his goal. The dam towered over him, and on the far side of the old streambed, a small water wheel slowly turned in the scant runoff. This far into the dry season the wheel had only enough power to turn the smallest grindstone. The dam had taken months to build, and the lake behind it now assured the humans they would always have sufficient irrigation water during the dry season for the vital Earth-grain crops—with their essential vitamins that the humans needed to survive in this alien paradise. But as much as the humans valued the dam, they valued their friends at the Jolly village more.

When the dam had been built, they had left an opening at the base that had allowed the water to run through until the construction was completed. When they sealed the hole on the lake side with boulders, a hollow was left that reached far under the dam. Now, Everett shoved his loaded backpack deep into the opening and strung a length of fuse behind him, leading to the safety of a small cave on the nearby hillside. He took the Teacher from his belt and called the comm unit in Carmen's house.

"Everett to Carmen . . . do you read me?"

"Go ahead, Everett." The adult's calm voice came over the speaker and soothed his nerves. The constant shaking of the ground beneath his feet, and his exhaustion from the long climb, had left him feeling tight and nervous. Richard had stressed the importance of waiting for the right time before taking any further action. Now, after all this hurry-up, it was time to wait.

"Tell Richard I'm all set up, and I'm ready whenever he is."

"Okay, Everett. Stand by."

Everett wondered if he should tell Richard that in addition to the black powder from the settlement's storage magazine, he had added the secret stash of powder the firstborn boys had managed to "collect" over the years, but he didn't want to tie up the radio in case Richard tried to call him just as he was trying to reach Richard. Besides, since the whole idea was to destroy the dam, a little extra black powder wouldn't hurt.

Richard was still working out the calculations when Carmen sent word that Everett was in position. Smoke from the distant fires flavored the air, and the ground was still rumbling ominously underfoot, reminding them constantly of the approaching disaster.

Under Seetoo's constant direction, some of the villagers labored along the irrigation ditch, widening and deepening it to increase the water flow to the seedling bed, while others gathered peethoo leaves and piled them up protectively around the seedlings, while soaking them thoroughly with water. Freeman, Dirk, Adam, and Shannon joined the Jolly work crews, preferring work to worry, as Richard and Nels refined the computations to produce a plan with the greatest chance of success. Richard had made it clear that this was all a matter of estimates and hope, but however great the odds were against them, they had to take the gamble. Now, they could only hope that fortune would smile on them and the wrath of Hoolkoor would be diverted.

Dark and sullen-looking in the reddish daylight, the flowing lava rolled relentlessly toward them down the river valley. The air above it shimmered with heat, as the liquid stone seemed to breathe and move like a living creature, leaving thick black walls of smoldering rock along its sides. Fires broke out all along its length, distant trees and underbrush bursting into flame under the extreme heat radiated by the molten rock. Shannon fixed the awesome scene in her memory while hating herself for thinking of art when her friends were in so much danger.

When it came, the rolling boom of the distant explosion made all of them look up. Even the Jollys stopped working to update their worldview. Shannon looked at Richard, trying to guess his reaction. The dam was *ten kilometers* away! Should the blast have been that loud?

With the explosion, Shannon abandoned all pretense at work and moved uphill to a better vantage point. Adam and the rest of the firstborn soon joined her, and together they looked up the river valley at the approaching danger. The lava was now close enough that Shannon could feel its odd dry heat on her face, and hear the rumbling crackle and hisses as it ate up more of the vegetation in the glen. Anything before it was swallowed into its expanding bulk. Even the dirt and stones in the now dry river bed were picked up and incorporated into its seething body. Along its heaving sides the plants withered, then blackened, and finally burst into flame. The lava passed the endpoint of the ridge marking the place where the stream from Meander Valley entered the river. It filled up the narrow cleft in the valley formed by the endpoints of that ridge and another one across the river from it. It flowed through the cleft and started eating into the shallow waters of Wide Pond, which slowed it down somewhat, but couldn't stop it.

Far up Meander Valley, something was happening. There was a rumble that built so gradually into a roar that Shannon didn't know just when she first became aware of it. Richard and Nels, down along the riverbank, were gesturing and pointing, imploring Seetoo to move away from the bottom of the valley. Finally they left the Jolly chieftain alone with his helpless seedlings and climbed up the hill to join the firstborn at their vantage point.

Shannon thought she knew what to look for, but when she first saw the incoming wave she didn't realize what it was she was seeing. At first she thought that the constant shaking had started a landslide—goodness knows water was never that color! It was a gray-brown wall filled with all the plants and rocks it had picked up in its headlong rush through the valley and across the many meanders in the twisting streambed. Shannon could make out wide boobaa leaves and long tangles of keekoo roots, twisting and writhing in the opaque water. Dirty froth highlighted the dark surface as it roiled and churned. Violent and deadly, the wall of water looked as dangerous as the creeping flow of liquid rock and Shannon's heart filled with fear.

"Oh, Adam," she whispered. "What have we done? How could we have let loose such . . . such a beast?"

Adam put his arm around her, but she wouldn't look away. They looked on with fascinated horror as the fire and water came crashing together at the juncture of the stream and the river. The flood climbed up on the back of the snakelike stream of lava like a mongoose attacking a cobra. The valley filled with clouds of steam as the surface of the lava exploded, as if attempting to shake the flood off. The hissing outburst of steam and the loud cracking of the rapidly cooling rock were deafening. Huge white clouds boiled up and filled the whole valley with its noisome dampness and set the humans to choking in the thick, stinking fumes. Small pellets of black glass rained down on them as the super-heated rock continued its fight with the cold wall of water. The lava hardened . . . and then melted again . . . its progress stalling until the building pressure from behind forced it onward. The lava piled up higher in the narrow cleft, filling the valley from wall to wall, while the flood of water climbed higher with it, continuing to flow over its top, attempting to submerge it. Boiling hot water flowed off the darkening lava tongue into Wide Pond and continued on down the riverbed, hiding the seedling bed and its lonely guardian in dense clouds of hot steam. . . .

The flow of hot water then slowed . . . and stopped. . . . The winds blew the steam clouds away and they could now see the far side of Wide Pond again. There was a large tongue of dark lava there. It had stopped moving! Along the riverside, Seetoo still stood sturdily by his young progeny—fronds wilted, but alive.

Shannon broke away from Adam and headed for the top of the ridge overlooking the point where the stream from Meander Valley emptied into the river valley. There was now a new lake at that point, blocked by a black mound of steaming rock. The river valley now contained a river of lava. It flowed down the steep valley until it reached the point where it too was blocked by the black mound of rock. There, the lava was forced to make a turn, sending it harmlessly off into an adjacent ravine.

Shannon looked around her and the world seemed for a moment to be holding its breath. Far up the valley, a whistling scream of gas could be heard escaping from a fissure. There was a final sharp jolt that knocked her off her feet, an earthquake more violent than anything she had felt earlier. With the jolt, the screaming stopped. The earth was finally still.

Richard looked up the valley. "The lava has stopped flowing out of the fissure in the side of the caldera. The magma chamber that was driving the lava flow must have collapsed."

As the lava flow diminished, the tube of hardened rock that had formed around the surface of the flowing liquid collapsed inward under its own weight. Later, except for the crusted remnants of the lava tube along its walls, the valley would be as empty of lava as it was now empty of water. Then, when the rains came again, the river would flow again down that valley. There would now be two "Wide Ponds" instead of one, but the Jolly village would be able to resume its normal life—safe until the next eruption—thousands of seasons in the future.

When the weary humans returned home to survey the

damage to their settlement by the earthquakes and flood, they concluded that it had been the final strong earthquake that had toppled Carmen's aerie. A landslide had brought her home down from its perch above the village. Her body was discovered beneath the rubble, still at her station by the comm unit.

ALOHA

Red slowly drifted out of her apartment on *Prometheus* and palmed the door closed. She paused and looked across the lift-shaft to the two doors that opened into Thomas and George's rooms. George was not in. He was probably down in the control room working with James on data reduction. Thomas had not been in his room for two years now. When they had floated him out the portal to take him down to the sick bay, Thomas had insisted that his door be left open.

"I'm not going to let a little heart attack keep me down. I'm going to get well and come back to my studio. I've got a lot of pictures to work on."

They assured him he would soon return to work on computer enhancements of his world-famous shots of the ring waves on Eau mountain, the ten-thousand-kilometer atmospheric volcano on Gargantua, and the elaborately decorated alien icerugs on Zulu. James, however, had been quite insistent that Thomas stay in the sick bay where there was better access to the medical equipment. Thomas had argued with the computer for a while, but after two more heart stoppages that would have been fatal if the Christmas Bush had not been there to apply shock treatment, Thomas finally stopped arguing and accepted the life of an invalid. The view-wall above his bed in the sick bay was identical to the one in his room, but it just never seemed the same. The real problem was that the complex photographic enhancement and display console that took up most of Thomas's private room could not be fitted into the sick bay, and Thomas was reduced to more modest processing of his picture pixels.

Red's eyes swept past the seven other doors ringing the lift shaft on this floor. They and all the doors on the floor above had been closed for a long time. Ten of them at once, some fifteen years ago, when Slam IV had crashed on Zuni, third moon of Gargantua. The others had died of one cause or another over the years while *Prometheus* slowly wandered back and forth through the Barnard system, collecting data on the planets and moons as the seasons changed. There were only three of them left on *Prometheus* now—all old, but still busy. They were presently engaged in a two-year survey of the star itself, following it through one of its sunspot cycles. For that job they had used the light from the star to slow *Prometheus* in its orbit, so that the spinning parasol of their ship fluttered down closer to the surface of the dim red sun. For the first time since they had come to Barnard they had to use filters over the viewing ports.

Red looked upward at the gaping maw of the central shaft and hesitated. In the past she would have simply flung herself up into the empty hole and used an occasional flick of hand or foot on the walls to propel herself through the shaft to her destination. She would still do that for a 'tween-decks jump—but now she wanted to go to the starside science dome nearly sixty meters away. They were getting close enough to the sun that the acceleration from the light pressure was becoming almost noticeable. Getting cautious in her old age, she called for the shaft elevator and took it to starside dome.

Her arthritic joints creaking in protest, Red wormed her way past a large telescope swung out under the dome. There was very little room left for a human. Red looked up to see a minibush working the controls. It was very busy, scrambling back and forth between the various control knobs at a speed that no human hands could have duplicated. Red was slightly puzzled, "Why are you using such a little branch, James?" she asked. "You'll wear yourself out running back and forth like that."

She heard James chuckle, both from her hair imp and from the minibush on the telescope. "I can handle the telescope fine this way," it replied. "It's a little more wasteful of energy than using a larger motile that can reach both knobs at once, but I felt that it was better to have most of the Christmas Bush elsewhere at this time."

Red's heart skipped a beat. "What's going on?" she asked in alarm, then instantly knew the answer. "There's something wrong with Thomas!" she cried, and started to wiggle her way past the slowly moving telescope.

"I didn't want to worry you," James said through her imp. "There's nothing bad happening to him, but I just thought it best to have more of my motile close to him since his vital signs are slowly worsening. Red! Elizabeth!! . . . Wait for the elevator!!!" the imp screamed in her ear as she dove headlong down the shaft.

"I'll pay for that later," Red said to herself as her adrenaline-anesthetized joints ignored their arthritic signals and brought her to a violent stop at the living area deck. She made her way to the sick bay. Most of the Christmas Bush was there, monitoring the medical instruments. Red noticed that Thomas's upper torso was naked and covered with a lacelike net of motile threads. She looked at Thomas and understood why James had been concerned. Thomas's face, usually a handsome and healthy light brown color, was now a muddy gray. He had aged well and usually looked much younger than his sixty-eight years. He didn't look young now, more like George's eighty-seven.

Thomas looked up as she came in. He grinned weakly at her and winked their special wink. She blushed, then put an exasperated frown on her face.

"Thomas," she scolded, "you're incorrigible."

"But it's been over two years, Red," he said. "A guy could die if he goes without getting it for that long."

". . . and he'd die if he did," she replied.

"But what a way to go!"

Ignoring his remark, Red moved over to him and put one hand on his forehead and one on his cheek. He moved his head and nuzzled his nose in her hand, his lips kissing her palm softly. She tried to hold back her emotions, but finally gave up, fell sobbing across his chest, and hugged him. Through her anguish and tears she could feel the motiles moving between them, keeping out of the way as much as possible, but still maintaining their vigil on the body of the dying man. Thomas ran his fingers through the brilliant red hair that he had loved for so long, grinned inwardly at the slight trace of gray at the root of each strand, and closed his eyes to rest.

After a while, Red got control of herself. She sat up and twisted her body until the sticky patch on the back beltline of her jumpsuit stuck to the holding pad of a workstation arm the Christmas Bush had swung out for her. Now she could stay beside the bed without drifting away. She looked at Thomas's closed eyes with concern, then turned to the Christmas Bush.

"He's just sleeping," said James, "but it won't be long now. In his weakened condition his usually benign sickle-cell anemia condition is flaring up and aggravating his other problems."

Red took Thomas's hand and waited, occasionally brushing him on the cheek with a wrinkled, freckled hand.

George was in his bed, staring up at the viewscreen in the ceiling and scanning through an old science fiction novel, *Dragon's Egg*. He'd read it many times before, but it was so full of scientific tidbits that he always enjoyed dipping into it before going to sleep. His favorite part was when the alien "cheela" came up from the surface of a neutron star to visit the humans in orbit above them, riding on miniature black holes.

George heard the rustle and the occasional odd noise of Elizabeth coming up the shaft. He looked out his open door to watch Red rise up out of the floor and bring herself to a halt at the railing. Instead of going to her door, however, she circled around the railing ringing the lift shaft and disappeared behind the edge of his door. He heard the splat of a human palm on the wall, the sibilant hiss of a compartment door sliding shut, and the deadly click of a bolt. He sat up under his tension sheet as his imp whispered in his ear.

"She wanted to tell you herself," James said.

Red appeared at his door, an inward strength glowing in the tall, green-suited body. Her red hair glistened in the bright corridor light as she said, "There's just the two of us now, George. Can I come in?"

"Sure," he said. "Just a second and I'll get dressed."

"Don't bother," she replied. "I just don't want to sleep alone tonight." She came over to the bed and, kicking off her corridor boots, climbed in under the tension sheet, her back to him.

"Just hold me," she pleaded, and George put the grizzled arm of an old man around the stricken woman and lay his head on the pillow next to hers, his imp scrambling around to his other shoulder as he did so. He closed his eyes and went to sleep, while James turned off the scan book, the bedroom light, and closed the corridor door.

Another year passed. George was now hanging loosely from a pylon on the control deck, monitoring the video data links from the deep space probes in the outreaches of Barnard. The screens showed little that was new, and James could have handled the data by itself, but George insisted on viewing all the scenes that differed in any significant aspect from those that had been seen before. A typical scene of frozen blackness on a distant moon nearly forty light-minutes away had changed to a scene of frozen grayness. The computer had asked the human element in its loop to evaluate the situation.

"Nothing here, James," George said. "Just another mound of dirty ice."

The screen flashed to a new scene, one that had been held up while the previous one had been evaluated. George scanned the picture, looking for anything that the well-trained senses of the computer might have missed. Suddenly, his eyes caught a flash of green out of the corner of his eye, and he turned to see a tumbled mass of green-colored satin clothing converging on his face. He brushed away the intruding jumpsuit and underwear just in time to see two tantalizing white mounds swim out of sight behind the control room door, tiny pink feet propelling them on their way.

It didn't take long. Within ten seconds he was stripped to the uniform that the "Game" called for and was searching through the downs and outs of the corridors that had made their life a heaven in the stars. They had tried other hiding spots, but the best—yes, the very best—was the exercise room.

George found her behind the exercise mats. She thought she was stretched out enough to be as invisible as a pea under the many thick mattresses. He noticed the slight mound, however, and, his body rising to the occasion, dove under the layers of mats and pulled a squealing, skinny, red-haired vixen into the open.

"*Stop!*" she cried. She twisted expertly in the air, trying to break his single handhold.

Her struggles to retreat were defeated by a single brushing kiss that he implanted on the tips of her hair. It was his turn to run now, and he bounded off the wall and entered the dim lounge that led to one of the video rooms. She smiled and stopped at the lift-shaft, her lithe naked body relaxing for a moment, clad in nothing but her glittering imp hairpiece. She waited, scanning the tumble of furniture and panels in the lounge, then dived full speed at a bulky gray form bouncing from one panel to another, his glittering imp hanging desperately onto his naked shoulder with all six paws. She caught him in midflight as they tumbled through the door into one of the video rooms.

Their play had risen to ecstasy . . . the dim lights of the video room adding to their games . . . they were coupled . . . her face flushed with pleasure until it was almost the color of her hair. Her body arched back . . .

"RED! GEORGE!! STOP!!!" imps shouted in their ears.

"Goddamnit, James!" George exploded with fury. "Can't you stay out. He grabbed the handful of brittle sticks from their perch on his naked shoulder and flung them at the far wall. The mangled twigs and wires hummed to a halt about a meter from his hand and buzzed back past him—heading toward Elizabeth.

George looked quickly around and watched his small wisp of imp merge into the imp on the side of Red's face, a face gasping for breath and wide-eyed with agony. He turned at another sound, a deep thrumming in the air. A thicket of brightly glittering sticks and twigs hit the two of them amidships and thrust him aside.

The fuzzy hands of the Christmas Bush then attempted to press life into Red's naked curvaceous chest, while a dense cluster of cilia pumped a pulsating stream of air into her lax mouth. The Christmas Bush worked on Red for a number of minutes, then the automatic motion finally stopped. Not abruptly, not slowly, but like some automaton given both stop and start signals at the same time.

"She is dead," said James, finally stopping.

"*NO!*" shouted George. "Don't stop! Save her! *Do something!*" He reached out and started pulling the Christmas Bush off her. "She can't die! I won't let her die!!"

"There is nothing either you or I can do," replied James calmly. "She has suffered a massive cerebral aneurysm."

"Oh . . ." said George, his hands coming to a halt.

He let go of the Christmas Bush and ran his finger-tips tenderly up over Red's face while he slowly calmed himself down.

"Thanks for trying," he finally said. He moved back and floated motionless, eyes staring longingly at her face.

"Are you okay?" said James, a large chunk of Christmas Bush breaking loose from the slowly falling nude to hover at a distance from him.

"I'm fine, James," George said, finally recovering. "Just take care of her, will you?" He went off to cry in a quiet place, his imp reforming unobtrusively on his naked shoulder as he left.

James waited patiently. George's grief eventually shed itself in a floating stream of sparkling spheres. George's imp tenderly flicked each tear from around his red-rimmed eyes, launching the drops toward the nearby air intake ducts. There was still a deep emptiness in him, however. That void would only be filled by the wash of tears from the intermittent floods of emotional catharsis that would return again and again in the weeks, months, and years ahead. The loss of the others had been hard, but there had always been someone to share the grief with. This loss he would bear alone.

When George finished his crying, he found himself in the starside science dome, lying back in the control chair and looking outward at the distant yellow star studding the end of Orion's belt. He had decided to get all the misery out of his system at one time and had deliberately worked up a good case of homesickness to add to his loneliness. He now had cried himself out, and getting up calmly, he floated away from the chair as it folded itself into its niche in the wall. He called for the elevator to take him to the control deck.

"I'd like to read a few words before you put her in cold storage, James," he said quietly to his imp.

"Red left some last wishes with me, as a verbal will,"

said James. "She didn't want her body to stay on board *Prometheus* with the others—even if there was a chance that someday it could be returned to Earth. She has no family or friends there. She felt more at home around this strange red star and wants to be buried here."

"A sailor of the skies, her body cast into the deep," mused George. "Okay. I'll look up a sea captain's farewell."

"It's going to be more complicated than that, George. She wants to be cremated in the star."

"We can't do that. If we put her out a port, she'll go into orbit," said George, puzzled. Suddenly, he looked up.

"Of course!" he said. "I forgot what kind of ship we're in."

"Shall I decelerate and assume a hovering orbit?" said James.

"Yes," said George. "How long will it take?"

"Two weeks. Less if you don't mind feeling a few percent of gee."

"*Sure!* I can take the gees!" grumbled George. "I may be old, but I'm not decrepit—you obsolete hunk of frayed wires and diffusing silicon. What'll we do with Red in the meantime? Put her in cold storage with the others?"

"Yes, we'll have to," replied James. "But before that, I'll have to make some preparations. She gave explicit instructions on what she was to wear and how her hair and makeup were to be done. The Christmas Bush is working on that now in the sick bay."

"I want to help," said George, pushing himself over to the lift-shaft as the computer began to tilt the huge sail to slow its orbit about the star.

"Are you sure?" asked James, with a concerned overtone in its voice. "I am perfectly capable of handling the whole thing myself."

"Yes!" said George gruffly. He padded into the sick bay and approached the still-naked body strapped lightly to the table. The thick red hair that was Red's crowning glory was now full of twigs from the Christmas Bush. One small clump of the Bush was controlling a plastic squeezer full of a reddish liquid and spraying a mist into the air. Each tiny droplet was snatched individually by the cilia on the twigs, carried to the base of each hair stalk, applied to the root, then carefully wiped off, as the few millimeters of gray hair became as red as the rest.

"I don't think she would have wanted you to see this," rumbled the Christmas Bush.

"She never fooled anyone," George replied. "We never talked about Red dyeing her hair, but we all knew that she did, and knew that everyone else knew, too."

James hesitated a little at that statement. It quickly sifted through sixty-eight years of conversation picked up and recorded by its imps. George was right. No one on the ship had ever talked with anyone else about Red's hair. They must have understood each other from facial expressions.

"I still have a lot to learn about humans," was the summary judgment it entered into its memory.

James let George brush, comb, and arrange Red's hair, but insisted on doing the makeup itself.

"She would come back and haunt me if I allowed you to mess up her lip line," James joked.

As they were finishing, one limb of the Christmas Bush appeared with a set of green satin clothing and a long pair of alligator-hide boots.

"Where'd those boots come from?" said George in surprise.

"She brought them on board as part of her personal baggage allotment," James replied. "She was planning to wear them for parties, but she forgot that her ankles swell in free-fall. After trying to get them on a few times, she gave up and shoved them in the back of her storage locker. Her last instructions about them were very explicit. I recorded them."

Red's voice emerged from the vibrating cilia at the tips of the Christmas Bush as the computer replayed the exact sequence of bits which it had recorded in that long-ago conversation. "'I want those boots on when I go out the port. Even if you have to cut off my feet to get them on. But don't you *dare* stretch them.'"

George winced visibly as he heard Red's hauntingly beautiful contralto emitted from the glowing Bush. "Please don't ever do that again," he finally said.

"I'm sorry," said James in a subdued whisper.

A few minutes of firm pressure on Red's lower legs by the massive paws of the Christmas Bush allowed the green leather to slide over the sheer green stockings. There was even plenty of room to tuck in the legs of the green satin slacks. As they were putting on Red's shirt, the Christmas Bush stopped, reached into a breast pocket, and took out a gold coin. It handed the coin to George.

"She didn't say what to do with this," James said. "I guess you should keep it."

"I'm sure I can think of a thousand ways to spend a sixty-billion-dollar gold coin in this thriving metropolis," remarked George sarcastically. He took the coin, folded it up carefully in one of Red's hands and crossed her arms across her chest. He leaped up toward the ceiling, hung onto the light fixture, and stared down at her critically.

"She looks fine," he said. "Now take her away before I get all soppy and smear her makeup."

The Christmas Bush picked up the stiffening body and headed for the lift-shaft as George, floating slowly downward from the ceiling, watched them go.

As the days passed, the huge sail tilted, then tilted back again. George noticed that the maneuver took almost two weeks, and that after the first day the acceleration had subtly changed from its earlier high level. He couldn't blame James for trying to take care of an eighty-eight-year-old man and let the computer get away with trying to fool him. Finally, the ship was hovering over the star. The light from the red globe shot straight up through the bottom science dome and illuminated the ceiling of the control deck. The ship was slowly drifting downward, for the star's gravity was slightly stronger than the push of the light on the sail.

George had been looking through the library for a suitable eulogy for Red. He had skimmed through the Bible and the prayer books for three religions, but hadn't found anything that really suited. Then he remembered a phrase. It was simple and short, and spoke of their last years together in this structure that was a combination of home and prison and tomb. He couldn't recall the exact words, however, and all of his reconstruction attempts seemed to lack the poignancy of the original.

The name of the author also persisted in eluding his searching thoughts, and it took George nearly four hours to track the phrase down with the help of James's library program. He finally found it, then realized why his brain had refused to come up with the source. He found the phrase in the humor section. The author was Mark Twain.

George followed the Christmas Bush in the two-percent gravity as it put the frosty body of the beautiful red-haired woman into the airlock and closed the inner door. The Christmas Bush waited, its colored lights blinking, while George read in a husky voice the words he had carefully copied onto a slip of paper.

"Wheresoever she was, *there* was Eden."

James, overriding the airlock controls, activated the outer door with the lock still pressurized. The rush of air twirled the body out the hatch, one elbow striking the side of the lock as it left. The last thing George saw before his eyes filled again with tears was a distant figure in frosted green, and between them, just outside the airlock door, flashes of red-gold light reflected from a spinning disk of metal. The coin was slowly dropping sunward as the sailcraft hovered above the all-consuming fire below.

Twenty-four hours and fifty-eight minutes later, the energy in a gold coin, a green-clad figure, and a misplaced alligator from Earth became a burst of photons bathing the farthest reaches of the universe with a minute flash of luminance.

It was two years later when George first picked up the beacon signal from the incoming space vehicle, *Succor*, carrying the crew of the follow-on mission. After coasting for a decade it had turned around and started to brake. It was decelerating rapidly as it neared Barnard, but it still had a year of thrusting to go before it stopped. George radioed the news to Maria, who had taken over her mother's place at the Eden communications post. This far from the planet there was a delay of several minutes and conversation was almost impossible, so George did little more than pass the *Succor's* message along.

Maria signed off. George had made it clear that the *Succor* was still almost a year away from Eden, but here on Eden it was time—time for the firstborn to call a meeting.

"What is *this* all about?" asked Reiki as she and Richard met Cinnamon and Nels at the door of the Meeting Hall. "Freeman just said we should come."

"I don't know," said Cinnamon, honestly puzzled. "The kids made it sound serious."

"Instead of wondering," said Nels querulously, "why don't we go in and find out." Using his two canes, Nels pulled himself up the step and into the building. His arthritis had grown progressively worse, and he once again had to use the strength of his arms to move about. Lately the ache had been gripping his fingers, and Nels feared losing all mobility. The pain and anxiety had turned the normally placid man peevish and sullen.

Cinnamon looked after him with anguish-filled eyes. She knew that he was in pain, and there was nothing she could do to help him. The antiinflammatory drugs that had been included in the last drop from *Prometheus* could ease the discomfort, but could do little to stop the progress of the debilitating disease. A cure for arthritis had been developed back on Earth, but James was incapable of manufacturing the cure. She followed him into the Meeting Hall.

Reiki entered on Richard's arm. They stopped just inside the door and looked around in surprise. The hall was packed. Everyone over sixteen was sitting there, silently waiting. *The children have called a meeting?* thought Reiki. Up to now, only the original castaways had called meetings. But then these were no longer children. The first-born were over twenty-one, and many now had children of their own.

Adam waited until the old folks were seated and then he rose to his feet. When the parents first reached Eden they had devised a very simple rule governing debates. Each person was allowed to speak without interruption. No one, however, was obliged to stay and listen. Adam took a deep breath, calming himself. Only by approaching this gently would he be able to keep the parents here and in their seats until he had said all that he needed to; until they had heard it all and understood.

"Maria has heard from George. The Earth ship *Succor* has started deceleration and will be in the Barnard system before the end of the year. They will be able to pick us up before the next high tide."

Nels turned to Cinnamon and his huge arms folded the tiny woman in a hug. Relief surged through his body as hope filled him. He longed to be back in space, free from the constant dragging pull of gravity. For decades he had lived in space moving freely with no legs at all. Once he returned, he would be able to leave the canes behind and go back to doing the work he enjoyed in the fields he had pioneered.

Adam waited for a moment until he regained the attention of Cinnamon and Nels. "Their intentions are to pick us all up, give us a drug that will put us in suspended animation, seal us in capsules, and take us back to Earth. The drug is an improvement on No-Die in that we will not age significantly during the entire fifteen-year return journey."

"Great!" said Nels. "With the great advances they have made in human medicine since we have gone, they can not only cure my arthritis, but even reverse much of the aging we old geezers have suffered. I can't wait to go home!" He turned to Cinnamon. "We'd better start packing!"

"But not all of us want to go," said Adam, dropping his bombshell.

Cinnamon, Nels, Reiki, and Richard looked at each other in shocked bewilderment. Then, as they looked around at the gathered children, it was clear that they were the last ones to hear of this ridiculous idea.

Nels forgot his pain and leapt to his feet. "Don't be absurd!" he bellowed. "This is not our planet! Already we have been interfering with the natural development of the natives. We have introduced them to cooked food, which they may love, but which they can't have without one of us to light the fires. We have stopped the war between the Jollys and the weresharks, which was providing a sort of natural selection. We even saved Seetoo's seedlings from the lava flow."

Shannon leapt to her feet. "Of course we saved the seedlings! They might have still been more plant than person, but they were still sentient beings! We would no sooner abandon them than abandon our own children." Shannon and Everett had just had a daughter, Shirley, and the baby had brought out strong maternal instincts in Shannon. She had even piled up her mass of red curls into a messy bun to keep Shirley's tiny fingers from tangling in the titian locks when the baby nursed.

"That's just my point. Humans are too emotional. We persist in getting involved because it is the 'right' thing to do," insisted Nels. "We lead with our feelings instead of our brains everytime. Think about it now. Think about that lava incident. What would have happened if we had let nature take its course?"

"All those wonderful little trees would have died," said Shannon through clenched teeth. "Weeshee, Taachee, Shaapoo . . . all of whom have grown up to be brave and intelligent stronglimbs would have been burned alive."

"Yes," agreed Nels. "All of Seetoo's seedlings would have died. But if Seetoo had survived, because his leadership had led the tribe into disaster, he would have been retired as chief."

"Seetoo is our friend! He has always helped us! Were we supposed to plot his downfall?"

"Not plot. No! That's interfering, too," said Nels, "but allow. . . . We must *allow* the planet of Eden to mold its occupants. If we had not interfered, the Jollys would have had a new chief and the next crop of younglings would be of a different genetic strain—one less likely to lead the tribe into future danger. The whole future of the Keejook Tribe was altered because we felt sorry for them . . . because we had to interfere . . . because we are only human."

Everett stood and Shannon yielded her place to him. Still a small man, adulthood had stripped away the last traces of softness from his features. Fine bones gave him chiseled features and a wiry compact frame.

"Okay, Nels. You're right. We are human. We are emotional and interfering and adaptable. We are also Edenites. We are as native to this planet as the weresharks and the Jollys and the boobaa trees. This planet has shaped us and we will shape the planet."

"You are an infection. You are ruining this whole island for study! That is why we came here, remember? To study the planet, to study the way it developed, study the lifeforms that developed here. Every Earth crop we plant, every waste product we dump, pollutes the island—taints it. If you really love this planet, you will leave it."

"Even if we did leave—" Everett started. Shannon's

hand reached up to grasp his, but he looked down at her and she held her tongue. "Even if we did leave, there would still be humans in the equation. Earth is sending more follow-on missions to study this whole section of space. There are going to be scientists studying the flouwen, the gummies, the icerugs, and the Jollys. Nothing is going to stop human interference. Call it pollution, call it infection, call it fate, call it salvation. This planet is going to have to deal with humans. The point is, which kind of humans do you want it to have to deal with?"

Nels could no longer stand. The pain shooting up from his joints forced him to sink back into his chair. He seemed smaller, older, than he had only moments before. Eve got to her feet and touched Everett's shoulder. Everett joined his wife, and gave the floor to Eve.

Eve moved gracefully over to her parents and knelt before her father so that she could look into his eyes, her head level with his own. Her long black hair swept the floor behind her and her young face, so like her mother's, smiled at Nels with love.

"You parents, you came from Earth with a mission, and even when it looked like you might fail, you carried on. You survived the crash and went on to study this planet the best you could without the tools that would have allowed you to do the job so much better and faster. But you did more than that. You thrived, you had us, and you raised us to help you with your work, learning about and studying Eden.

"We didn't sign up for this mission, but we were born into it and raised with it. It means as much to us as it did to you. We have all learned from the Teachers. Even on Earth we would be considered to hold advanced degrees. Earth is sending scientists? Eden has scientists right here. Scientists who know this planet, scientists who love this planet . . . who better to finish what you started?"

Nels loved his daughter. He loved all his children and

it was clear that they had made up their minds. But he didn't agree with them, he would *never* agree with them, and he had only one option. He struggled to his feet, trying to leave the room. Cinnamon tried to help him, but Eve slipped her arm around her father's waist while her husband Freeman supported him from the other side. Together they helped Nels back to his home. Cinnamon paused before following them out of the room.

"Whatever the rest of you decide," she announced, looking around the room and seeking out her daughters, "Nels and I will be leaving with the *Succor*. For us the ship is aptly named. If Nels is to survive, if this brilliant man is to continue his work, he needs to get away from the painful pull of this planet. If any of you are staying, I suggest that one or more of you start advanced medical training, because I will have gone with him." She went to join her husband.

Attention focused on Reiki and Richard. Richard sighed and got to his feet. "I think I understand what is *really* going on here. I think that you are all just afraid of going to live on a planet you have never seen."

A chorus of denials rumbled through the room. Adam rose to the challenge. "Afraid? Is that your plan, Richard? To shame us into going back to Earth?"

"I thought I'd give it a shot." Richard smiled. He studied Adam's face as he laughed. Adam had grown tall and strong with his father's Kennedy features and blue eyes, and his mother's dusky skin and dark curls. But Adam had inherited something more from his mother. It showed as a way of standing, a way of holding himself, but it was deeper than that. It was a whole way of thinking, an innate sense of superiority—of command. The son of their highest ranking officer, Major General "Jinjur" Jones, the first of the firstborn, Adam had, since birth, been the leader of everything the children had ever planned. He stood tall and strong at the head of the Meeting Hall and the others looked to him to guide them. If Richard hoped to sway them, he would have to win Adam to his side.

"The move to Earth will be a big one," Richard started. "And it will mean a big change in your lives and the lives of your children. All the technology that you have seen and studied on your Teachers will be available to you. All the things that steal your time away from research and learning—the farming and hunting and latrine digging and cooking— all that will no longer interfere with your lives. You, *and* your children, will have all the advantages of all of humanity's past achievements so that you can add on achievements of your own. Mankind has been growing and expanding all the years we have been away. Things have been happening so quickly, even the six-year communication delay from Earth to here means that our latest updates are already obsolete. By the time you reach Earth, fifteen more years of learning and growth will have improved things even more. Your parents, all of us, knew when we had you that you would be able to return to Earth one day and claim your inheritance, your birthright as members of the human race. All of mankind's achievements are waiting for you to reach out and take them!"

Richard started pacing the floor. "We have worked on this planet for twenty-five years and we have literally only scratched the surface. Why? Because we have had to do all our research without the benefit of mankind's technology. Can you imagine how much more we would have accomplished if we had had even half the tools available on *Prometheus*? Far, far too much of our time and energy has been eaten away just trying to survive, to find nourishing food . . ."

"And to raise your children?" interrupted Adam. "We don't need to go to Earth to benefit from Earth technology. Earth technology is coming to us. The *Succor* will bring us new tools to aid our research here and in the rest of the Barnard system. As for our other chores, the growing of food, the hunting of game, the raising of children, we have no desire to be free of these tasks. Maybe on Earth they are no longer necessary, but some of us not only are good at them but enjoy them, enjoy being good at them."

"So you are afraid," challenged Richard. "Afraid that your skills in farming and cooking will no longer have worth in a place where robots can do them just as well. Too much of your ego has been invested in your skills at low-tech living. You are afraid to test yourself in a new world where more of yourself than you've ever explored will be allowed to stretch and grow. Adam, don't you see? You will be limiting yourself if you stay here . . ."

"Oh," Adam interrupted again, "I'm not staying. I want to go back to Earth. I'm just arguing for the right of some of the others to stay. They feel . . ."

"We feel," said Lavender getting to her feet and looking at her father, "we feel happy here and we see no other way to insure our happiness than by staying here."

"Oh, Lavender . . ." Reiki sighed.

"You called this planet Eden because it seemed like paradise to you," replied Lavender. "It is more than just a comfortable home that we are afraid to leave. It is a planet of fragrant warm oceans where we can swim and fish and play with the flouwen. Can you say the same for Earth? For Mars? For any other planet Earth has colonized? Yes, space is large. Yes, there are new worlds discovered every year. But why go looking for happiness when we have it right here?"

"But the flouwen aren't staying!" Richard protested.

"Are you sure?" asked Lavender. "They want to go back to visit their primary bodies on Eau and tell them what they have learned, but they also want to stay here and explore some more. Fortunately for them, they can do both. They will send buds back to Rocheworld while the rest of them stay here. They told me they will stay as long as there is ammonia enough to keep them healthy, and we are their best source of the chemical. As long as there are humans on Eden, there will be flouwen."

"Okay, so you're happy here, and even though you admit that you might also find happiness on Earth, you don't want to leave the life you know. Right?" Richard looked around. Most of the young people were nodding.

"But for all that we named this planet Eden, it has hardly been a paradise. Of the original ten crew members, six have died! We have faced flood and tsunami, lava and earthquake. There will always be accidents and drought and disease. Now that *Succor* has arrived, you will have some of the advantages that it will bring, but you will still be living out here on the edge of human space, on the frontier, in danger. Can you understand why we want you to move to Earth to bring up your children, our grandchildren, with all the safety and advantages that Earth can offer you?"

Adam took Lavender's place. "*Succor* is only the first of many ships, and 'human space' is growing right toward us. We won't be on the frontier long. Your children and your grandchildren will help give mankind a foothold here, a foundation with which to build on, and we will have an advantage—by being here first."

Richard knew he was losing. Adam was going back to Earth? Earth would never be the same. "Reiki, why aren't you helping me out here?" he whispered down to his wife.

"Because you were beaten before you began, dear," she answered him calmly. Stunned, Richard sat down. Reiki moved to the head of the room and gestured for Adam to yield to her.

"Of course," she started, "anyone who wants to stay should do so. They are quite right to fear that there are things they enjoy about their lives here will be available nowhere else. Earth's oceans are hardly swimmable anymore, and farming, hunting, even child-rearing are no longer valued on high technology worlds. But just because robots can do something doesn't mean that those who enjoy them must give them up. I suspect all of you will find aspects of life on Earth at least as enjoyable as you find life here on Eden. But you are big enough to make that choice for yourselves. We have raised you well, and I am proud of all of you and whatever decision you make; whether it is to go, whether it is to stay, or whether it is to go to Earth later on another ship, I trust that all of you will be making the best decision for yourselves. We all have to make the best decisions for ourselves and . . ." she paused and looked at Richard " . . . unless my husband can come up with some better reasons than he has so far for going back to Earth, I will be staying here."

Lavender hugged her mother as Richard jumped to his feet.

"What?" he cried.

"I am happy here, too, Richard," Reiki said calmly. "I am ninety-nine years old and I have no desire to do any more exploring. When we left Earth, we had no expectation of ever returning. I said good-bye to Earth forever at that time, and I have had no regrets. Eden is my home, and if you will stay here with me, Eden is where I'd like to stay. To me, this place has always been paradise, even during the droughts and the floods, even when I've lost friends. Don't you see? The original ten castaways didn't dwindle into four survivors; we blossomed into twenty-seven!"

Richard threw up his hands. "Alright, alright. I give up. You're going to stay . . . we're going to stay." He paused, then looked around at the group thoughtfully before continuing. "There is one minor problem. Up on *Succor* is a group of people that were sent here by Earth with instructions to 'rescue' us and ship us back to Earth in cold storage. The head of the expedition is a General Winthrop, which means this is Earth military we're dealing with. General Winthrop is not going to want to sit around twelve years waiting for permission from Earth to change his marching orders. He has instructions to bring us back, and if I know the military mind, he is going to do all in his power to follow those instructions. How exactly are we going to convince him and the others to do things our way?"

Reiki smiled. Richard knew that smile. He'd better get used to the idea of staying on Eden.

"That," she said softly, "is all just a matter of diplomacy."

George's first communication sessions with the people on the incoming ship were brief, for a roundtrip message time of one hundred days made it difficult to engage in brilliant discourse. Besides, both of them were busy collecting data. George now had *Prometheus* in a slow spiral about the north pole of Barnard, mapping it from the polar regions outward. As the year passed and the rocket ship of the follow-on expedition drew closer, George visited the communicator more often. When they were a month of travel time away, the roundtrip communication time became about twenty-four hours and he enjoyed a short one-way conversation each morning at breakfast. It was about this time that he was able to use the science telescope to pick up the faint speck of the blazing exhaust from the braking antimatter rocket as it entered the outskirts of the Barnard system. A few weeks later, when the time delay was only an hour, and they were only a few days from zero relative speed, George suddenly realized that he was going to have visitors and the place was a mess. He canceled the science plan, put the Christmas Bush to "cleaning up," and began to prepare for company.

The huge interstellar exploration ship dropped into an orbit about Barnard. A small sleek flitter from the ship flew smoothly in under the giant sail of *Prometheus* on a nearly invisible jet of antimatter-energized hydrogen. George watched them approach from the bottom science dome, then floated over to the airlock console and readied the lock. The first to cycle through was one of the new general-purpose robots. Built along the same lines as a human, they could replace a human at any station. They, of course, did not need spacesuits.

The robot exited the lock. It looked carefully around, then fixed its eyes on the human. George noticed a gold caduceus on the breastplate of the shiny black plasticoid. Probably a medic of some sort. There was a dramatic increase in the light display on the Christmas Bush, and George realized that James and the robot were trading information. The robot drifted toward him, propelled by a precision flick of its foot on the airlock hatchway, and drifted to a halt just an arm's length away. It spoke in a deep baritone voice.

"I have received a report on your state of health from the ship's computer, but I would like to calibrate my medical sensors if I may," it requested.

"Sure," said George. The robot placed its right hand on the side of his neck, its thumb resting on his jugular. As the hand approached, he could see each finger was a complex maze of tiny sensors. He was surprised to feel that the hand was warm, despite its cold-looking appearance.

Nice bedside manner, thought George as he felt an ultrasonic hum pass through his body, while at the same time a tiny section of the robot's chest plate emitted a multicolored display of lights that explored the front portion of his body. After a second, the robot moved both its hands to place them at opposite sides of George's head, then dropped them at its side.

"Thank you," it said, then backed away.

George cycled the lock to let the next visitor in. A spacesuited figure stepped through; the spacesuit had a single silver star on the shoulders and helmet. The plasticoid was very efficient and soon the spacesuit was off the human. Instead of the uniform George had been expecting, the young man was dressed in "civvies": a plain black jumpsuit. Obviously, he was stressing the nonmilitary humanitarian rescue aspect of the mission.

"Hello, there," said George with a twisted smile. "Welcome to Barnard."

The visitor looked at the ancient astronaut. George was dressed in a neatly pressed coverall, but that couldn't hide the angular structure of a computer-controlled motile exoskeleton activating his arm and leg on the left side. The visitor estimated it must have required about one-third of the Christmas Bush. As he looked, his computer implant fed him the background information that had been picked up from James and the recent examination by the medic. George had suffered a massive stroke just eighteen months ago and had only barely survived to greet them. He was getting better, though, and probably had a good many years left.

"Hello, George," said the young man. His method of talking was slow-paced and carefully enunciated, as if he were repeating a well-rehearsed speech. "I bear a proclamation from the President and Congress of the Greater United States, and a personal message from my great-grandfather."

"Your great-grandfather?" asked George in bewilderment.

"I am cursed with the jawbreaking name of Beauregard Darlington Winthrop the Sixth," the young man replied with a faint smile. "But just call me 'Win.' My great-grandfather was Senator Winthrop, formerly General Winthrop, one of your old friends in the Air Force."

George clouded up. Far from being his friend, General Winthrop had been George's personal nemesis when Winthrop had served as Head of the Joint Chiefs of Staff before switching to politics. He had blocked George's promotion to General and had nearly kept him from going on this mission.

"Winthrop?" he said. "What was his message?"

"I don't know," said Win, "it's here in this envelope. Since he was the person in Congress that knew you best, they asked him to write you a personal note to go along with their formal commendation."

He handed over a yellowing ancient envelope with the

embossed imprint of Senator Beauregard Darlington Winthrop III in the upper left corner. George tore the envelope open and pulled out a folded sheet of Senate office stationery. There in fading black ink was a short note dated July 4, 2056.

Your goddamn friends in the goddamn Congress finally finagled you a goddamn star. May you be dead and frozen in Hell before it gets to you!

There was no signature.

George smiled quietly, folded the letter carefully, his motile-assisted left arm acting in near-perfect coordination with his good right one, and put the letter into his breast pocket. There was no need for this puppy-dog of a young man to know the contents of the message.

"What did it say?" asked Win, eager to know the family secret. As a child he had become fascinated with the time-spanning history of the piece of paper, and he had worked until he was chosen for the follow-on mission to Barnard so he could deliver it personally.

"He mentioned a star," said George.

"Oh, yes!" said Win. He reached into another pocket and pulled out a small box.

"In recognition of your services to the country," he parroted, "the President and Congress of the Greater United States hereby promotes you to the rank of Brigadier General of the Air Force." He handed him the box and George opened it. He took out one of the silver stars inside, snapped the box shut and looked at it contemplatively.

He hobbled over to one of the viewing ports in the side of the command deck and stared out at the dull red ball off to one side. He turned to face the two robots and the human, and said, "James, send the Christmas Bush over here next to me."

The computer obeyed and soon the scraggly looking motile was floating in front of him. He reached up and stuck the shining silver star into the branches at the apex of the Christmas Bush, where the cilia automatically gripped it. George leaned back against the viewport and looked at the greenly glowing Christmas Bush, its colored lights blinking on and off in its never-ending communication with the main computer. The five-pointed silver star stuck in the top branches glittered brightly as it reflected the reddish rays streaming in the viewport window from Barnard.

"I think you're the one that deserves a General's star, James, so why don't you keep this one?" Stiffly, he turned his back on the group and looked out the window at the dull red globe that was six lightyears away from the home to which he had thought he would never return.

"I already have my star."

SOLARIANS

"Cal'n Ed'n, dju'earme? Thiz Gen'l Beau'gard Dar'ton Wint'up t'Sixth, uvth' *Succor*, cal'n crash s'viv'rs 'n Zuni. Djurea'me?"

Maria sat back on her heels, stunned. The sounds coming from the communicator resembled human speech, but were so slurred together as to be almost indistinguishable as separate words. She looked about at the people gathered around the communicator that occupied one end of her ridgetop dwelling. Reiki nodded to her to respond, so she pressed the "talk" button and spoke.

When her reply was broadcast aboard *Succor*, Win and the others looked at each other in puzzlement. The slow rhythm of Maria's reply was like a dreamy song in their ears.

"Hellooow, theah. This is Maria, talking to you. We are all waiting heah, and wanting to speak with you directly, but Ah'm ver-ry sorry to have to tell you, that there is a sur-prising amount of garble in your transmission channel, and we cannot understand your message."

Win blinked. Did the word "s'prisin'" really have two "r's" in it?

He spoke again, slowing down and trying to enunciate carefully. "Le'me speak to Comoff of landin' party, mejitly." There was a long pause. On Eden, the humans exchanged puzzled looks.

"Perhaps our speech patterns have slowed down
312

somewhat," said Reiki. "Because of our more relaxed living style, or altered, because of our new circumstances. And, if that was English he was speaking, it certainly is different!" Moving to the radio, Reiki tried to recall the terms and expressions they had all used on *Prometheus*. "This is Ranking Officer of the Landing Party, Reiki LeRoux. We can comprehend your words when you speak them clearly, therefore the transmission channel is not the problem. Can you understand me?"

Win, impatient with the delay, had been about to bark a brusque order to his comm robot, but Reiki's cool tone made him pause. With an effort, he slowed his speech even more. "Ma'am, we are entrin' into orbit about Zuni. We require information on safe landin' sites. Our mission to rescue you will go much smoother if you will respond promptly to my commands."

Unconsciously, every human gathered around the little radio stiffened. Reiki replied with chilly calm.

"Are you requesting permission to land?"

This brief message seemed to please the people aboard the orbiting spacecraft.

"Yes! Course w'are, tha'swhy we've come. Wha' djuthinkwe wanted?"

This was rattled off almost too fast for the listening Edenites. Again there was a pause. This time, Reiki used carefully enunciated proper Solarian English phrases, but spoke them at the leisurely pace of Eden.

"We shall consider your requirements, most carefully, and shall let you know in good time of the most suitable landing site for your vehicle. We have managed to maintain ourselves quite satisfactorily for some time, and it is imperative that we not be exposed to bacteria, viruses, or fungi which you may have unwittingly brought with you. Therefore, you must understand the necessity of strict quarantine, including the wearing at all times, on your part, of environmental isolation suits which will not permit contamination of our health. If that is understood, we shall proceed to survey possible landing sites for you. I suggest that we resume radio communication at eighteen hundred, Zuni time, which will give us sufficient time to prepare for your arrival. Do not call us. We will call you."

The Solarians had no difficulty understanding the words, slow and flowing though they were, but they were somewhat puzzled by the tone.

"Not the welcome I expected, dju?" remarked Win to Orson.

"Chilly . . . on all fronts," agreed Orson. "Wha's this nonsense about wearing isosuits? After all this time in space we're 'clean-room clean,' are'nwe?"

"D'know," said Laura grudgingly, "they've a point. I had the Yugocold a week ago, 'member? And, their immunity's prolly way down, wha'wi sufferin' years of malnutrition and stress."

"Ovr'n'out," barked Win brusquely. He moved to terminate the transmission, but Reiki's voice stopped him.

"I beg your pardon? That last phrase. Did that signify a yes or no, or something different entirely?"

Win shook his head.

"It signified som'thn difrn't . . . that is . . . *diff-er-ent*. We unnastand, and will comp . . . comply." He clicked off the channel and swore irritably. "Damnation, this is going to take some work."

Down below, the Edenites looked thoughtfully at each other, and Cinnamon chuckled.

"You said 'eighteen hundred, Zuni Time,' Reiki! Just when is that?"

Reiki grinned back at her.

"Oh, sometime after dinner, more or less! But we have things to talk about before that. Now, what do you think . . ."

That evening, after a long dinner and discussion, they all went to Maria's hut and contacted the rescue ship through the communicator. In the interval, the ship's computer had used its implant connection to Win's brain to run through some language training lessons in old English vocabulary and pronunciation. After Maria opened up the channel, Win spoke.

"Rescue is finally here, survivors. We'd like to meet with you immediately to assess the general situation, then get you out of there and back to civilization. Have you identified a good landin' site? We'll want level ground so that our robogangs can unload our equipment easily."

The Edenites smiled and listened with pleasure to Reiki's response. The slow lilt of Eden's speech did not disguise the firmness of her directions.

"We shall all be most happy to welcome you to our home, and we all will do our best to make you comfortable for the duration of your stay. I must remind you that it's imperative for our safety, as you will be the first to acknowledge, that you remain in your environmental isolation suits at all times. I'm sure we are most interested in observing the wonderful new materials of which they are constructed! Of course, your robots must be sterilized also. As for landing, the best procedure will be for you to bring your rocket down over the enclosed bay on the island we call Crater Lagoon—you will readily observe it upon your maps. The exhaust flames emitted during your deceleration phase will be less likely to cause forest fires from there. After bringing the lander to a hover some meters above the surface of the water, you can translate across the water and land among the dunes. We will be waiting, a safe distance away, to greet you in person."

"Oh, hell," muttered Win privately to Orson. "Sterilizin' the robots will take a while. That's a beefin' nuisance. But, for now, anyway, we gotta do it their way, at least till we actually meet 'em."

"Sterilizin'," reminded Orson. "That does make some sense. They already warned us about that, and we agreed."

* * *

The various representatives of the United Species of Eden were gathered on the shores of Crater Lagoon to await the arrival of the Solarians. The incoming aerospace rocketplane announced itself with a double-crack boom as it entered the upper atmosphere of Eden. Having heard the noise before at the time of the aeroshell drops from *Prometheus* bringing supplies to the humans, it didn't bother the waiting Jollys and flouwen, but the weresharks basking in the shallow waters of the lagoon were perturbed by the noise and all their eyefish scurried into their sockets and closed their eyes in fright.

Cinnamon, having discussed with Laura the safety perimeter needed for the landing of the small rocketplane, had the multicultured collection of Edenites placed about a half-kilometer down the beach from where the rocketplane would touch down. The winged vehicle flew in from the west on its stubby wings, and with bluish-purple jet bursts flickering from its wings, sides, and tail, it assumed a nose-up attitude and lowered itself down, landing tail first on an almost invisible blue-purple flame.

"The exhaust is throwing up lots of sand, but no smoke," remarked Richard. "Wonder what it uses for fuel?" As he was speaking, a strong wind arose from the direction of the rocketplane and his voice shifted upward in register between sentences. He turned in surprise to Cinnamon when he heard the way he now talked.

"Helium!" he exclaimed, continuing in his weird high-pitched voice. "I remember it from sucking balloons as a kid."

"According to Laura," said Cinnamon, also speaking strangely, "it's liquid polynitrometahelium—a polymer made of excited helium molecules stabilized with nitrogen. It's a simple monopropellant that outperforms lox-hydrogen by six times, while its exhaust fumes are about as nontoxic as you can get—pure helium, with a little bit of nitrogen."

A door opened at the base of the rocketplane and a

gang of robotic androids exited down a ramp to inspect the five landing pads. After assuring themselves that all was safe, they turned to the task of escorting the three humans down the short ramp to the sandy beach. The humans then started their long walk around the lagoon to where the Eden contingent was waiting. As the Solarians approached the mixed group of Edenites, the two groups got a chance to inspect each other.

"That Win fellow looks like Buck Rogers to me, straight from the twenty-fifth century," giggled Maria, patting her curls. "He's cute."

"And that Laura looks like she's right off the cover of an ancient science fiction pulp magazine," remarked Richard. Laura was dressed in the short skirt, bare midriff fashion of the climate-controlled enclosed cities of Luna. Her skin, rarely exposed to the damaging light of the Sun, was as soft and smooth as a baby's, and her long willowy frame left plenty of it visible between the colorful wisps of her costume. She, like the other two humans, was wearing a helmet and a backpack air exchanger, while their bodies were covered from neck to toe by a monolayer isolation film. But, while the men had chosen brightly colored film, hers was transparent.

The tall amazon strode closer. It was now obvious that when she arrived, her head would tower high over Richard's nearly two-meter height.

"What do you think of her now?" whispered Reiki from beside Richard's elbow.

"Impressive!" he gulped.

"O'm'gahd! They're *all* aliens!" chatlinked Orson through his implant to the others. "Even the *humans* are alien."

Win understood immediately. Instead of a bedraggled band of desperate stranded astronauts in tattered remnants of spacesuits, they were instead confronted by a quiet group of calm, but odd-looking people; well-fed, healthy, immaculately clean, and dressed in exotic but lovely brightly colored costumes that looked like those on the android dancers at Polynesia-Land. But they were too short and compact, and their arms and legs bulged strangely with muscle. With all the physical labor in the Solar system done by robots, only those of the lowest castes ever developed more muscle than was needed for optimum health. The skin of these people seemed too thick, and all of them, even the blonds, had the same golden brown skin. Probably there had been more inbreeding than they wanted to admit. But the oddest thing was the elders. Win had been amazed at how little time had affected George Gudunov up on *Prometheus*. He looked remarkably young. Here in the gravity well of the planet, however, the skin of the four original survivors hung in loose folds under their eyes and necks and gathered into deep wrinkles as they smiled at the new arrivals. Win had to swallow his revulsion and look away. Thankfully some of the younger females were really very attractive, although in an alien sort of way. One girl was smiling at him boldly and patting her thick black curls into place. The last time Win had seen fat-laden curves like that was in a holoporn.

The humans were waiting on the shoreline of the lagoon, with the waves occasionally washing up around their bare feet, while some of the younger ones in the deeper portions of the water seemed to be "sitting" in the water. Standing further up on the beach, well out of reach of the waves, were a half-dozen tall trees, about four meters tall, with a crown of blue-green fronds and six massive curved roots that looked like brown elephant trunks. From nests in the fronds of the trees there came owl-like birds with a single large eye that flew around the party of Solarians and their escort of robots and then flew back again.

Further up on the beach was a strange metallic-looking object sticking up out of the sand. It looked like a cross between a totem pole and the tail of a rocket. It had four fins, and below each fin was a circular grid that looked like a ventilation grating or a loudspeaker grill. The surface of the almost metallic-looking structure had the patina of age, and Win wondered whether the "totem" was a human artifact left over from the crash, or something the alien trees had erected on this shore for religious purposes.

In the shallow water along the shoreline, the Solarians could now see large blobs of colored jelly, each blob a distinctive color—red, purple, milky, pink, and blue. The younger human children were sitting on these blobs. Beside each child a small colored pseudopod rose out of the colored body. On the ends of the pseudopod there was a clear lens, which also looked like it was made of jelly.

Out in the deeper water there rose four large dorsal fins, each riding on the top of a massive gray-furred shark-like body, the top of which was occasionally revealed as the wave troughs passed over them. A multitude of eyes gazed in seeming malevolence from the massive shark-like heads. What made the gazes even more evil-looking was that some of the monsters seemed to have had their eyes gouged out, for all that was left was an empty socket!

As prepared as the Solarians were by their briefings on the physiology of the aliens, Win and Orson were still unnerved by the strangeness of the alien eyes. To Laura, however, the massive shapes of the Jollys, the lethal-looking ranks of weresharks, and the strange colors of the flouwen in the shallows seemed to blend harmoniously with the relaxed but watchful humans. The human children, shining with health and youth, stared back at the Solarians with eager, unafraid curiosity.

The Edenites, mindful of the audience they would have, had planned that this first meeting would be controlled as far as possible by themselves. It would be as formal as barefoot Reiki could make it, and as amicable as the Solarians would permit.

Reiki took three steps forward, bowed deeply, and began to speak—loudly and clearly—fervently hoping the man before her would not interrupt. Fortunately, he found her words too surprising to do so.

"As duly elected President of the United Species of Eden, I welcome you to Eden! All here give you welcome! I am honored to speak for our friends, the Jollys, whom you see on my right. I am honored to speak for our friends the flouwen, whose colors and eyes are visible in the water beside you. And I am honored to also speak for our friends the weresharks, resting in the deeper waters of the lagoon. We shall all become known to each other more fully as your visit progresses." She took a deep breath and changed her tone slightly. "First, however, it is my duty to ask you for your passports. Please present them at this time to our customs officer to be stamped."

Dirk, wearing an official-looking sash over his bare chest, stepped forward, holding out one hand for the passports, while the other hand held an inked stamp carved from a piece of wood.

"What? Passports! Wha'in Orion are you . . ." Win was stunned, but with reflexive formality he adjusted to this strange situation and responded, carefully slowing his own speech to do so, while at the same time trying to regain control of the situation.

"I beg your pardon, ma'am. Our government—which is also your government, I may remind you—did not provide us with passports as such. But I assure you—"

Reiki had not interrupted anyone for years, but she did so now, firmly.

"That was remiss of your government, indeed. But we are quite willing to grant you temporary visas for the duration of your stay. Your possessions and equipment—in point of fact, everything which you have brought with you both today and which you may see fit to bring here during your visit, including your robots—are subject to customs regulations. Our regulations require that they must be taken with you on your departure. There can be no exceptions to this, unless mutually agreeable between all parties. All items will, of course, be tagged for identification, and you understand that you must not trade or sell them while you are in residence."

There was a silence. Then Win said slowly, "If I understand you, ma'am . . . President?"

Sweetly Cinnamon intervened. "That is correct. Reiki is the duly-elected President of Eden. She is our first, we trust, of many. And now you shall have the privilege of being the first Solarians to hear our cherished Declaration of Independence!"

She motioned to Richard, who stepped forward, gave a low bow, and rose again to his full height, unrolled a long scroll, and proceeded to read it in loud and firm tones.

"When in the course of events, it becomes necessary for the peoples of a planet to dissolve the political bands which have connected them with another planet, and to assume the separate and equal station to which they are entitled, a decent respect to the opinions of all concerned requires that they should declare the causes which impel them to the separation. We hold these truths to be self-evident, that all intelligent species are created equal . . ."

" . . . and for the support of this Declaration, we, the United Species of Eden, mutually pledge to each other our lives, our possessions, and our honor."

Richard concluded these ringing words with another deep and formal bow, which struck the astounded Solarians as even more alien than the startling document they had just heard. The precious piece of barkcloth on which they had all worked so carefully bore strange signatures and marks, and was displayed proudly to the gaze of the Solarians before being rolled tenderly into a scroll and carried away by Eve.

"This is ridiculously unnecessary, ma'am," said Win. "No one from Sol is proposing to tax your tea. What was the purpose of this absurd exercise?"

"It was simply the first step in the logical, legal development of this world for the benefit of all its citizens. In addition to the Declaration of Independence, which you have just heard, the United Species of Eden also has a Constitution, witnessed and agreed upon by representatives of all known intelligent lifeforms on the planet. It's a very simple document, flexible and general enough to provide mutual cooperation for us here and protection for all of its citizens, no matter what species they may be. More important for *you* to know, however, is that you four are *not* citizens here."

Win had listened to enough of this farce. He lost his temper and exploded. "I may not be a citizen of this goddamn planet, but all of you goddamn humans are still citizens of Earth, and are still bound by Earth laws and Solar Worlds laws—despite what is written in that goddamn ridiculous Declaration of Independence." Reiki tried to object, but Win just bellowed louder. "I was sent here to rescue you and take you back to Earth, and I'm going to do just that . . . whether you like it or not!"

"I'm not going!" exploded Mirth.

Dirk lay a restraining hand on his daughter's shoulder, but the seven-year-old shrugged it away and stepped forward boldly. With arms akimbo she looked up undaunted into Win's face as he towered over her.

"You can't make me!"

Win exploded. "I have not come halfway across the goddamn galaxy on a mission for the Solar Worlds Congress just to be told by a spoiled child that I will not be allowed to carry out my mission!" he bellowed. "I have my orders and I mean to carry them out!"

"You have not come halfway across the galaxy, you have come six lightyears, just as we have," said Cinnamon. Her gray hair was starting to come loose from its braid and fly in wisps around her brown wrinkled face. Win's upper lip curled in disgust at the ugly creature. "We signed on for a mission that would last our lifetimes, and as long as one of us has a breath left in us, it is our mission that is going to be carried out."

"You people asked for this rescue," said Orson, trying to defuse the situation. "All that we're doing is answering your request."

"And we appreciate the rescue," said Reiki to Orson. "And there are those among us who do want to go back. But things have changed since we first called for help— here, and on Earth. We have stumbled onto a planet that is full of amazing discoveries. It has given us a home, for ourselves and for our children. We owe it our allegiance and we intend to stay and see that it is properly respected and nurtured, just as it has nurtured us these last twenty-five years."

"These last twenty-five years, while you have been playing in the surf and making babies," Win sneered, "the Solar Worlds Congress has been spending trillions of credits and millions of personyears on a rescue mission! This rescue mission! We are not the goddamn bad guys! We come in *peace*, goddamnit! We don't intend to hurt your pla— *this* planet, or these Bug-Eyed Monsters, but you humans are going to get into our ship and you are coming back to the Solar system and that's all there is to it!"

"We have told you that this planet had declared its independence!" said Reiki, almost starting to lose her temper. "These species have never been under the authority of the Solar Worlds Congress and we humans here have just seceded!" She saw no need to explain now that in fact many of them had decided to retain their Earth citizenship. For the moment it was best that they appear united. "You have no authority in our nation, General Winthrop, and unless you respect the wishes of our citizens, I'm afraid I'm just going to have to declare you persona non grata."

It took a moment for Win's computer link-up with the lander to translate Reiki's last remark and it reminded him that if threats were being made, he could make a few of his own.

"Madam President. You might consider yourself the representative of the United Idiots of Eden, but with a twelve-year comm lag between here and Sol, I, as the highest ranking officer, represent the Solar Worlds authorities and have their full powers invested in me. It is up to me just how our state will deal with your defection." He touched his wrist-communicator and a cargo door slid open on the distant landing rocket. Out came a large swarm of androids, who started trotting across the sand toward them in military formation. "You have twenty-four hours to pack. These androids will insure that you are back here in time for the liftoff."

"Dad!" said Freeman, looking up at Richard. "Can he do that?"

"I'm afraid so, son," said Richard, looking at the phalanx of metal bodies trotting across the sand, each larger and infinitely stronger than he was—the strongest human on Eden.

Just then, a loud click, followed by a hissing sound, came from the "totem pole" on the hill. Win turned to look at it in surprise. The hissing grew louder.

"General Winthrop!!!" roared the totem pole in obvious anger. The last time Winthrop had heard that tone of voice was when he had broken a window at the family mansion with a baseball. For a second he felt ten again. Win then realized that the voice coming from the "totem pole" was that of Gudunov. *General* Gudunov, Win suddenly recalled.

"Yessir!" Win called back. He closed his eyes, pretty sure what he would hear next.

"What is the date of your promotion, General Winthrop?"

"April second, 2080," replied Win. "Sir," he added.

"Mine, as you well know, is the fourth of July 2056," said George. "I believe that I outrank you by nearly twenty-five years."

"Yessir."

"I therefore command that instead of invading this fledgling nation and returning these people back to Earth by force, that the exploration mission they are on be allowed to continue. They volunteered to come here, at great cost and risk to themselves, and they should be allowed to continue to carry on their assigned task—to explore the Barnard star system, its planets, and its lifeforms. Their task is not done—in fact, it will not be completed in their lifetimes. While you are in this system and under my command, you are instructed to assist them and any of Eden's citizens in any way that you can, including supplying transportation between planets. You still have an obligation to return to Sol. When you go, you will take those who wish to return with you."

"Yessir," replied Win. Inside, he was furious at the goddamn Gudunov. Yet he didn't dare rebel. He would soon be back in Sol at the head of a successful rescue mission, and Brigadier General in the Space Force was only the first step in what he knew could be an illustrious career that would reflect proudly on the Winthrop name. He would cooperate with the goddamn Gudunov, but he goddamn didn't have to like it, and one of these days Win would be glad to carry out grandpapa's wish and spit on that goddamn Gudunov's goddamn grave.

"Carry on, General Winthrop," said the totem pole, and with a loud click, it became silent.

Reiki stepped forward again. "General Winthrop," she said, smiling sweetly, "it would really be of great assistance to our exploration objectives if you could somehow arrange for transport between the various moons of Gargantua and to Rocheworld when it comes near us each season."

"Tha'll be easy," interjected Orson. "Gravity is low enough on these moons so that a tether transport system will be easy to set up. I'll have my robogangs get to work on it. . . ."

Adam strolled casually up to Laura and looked her up and down. Although she was considerably taller than he, she found herself standing straighter to widen the gap.

He smiled, his teeth flashing whitely in his dark face, blue eyes twinkling up at her.

"Bug-Eyed Monsters?" he asked.

"Standard slang for all alien beings," explained Laura. "He wasn't trying to be insulting."

"Oh . . . and I guess he didn't really threaten us with his robots either," said Adam.

Laura colored briefly. She hated being forced to defend the overbearing Win.

"Come on," Adam continued, "I'll show you around." He slipped an arm around her waist, and Laura could feel the heat of his lumpy arm muscles though the plastic.

Those oversized muscles would come in handy on this world, thought Laura. Besides, they were oddly attractive.

As if reading her thoughts, he added, "We'll find a place where you can get out of that isosuit . . . someplace where Reiki won't catch us."

LEAVING

Two years later, Reiki was standing on the beach at one end of Crater Lagoon, watching the panorama of the now busy heavens. Standing around her were many from the settlement who had come with her to the beach, while in the waters offshore floated the flouwen. Floating among the flouwen was a canoe with Everett and Freeman at the paddles. Barnard was about to set, and in the clear evening twilight, all the new structures that had blossomed in space now were visible in the darkening skies. It was the time of the season when Rocheworld loomed large beyond Zouave on its once every three-orbit visit to the outskirts of the Gargantuan moon system. In the distant eastern sky, opposite the sinking Barnard, both Rocheworld and Zouave loomed bright in the sky with their glittering new attendants. The sphere of Zouave now sported a number of disk-shaped "wings": large thin-film mirrors levitated in space all around it. The light from Barnard reflected off the mirrors and produced warming spots of reddish light on the surface of the cold planet, awakening its inner volatiles in order to raise the dead planet from its ecological grave. In addition, the globe of Zouave, as well as both lobes of Rocheworld, now sported thin white "antennae" oriented at various angles above their surfaces. As Reiki patiently waited and watched, one of the lines above Zouave slowly touched down at the southern pole of the planetoid and lifted slowly off again. Similar lines were also visiting various spots on the rapidly rotating double-lobed planet of Rocheworld.

Reiki looked back toward the fading red glow in the west, where, rising up from where Barnard had set, there grew a spear of light that had a "red-white" luster in contrast to the deep red sky glow. The spear grew longer and longer, and as it approached the zenith, the tip seemed to slow as it tilted down toward where she was standing. This was the eastward-traveling rotating space tether, the "rotovator," coming down in one of its periodic visits to this part of Eden.

Just offshore from the beach there was the noise of splashing water. Rising up out of the waves was a large metallic platform, coming up from its normal stowed position on the top of a submerged seamount—hidden underwater so its presence wouldn't spoil the view from the beach. The warm ocean waters of Eden dripped rapidly off its water-repellant and barnacle-proof shell-like cover, which opened like a flower to reveal a landing pad. In one corner of the landing pad was a futuristic-looking control building, while near the center sat an object as big as a bus, with heavy glass portholes in the front and back and along the sides. From the four corners of its base there projected four squat landing skids, while from its top corners there extended four heavy grappling rings. This was one of the many space capsules that the rotovator and its similar counterparts moved from place to place in the Barnard system.

Normally, when there was no need for their services, the rotovators just touched their tips down high in the upper atmosphere as they passed over. This time, however, they had a cargo to be delivered. Long before the actual tip end of the rotovator had arrived at its lowest point, the space capsule at the end of the tether had been released on the end of its own failsafe multistrand tether made of strong, heat-resistant polymer fiber. By using a combination of rocket jets to speed up, and braking on the tether to slow down, the space capsule reached the upper atmosphere long before the tip of the cable, and slowed down enough to penetrate the air at speeds and acceleration levels well within the safety margins for both the capsule and the tether material.

As the rotovator structure itself continued its ponderous rotation overhead, it seemed to shrink in length as it started to point down directly at the observers standing near the landing point. They first heard the sonic booms of the capsule entering the skies above them, then shortly afterward they could see the space capsule itself, brightly lit not only in the light from the setting sun but also from the glare of its polynitrometahelium jets. The observers could now see that the capsule was hanging from a complex grappling mechanism that contained the jets and the large reels that released or pulled in tether as needed during the landing maneuvers. The capsule and its grappling mechanism initially seemed to be dropping downward at a terrifyingly dangerous speed, but with a combination of jets and tether reel control, the robots running the system brought the incoming capsule smoothly down to a halt next to the outgoing capsule that was waiting there. The grapple mechanism hovered, supporting itself by pulling in tether as fast as it came down from above, then carefully released the incoming capsule while at the same time picking up the outgoing capsule so that the load on the end of the tether never changed. The grapple mechanism, with its new load, then took off again, its reels pulling in cable ever faster as it accelerated upward toward the top of the atmosphere, where the momentum of the gigantic rotovator would take over to lift the capsule up from the planet, until it was high overhead. Then, at just the right time, it would sling it at high speed to an intermediate "momentum-bank" rotovator in orbit elsewhere in the Barnard-Gargantua system, which would pass it on to a rotovator around one of the other planetoids in the system.

Even as the capsule landed, Freeman and Everett were paddling in the canoe toward the landing pad to pick up their arriving guest. The Edenites had allowed the Solarians to set up high-technology landing pads at selected points around Eden for storage and servicing of the rotovator capsules and the other pieces of high-tech equipment, such as spacesuits, that the humans and flouwen required for operating in space or on planetoids with dangerous atmospheres. They wanted to keep Eden the way it was as much as possible, however, so instead of allowing helicopters and motorboats, even low-noise ones, they insisted on providing their own transportation. As a result, their guest, who had arrived in a supersonic metal space capsule, would be slowly paddled ashore in a wooden dugout canoe.

As Reiki and the other humans watched the floodlight-illuminated platform, they could see a human figure getting out of the capsule door while brushing off the attentions of one of the ever-present androids. At the other end of the space capsule, another android was screwing off what looked like the cover cap to a fire hose connection. As the cover came off, there was a rush of water, which started out clear and quickly turned a bright vermillion color.

"LET'S SURF!!!" came the shout across the waves as the red puddle flowed to the edge of the landing pad and slipped into the water. The red blob was followed by a white one and a purple one.

"Little Red's back," remarked Richard with a smile.

"I hear me!" said the red blob waiting in the shallows off the beach. "I go see me!"

"Hmmm . . ." Richard pondered. "Can't call the new bud of Loud Red, Little Red, 'cause Little Red's still here. Or at least the part of him that didn't go back to Roche-world to tell his primary self what he had learned on his exploration trips with us. Newer Red?"

"I don't think it really matters, dear," said Reiki. "They don't come when called anyway. Besides, from what we have observed before, they don't really like being separated into pieces—lowers their intellect level—so I suspect they are going to soon be joined into one entity, and we will be back to one Little Red, anyway."

Just then the red blob returned—much larger than it had been before. It seemed to be talking to itself.

"Stuck in capsule for days! Go surfing!"

"Just been surfing! Tell me about Water!"

"Surf first!"

Another flouwen voice interrupted the argument.

"Laugh . . ." rasped Little Purple, who had recombined with his newly arrived portion with little problem.

There was a long pause as both humans and flouwen tried to understand why Little Purple had made the comment. Then the red flouwen understood. With a whoop, the back of its body pushed through the center and out the other side, turning the red blob into a whirling red smoke ring, shrieking with laughter at the ridiculousness of its recent argument with itself. Soon the cells in Little Red had been thoroughly intermixed and were all sharing the memories of not only all that had happened on Eau since the original Little Red had left with the humans, but also the memories of a recent long session of surfing. Now completely satisfied, Little Red became calm and went out with the rest of the reconstituted flouwen to escort the incoming canoe to the shore with its important visitor from space. The visitor nimbly jumped off the bow of the canoe and onto the shore without getting his feet wet.

"Is that really you, George?" Reiki asked, not quite sure in the dimmer moonlight from the half-phase Gargantua that had replaced the stronger light from Barnard. The last time she had seen a picture of George, he was wearing a half-body Christmas Branch brace as an aid.

"Sure is!" said George, giving her a hug with one hand while shaking Richard's hand with the other. "And it's great seeing all of my old friends again." He looked around at the tall, lanky youngsters. "And my new friends, too," he added. "Where's Cinnamon and Nels?"

"They're back in the settlement preparing a welcome feast," said Reiki. "It's a bit of a walk. Because of your stroke, and this being your first time in planetary gravity, I had the youngsters bring a litter chair to carry you."

"No need," said George cheerily as he started up the beach with an active stride. "Lead the way, and on the way I can tell you more about what the Solarians are doing out there."

As they made their way from the beach and through the moonlit forest paths, the trails became steeper, and soon Reiki and Richard found themselves trailing George, who had no trouble keeping up with the youngsters.

"You are in good shape," puffed Richard as he caught up with George at a level portion of the trail. "How do you do it? You're much older than Reiki and I."

"The Solarian robodocs fixed me all up," said George. "You two ought to consider visiting them before the big ship leaves for Sol. They have these little nanomachines that go inside you and correct all those little things that have gone wrong. They can't rejuvenate your cells—they still are designed to die. Seems it's good for the survival of the species to get the old versions of the species out of the way, so the younger versions have enough food and room to try out their new gene-recombination models. They also can't restore memory loss due to brain cells dying, but they can at least make you feel decent, until one day every part of you collapses at the same time— like the proverbial one-horse shay.

"Besides, this is only twenty-eight percent gravity. I've spent the last month at thirty-four percent, out on Zapotec visiting Laura and Adam as they start Laura's robogang on terraforming the planet for the first wave of Solarian colonists. A few primitive lifeforms were found out there, surviving in the sand, but it was quickly established that all of them had originated elsewhere in the system and had ridden there on debris tossed up by large meteor strikes on the other moons and planets. They even found some primitive versions of flouwen cells from Rocheworld. The primitive Rocheans and the other lifeforms failed in their attempt to colonize Zapotec, but the Solarians now think they can do it by applying brain instead of brawn."

"But the planet is as dry as a bone," protested Richard as he unfastened George from the sling seat that had carried him across Lava Canyon on the cable crossing.

"Lots of frozen water and other volatiles in the permafrost," answered George. "That's why they constructed those large space mirrors to raise the temperatures at the poles. Besides, there's another barren planet with an excess of water and organic-type hydrocarbons—Zouave. It's covered miles deep with ice and has enough organics in its atmosphere to provide plenty for fertilizing the soil of Zapotec, while still leaving more than enough to feed the plant life on Eden for hundreds of millions of years. The Solarian robots are going to strip most of the organics out of Zouave's atmosphere and store them as frozen balls in a safe holding orbit until they are ready to be delivered to either Zapotec or Eden as needed. Then, they will mine away the ice where it is shallowest until they get down to dirt solid enough for the colonists to start building on. The ice removed will go to Zapotec, and the rest will turn into oceans as the planet heats up from the space mirrors."

"Speaking of Zouave," said Reiki, "how is my darling Lavender doing as Orson's apprentice?"

"She's having a great time, ordering around massive gangs of robots through her control screen. Orson mostly lets her do the work and just sits watching over her shoulder and giving her advice once in a while. Little Purple was disappointed with the trip, though. He had gone along to Zouave with Lavender and Orson in case they found liquid water under the ice. They were going to drill holes until they found water, then pour Little Purple down the hole to see if there were any lifeforms there before they started terraforming. Not only did they not find any indigenous lifeforms, either under the ice or on the surface, they didn't even find water. It was solid ice all the way down to bedrock—just like drilling in the center of the main glacier covering Greenland. Little Purple was so annoyed he left. In fact, he was in the habitat tank on the water side of the capsule that I landed in. He joined us at the Rocheworld-Zapotec transfer rotovator station and rejoined the part of himself that was returning from Rocheworld."

"I guess I really ought to take Mirth to see all those things before we go back to Earth," said Dirk quietly.

"You really should," said George. "There's all kinds of things to see out there. Those robots can make a silk purse out of a sunbeam. They have a robot replication factory and a tether manufacturing plant set up on Zen, between here and Zapotec, and they have a space mirror fabrication facility on and around Zeus. At twenty-four kilometers across, Zeus provides plenty of raw materials for the space mirrors, while its gravity is low enough not to cause problems with fabricating the large flimsy structures. Your daughter will be amazed to see a mirror as wide as an ocean and thinner than an oil film. We could have used that technology when we were building *Prometheus*."

"I notice that the Solarians are building a large sail near *Prometheus*," said Reiki. "What is that for?"

"It's a retromirror," said George. "Remember when we came to a halt at the Barnard system? We had two sails, then. The circular one that *Prometheus* has now, plus an outer ring sail that was ten times larger in area and slightly curved. Before we arrived, we separated the sails and let the ring sail go ahead, while turning the inner sail carrying our habitat around so that it faced the ring sail. The laser beam from the solar system then hit the ring sail, and was reflected off from it and focused down on the smaller sail carrying the habitat. There was now ten times as much reflected light pushing on the sail to slow it down as there was coming from the solar system trying to speed it up, so after a year we came to a halt in the Barnard system. Unfortunately, that same laser light pushed the ring sail mirror out of the Barnard system, so we couldn't use it again. The Solarians are building *Prometheus* a replacement mirror. There is a slug of laser light on its way from the solar system. According to the plans, it was supposed to be started on its way about five years ago. When it arrives next year, it will bounce off the big mirror the Solarians are making and be reflected onto *Prometheus*'s sail, pushing it back to the solar system, where fifty or so years from now, it will be brought to a halt with one last burst of laser power. It will then be the main exhibit in the Solarian Space Museum at L2."

"I guess they'll give the bodies of the crew in the deep freeze on *Prometheus* a burial then," remarked Reiki somberly.

"That's too long and risky," said George, also in a somber tone. "I'll be taking them back with me on *Succor*." He paused. "It's the main reason I'm going back instead of staying here on Eden with you. The last duty of a commander is to see that his troops are returned home."

They had passed through the moonlit forest trails and were now crossing over the ridge to Meander Valley. From their vantage point they could look down on the Jolly village, with all the tall trees slumbering quietly in front of their tall huts. The winds were quiet this night, and there was no danger of being blown over, so the Jollys rested outside so their fronds could pick up any light and nourishment that might fall from the sky.

"I understand that none of the Jollys want to go back to Earth with us," said George quietly.

"The elders are too rooted in their ways, and the young, while interested in the possibility, have not developed enough self-assurance to challenge the wisdom of their elders," said Reiki. "I expect that in five or ten years, however, we may see a young stronglimb decide to venture into space rather than challenge the chief."

"It is the same with the gummies," said George, "although I expect it will happen faster with them. Did you know that the gummies are now the primary pilots for *Dragonfly II* on Rocheworld? Since they don't need drysuits to board the plane, they are much more mobile in the cockpit and at the science consoles. Even though they are burrowers by breeding, they seem to be natural fliers."

"Nels mentioned once that if we humans had waited a few more thousand years before coming to Barnard, the gummies would have come out to meet us, whereas the flouwen could never have made that transition," said Richard.

"Similar to the unreasonable effectiveness of the anthropoid brain," said George.

"What do you mean by that?" asked Richard.

"We humans are just naked apes," explained George. "We have brains that evolved from the anthropoids—tailless, omnivorous, tree climbers. Yet that same basic brain allows us to be expert space pilots, graphic artists, baseball pitchers, operatic singers, bridge builders, and mathematical cosmologists, while displaying thousands of other talents. What is it about the anthropoid brain that makes it so unreasonably effective in doing all of those things that have nothing to do with surviving in the jungle? There is no good answer.

"The brains of the gummies seem to be like that: very good in many things that have nothing to do with gummie existence. That's in addition to having the terrific IQ and memory of the flouwen, since nearly all their body cells are also brain cells. It is a good thing we have a few hundred thousand years head start on them in the evolutionary race.

"I took a ride with a gummie pilot on *Dragonfly II*. We were going from 'Gummie University' on the outer islands of Eau to the gummie settlement on Roche, and when going through the stormy region between the planetoids, he performed some spectacular acrobatic maneuvers while avoiding a stray twister—I though it was Arielle at the controls."

The reminder of their long-lost comrade brought another long period of silence while the group continued its journey through the moonlit forest. When they came to Tarzan Highway, however, the pure joy of flying from platform to platform raised their spirits again.

"The swings cut almost a full hour off our trek through Meander Valley," said Richard, leading the way.

"I'm looking forward to this dinner," said George as he landed on the platform next to Richard. "I'm tired of those perfectly prepared artificial foods that the Solarians eat now. Even the bones in the slices of the rare prime ribs are artificially manufactured."

"We're having jookeejook steaks, Reiki-dough bread, and steamed keekoo sprouts for dinner, with jookeejook fruit shortcake for dessert," said Richard, taking off again.

"I brought the last three bottles of James's Pinot Noir '64 with me from the cellars on Prometheus," said George. "It's in that pack Freeman is carrying for me."

"Should make for a civilized dinner," remarked Roiki as she swung to join them on the platform.

A few months later, a smaller group gathered for the communal dinner at the Meeting House. Afterward, they all went out to the bend in the river that gave them the best view of the skies, except for Rebecca and Christopher, who stayed behind to do the dishes. As they sat in the warm sand and shared their bowl of fruit for dessert, the last red rays of Barnard on the evening clouds faded and the stars started to come out. With Everett's help, Shannon set up a frame holding a large cloth that one day would be a sarong, and cradling Shirley in one arm, she started painting the sunset in bright colors. Almost above them were four bright stars in a row, with another star below that looked large and fuzzy.

"The plume on that incoming science ship is getting bigger every day," remarked Richard as he cracked open a boobaa fruit and gave half of it to Reiki sitting beside him.

Eve cut off a small bite from a Jolly self-fruit and fed it to her son Nathan, who was sitting quietly on Freeman's stomach while his daddy tried to teach him the constellations.

"Look, Nathan," said Freeman pointing at the sky. "One . . . two . . . three . . . four . . . stars in a row. That's the constellation of Orion."

"Which one is Sol?" said Orson as he lay down in the sand next to Lavender.

"And you call yourself an astronaut," said Lavender.

"Those details are what robots are for," replied Orson. "I know that one end-star is Sol, but which one?"

"You expect me to be your robot?" said Lavender, laughing, then she answered. "It's the yellowish one on the right." She paused. "Are you going to miss home, now that Win and Laura are leaving to go back?"

"I'm enjoying the company here," he said, taking her hand.

"I wonder how the others are doing?" asked Maria pensively.

"When I left the *Succor* they were all settling in," said Orson. "The two flouwen buds from Loud Red and White Whistler were already in their tanks and rocked up for the duration. Since I wasn't going to be using my suite, the ship construction robots converted it into a series of separate apartments. Cinnamon and Nels and their kids, Ruth, Sarah, Justin, and Ernest are sharing the largest area, while Dirk has a separate apartment with Mirth right next to them. George has the high-gee penthouse at the end. Of course, none of them are going to be living in them long except when they are approaching the solar system. They go into deep sleep as soon as they leave the Barnard system."

"Where's Adam staying?" asked Reiki, then wished she hadn't asked.

"He's a permanent 'guest' in Laura's suite," said Orson, then chuckled deeply. "Win was sure pizz'd when he found out. Not that he was that interested in Laura himself. He is 'saving himself' for a proper breeding partner. That's why he refused to donate sperm for storage in the medic unit at the lander site to help diversify the gene pool on Eden. But since Laura had shown no interest in Win, it ruck'd him that she had taken a liking to—as he remarked to me: ' . . . that half-breed savage—I bet he doesn't even know who his father is. . . .' "

Orson, who had been expecting some shocked responses to his quote, was instead surprised when nearly everyone broke into laughter. All except Reiki, who instead had a Mona Lisa smile on her face as she spoke.

"If I recall," she said calmly, "the latest news in from Sol is that a new Solar Worlds government was formed shortly before you left."

"That's right," said Orson. "And Win's father is vice president for the North America Region. By the time Win gets home in fifteen years, he is going to be in a position to pick his next job. But what's that got to do with Adam?"

"And who does Win's father report to?" Reiki continued, deliberately not answering the question yet.

"Why, President John Quincy Kennedy, of course, the present head of the Kennedy clan. With his youthful looks, great popularity, and system-wide political machine, he is going to be President of Solar Worlds until he decides to turn it over to a younger Kennedy. But what's all this got to do with *Adam*?" he persisted.

"Adam's father was a Kennedy," Reiki finally explained.

"I'll be . . ." exclaimed Orson. "I'm sure Win doesn't know that."

"And after all the holovideo exposure Adam will get

when he returns to Earth," Richard added, "he will soon be one of the best-known Kennedys, which can only help his political chances. It wouldn't surprise me one bit if 'half-breed savage' Adam Kennedy were the next Solar Worlds President after John Quincy, *if* he wishes to set his sights that low. . . ."

"Win is really going to be surprised when he finds out," said Orson chuckling.

"He has another surprise coming," said Maria.

"What's that?" asked Orson.

"He's going to be the father of a baby," she said. "The robodoc at the landing pad medic station tells me it's a boy. I'm going to name him after his grandfather— although I'll give Win second billing: John Winthrop Kennedy."

Just then Freeman heard a beep from Nathan's Teacher that he had set up in the sand.

"Five minutes to ignition!" he announced. "Rebecca and Christopher, come on out . . . it's almost time!"

Up on the starship *Succor*, the slow rotation of the vehicle nose that had provided artificial gravity to the crew compartments had been brought to a halt. The two-kilometer long ship now pointed at the yellow star at the end of Orion's belt. Amidships, a sextet of laser beams reached through portholes in a vacuum chamber cooled to nearly absolute zero and selected out a tiny clear crystal floating on the electromagnetic fields inside. With a flick, the laser beams sent the crystal off through a hollow tube, where it was passed along by radio pulsations to the engine at the aft end of the ship. As soon as the first crystal was sent off, it was followed by another. The crystals of antihydrogen shot through a series of locks and entered the engine where they met a stream of gaseous normal hydrogen. Each tiny crystal of antimatter annihilated in a tiny explosion of energy more powerful per gram than a nuclear bomb. The high energy particles streaming from the mini-explosions heated the rest of the hydrogen gas into a blazing blue-white plasma that expanded against the magnetic bottle that contained it, until it was forced out the magnetic nozzle of the engine as a blazing exhaust, lighting up the moonscapes below.

The blaze of light that came from the blue-white plasma exhaust of the starship fell on the upturned faces of the people below, some of the eyes glistening with teardrops. They had said their good-byes earlier, so there was silence now as their loved ones left. . . .

Suddenly there was a sneeze.

"Excuse me!" said Maria. "I guess a baby isn't the only thing Win left me with. I'm afraid I've caught a cold!"

ABOUT THE AUTHORS

Dr. Robert L. Forward writes science fiction novels and short stories, as well as science fact books and magazine articles. Through his scientific consulting company, Forward Unlimited, he also engages in contracted research on advanced space propulsion and exotic physical phenomena. Dr. Forward obtained his Ph.D. in Gravitational Physics from the University of Maryland. For his thesis he constructed and operated the world's first bar antenna for the detection of gravitational radiation. The antenna is now at the Smithsonian museum.

For thirty-one years, from 1956 until 1987, when he left in order to spend more time writing, Dr. Forward worked at the Hughes Aircraft Company Corporate Research Laboratories in Malibu, California, in positions of increasing responsibility, culminating with the position of Senior Scientist on the staff to the Director of the Laboratories. During that time he constructed and operated the world's first laser gravitational radiation detector, invented the rotating gravitational mass sensor, published over sixty-five scientific publications, and was awarded eighteen patents.

From 1983 to the present, Dr. Forward has had a series of contracts from the U.S. Air Force and NASA to explore the forefront of physics and engineering in order to find breakthrough concepts in space power and propulsion. He has published journal papers and contract reports on antiproton annihilation propulsion, laser beam and microwave beam interstellar propulsion, negative matter propulsion, space tethers, space warps, and a method for extracting electrical energy from vacuum fluctuations, and was awarded a patent for a Statite: a sunlight-levitated direct-broadcast solar-sail spacecraft that does not orbit the earth but "hovers" over the North Pole.

In addition to his professional publications, Dr. Forward has written over eighty popular science articles for publications such as the *Encyclopaedia Britannica Yearbook, Omni, New Scientist, Focus, Aerospace America, Science Digest, Science 80, Analog,* and *Galaxy.* His science fact books are *Future Magic, Mirror Matter: Pioneering Antimatter Physics* (with Joel Davis), and *Indistinguishable From Magic.* His science fiction novels are *Dragon's Egg* and its sequel *Starquake, Martian Rainbow, Timemaster, Camelot 30K,* and *Rocheworld* and its four sequels: *Return to Rocheworld* (with daughter, Julie Forward Fuller), *Ocean Under the Ice, Marooned On Eden* (with wife, Martha Dodson Forward), and this final sequel, *Rescued From Paradise* (with Julie Forward Fuller). The novels are of the "hard" science fiction category, where the science is as accurate as possible.

Dr. Forward is a Fellow of the British Interplanetary Society and former editor of the Interstellar Studies issues of its journal, Associate Fellow of the American Institute of Aeronautics and Astronautics, and a member of the American Physical Society, Sigma Xi, Sigma Pi Sigma, National Space Society, the Science Fiction Writers of America, and the Author's Guild.

Julie Forward Fuller turned to writing in desperation after running out of things to read. This is her third novel, the first being a fantasy, *Wyrmmount,* presently making the rounds of the publishers, and the second being *Return to Rocheworld,* the first of the Rocheworld sequels, written with her father. She writes while others sleep, which lets her avoid the distractions of telephone, television, and talk, and gives her an excuse to sleep until noon.

Mrs. Fuller grew up as a happy, active member of the Forward family. She now lives in Palmdale, California, with her husband of ten years, Charlie Fuller, and enjoys, most of all, the mothering of their three wonderful daughters.